CW00381656

Alfie Jaeger;
Power-less Kid

By A.Haigh

About the Author

Alfie Haigh is a 15-year-old lad from the heart of Yorkshire. In lockdown 2020 he started writing in his spare time. Once the pandemic was over, this was the result. A 110-thousand-word story about a teenage boy, who is really a no-one, who wants to be a someone, and who goes on to... well, you'll see!

He hopes you enjoy this book...
and look forward to the movie next year ;)

Acknowledgements

Massive thank you to my Dad, who was my editor throughout this whole process and helped me a lot, and thank you to my Mum and Emma for their support also. Thanks also to Jake, for allowing me to use his name, thanks Jake!

Contents

1. The Beginning
2. The Exams
3. The Tourney
4. Light itself vs a guy in sunglasses
5. I start school (it's an interesting place)
6. Our first day
7. Woohoo! Combat!
8. The Final 5
9. I'm getting demoted?
10. My Birthday is worse than Christmas this year, I think
11. Okay so maybe Christmas was worse
12. The contest with lots of smaller contests and no overall winner!
13. A slight detour for something far more important...! And then back to the regular schedule...
14. The rest of our lives starts now
15. School starts again, with one small difference
16. I beat up an old guy (he started it)
17. The Global Sports Festival Begins!
18. Basketball!!!
19. The Finals!
20. Not much to say here... It doesn't go well...
21. Tennis is dull until it gets exciting (words of wisdom from me)
22. Practise... More practise... And some tricks...
23. Football with Powers, what could go wrong?
24. I really hate dreams, there is no point...
25. I don't like losing
26. This just got interesting!
27. Fight Night! But over a couple of weeks!!!
28. Well... There's the Third...
29. Woohoo! Another finals appearance!
30. I lose a fight, well, you'll see...

31. Oh yay, it's the end of the school year... And you know what that means
32. Oh no! A prison escape?
33. Home Time!!!

1 - The Beginning

Hey, I'm Alfie Jaeger.
I was an odd kid, at an odd school for power-less kids.
And I got lucky.
I got so lucky that… Well… You'll see…
I wanted to become a hero, well, *the* hero. More than anyone in the world. But I was a nobody. From a school of nobodies. My chances were next to none. But your chances are never zero, and you should never forget that. I trained, all day every day. Even in school, I was always getting scolded for that. Everyone had lost hope in us. That's why we were in that school.
So we didn't get in anyone else's way.
'Cos that's what we were known for, getting in power user's way.
Our chances were next to none, but never zero, and I got lucky.

I was 1 month off turning 16 when I took the entrance exam to the best school in the country. I was the only powerless kid there.
I could see kids making portals. Flying around. Slipping through walls. Manipulating elements.

And I was the only powerless one there.

'Hey there!' This girl shouted, popping up out of nowhere. She had golden, long, straight hair and green eyes that glowed with power. She seemed to have one speed, super speed. She probably lived off of caffeine.
'Uhh, hey...Wait… Jessica?' I said, awkwardly.
She squinted at me, 'Alf?'
I nodded.
'Oh my god!' She squealed, wrapping her arms around me, 'I haven't seen you in ages! It must have been what? Four years?'
I nodded, 'Something like that.'
'What's your power?' She shouted.
'Hey, quiet down will you,' I muttered, 'I don't have one.'

She wrinkled her nose, it was kinda cute, 'And you're taking the exam for *this* school? Have you lost your mind since I last saw you?'

'Nope.' I said, adamantly. 'I just want to.' I replied, shrugging.

She smirked, 'Alright then, see you at the end!' She shouted, running off.

'They sure are a handful.' Said a guy coming up behind me, hands behind his head. The guy had this air of confidence around him, almost the opposite of me. Dark hair and built like an athlete, dark eyes. Tall and *very* pale. Sounds like most girls' dream guy, right? He was similar to me, except for the girls part and well... Okay maybe scrap that part.

I stared in the direction she ran off to. 'They sure are...'

'Anyway, I'm Barukko.' He said, holding out his hand.

I shook his hand 'Oh, hey! I'm AJ. You here for the exam?'

'Not the one you're taking; I've got the recommended one.' He said, sighing.

My jaw dropped, 'I'm sorry what? Why on earth are you talking to a guy like me?'

'Because why not?'

'I mean, it probably looks bad for you, a super-powerful guy like you talking to a nobody like me.'

He shrugged, 'Look, if you're powerless and still have the audacity to take *this* exam, I don't care what anyone else thinks, you're good in my books.'

I studied him for a minute, 'What is your power anyway?'

'Darkness,' I raised my eyebrow, 'I can control darkness, manipulate it if you will, as long as there's a shadow, I can do pretty much what I want.'

'I feel like I should bow down to you.'

The corner of his mouth turned up. 'Yeah well come see me after the exam, if you get in then I'll be the one bowing down to you.'

And with that he walked to the recommendations entrance. And I set off to the normal entrance, to the worst exam that I'd ever take...

I entered and sat at the back of this huge gymnasium, with an empty stage at the front. I strained my neck trying to find the girl from earlier, but it was hard with the variation that was in that hall. It looked like something from a film.

The last of the examinees filed in and a light lit up the stage. The principal walked on. The principal was this 82-year-old guy who was crazy smart, even though he didn't look like it at first. His power was what everyone calls IQ, which, as you can probably guess, means he has a crazy high IQ. That's the only reason he's the principal of this school. He has, no had, no wait… both, like no athletic ability whatsoever.

Anyway, he made this long speech thanking us all for coming and talking about what the exam was about. But I'll shorten it down for you…

The exam was split into two parts: The mental part, and the physical part.

The mental part was a series of tests assessing your ability to do the basic stuff, maths, English etc. But also you're ability to think in a dangerous and problematic situation. That stuff is easy.

The physical part is the problem. Without a power the exam is nearly impossible to pass and if I did I'd be bottom of the pack. So I would have to perform amazingly in the mental exam to just scrape in. And even then, it still depends on how everyone else does.

The first exam was the mental exam, Maths and English were easy, not a problem. The dangerous situation stuff was a bit trickier but still, I'd come prepared. All in all, I'd done well so far.

But the next test was the problem.

The next test was split into two smaller tests.

The first of the two was an obstacle course. 2km in length and was littered with obstacles. A lake, a cliff we had to climb, and a minefield, yes you heard that right. A MINEFIELD. I was regretting my choice to take this exam more and more by the minute. But I had to get here to achieve the dream.

The second test was combat-based. A 1v1 bracket-style tournament that would account for a third of our scores. And our placement in the race would decide our placement in the tournament. The best would go up against the worse, etcetera. I was screwed.

We all began to line up for the race when the principal's voice began blaring through some speakers.

'Oh and we forgot to tell you, only the first half of you will get through to the tournament. The rest might as well go home after this!'

Panic erupted from amidst the crowd. *What?* I thought, *okay this just got a whole lot harder.*

I lined up at the line regardless and got ready to run like my life depended on it.

'Three…Two…One…GO!'

A dozen people flew away from the start line, (for some that's literal) and all hell broke loose around me. 90% of the participants tried to use their powers to get away from the start and that meant that everyone got mixed up in each other's powers. All around me there was an explosion of colour as everyone's abilities went off. It was like something out of a dream. But I kept on running, I couldn't afford to stop. I somehow managed to get away unscathed but I was already tired and now I was behind the main pack, and one guy had already finished. The first major obstacle was the lake and most people had just jumped in and started swimming, but it must have been 200 metres long. I stopped and scanned the outskirts of the lake for a second and happened to see Jessica from earlier sprinting along the edge of the lake on a thin ledge that you probably weren't meant to run on. A longer route but it was quicker.

Hmm, smart girl. I thought.

So I did the same, I launched myself past one girl and set off running around the lake and before I knew it I was around the other side and running down to the next obstacle.

The minefield…

Now it was a pretty bad minefield, you could see where they had put the mines, but I guess that was purposeful so that you didn't necessarily get blown up. But it was going to take a while, I had lost sight of Jessica.

Come on there's got to be a quicker way.

I stared at the field and saw this one guy just running in a straight line across the mines, blowing them up as he did so.

Hmm, I guess I'll just use the path he cleared then.

It was easy once I got to the path, however it took too long to get there, and I nearly stepped on a mine when a runner brushed my shoulder as he passed.

But I cleared it as quick as I could and I ran to the final major obstacle. The mountain. By this point I was shattered and my whole body ached with pain.

But I only had one objective, and I had to get there.

One-quarter of all contestants had finished. I couldn't waste any time. I didn't try anything smart this time, I just began to climb. Every muscle ached; I nearly fell once. The rock my left hand gripped came loose and fell, but I held on. Just.

Amazingly, my choice to just climb ended up being the "smart choice" because this guy with power over the earth ran past me, building a staircase as he went. So, I just jumped onto it and climbed after him.

Well, I say it was a smart choice, more like a temporary solution. Because as soon as the guy got off at the top the whole staircase crumbled and I leapt for the ledge at the top. Grabbing on by my right hand. I gasped, the pain in my arm was unbelievable but I couldn't give up now. I was at the top. I was so close. I summoned all my might. And pulled myself up. Right as I did so the ledge I had hold of crumbled away.

'That was too close.' I said turning and making my way to the finish.

It turns out I was a lot closer than I thought I was. I ended up being part of the last 50 (15) that finished and got through. I was relieved, but it meant whoever I was up against was going to be strong, or at least quick.

As I crossed the line Jessica came up out of nowhere.

'Oh my god you made it!' She exclaimed, tackling me in a hug. My face went bright red, 'Ahem, er yeah I did I guess.'

'That's amazing.' She said, still holding onto me.

'Errm yeah, can we... untangle now please?'

Now it was her turn to go red. 'Oh my god I'm so sorry, it's so embarrassing.'

I held my hands up, 'Na it's good just... we just met again you know?' I said, grinning.

She brushed herself down, 'How are you so dirty?'

'It's a long story.' I replied, glancing down at my clothes, they were covered in muck. 'Anyway... the tourney's next.'

'Yeah!' She said, clenching her fist. 'I can't wait!'

I smiled.

I could...

All the remaining participants were gathered around the stage that sat in the middle of an arena. We were staring at a screen that was about to announce the brackets for the tournament, that was due to be underway in half an hour.

'Hello everyone! So as you all know you have successfully made it through to the combat stage, now as you will see your brackets are appearing on the screen... now.' Said the Principal, his voice blaring through some loudspeakers in the corners of the room.

I scanned the brackets, searching for my name.

Alfie Jaeger vs Tan Orugun

Who is that? I thought, scanning the crowd. I caught the eye of a guy standing on the other side of the stage. He was glaring at me. He looked terrifying, kind of like a mad scientist with his spiky, grey hair.

This wasn't going to be fun...

There were 400 people in the tournament. I know. 400 HUNDRED! My match was pretty early on, but I still had some time to prepare.

'Do you know what you're going to do?' Asked Jessica.

I shrugged, 'Nope, I'll just wing it I guess.'

'Do you not have a weapon or anything?'

'You're allowed weapons? I mean I don't have one anyway but it's nice to know.'

She turned to me, a sword in her hand. 'Here, take this.' She said, tossing the sword to me. I caught it and unsheathed it. The sword was a metre and a half one-handed longsword. Black and red handle, black hilt, grey steel double-edged blade. Elegant.

A wonderful sword to lose with.

'It's nothing amazing but-'

'It's amazing.' I interrupted, she blushed, 'I can't wait to lose with it!'

'You won't lose!' She demanded, 'At least not until you fight me.'

I shrugged again, 'Okay, I'll try my best.' I replied, walking away. 'Anyway, I gotta go to the arena. See you later!'

She waved, then I turned away and steeled my face. It was time to battle.

I walked up the stairs to the arena, sword in hand. Staring at the sky above me, wondering what my plan would be. *I've gotta figure out what his power is first* I thought. And so with my "master plan" in place, I stepped onto the battlefield, only to find Tan already there, grinning.

'You're late.'

'You're early,' I grumbled, 'anyway, let's get on with this.'

'You ready to lose punk?'

'Three...Two...One...Fight!'

He set off running at me, grey hair flowing as he bared down on me. I raised my sword, ready to defend when he sped up, and I mean *sped up*. Like he went from 20mph to 60. I couldn't react. He hit me, hard. Then sped away, slowing down again.

'What the?'

He sneered, 'Do you like it, it's my ability. I won't tell you what it is... Actually... I will. If you win, which you won't.' He shot towards me again, but this time I was ready. I swung earlier than I would do, to counter his attack, but he never sped up so I overcommitted and he hit me again.

'Aargh!'

What can I do? His attacks are too unpredictable.

He hit me again, and again, and again. I couldn't do anything about it, so I wracked my brain. Accepting the fact I was going to get hit and so tried to defend myself from the impact.

What can I do to counteract both attacking options?

My eyes widened. I'd got it.

BOOM!

Before I knew it I was flat on my back and coughing up blood.

'What?'

A voice came blaring through the loudspeaker, I think it was counting down but my ears were ringing so I couldn't tell. I was so disorientated I had no clue what was happening. Was this it? Was I falling at the first hurdle? No...

I climbed to my feet when the speaker reached 2 and raised my sword. My eyesight was blurry but I could still make out Tan, was he, laughing?

'You've got spirit all right... but it's time to die.' He shouted, charging towards me one final time.

I slashed out of desperation, and missed.

'Hah! Missed!'

'Did I?' I muttered, completely overcommitting and spinning in a complete circle, slashing a second time. Tan didn't make a sound as I cut deep into his chest. He coughed blood directly in my face and collapsed.

Blood pooled around his body whilst I stood there, staring down at the man I'd just defeated.

What a lovely time for my eyesight to return.

I glanced around, trying to find any indication of what to do next when I finally heard a voice come through the speakers.

'Uhhh? What just happened?' It wasn't the principal, it was someone else, 'Ahem, erm anyway congratulations Jaeger on the victory! Please proceed to the waiting area where you will be treated for your injuries for your next fight.'

I stumbled off the stage and wandered towards the waiting area I'd originally come from, passing another competitor as I did so. 'Not bad kid.' She said as she brushed my shoulder. I glanced back at her, tall, slender, with a powerful aura. She was dangerous. I turned back around and headed to the waiting area, where a certain person was waiting (again).

I walked through the open doors and got tackled into another hug.

'Owww.' I yelped, 'Hey Jessica.'

'How on Earth did you pull that off?' She said, pulling away from me.

I shrugged, 'Just good I guess.'

She grinned, nodding towards the sword in my hand, 'Did that help?'

'Oh yeah... it basically won me the fight not gonna lie.'

'Good, I can't wait to beat you whilst you're using it.'

'You've got to win first.' I noted.

She smirked, Oh please it'll be easy. The guy's power is sludge, like, how bad can you get?'

I looked down, 'I mean, you could like, not have one.'

She paused... 'Oh my god no I didn't mean it like that!'

I grinned, 'I know, I'm just messing with you. Now go out there and kick Sludge guy's butt!'

'But it's not my turn.'

I groaned, then shrugged and turned to one of the huge screens that were displaying the fights. That girl that I'd passed earlier had already won and the next fight was starting. What had it taken her? 20 seconds? She was powerful. The next few fights were boring, but they were over quickly and before I knew it was Jessica's turn to fight.

'Alrighty then!' She said, turning to me, hands behind her back, 'Wish me luck!'

'You make your own luck.' I replied.

She frowned, 'Great thanks.' I grinned.

'Go get 'em!' I shouted as she walked out the doors. I turned back to the screen; it was time to see what her power was really about.

She was first on the stage, with the other guy (I can't remember his name for the life of me so I'm just going to call him gloopy) entering soon after. There was a short exchange of words before the battle began. Gloopy started by lobbing a couple of sludge balls towards Jessica, but she dodged them easily. He then launched a huge sludge bomb towards her face, which she dodged easily but as it passed her by it exploded in her face, blinding her momentarily.

'Come on.' I muttered.

Gloopy (I love that name) closed in on her whilst she was still trying to clear her face of the sludge. She realised what was happening right at the last second, generating a blinding light right before Gloopy hit her.

Now I can't say for sure, but the look of pure shock on the poor guy's face suggested that he did not expect that. But to be fair neither did I. The light she was emitting was so ridiculously bright that I could hardly look at the screen. I couldn't imagine

18

what it must have been like for the guy fighting her. But now it was Jessica's turn to fight back, the light appeared to have melted the sludge or something, because it wasn't there anymore and now it was Gloopy's turn to stumble around blindly, Jessica didn't wait around, she charged straight at him and hit him in the temple.

'Won't that kill him?' I muttered.

'Na she didn't hit him that hard.' Said a voice next to me.

Now I'm not going to lie, I get scared easily, but when I say I jumped, I mean I *JUMPED.* I glanced to my right, 'Barukko?'

He turned to me, 'Wassup?'

'I thought you were in the Recommended competition.'

'I was, but it's done so I thought I'd come and watch the fights.'

I stared at him, 'Did you get through?'

He put his arms behind his head, 'Of course, who do you think I am?'

I shrugged, 'Fair enough.'

'Oh, before I forget, here take these, you won, didn't you?' He asked, handing me a pair of sunglasses.

'Uh, yeah I did,' I glanced down at the sunglasses in my hand, 'Thanks for these... I guess.' I muttered, putting them on my head.

'Trust me, you'll need them.' I stared at him, what did he know that I didn't?

In the time we were talking Jessica had finished her fight and was already heading back to the waiting area, victorious, of course.

'Hey Alfie!' She shouted, entering the room.

I rubbed the back of my head, 'Uhh, hey Jessica.'

She stopped 10 yards from us and tilted her head, frowning, 'Who's that?'

I turned, 'Huh? Oh yeah this is Barukko, he's a... friend?'

He smiled a little, and stepped forward, 'Pleasure to be of your acquaintance.'

Is he a businessman or something? I thought.

Jessica's smile wavered, she took a step back, 'Umm Alfie? A word please.' She said, her face paling, I glanced at Barukko, who just shrugged. So I went to talk to her.

'Heyyy, what's up?'

'I don't like him.' She muttered, glancing over my shoulder.

'Why, 'cos he's got the opposite power to you?'

She stared at me, 'WHAT?'

'Well you know, your power is light and his is darkness.'

Her face turned as white as a sheet. 'That... that must be it.'

I grabbed her arm, 'Hey you okay?'

'Yeah... I'm fine.' She said, pulling away and staggering off, I watched her go, before realising she was about to fall over when I grabbed her again and pulled her towards me.

'No you're not.' I replied, sitting her down.

'I don't know what's happening.' She muttered.

'You'll be fine, just give it a-' I stopped because she'd slumped on me, she'd passed out.

I caught Barukko's eye from across the room, he just shrugged again then turned around to watch the fight.

I glanced down at Jessica's face, *What was that about?*

Anyway, she slept through the rest of the fights and even the draw for the next round...

After all the fights had finished and everyone still participating was in the waiting area, the principal popped up on screen, congratulating all the remaining contestants on making it this far, I glanced down at Jessica again, she still wasn't stirring.

'And now,' the Principal continued, 'here are the fixtures for the next round of fights.'

The brackets appeared on the screens and I scanned through the list, looking for both my name and Jessica's. I found them both at once.

Alfie Jaeger vs Jessica Verose.

I glanced up at the sunglasses that sat on my head, then scanned the room for Barukko. *How did he know?* I thought.

I shook my head, *it doesn't matter now, the first problem is-* I looked down at the girl, who I now had to fight, who was asleep on me.

More and more fights passed, and she didn't wake, thankfully we were towards the end, but still, if she didn't wake what would happen?

Thankfully it couldn't come to that, although what happened was weird…

3 fights before ours a girl wandered over, I knew she was coming, she had stared straight at me for like 5 minutes beforehand.

'Err, hey there.'

'Hi.' I replied, 'What do u want?' I asked, slightly passive-aggressive

'To help with your little, err situation there.' She replied, nodding to Jessica.

'Why?'

She blushed, 'Er, err, 'cos why not?'

I shrugged, 'Fair enough, but anyway, what can you-'

I stopped as the girl touched Jessica's arm and all of a sudden, she started to stir. I turned back to thank her, but she had already disappeared.

She rubbed her eyes, 'Hey Alfie.' She said,

'Wassup sleepy head.' I replied.

'Sleepy head?' Her eyes suddenly widened, and her face reddened, 'Oh my God I'm so sorry. How long was I out for?'

'Oh a good hour and a half.'

Her face got even redder, I thought she was gonna burst into light. She shoved her face into her hands, 'I'm such an idiot.'

I rubbed the back of my head, embarrassed. 'It's good, but you missed a fair bit.'

'I haven't missed my next fight have I?!'

'Na you're good, but you should ought to know who you're up against in a good, 10 minutes.'

'Who?'

I grinned, 'Me.'

Anyway, 10 minutes later I found myself facing Jessica, with my sunglasses on. Ready to fight for my life. I squinted in these sunglasses, it was almost too dark to see, I hoped they worked.

'GO!' The voice shouted through the speakers.

I charged, and as soon as I got within 10 metres Jessica was enveloped in blinding light, I flinched, but it really wasn't that bad. *Thanks Barukko.*

I continued my charge, and I even saw Jessica's attempt to hit me, thinking I was blinded by her light she came straight at me, but since I wasn't I dodged easily and swung with my sword, grazing her shoulder.

She grunted. 'What the?' She shook her head and her light brightened, I imagine it was like looking at the sun, but for me it wasn't so bad. These were good sunglasses. Jessica charged at me again, putting all her weight behind her punch, aiming for my chest. I saw it coming and dodged again easily.

Jessica overcommitted and stumbled right past me, leaving her wide open.

'I'm sorry.' I muttered, right before slicing my sword across her back.

She screamed again, and the surge of pain must have surprised her because her light shut off, now I was blind, it was too dark!

Jessica turned around, her eyes blazing in the pain – I could see that clearly enough – 'Aaargh!' She yelled, charging at me. This time I couldn't dodge in time and she smashed her fist into my stomach, winding me, then into my jaw, reversing the direction it was previously going in.

Before I knew it I was flat on my back, coughing up blood, with Jessica stood above me, bleeding badly.

'I'm not.' She replied, her light blazing again. Her fatal mistake.

She raised her fist, thinking I was unable to see (even though I'd proven I could).

'Bye-bye.'

SMASH

'Wha-'

Swish, **Crack**

She screamed again.

And before anyone knew it, I had won.

A horn sounded; I hadn't heard this one before, or maybe I just was too injured and tired to notice last time, and 4 people ran onto the arena. I just stood there, blood trickling out of my mouth, whilst they took Jessica to some exit on the other side of the arena.

I followed their path with my eyes and once they had left, I turned around to head back to the waiting area.

I don't know what I expected to hear when I got back, but I definitely didn't expect a massive roar of applause from just about everyone.

As soon as I walked into the room everyone turned to me to congratulate me, I'm not going to lie I was completely overwhelmed so I scanned the crowd and found the girl who helped me out earlier. She blushed then turned around, my eyes drifted to the person stood next to her. *Barukko?* He nodded, smiling, then tapped his head. I realised that somewhere at the end I'd lost my sunglasses that he'd given me. I just shrugged to him and he shrugged back, then turned around too.

Do those two know each other? I wondered.

The attention dialled down a fair bit once the next fight had begun, but I still had people come up to me about that fight years later, and I still don't really know why...

I didn't catch any of the fights after mine, I was too busy getting healed up.

It turns out Jessica did more damage than I thought, a broken rib and a fractured jaw were the worst of it though. Thankfully I was done by the next round draw and I was able to see who I had to fight next.

Barukko and I were stood in the middle of the room, staring at the screen with all the remaining contestants on.

'You've lost.'

'What?'

'This guy is a year older than you, that's how far you've made it in this tournament. I'm sorry, but this guy is out of your league.'
'What do you mean he's a year older?'
He sighed, 'Once you've made it to a certain point, they merge you with the older guys who are also taking the entrance exam. You've done well to make it this far without any power, but you're done. This guy has had a year longer to train with his power, he might win this thing.'
I sighed, 'Great. So what should I do?'
'Try not to die...'
And with those cheery words of wisdom he turned around and went to talk to that girl he was with earlier.
'Great.' I muttered again, 'Let's do this.' I walked outside preparing myself for a beating.

I was the first fight on the board, so I entered the arena immediately, where my opponent was already waiting.
'Hey kid, I'd just like to apologise for this in advance.'
I grinned, 'I'm not going to make it easy for you.'
He shrugged, 'There's not much you can do about it. My name's Leonardo.'
'Alfie.'
The horn sounded, 'I know.' He replied.
He set off towards me at an incredible speed, but straight at me, easy to predict where he was going to run, and so easy to attack.
He continued running until he got within range, where he seemed to stumble, my chance opened up, I swung my sword...
A direct hit, against myself...
Blood gushed from my stomach, where my sword had impaled itself.
'What?' I mumbled, stumbling. Leonardo regained his balance and grinned.
'My sword... it bounced right off you.' I coughed up blood, the world seemed to spin.
'I'm sorry kid.' He replied, catching me as I fell.
The last thing I heard was the sound of the horn.

I had died...

Not really, that'd make a pretty bad story if I died in the first 11 pages wouldn't it?

The next thing I knew I was in a hospital bed. I looked out the window, the sun was going down. I glanced down at my stomach; I was wrapped in bandages. What day was it? Is it the same day? Had I passed?

'Oh! You're awake.' Said a Nurse.

I rubbed my eyes, 'How long was I out?' I asked, swinging my legs around off the edge of my bed.

'Woahh, you can't get out of bed.'

'Why not?'

'You'll pass out.' She said, turning away.

'What do you mean?' I said, standing up.

She turned back around, 'What are y-... How...'

(My body was always a quick healer, wasn't a power, just... high metabolism or something)

I shrugged, 'My body is really stiff though.'

'Yeah it will be, you took a lot of damage.'

'I only took a sword to the stomach.'

She shook her head. 'You took a lot more damage than you think, from ways you don't understand.'

I scratched the back of my head. 'Let me guess, when I hit Leonardo my sword bounced back, but also all the force I hit him with reverberated to me, with, presumably, increased power?'

Her eyes widened, 'How?'

'Just 'cos I don't have any power doesn't mean I don't know my stuff.'

'Of course, I'm sorry.'

'Na it's not a problem, happens all the time... Anyway, is Jessica still here?'

That question caught her by surprise. 'Who?'

'Jessica, light girl.'

'Ohh yeah, she's 3 doors down.'

'Okay thanks.' I said, slowly walking out the room, trying to loosen my joints. It took me a whole 30 seconds to walk 20 metres, I felt 90.

I knocked on her door and entered, leaning against the doorway.

'Hey.' I said.

She looked up, 'Oh, hey, why are you here?' She blushed.

'Just checking in.'

'Oh, okay.' She nodded at me, 'What happened to your shirt?'

'Hmm? Aah!' I noticed that my shirt had indeed disappeared and that my chest was now I wrapped in a bandage. I crossed my arms, 'Ugh, it kinda got wrecked.' I replied, rubbing the back of my head.

'And the bandage?'

'How do you think the shirt got wrecked?'

'How bad is the injury?'

I unwrapped the bandages, revealing a massive scar where the sword had been, just to the left of my heart.

Jessica covered her mouth, her eyes watering.

'Hey, it's not that bad.' I said, walking over to her. 'How are you anyway?'

'Okay, it was just mainly blood loss anyway, but how are you even alive? Let me check your back... AJ!' She scolded after seeing that the cut went the whole way through.

'How do you know about the J?' I said, looking over my shoulder

'I think you forget that we know each other.' She said casually, 'But seriously, you have an exit wound. How are you not dead?' She questioned, her eyes full of worry.

I just shrugged, 'I'm just good.'

She smiled a little bit, 'Just be careful.'

'Okay Mum.'

She laughed, 'Don't call me that. Anyway, did you pass?'

'I have no idea,' I replied, putting my hands behind my head, 'Probably not.'

'Why?'

'Because I'm a powerless kid.' I said. 'Anyway,' I waved my hand, 'I'll be off. See you later.'

'But what if you don't?' I stopped, 'Here, do you have your phone on you?'

27

'Er it's in my room back there,' I said, waving towards the direction I came from, 'Why?'

'Just give it to me.'

'Okay, gimme a sec.' I went and fetched it.

'...Okay... and done, here, now you've got me number.'

I blushed, 'Err, thanks.' She smiled, 'Okay I'm gonna leave now bye.' I said, casually walking into the doorway on my way out.

I exited the building and gasped for breath, 'Real smooth Alf.' I muttered, leaning against the wall.

'Okay well, I guess it's time to look at that other school I'm going to have to go to then.' I said, setting off in the direction of the train station.

I was back at 9 o'clock, I'd been at the exams for over 11 hours.

'You're back!' Shouted Mum, gripping my arms as I walked through the door.

'How'd it go?'

'I have no idea.' I said.

'Well this might tell you.' She replied holding up a letter with the school's golden logo imprinted on the centre of it. I grabbed it and flipped it other. Sitting down at the kitchen table, my hand trembling. *This is it, make or break time.*

I ripped it open and unfolding it, skimming through the larger body of text, trying to find the important part.

Congratulations

'Wait... what?'

I read through the whole thing, properly.

You have been accepted into Super Schola

(I know, the name's dumb, it's just a fancy way of saying "super school")

Tears formed in my eyes

'What? Have you made it in?'

I nodded

'Oh my God!' Her eyes turned to the sky as she hugged me and muttered something under her breath.

'What?'

'Oh nothing.'

Now my Mum doesn't believe in 'God', no one does nowadays because everyone has powers now, so I don't know what she was doing but she definitely appeared to be thanking someone. She stopped and grabbed me again.

'What?'

'You've got to pack your things.'

I stared at her puzzled, 'What?'

'You move into the dorms tomorrow don't you?'

'Oh sugar yeah.' I said, scrambling out of my chair.

'I'll get the bags.' Mum yelled.

I paused as I entered my room, which wasn't very interesting, grey walls, one wall with a pretty big window in it. A desk with a PC sat on it. And my bed tucked into the corner. I didn't sleep much normally.

I ran my hands through my hair. 'I can't believe it!' I yelled.

'Neither can I.' My Mum chuckled. Patting me on the cheek.

'Now stop standing there and start packing!' She said, lugging two suitcases into the room.

'Right.'

My phone vibrated in my pocket.

Zzz...Zzz...Zzz...

'Are you going to answer it?'

'Uhh, yeah.' I muttered, pulling my phone out of my pocket.

I answered the phone and put it to my ear.

'I MADE IT IN!' Yelled a voice from the other end of the line.

'Oh, hey Jess.' I said, my Mum looking at me strangely as I walked out the room, I waved at her to carry on. 'Congrats.'

She panted, 'Thanks.'

'Have you been running?'

'Yeah... I ran all the way home I was so excited.'

'So I'm guessing you're all healed then.'

There was a pause, '...Yeah... I'm fine. Anyway, how about you? Did you get in?'

I rubbed the back of my head, 'Yeah I kinda got in too.'

There was another pause. 'Oh my god! I'm so happy for you!'

I literally blushed, I WAS ON A PHONE CALL. 'Thanks, anyway I've gotta pack but I'll see you tomorrow?'

'Wait you've got to pack?'

'Yeah well I didn't exactly expect to get in.'

'Ah okay, well I'll leave you to it then. See ya!'

'Yeah see you.' I replied, ending the call.

I walked back into my room, my Mum raised her eyebrow, 'A new girlfriend?'

I went bright red, 'No she's just a friend.'

'Umm hmm, okay, anyway let's get packing.'

We were done by 9 pm. My stomach rumbled, 'I'm starving.' I moaned.

'I'll order take-out.' She said, pulling out her phone.

'Ohh yes.' I said, falling onto my bed.

I didn't get to sleep quickly, I tossed and turned all night, thinking about all the adventures that awaited me. But when sleep did finally find me, I slept like a baby.

5 – I start school (It's an interesting place)

I awoke early the next morning and got dressed into my usual clothes. White high tops, black joggers, a white t-shirt and a green jacket. This school was one of the few in the country that actually had loose clothing policies.

I was on campus at 10 that morning, I got off the train, having said bye to my Mum at the station before she headed off to work, and walked into the entrance, joining the queue.

The entrance building was basically just one huge foyer, massive marble pillars and floor-to-ceiling windows spaced out along the walls.

'Name?' Said the lady at the desk as I got to the front of the queue.

'Uh, oh, Alfie… Jaeger.'

She typed on her keyboard, undoubtedly looking me up in the database.

'You're in Dorm 1-A, you're the first here so you get first pick of the rooms.'

'Nice.' I said.

'You'll find the keys to all the rooms there. The higher the number the higher the floor, and the letter correlates to the specific room, you can figure out the rest.'

'Okay thanks.' I said, turning and heading off to find 1-A.

It was the third to last one on the whole row, it took me a good 5-10' mins to get to it.

'Okay.' I said, entering and flipping the lights. 'Nice.' I said, grinning.

The living area, washing, kitchen, communal area, and gym were all on the bottom floor. I stared at the board full of keys, the highest number was 5 and the highest letter was E. As I stared at the keys I realised something, letters A-C were blue and the rest were pink. *It must be boys and girls, bit sexist isn't it?*

Wait, there are 30 kids in this dorm? I thought. Grabbing the key 5-C assuming that the middle top one had the best view. I took the elevator up to the top and exited, unlocking the door to my room and walking in.

'Whoa.' I said. But it wasn't the room that was amazing, it was the view. I walked out onto the balcony, dropping my cases as I did so. The view opened up to the private park that sat behind the school, you could see the whole thing from here, the massive lake that sat in the middle, and even some of the previous year's students who had already arrived and were enjoying a walk.

I started laughing. 'This is amazing.' I muttered. I took one last look before I went back inside and closed the door and then unpacked my stuff. It was pretty empty at the moment but I was getting my PC sent over tomorrow, and that was all I needed, I didn't plan on spending much time staring at the walls. After I'd unpacked, I headed back downstairs and checked out the other floors, quickly noticing that the guys' rooms were always the ones closer to the elevator. I'd finished checking out the Dorm and still no one else had arrived.

'There's no way I was this early.' I said.

'You're not that early.' Said a familiar voice.

'Aah!' I shouted, scrambling to my feet. 'Jess?'

'Hey.' She said awkwardly, blushing, standing at the doorway with 4 suitcases behind her. She looked good, green high tops, jeans and a green shirt worked on her.

'Wait, this is your dorm too?'

She nodded, 'Can I come in?'

'Why are you asking me? You're living here too.'

She looked flustered as she closed the door, leaning against it.

'Hey you okay?' I asked.

'Yeah... it's just... nothing... Anyway.'

I grabbed her arm, 'You sure?'

'Yeah, anyw-'

'Ahem.'

I turned, 'Barukko?'

He grinned, 'Wassup.'

Jess turned white as a sheet. 'Do you mind if I take her?'

He shook his head, 'Go, I know what I'm doing anyway. My brother told me a while ago.'

I decided I'd question him about that later and got going.
Getting Jess to choose a room and herding her into the elevator
with her cases.

'Which room did you take anyway?'

'Err, 5-D.' She said, staring at it.

'That's right next to mine.'

She blushed, then smiled, 'Is it?' (Now that I think about it…
That was definitely purposeful

'Yeah, the view is bonkers by the way.' I said as the doors
opened at the top. She ran off ahead, lugging 2 of her cases
behind her while I strolled behind, walking down to her room.
She paused for a minute, key in hand, facing the door.

'What are you waiting for?' I said, 'Open it!'

'But…'

'But nothing, open the flipping door!'

She shoved the key into the lock and opened the door.

'Oh my gosh!' She gasped.

'I know right?'

'The view is absolutely amazing!' She said to me, I didn't reply,
she turned to find that I had disappeared. 'Alfie?'

'Hey.' I said emerging from the door from my room, scaring the
life out of her.

'Don't do that!'

I grinned, 'Sorry.'

She panicked for an instant when I leapt over my balcony to
hers, then she turned out towards the park sprawled out below
us. 'It really is amazing huh?'

'It sure is.' I said, staring at her.

'What is it?' She asked, glancing at me.

I turned away, leaning against the balcony edge, 'Nothing…
Anyway, shall we unpack your stuff?'

'Na.' Her reply took me by surprise, 'I will, you go talk to
Barukko.'

I glanced at her, but she was facing away from me.

I sighed, 'Okay… See you at dinner then I guess.' I replied,
leaving to go find Barukko.

I found him on the first floor (or to you uncultured Americans, the second floor) with his door wide open, I knocked on the door frame, 'Hey can I... My god, it is so dark in here.'

He turned to me, 'Just the way I like it.'

I nodded, 'It's cool in a... mystery kinda way.'

'Thanks.'

I cleared my throat, 'Anyway... Your brother.'

He shot me a glance which told me to go no further, all the danger sensors in my body were popping off right now.

'Okayyy... never mind.' I turned to leave, feeling quite awkward.

'Hey AJ... I'll tell you about it... Someday...'

I nodded and continued walking out, heading down to the common area to see if anyone else had turned up.

I got downstairs and went to check if any more keys had been taken, nope, just the three of us. *Where is everyone?*

Over an hour later we were all in the common area, Jess had gotten used to Barukko enough to be in the same room as him, but she was sat as far away from him as possible, and she looked pale still.

Jess and I were watching TV on the sofas while Barukko appeared to be sleeping at one of the dining tables. I kept checking on Jess to make sure she hadn't passed out or anything.

'Where is everyone?' I said to her.

'I have no clue.' She replied, her eyes fixed on the TV.

'They're coming.' Replied an apparently not sleeping Barukko.

And he was right, 5 seconds later a group of 20 or so kids burst through the door.

'AHA!' Yelled the guy first through the door, 'I am the first in the d-'

He stopped, 'Who are you lot?'

Barukko was on his feet before you knew it, 'Barukko Knox.' He said.

The power that had filled the room was mind-blowing, before our eyes we had 2 "Alphas" facing off.

'I know,' He replied, his attention turned to me, 'And you are?'

'Alfie... Alfie Jaeger.'

34

'Oh I know all about you.'

'You do?'

'Yeah, you're that powerless punk that just scraped in.'

I swallowed, 'O...okay and?'

'Don't get in my way.' He said, barging past me and Barukko. 'Now you,' He said, sitting dangerously close to Jessica, 'I can deal with.' He said, attempting to put his arm around her.

'Eww.' She replied, jumping up and hiding behind me, I glanced at her, she glared at him.

He glared at me, 'And you are?' I questioned.

He laughed, 'You don't know me?... I am the number one prodigy, San Wukong!'

'Wukong?' Jess said, 'I've heard that name before.'

'Yes! I am the descendent of the greatest warrior ever!' He exclaimed.

I rolled my eyes and sat down on the opposite sofa, facing the TV, Jess came with me.

He stood up furious, he opened his mouth, then closed it again. I ignored him, he just took one last glance at Jess and then stormed off. The other 20 or so kids had just stood there in dumbfound silence the whole entire time. I waited for "Numero Uno" to grab his key and leave. Then I stood back up again to greet everyone else.

'Hey everyone!' I said, waking everyone out of their daze, 'As you probably heard, I'm Alfie Jaeger, yes I'm powerless, and that over there is Jessica Verose.' She raised her hand, not taking her eyes off the Screen, 'And this is Dorm 1-A, I'm also new here, I just got here early.'

'You weren't early, these lot were late!' Jess cut in. I shook my head.

'Anyway, this is the communal area, there are 5 floors above us and the keys to the rooms are there.' I said, waving to my right, blue keys are boys, pink keys are girls. 'You can fight over them yourselves.' I glanced at the board, noticing San had taken 5-A, he was on the same floor as me, *Great*. 'Erm... yeah, any questions?'

One kid in the middle raised their hand, I don't know why, I wasn't a teacher.

'Err, hi.' This little boy said, he didn't look older than 12? But he must have been a lot older, 'I'm Jason Webber, and you said you don't have any power so… how did you get into *this* school?'

I shrugged, 'Not a clue.'

'It's cos you beat me.' Jess butted in again, her mouth full of crisps.

'Where did you get the food from?'

She jutted he thumb towards the kitchen, where a cupboard door sat half-open. I sighed, 'Of course… Anyway!' I said, returning to the group in front of me, 'Enjoy!' I said, quickly retreating to the safety of the sofa as the kids tussled for the best rooms.

'This'll be fun.' Said Jess, peeling her eyes off the TV to watch the arguments sprouting up. I just shook my head, studied her for a second, watching the enjoyment light up her eyes as she watched the carnage unfurl, then glanced over to find Barukko, only to find that he had disappeared at some point.

Anyway by the end of the day (mostly) everyone had sorted themselves out and introduced themselves to us at some point. They seemed to look up to me, Jess and Barukko as the unofficial leaders (as for why… I have no idea), and San just kinda did what he wanted. Anyway I quickly realised how badly I was going to struggle, all the kids in this dorm appeared to be the most powerful of our year, *I wonder if they put me in this one by mistake,* I thought.

Anyhow, most of us were hanging around in the common area, talking and whatnot, when Wukong came bursting through the elevator doors screaming.

'Barukkoo! Come here you scumbag.'

I didn't even bother turning around, 'He's not here you dimwit.' I replied.

'What did you say?' he demanded, storming over to me, Jess started to glow a little bit, I shot her a warning look.

'You heard me.' I sighed.

Everyone's heads were bouncing back and forth like they were watching a tennis match. They all looked terrified; I couldn't care less.

He grabbed my shoulder, 'Look m-'

I shoved him off and stood up. 'He's gone, you wanted to know where Barukko is? He went for a walk, go find him if you're that bothered.' I replied, sitting back down. Jess glanced over, frowning, then returned her attention to the TV, she loved the thing.

'Hmph.' He grunted, turning around and walking off.

I sighed, everyone remained silent, staring at me. 'What?' I asked.

'How are you not intimidated by him?' Asked Queenie, a tiny girl with flaring red hair that was all over the place.

'Oh he's not that scary.'

'No not scary, intimidating.'

I turned to Jess, confused.

Her mouth was wide open, 'You don't know do you?'

'Know what?'

'One of that guy's powers, intimidation.'

'Intimidation?'

'Yeah, he just has this power to intimidate everyone around him, and I mean everyone.'

I shrugged, 'I don't feel anything, he just annoys me.'

'You don't feel anything...? Hmm... That's, odd.' She frowned.

I shrugged again, 'Oh well. Guess I'm just good.'

'That's your answer to anything you can't explain.'

I didn't answer that time, Jess grabbed my hand, then shot everyone a look to everyone else, they all got back to whatever they were doing.

'Let me look at you.' She said.

I sat down next to her. 'What?'

She studied me, then traced my hand. This went on for a solid 5 minutes.

'I don't get it.' She finally exclaimed, 'I do not get it!'

At least half the room glanced over in surprise.

'Get what?' Asked Alexander.

'Him... Alex... Him...' Jess replied, nodding to me.

'I don't get it, so what if I'm not affected by his intimidation, it's not anything amazing.'

'That's what you think.' Muttered Sam his eyes full of admiration (or so I was told).

'I heard that.' I said, chuckling.

'It is seriously weird though.'

I rubbed the back of my head, 'I know.' I stared out of the window into the park. I needed to talk to Barukko.

Speaking of the devil, well, thinking of the devil, darkness enveloped the dorm, the lights didn't turn off, they just dimmed severely. There were a few panicked shrieks. I glanced at Jess.

'What is happening? You don't think this is-'

'I hope not.' She replied, starting to glow.

I turned to the rest of the group, 'Okay guys just wait here, we'll be back.'

Jess and I exited through the back, Jess leading the way, like some sort of human torch. I was close behind, sword in hand.

'Did you see where the darkness came from?' Jess asked.

'Yeah… kinda… it came from just over there.' I said, pointing just slightly over her right shoulder.

She continued walking forward, getting more and more cautious as we got further and further into the darkness. It was getting thicker by the minute, I was struggling to see Jess now, and she was a metre in front of me.

She paused for a second, let me catch up, and then grabbed onto my arm. I stared at her, 'You're the powerful one.' I stated.

'I know it's just…' She shuddered. 'It's dark.'

I exhaled, 'I know.' I smiled a little bit, 'Should've brought Jake.'

She glanced at me, looking slightly annoyed, 'Why?'

'Because he can do what you do, and probably isn't scared of the dark.'

'Just 'cos he can summon fire doesn't mean he can do what I do.'

'I know… But still.'

'You're unbelievable.' She said, storming off.

I didn't chase her, I just waited.

Soon enough she came running back and grabbed me again.
'Okay I'm sorry.' She said, panting. 'It's scary.'
I grinned but didn't reply. Instead, I started walking onwards,
towards where I hoped Barukko was. The darkness got so deep
I could only see Jess's face because it was a few inches from
mine, but at least now it wasn't getting any worse.
'He must be close.' I whispered
'Mhmm.' She replied, her hands gripped my arm so tightly I
thought it was going to drop off.
'How bright is your light?'
'About fifty percent.'
'Can you up it?'
'Yeah but I'll tire quicker.'
'That's okay, I've got you.'
She appeared to blush, but I couldn't tell in this light, then our
surroundings lightened and I could just about see Jess. Then a
voice rang out in the darkness.
'Helloooo?'
I stopped, 'Who is that?' I whispered.
'Who is what?' Jess whispered back.
'Helloooo?'
'That.'
'Helloooo?'
Jess frowned, 'Is it the principal?'
And with hearing his name he appeared in front of us. 'Oh!
Hello! You two aren't the ones responsible for this are you.' He
asked, gesturing around us.
I shook my head, 'No sir, we're out here looking for the two
who have done this too.'
'Do you know who have done this then?'
Jess nodded her head, still holding onto me, 'We think so,
Barukko has the ability to do this thing and San Wukong went
to find him earlier, those two don't really like each other.'
'Aah, I see... Well dear.' He said, squinting at Jess. You appear to
be able to control light?'
'Uhh, yes.' She replied.

'Let me, um, amplify that for you.' He said, and as he did, the darkness around us seemed to melt away, and I could actually see what was around me, well, 5 metres around me anyway.
'How?' I asked.
The Principal chuckled, 'You don't just think I'm principal of this school because of my IQ do you? I am a man of many talents.'
All of a sudden pain flared all over my body. 'Aargh.' I yelled, my legs collapsed from underneath me.
'Alfie!' Jess exclaimed, catching me.
'Are you alright young man?' The principal asked.
The pain had subsided, and I stood up. 'Ugh, yeah, I... I don't know what just happened.'
Jess studied me, her eyes wrought with worry.
'I'm fine, promise.' I gasped and pointed in front of us. 'There they are!'
'Where?' Jess asked, squinting.
'You can't see them?' I asked.
'No.'
'Neither can I.' Said the principal.
'Well I ca- Wait... I can't now.' The pain had completely subsided, and so had Jess's light.
'Are you sure you're okay?'
I nodded, I wasn't sure if I'm honest, but I set off walking towards where I'd seen them anyway.
The darkness suddenly stopped, and a clearing opened up before us.
Jess gasped, 'There they are!' She said, pointing, 'You were right!'
And indeed I was, on one end of the clearing stood Barukko, shrouded in an aura of darkness, and on the other stood San. Neither moved, they both stood panting, and staring at each other, both were bleeding, but San was the worst of the two. He clutched his arm, it was probably broken. Barukko had an alarming amount of blood tricking from his chin, and there was a piece of glistening red wood sat on the floor, but otherwise he appeared to be unharmed.
The principal clapped his hands together. 'Okay chaps that's enough.'

Barukko's eyes flicked towards us, and his stance relaxed. But the darkness remained.

San didn't move a muscle.

'I said that's enough…' Nothing happened. 'Barukko is it? Lay off the darkness.'

'Not until San relaxes.' He grumbled.

The principal's attention switched to San. 'Boy,' He said, his tone angry, 'Relax.'

San appeared to tense his body further, as if preparing to attack.

Barukko dropped his darkness, apparently seeing something different.

I glanced around us, all of a sudden I saw 5 or 6 pairs of people turn in our direction and start heading towards us.

I readied my sword and Jess tensed up. San hadn't relaxed. We were right, Barukko turned his back to leave and San launched himself at him, but we were all ready, the Principal amplified our powers and I felt stronger, even if I didn't have any, and Jess blasted San with a bolt of light, sending him flying into the nearest tree.

I flew (not literally) after him sword ready, he quickly got to his feet and, dazed by rage, literally tore the tree out of the ground and launched it at me.

'Alfie!' Jess screamed.

I brought my sword down and sliced the tree in two. *Just good I guess.* I thought. San was completely dumbfounded when he saw me continuing my charge, 'Wha? How?' He exclaimed. Right before I kicked him into the next tree.

'That's how.' I replied, lodging my sword through his shirt into the tree.

I collapsed to my knees, all the energy had just drained out of me. Thankfully it seemed that somewhere along the way I had knocked him out. So I was safe, ish.

Jess scrambled over and hugged me right as everyone else arrived. 6 pairs of ex-pros who are now teachers had come to stop the problem, only to have 2 first years beat them to it.

'What on Earth was that?' Jess sobbed, I patted her on the back, weakly.

'Not a clue.' I said, smiling.

The Principal came over, studying me, he then shook his head in dismissal.

'Well done!' He said, walking past us and staring at San, shaking his head again.

Jess turned her head, still holding me, 'What's going to happen now?'

I turned to find all the teachers staring at us and mumbling to one another. *I wonder if one of them is our new teacher.* I wondered.

'Well... I guess we'll hand out the appropriate punishments and address the school.'

'Barukko... He didn't start this.' I muttered.

Jess nodded. 'And we'll take all of that into consideration.' Replied the Principal. 'Now let's get you back to your dorm.' He said, signalling to one of the teachers to come over.

Jess grunted, 'No it's good you lot deal with these two. I'll take AJ here.' She said, she looked like she was about to cry.

The Principal looked concerned, but agreed, and having pointed us in the right direction, let us be. By this point I could walk but Jess still had to support me.

Once we'd entered the forest Jess lost control of her emotions and tears flooded from her eyes. 'Why? Why'd you dive in like that? Even though you're powerless...' She demanded.

'Cos he was going to go after you since you blasted him with your light.'

That answer caught her by surprise, she paused for a moment then buried her face in my shirt. I wrapped my arms around her and we stayed this way for a good 5 mins before Jess gathered herself and stood up.

'Okay.' She said, wiping her eyes, 'Can we go now?'

I smiled, nodded, and stood up, putting some of my weight on Jess.

We made it back 5 minutes later, slamming open the front door.

Everyone massed towards us and began asking questions, I waved them off.

'There goes our sneak entrance.' I grumbled, Jess chuckled and continued walking, we sat down on the sofa.

'So, what happened?' Asked Sam.

I glanced at Jess, who had stood up and was almost running to the elevator, 'I'll tell you in a bit.' I said, getting up and following Jess. 'I'll be back in five!' I shouted back. The elevator doors closed before I could get in after her.

I moaned, annoyed at myself for not being quicker, and waited for the elevator to come back down.

I quickly got in the elevator and hit the button. When I arrived at the top the doors opened to reveal Jess, tears streaming down her face.

I approached her slowly, 'Jess...'

'You scared me!' She screamed. 'I can't lose you too!'

I paused, *too?* 'Jess.'

She slammed the door in my face.

I rested my head against the door, 'Look... Jessica, I'm sorry, I didn't...' I sighed, slammed my fist against the wall, and turned away, walking back towards the elevator, where I told everyone exactly what had just happened, skipping a couple of bits, of course...

6 - Our first day

I know… a lot had happened over the course of two days.

Anyway, I woke up the morning after feeling awful, it seems like whatever I did yesterday really took its toll on my body. I got up and threw open the curtains, then the door, and took a step onto the balcony.
I took a deep breath and opened my eyes, only to see Jess slamming her door shut.
'Well, I guess she's still mad then.' I muttered, going back inside and getting dressed.
Green high-tops (I love high-tops), black joggers and that green jacket. (I know, varied.) Then I got in the lift and hit the button for the ground floor, it stopped another 3 times before we got to the bottom.
Should've taken the fire exit down. I thought
I said hello to everyone regardless, and when we got to the bottom found out that I was one of the last ones to get up, barring Barukko and San of course. Apparently, they still hadn't returned. There was a lot of excitement that day, it was the first day of school! There were loads of gossip about who our 'dorm teacher' or 'form tutor' or whatever you wanted to call it would be. But no one knew for certain. Jess didn't say a word the whole time, she just sat on her own on the sofa. I wanted to say something, but… what?
Sylvia kept frowning in mine and Jess's direction, I knew why, she could read our auras, but I never said anything to her…
At 9 o'clock on the dot there was a knock on the door, just as expected. I went and opened the door, having already gotten everyone ready. Equipment and all, it was a pain to organise.
'Hey… Sir?' I said, tilting my head to one side, 'Principal?'
Everyone looked on in awe, even Jess was looking.
'What are you doing here?' I asked.
'Well, I'm your new dorm teacher.' He replied, walking in.
I closed the door behind him.

'Wait… Is that why you knew our names and abilities yesterday?'

He nodded, then turned his attention to the rest of the dorm. 'Hello everyone!'

His greeting was met with a chorus of 'Hi!' and 'Hello.' From the others.

He continued, 'Yes I am your new teacher, and I also know all of your names, so don't worry about introducing yourselves.'

I went and sat down between Alexander and Alexandra Pendrakon.

This went on for a solid 2 hours, he went over all the rules and stuff, we also found out our timetables for lessons and he answered any questions, then left, giving us an hour and a half to do what we wanted before our first lesson.

Hero basics.

After Sir left, I looked around for Jess, but Sylvia told me that she'd already gone up to her room, I groaned.

'Wait till tonight, then go talk to her.' She said, I just nodded then went to join some of the lads, who had convened around the recently discovered games console. I absolutely destroyed them. I had to leave halfway through though as we had a load of parcels for the whole dorm that we had to pick up. So, there we were, Troy and I, stood in reception staring at the mountain of parcels in front of us.

'There must be at least a hundred.' I moaned. 'I know you can enlarge body parts, but can we even carry this stuff in one go?'

He nodded, 'But not in here, you're going to have to give me the stuff outside.' He said, walking out the doors.

I sighed, and picked up 10 parcels, carrying them outside, I did 8 trips and still had some left!

'I can't carry anymore.' Bellowed the 25ft giant stood next to me.

I nodded, 'I've got the rest!' I shouted up to him, and so we set off on our 5-minute journey back to Dorm, a giant and me, walking down a path, with a ridiculous amount of boxes. What a sight to behold…

We got back and I blew open the door. 'COME GET YOUR BLOODY PARCELS!' I panted.

Alex looked up, 'Can't you bring them inside?'

I glared at him, 'Do you want to move a mountain?'

He walked to the door, then turned to look at me, 'Yeah okay I see your point.'

Everyone grabbed their things, I actually only had 3 boxes, it seemed like the girls had most of them.

Anyway, I unpacked my Pc and set it all up, then went back downstairs, I was about to close the door when I saw Sam stood by the remaining 5 parcels.

'Whose are those?' I asked.

'Jessica's.' He replied.

I sighed, 'I'll take them.'

I gathered them all up and took them up to the top floor. Knocked on the door, leaving the parcels at the foot of the door, hesitating and then turning away, walking towards the elevator, as I got in, I heard her door open, but I didn't turn around. Not until the doors had closed anyway.

When it was time for our first lesson, I gathered everyone at the entrance to that day's classroom, or 'Training Area Delta', as it was named. We were all stood around chatting when suddenly we heard an 'AHEM!' From the entrance to the training area. We all shut up rapidly as a 7ft tall, mountain of a man, appeared from the entrance.

'Hello everyone.' Bellowed a deep voice. 'I will be your teacher today, my name is, officially, One Hit, but you all can just call me Sir.' He continued, 'And today we will be going through the *basics* of what a hero is and does.'

Excited chatter erupted around me.

'However!' He interrupted, 'We will NOT be doing any combat today!'

A lot of disappointed groans followed; Sir just smiled.

'Now follow me!' He bellowed.

We followed him down a single corridor, past the open door that led onto the battlefield, which led to even more disappointed faces, and into, yep, a classroom.

'Are you mad?' Paris complained.

One Hit just chuckled, 'Here is your seating plan.' He said, and sure enough one appeared on the board.

I was sat next to Jess and behind Barukko.

'These have been organised by your Dorm teacher by the way!'

'Great.' I mumbled, Sylvia winked at me, then went to sit down. I took my place next to Jess, sitting with her arms folded, she glanced at me once and then ignored me for the rest of the lesson.

I won't bore you with the details, but it was basically just a recap lesson on what every single person on this planet knew – what a hero was.

Anyway, the lesson ended, and One Hit announced some certain things that the Principal hadn't told us.

'Lesson times vary from day to day! Some may be fairly short whilst others may be a lot longer. So, you may get more free time on some days than on others. You will be given your timetables on the Sunday of every week.' He said dismissing us. Everyone drifted off in little groups, going off to do their own thing, it was only 3 o'clock. I walked back on my own, and when I saw Jess get back and get in the elevator I glanced at Sylvia, who just shook her head. So instead, I grabbed my basketball and went to shoot some hoops on one of the courts situated across from every dorm. When I got there, I was surprised to find Zoe and the Ramirez triplets, Bianca, Natalia and Gabriella, all playing a 2v2 half-court game.

'Hey, do you mind if I play?' I asked.

'I'll join too.' Said Sam, behind me.

'3v3?' I said, 'Ramirez sisters take?'

'They shrugged, yeah sure why not?' Gabriella said.

I turned to Sam, 'Can you even play?'

He grinned and nodded.

And he could, he was too small to defend well, but the guy could shoot.

We played until we could play no more, we ended up sprawled out around the centre of the court, too tired to stand.

'What time is it?' Sam asked.

'6.' Bianca replied.

'3 hours.' Sam exclaimed.

'Good maths.' I muttered, jokingly.

'What was the score again?' Natalia asked.

'457 – 424, to us' I replied.

'UGH! Can't believe we lost.' Groaned Gabriella.

I just smiled.

'I'm soo hungry.' Sam complained. 'I want pasta.'

'You always want pasta.' The Ramirez lot said simultaneously.

I laughed. 'Come on then.' I said, getting up on my feet. 'I think we all need a shower.'

We all wandered inside, much to the disgust of some of the girls, who thought we were some sort of demon after doing all that exercise.

I went and had a shower, then grabbed some food from the kitchen, Sam had cooked a ridiculous amount of pasta, so I had that. And at around 8, after thrashing the lads at more videogames, Sylvia tapped me on the arm in the middle of a match, 'Anytime now.' She said.

That got a couple of confused looks from the boys, but I waited till after I'd whooped Jake at virtual basketball before going up. 'Haha, the best at real and virtual ball.' I claimed confidently. Clambering to my feet.

I glanced at Sylvia, shook my right hand with only my pinkie and thumb sticking out, and said 'I'll be back.'

She nodded, 'Good luck.'

I stepped into the elevator and hit the button for the top floor. Taking deep breaths, preparing myself for what was to come.

The doors opened at the top and I walked over to Jess's room and knocked... No reply.

I considered knocking again but instead went with a different option.

I put my forehead against the door again. 'Jess?... It's AJ... Can we please talk?'

No reply.

I sighed, 'Okay well... I'll be in my room.' I stayed there for another second, before turning around and beginning to make my way towards my room.

Just as I turned around, I heard the door open behind me.

'Alfie.'

I turned back around to see Jess stood with the door open, her hair was a mess, her eyes were red as if she'd been crying, she raised her arm like she was about to hit me. Instead, she ran to me and wrapped her arms around me, hiding her face in my shirt again.

'I'm sorry.' I whispered. Embracing her.

'No, I'm the one who over-reacted, it's just…'

'I know… I know…' I replied.

'Can we go sit down?' She said, gesturing towards my room.

'Yeah.'

I picked her up, and carried her into my room, sitting her down on my bed. She sat up and put her head against mine.

'It's just…' She wiped her nose with her sleeve, 'I really like you and…'

'I know… I'm sorry.'

'Do you wanna, play something?' She asked, sniffling.

I nodded, 'Sure, like a board game or a video game?'

She sniffed, 'Do you even have any board games?'

'Nope, I got one on my computer though.'

She smiled, 'Hang on then.' She said, walking out and going to her room. I fell back onto my bed. My mind blank.

'Here…' She said, entering my room and closing the door behind her. 3 boxes in her arms, 'Games!' She laughed.

I sat up, 'Okay, what do we play then?'

'All of them, obviously.' She had seemed to have recovered a bit now.

I grinned, 'Okay, but prepare to lose!'

She shook her head, 'I've not lost in 3 years,' She claimed, 'so, good luck.'

We both sat on the floor and got ready.

The first game took an hour and Jess absolutely smashed me, I'd like to say I let her but, well, I didn't.

In the second game however I fought back in force, winning with a resounding victory.

In the third game we didn't finish, it was half ten at this point and Jess was shattered. So we just abandoned it on the floor and agreed on a draw (but she'll claim she was winning).

She yawned, 'I won that.'

I climbed onto the bed, 'That's what you think.'

'You're right.' She said, joining me.

I put my arm around her, 'Whatever…'

Before I knew it Jess was asleep in my arms, and I was stuck.

Zzz…Zzz…Zzz

My phone was buzzing, I unwrapped myself from Jess and answered the call.

'We've got two problems.' A voice said.

'Sylvia?' I replied.

'Yeh, duh. Anyway, Jess is missing.'

I yawned, 'She's with me.'

'Can I talk to her?' I glanced behind me.

'She's asleep.' I replied, 'What's the second problem?'

'We've got newcomers.'

I wrote Jess a note and stuck it to the door in case she woke up, and then quickly got to the communal area, where there were only 5 of us still up.

The doors opened to reveal Sylvia, Barukko, Sam and Gabriella, all stood in a sort of semi-circle. I rubbed the back of my head, yawned then walked in between Barukko and Sam.

'Hey guys, wassup?'

Sylvia cleared her throat, 'Ahem, err… Alfie these are-'

'CJ and Talia.' The guy interrupted.

'I'm assuming your CJ then?' I said, shaking the guy's hand.

He nodded, CJ was slightly taller than me, dark hair, dark-skinned, and built like a basketball player. His pearly white teeth seemed to glow in the darkness of the room. It was weirdly blinding.

I turned to the girl, Talia, she was that girl I'd seen at the tournament earlier.

Tall, dark, long, straight hair, slender body, and that powerful aura I sensed earlier, I bet Sylvia was having a field day.

'Hey, I'm Alfie.' I said to the two of them, 'I'm assuming one of these lot have given you the run down?' They nodded, 'Okay great.' I said, clapping my hands together. 'Barukko, a word.' I said, turning to find that he'd left, I sighed.

Sylvia turned to me, 'I'm going to have a word with you.'

Great. I thought.

We went to the corner of the room, leaving Sam and Gabriella to give them a tour.

'Soooo, what's happened?' She asked, smiling.

I rubbed the back of my head, 'Nothing much.' I replied.

'Mhmm, okay, it's that way in see, I know you're lying... But fine.' She winked at me, 'Go back up.'

I nodded and was about to get in the elevator when I realised how thirsty I was. I made drinks for Jess and myself then went back upstairs and was about to go into my room when I noticed Jess's door was cracked open.

I put the drinks down and went to see what was up.

'Jess you o... You're not Jess, what are you doing here?' I said to CJ, who was just stood in the room.

He didn't say anything and instead ran straight past me and out the fire exit.

That's very weird. I thought, making a mental note to ask Talia later.

I went back to my room and found that Jess hadn't moved since I'd left her, and having grabbed her keys and locked her door, laid down on the bed next to her, and shut my eyes, Jess immediately rolled over onto me.

I promised myself I wouldn't tell her about CJ being in her room.

It took me a while to go to sleep, and once I did, I had my first dream in a while.

I woke to find myself stood, staring at a warrior, a white, perfect, two-handed longsword in my hand.

He said something I didn't quite catch, then charged, and right as he was about to slice my face into bits, I heard a voice.

'Alfie.'

'Jess?'

7 – Woohoo! Combat!

My eyes opened and I found Jess, dressed and ready, stood over me.

'What time is it?'

'Eight.' She replied.

I yawned, stretched, and sat up.

'We had some newcomers whilst you were asleep.'

'I know, Sylvia told me.'

'Of course she did.' I muttered. 'Okay, are you gonna go down then?'

She nodded, 'Yeah, I'll see you in a bit.' She said, kissing me on the head, which caught me off guard, then turning and exiting.

I sighed, *what are we gonna do today?* I wondered.

I quickly showered and got changed. Then went downstairs, my stomach rumbling. I met Sam in the elevator and said hello, then the doors opened to a sight that I was beginning to get used to.

Everyone was milling around, eating, chatting and getting ready for the day.

'Hey, what have we got today?' Shouted Jason.

'Normal lessons in the morning then combat basics in the afternoon!' Replied Helena, her nose in another book.

Jason grinned, then panicked, then grinned again, but it seemed forced this time. *That's weird.*

I went to the kitchen and found Darius cooking up something, 'Mmm,' I said, 'Smells great.'

He smiled, then turned back to his cooking. I patted him on the back then stole a piece of Sam's toast.

'Hey!' He complained.

'You've got like, ten pieces!' I replied, he just shrugged then went back to eating, he had a hell of an appetite.

I glanced across the room and saw Jess sat across from CJ and Talia, they were chatting about something, well CJ and Jess were, Talia was just watching the Tv.

I sat next to Jess, 'Hey guys.'

'Yo.' CJ said, Talia ignored me, and Jess put her head on my chest. CJ gave me the once over then turned away.

I sighed. 'You ready for today?' I whispered to Jess.
'Mhmm.' She nodded.
'Good, 'cos I'm not I'll be back in a min.' I replied, getting up and going to get my stuff for later.
I got to my room and packed my bag for this morning, books, pens, pencils, all that *fun* stuff. Then went back downstairs, the elevator doors opened and I started to move towards the sofas where Jess was before. I stopped, CJ had swapped sofas, and both Jess and Talia had disappeared.
'Alfie!' Shouted Jess, I turned around. Talia and Jess were both sat at one of the dining tables.
'Sorry,' said Talia, 'CJ was being weird.' She smiled, embarrassed.
'It's good.' I replied, glancing at Jess she looked, panicked...
What is this guy's deal?
I decided I'd talk to her later about it. 'You okay?' I asked her. She nodded.
'Okay... I'm gonna go play with the lads I'll see you later.' I said. She looked up like she wanted to say something, but then turned her eyes to the table again, I turned to Talia.
We locked eyes; *I'll watch her.*
Neither of us reacted, I just turned and left.
Sylvia looked worried, I just shrugged at her and carried on walking, we'd have to keep an eye on CJ...
The boys were using swords to dice up zombies. At half 8 in the morning.
'Lads, it's half eight in the morning.' I stated.
'Yeah, and?' Tiago replied, not taking his eyes off the screen.
I shrugged, 'Fair enough, I've got next game!'

The morning went pretty slow, the morning lessons were uneventful, just a maths and English test, to see what we could do. That was easy.
Next came combat basics, this could have gone one of two ways; great, because they do a no power rule, or badly because

53

they allow powers, and since I don't have one, well, you get the idea.

'So...' Jess said, stuffing her mouth. 'How do you think you'll do?' She asked as we walked to the training arena.

'It depends.' She nodded, appearing to have understood, 'You need to be careful, you're gonna feel sick.' I said.

Jess shrugged, 'Oh well.' She replied, skipping on ahead, 'I'm just so excited to have a chance to beat you!' She shouted, spinning round, her eyes glowing.

I stopped.

'Just kidding!'

I smiled, she scared me for a second there, it was just like back at the tourney. I joined her again and we arrived at the entrance to the training area, meeting the Ramirez lot who were already there.

Eventually One Hit arrived and announced that it was none power combat.

I breathed a sigh of relief. *Thank You,* I thought, eyes to the sky, *I actually stand a chance.*

You stand more than a chance, my descendant boomed a voice.

I searched my surroundings, where had that voice come from? Jess stared at me, frowning, I guess I must have looked panicked. 'You good?'

I shook my head, 'Yeah... Yeah I'm fine.'

She gave me the once over then turned back to Bianca.

'AJ, you've forgotten your sword.' Noted Barukko.

'Huh, wha? Oh sugar!'

He smiled, 'Here, take this, it's not my style but it seems to fit you.' He said, handing me a white two-handed great sword. *Wait, this is...*

'T...Thanks Barukko.' I said, swinging the sword, testing the weight, it was perfect, no, a little too short.

'Hang on, where's the sword I gave you?' Jess asked.

I rubbed the back of my head. 'In my room. I kinda forgot it.'

'You're such an idiot.'

I grinned. 'Hey where's San anyway?'

'Oh no. Don't change the subject!'

I backed up, 'What's gotten into you?' I knew she could be a bit loud, but this?

'How did you forget the sword?' She said, her eyes glowing.

'Uh? Barukko? Lil' help please.'

Nothing happened, then all of a sudden, a dark line appeared in front of Jess, she stopped. By now everyone was too startled to move, only now had One Hit realised he should step in.

'Okay now folks!' He bellowed, wading into the crowd of people, 'That's enough.' He said, picking up Jess, 'I'm going to take this one to the classroom, the rest of you go on up to the training area and warm-up.'

Jess didn't react, even after being picked up and carried away. Everyone trudged off into the training area until it was only me, Barukko, Talia and Sylvia. Talia paused at the door, like she wanted to say something, but then went in.

'What was that?' Sylvia asked.

I looked at Barukko, then shrugged, 'Not a clue.'

Barukko stared at the door One Hit had taken Jess through, 'That was… Weird.'

And with that, I strapped my sword to my back and walked on in, trying to act confident about… That…

The part of the training area where we were situated was in the northeast corner, a massive concrete slab surrounded by sets of what seemed like stairs, it looked like a football stadium without seats.

'This is huge.' I said, spinning in a circle in the centre of it all. Jake turned to me, 'I know! Now warm up you don't want a stitch!'

We warmed up for a solid 20 minutes before One Hit came outside.

'Right!' He bellowed, rubbing his hands together, 'You're going to compete in a 1v1 tournament, the winner gets no homework for a week! Helena and Sylvia, you are exempt from this one by request. And due to the awkward number of people when you get to the last five contestants you will have a 5-way brawl to decide the winner! I will be up there,' He said, pointing to a glass screen halfway up a 50ft wall, 'and will announce everything from there. The first fight is Samuel Caesar Vs Ulva Hoights, good luck!'

Ulva said something none of us could discern, she speaks fluent English, we think, her German accent is just so thick...

Sam pulled out a knife, a black steel blade so dark it looked like night itself.

'You a ninja?' I asked him, laughing.

He smiled, 'I wish.'

'All righty folks!' Said a voice from the speaker, 'Everyone else please clear the stage!' There was a pause as everyone shuffled away from the fight. 'Okay... Three...Two...One...GO!'

Ulva raised her fists and stood, feet firmly planted, waiting for Sam to make his move.

He didn't hesitate, Sam set off with blistering speed, baring down on Ulva, who didn't move.

'I've gotchu!' he shouted, diving at her, if he got one touch on her, she had lost.

BAM

Sam was sent flying in the other direction, now Ulva was moving, she was halfway across the arena before Sam had even stopped sliding.

'What just happened?' Tiago asked.

'Kick to the face' Barukko said.

'Na,' I replied, 'Two kicks, one to the face, and one to the chest. That's what sent him flying.'

Barukko stared at me. 'How'd you see that?'

I shrugged.

Ulva was about to bring the hammer down on Sam when she made a fatal mistake, she put her foot right by his hand.

'Argh.' She collapsed.

Sam struggled to get to his feet, but it didn't matter, he had already won.

Tiago stared at Samuel, completely dumbfounded at how he'd won. Sam moved so quickly his eyes never even registered the movement.

A horn sounded and One Hits voice boomed through the speakers again, 'Congratulations Samuel!... The next fight is Alfie Jaeger Vs Jason Webber!'

I glanced across the arena to him, he looked terrified.

Barukko looked at me, 'If you lose this-'

'Don't worry,' I replied, 'I've got your sword.'

'You mean *your* sword.'

'Exactly.'

Barukko looked confused, Sam fist-bumped me, and I walked down onto the arena.

I turned to Jason, 'I'm sorry about this.' I shouted, twirling my sword.

'Don't g...get too cocky!' He shouted back.

I chuckled, that boy was scared out of his wits and he knew it. 'Three...Two...One...GO!'

Jason immediately charged towards me but tripped over his own feet and fell onto his face. A ripple of laughter erupted from the rest of the class, even Barukko cracked a smile. Jason laid there for a second in his own humiliation, then got to his feet, his nose bleeding. He looked fuming but I couldn't help but laugh.

'I'm sorry.' I said, trying to compose myself, I raised my sword, 'Shall we continue?'

Jason charged at me again, thankfully not falling this time, and got within swinging distance, he pulled his arm back and was about to try and knock me out with one punch when I hit him with the flat of my blade. I was surprised he didn't dodge it since I made it amazingly obvious, it looked like I was going for a home run in baseball, but clearly, he wasn't paying attention. Because before he knew it, he had a bad bruise forming and was flat on his back, coughing up a little blood.

He struggled to his feet, 'You're pulling your punches.' He muttered.

I planted my sword into the ground, it cleaved into it surprisingly easily. 'Of course I am, I don't want to break anything.'

His eyes blazed with fury and then started glowing.

A voice emerged from the speakers, 'NO POWERS.'

I looked up at the screen, 'It's fine! It's useless at this moment anyway.' I replied, pulling my sword out of the ground and dragging it towards a charging Jason.

'I'll kill you!' He screamed.

'I *highly* doubt that.' I muttered.

He got within my swinging range and that was where he lost, because in an instant he was on his back, with a sword lodged in his shirt, just grazing his shoulder and impaling the floor. Stunned silence.

'C...Congratulations Alfie Jaeger! The next fight is Gabriella Ramirez Vs Zoe Zane!'

No one moved, I pulled my sword out of the ground and swung it over my shoulder, walking back to where I'd watched before.

'What the Hell was that?' shouted Ajax.

'You're telling me you didn't see?' Called Barukko.

Ajax shrugged.

'Jaeger here swept Jason's feet out from beneath him then lodged his sword into the ground, nothing special.' Barukko said.

'Nothing special?' Shouted Jake, 'He did it in like point two of a second.'

Barukko shrugged, Zoe and Gabriella finally stepped onto the arena. I sat down with the sword strapped to my back.

Barukko leaned towards me, 'Umm, how'd you do that?'

I stared at him, 'Do what?' I whispered back.

'Change the size of the sword.'

I stared at him, dumbfounded, 'What?'

Sam glanced over at us. I smiled at him, he turned back around.

'I have no idea what you're on about B.'

The name caught him by surprise, but he got back to the point. 'Seriously?'

I looked him dead in the eyes.

'My god.' He put his hands to his head. 'You've got to have a power.'

I turned around to watch the fight, 'I don't...'

I used to be certain about that, now, I wasn't.

The rest of the first-round fights flew by, but that's because I was too busy thinking, neither myself nor Barukko said another word.

The next round matchups were announced, I was against Sam who, after my previous performance, looked a tad bit worried. We were the first fight, so I got to my feet and strolled down to the arena, sword over my shoulder.

'How do you carry that thing? It's huge!' Exclaimed Sam.

I shrugged, 'It's easy.'

'Give it here.' He said, his arms out.

'Uhh, I wouldn't do that if I was you.' Barukko shouted.

'What do you m- OH MY GOD!' The sword fell to the ground, I picked it back up.

I frowned, 'What?'

'It's so heavy.'

I laughed, 'You're kidding right?'

He looked me dead in the eyes.

Tiago walked down, 'Now come on, it can't be that hard... Give it here.' He held his hand out.

I sighed, 'See look it isn't-'

CLANG

I stared at the sword which was currently embedded in the concrete. 'What?'

Barukko finally came down, 'We'll talk after,' He leaned towards me, 'Try to do what we talked about.'

I glanced around the arena; everyone was murmuring excitedly. I sighed, 'Okay.'

Sam and I walked to our respective ends and got ready. My mind was running at one hundred miles an hour, *Is this sword really that heavy? Do I have some hidden power? What is going on?* I didn't even realise we had started until Sam was 20 metres off me.

'WAKE UP!' Sylvia yelled.

I snapped out of my daze in an instant. I instinctively swung my sword, but he was still out of range.

Riiipppp

'Huh?' I said, pulling my sword away and lifting it upright, it WAS abnormally long, 'Wha?'

I glanced at Sam, who was stood, breathing heavily, his shirt ripped, 3 metres from me, 'I only just dodged that,' he muttered, 'Who are you?' he gripped his knife.

I twirled my sword, 'I'm just a powerless guy.' *Or am I?*

Sam launched himself at me, trying to get close enough to grab me, but with the size of my sword, he couldn't get close enough.

He backed off, 'How can you move it that quickly? It looks way too large for it to be that agile.'

I stopped twirling it.

'Wait. It's, smaller?'

'That's what she said!' Tiago yelled.

I smiled and gave him a thumbs up.

'No...No...NO NO!' He said, stomping his feet. That, I'm not going to lie, cracked me up.

'How are you doing this?' He complained, 'You aren't even allowed to use your power in this tournament!'

I saw Barukko panic for a moment out of the corner of my eye. Thankfully he regained his composure and shouted, 'It's not him, it's the sword!'

I caught his eye, they sent a silent message, *Talk later, get this done.*

Sam turned to the glass screen, 'Is that allowed?'

There was a pause, 'Yeah, I don't see why not.' Helena's voice rang through the speakers, 'I made the rules and well, there isn't anything that says you can't so...'

Sam muttered something, presumably rude, in Italian.

I raised my sword, 'You ready?'

He opened his mouth, but I wasn't waiting for an answer. My sword was already at his throat.

'You lose.'

He smiled and dived down the edge of the sword, I was ready for that, I swung the flat of the blade into him, sending him flying past my shoulder. *Totally not accidental.*

I spun around, Sam was already on his feet, his nose was bleeding. He sneered, holding his ground. I twirled my sword,

I'll come to you then. I took my time, searching for an opening, constantly twirling my sword, keeping my defence up. I'd practised this a million times, it's a necessary precaution when you want to do what I want to do against a guy like Sam.

Sam was forcing all his weight to the bottom of his feet, I've not a clue why. But there was my advantage, it would take him too long to react and dodge, as long as I got close enough.

I kept on advancing, being careful as to not get too close, just the right range. If Sam got a hit on me it was over, even without paralysis, the guy could throw 10 punches about as quickly as I beat Jason.

I carried on walking. 'That's enough.' He growled.

Perfection, he'd stopped me right where I wanted to be.

He remained flat-footed, 'Now.' I muttered, launching myself at Sam, my sword flashed, his eyes widened.

CLANG

He caught my sword with his knife, 'How?'

He trembled under the force of the sword, if he didn't do anything he would lose.

'I can't... HOW?'

I pulled the sword away, flinging his arms into the air, then brought it back down, too quick to stop, and I was a lot closer now. This time I connected, slicing a thin line down the middle of his chest.

He sunk to his knees, then fell on his face.

I winced, 'Sorry.'

I rolled him over, he opened his eyes and sat up. 'I lost.'

I grinned, 'Yep.'

We walked back to the stands, Barukko and Jake walked past, they were next.

The rest of the fights went by and then there were only 5 of us left; myself, Barukko, Gabriella, Queenie and San, who kept disappearing after every fight.

It was time for the 5-way rumble...

We all entered the arena once we were ready, and spread ourselves out, me and Barukko agreed beforehand to take San out as quickly as possible, for the better.

Unfortunately, both myself and Barukko were on the opposite side of the arena to him, so we'd have to run past Queenie and Gabriella, which would be a problem. Queenie could turn into an elemental phoenix and Gabriella could fight very well, like incredibly well.

One Hit started the match and Barukko and I didn't hesitate like everyone else, we darted towards San immediately, flying straight past Gabriella and Queenie, who were too stunned to react.

Barukko got there first, dodging under San's jab and smashing his fist into his gut, sending him flying into the air. I then arrived, plunging my sword into the ground and leaping into the air, launching San behind me with a full force roundhouse kick (I'm not going to lie I enjoyed it).

I spun around and saw a very stubborn man, struggling to get to his feet.

I sighed, 'Why doesn't he just quit?'

San pulled the zhanmadao (I had to search up the name, but it's basically just a single-edged sword) he had from its sheath, planted his feet, and yelled 'Come at me!'

We happily obliged, Barukko started towards him immediately and I followed suit, San was ready this time though, slashing at Barukko, who was forced to dive under his sword, then smashing it into his back, sending him flying. I hesitated slightly, waiting for an opening, it came when he reset his stance, holding the sword level with his head he revealed his tactic, he was going to do the exact same thing to me that he did to Barukko.

So unimaginative...

I charged in and willingly slid under his blade, but when he came to smash it into my back, he was surprised to have found that I had spun around mid-slide and was now facing the oncoming sword. Still rotating, I flicked his sword into the air and carried on swinging the sword, slashing into San as I slid past.

He crumpled.

I expected a cheer or something, but all I got was stunned silence, Barukko got to his feet, he looked a lot worse than I thought he should of.

'What was that?' he said with a beaten smile.

'Practise...'

'Fair...'

By now there were only 3 of us left, Gabriella had taken out Queenie with very little damage, and Barukko had sustained a lot from just one hit. I was unharmed. We all stood in a triangle, facing off against each other.

I am not taking the first move. I thought.

I made the first move...

No one moved for a solid 20 seconds and I got impatient, so I feigned charging at Gabriella, knowing Barukko would come with me, then suddenly changed direction, hoping Gabriella would be too surprised to react, darting straight towards a surprised Barukko and clattering him with the flat of my blade and reversing his own momentum, sending him out of the competition.

I turned to face Gabriella, thinking I had this one in the bag when I crumpled to my knees, my head throbbing.

What? I thought back to when I had hit Barukko just now and realised something, right before I hit Barukko he caught my face with his fist, not doing as much damage as he would have probably liked but doing enough.

I glanced over to where he laid. *Fair play.*

I got to my feet and raised my sword, I raised my sword and launched myself at her, swinging my sword when I was in range.

Or when I thought I was in range...

My swing completely missed... The sword wasn't long enough.
'Huh?'
Bang
My face hit the concrete.
Oww
I got up again, Gabriella cracked her knuckles and came in for
the finishing blow, I swung for her again and missed, she hit me
in the gut.
I threw up.
She stood over me, not saying a word.
My vision was blurred, but I could see where she was, and I
could see my sword. She was definitely in range now.
I hesitated, then grabbed my sword and swung for her ankle,
hoping to knock her off balance. Instead, she kicked me in the
jaw, flipping me over and knocking me flat on my back.
I couldn't get up again. My body simply didn't allow it.
I stayed down; Gabriella had won.

My vision was still bad, and I had broken my jaw. Safe to say it
hadn't ended well for me.
'Sorry about that.' Gabriella said, offering me a hand, I took it
and she pulled me up, 'I really wanted to win.'
I wiped my mouth of the blood, 'It's good, so did I.' I replied,
rubbing the back of my head.
I saw Barukko storming over out of the corner of my eye.
'What did you do that for?' He complained, his competitive side
getting the better of him.
I laughed, which hurt, 'Sorry, I thought it was the best strategy
at the time.'
He grunted, 'Agh, whatever.'
One Hit, Helena and Sylvia came over to congratulate Gabriella.
Sylvia looked worried.
'Hey Gabriella,' I said, turning to her before the others arrived,
'I'll beat you next time.' I said, holding out my hand. She shook
it, 'I doubt that... Oh, and call me Gabby, Gabriella is too long.' I
nodded.

Everyone else arrived, and Sylvia took me to one side, 'How is she?' I asked.

She shook her head, 'It's weird, her aura's fuzzy but it's obvious, she is not happy.'

I sighed, 'I'll go see her.'

'Err no you won't,' she said grabbing my arm, 'Not until you get cleaned up anyway.'

I glared at her, but she refused to back down, 'Ugh, fine.'

So, there we were, myself, Barukko, Queenie and San, who was asleep, in the nurse's office getting checked out by the resident nurses.

Barukko was okay really, his muscles had taken a lot of damage from repeated impacts, but all he needed was rest. Queenie was a bit worse off, she had a broken leg, but they said it would be fine by Saturday. I thought I had the worst injuries, but most of my cuts had faded and my jaw was only just broken, they said it would be fine by tomorrow but that I should only eat soft food tonight.

San was out cold, so I had no clue how he was.

Anyway, an hour after the fights had finished, I was outside the classroom that Jess was being kept in, my jaw bandaged, but that was all. I was staring at the door, wondering whether I should go in or not.

Sylvia popped her head round the corner, 'Go on in, there's no real way of telling what's wrong unless you go see for yourself.'

I took a deep breath and walked through the door, leaving my sword on the outside.

I thought she was asleep, with her head upon the desk, but she raised it when I walked in the room. I leaned on the desk at the front, a few metres away from her.

I sighed, 'Hey, you okay?' I asked, she ignored me putting her head on the desk.

There was a moment of silence, finally I said, 'If you don't want to talk fine, I'm going then.'

'...I watched you.' She said.

'What'd you think?'

'You're good with that sword.' She grunted.

65

'Yeah?'

She nodded, then sobbed. 'I don't know why I snapped earlier. I wasn't like me.'

She caught me by surprise, I didn't say anything.

'I just felt so... weird... I... I think it's better if you stay away... For now at least...'

'Jess...'

'NO!' She shouted, tears streaming down her face, 'It's for your own sake. Now go... Please...'

I retreated out of the room and closed the door behind me, picking up my sword and driving it through the opposite wall, embedding it up to its hilt.

'It didn't go well then.' Sylvia said.

'You think?'

'She wasn't angry at you, just...'

'Scared.'

'Of herself.'

'That's so much worse.' I complained. 'At least if she was scared of me I could do something about that!'

I yanked my sword, out of the wall and stormed off, going to find Barukko. I passed CJ on my way out, he seemed deep in concentration, I didn't give him another glance as I walked out.

I got back to the dorm and Jake told me where Barukko was. I slammed open his door and sat down on his bed.

He looked up at me, 'You alright?'

'No! But I'm not here to talk about that.'

He nodded, 'The sword.'

'Mhmm.'

'Okay I don't know what's happening, but it definitely is not the sword, 'cos I can't do that, as much as I'd like to.'

I studied my own hands, he sighed.

'So...?'

'So you probably do have a power.'

'There's no way though, I've been training with swords my whole life, this has never happened before.'

'Has it not, or has it been too subtle to be obvious?'

I thought back to all the times I'd fought with a sword, there wasn't one occasion. Then I thought back to recently, when I had all kinds of weird encounters. *Is it possible?*
Barukko shrugged, is there anyone in school we could ask?
'There's the Principal, he's got all kinds of weird abilities, but I doubt power sensing is one of them.'
He sighed again, 'I'll do some research, but I guess we'll just have to wait and see if anything else happens.

Nothing else did happen. Not for a while anyway.

9 – I'm getting demoted?

We continued our lessons and nothing else interesting really happened for a while, I kept working out, playing sports, Jess kept away from most of us, CJ, Sylvia and sometimes Barukko were the only ones who had any luck. And we continued learning the basics of being a hero.

About a week and a half later the Principal told us that in the afternoon we were going to have a lesson with Class 1-B. Now, I didn't really know any of that class, but whenever we came into contact with them, they made it clear that they wanted our places at the top. Especially mine.

We all immediately took this to be a competition, even though the principal told us it was not a competition.

So, there we were, every person in our class, outside training area Alpha, raring to go.

The principal and Class B's teacher, Taper (He has tape powers), came outside.

'Hello class!' The principal exclaimed, 'And welcome to your first rescue.'

Everyone glanced at each other, murmuring excitedly.

'What does Class B have to do with this?' Tiago asked.

'Well… they're the villains of course.'

San cracked his knuckles, 'So I get to beat them up?'

The principal smiled, 'Well, kind of…'

'Hahaha! Yes.' He said, sprinting inside, only to find that Gabriella had hold of his hood.

Taper cleared his throat, speaking for the first time, 'Er, yes… anyway, you guys, in this scenario, are the heroes. You will be saving the civilians, or in this case, dummies, from the villains. You will be recorded on speed, safety, and choice.'

'Yes,' the principal continued, 'So you won't always fight your opponents, but then again, you can, but it may cost you.' He winked at San.

'Why'd you do that!?' He demanded.

The principal said nothing and instead signalled for us to enter the training area.

I was one of the first to step through the doors, 'Woah…'
This place was even bigger than training area Delta, easily the size of inner London, but we were only using the city area which made up the centre.
The teachers walked in after us, 'You have thirty seconds to plan, go.'
Honestly, we all spent the first 10 seconds panicking, then Helena said,
'Alfie, Troy, Shanelle and Jake, you take the east corner, Alfie and Jake you protect the other two. Next, Barukko, Paris, Alda and Alexander, Barukko and Alda protect. You take the west corner.' We all took a moment to process that info, then she continued, 'Tiago, Kareem, Ajax and Queenie, you take the south side, you can all fight so switch out depending on the situation. Next, San, Sylvia, Jess and Talia, take the North side, Jess and San should defend.' Helena really emphasised *defend*, staring at San. 'In fact, CJ, go with them, in case San runs off. Now, myself, Jack, Maddison, Alexandra and Bianca, we're on support, we're going to sit on the roof of that building there,' She said, pointing to the tallest one, 'and we're going to run the operation and pick off any targets. Finally, Sam, Ulva, Natalia and Darius, you're on stand-by, I'm going to send you where you're needed once I know where you're needed, just patrol the centre for now.'
Everyone nodded, seeming to understand.
The principal clapped his hands, 'Okay, that took slightly longer than thirty seconds but that's fine.'
A horn sounded, and we all sprinted off to our various corners, myself and Jake in the lead, however, we were quickly overtaken by Shanelle, who could fly.
'I'll go on and scout ahead!' She called to us, I just gave her a thumbs up and carried on running. By the time we'd arrived Shanelle had already saved 5 people. But she was in trouble. 4 of the "villains" had found her. We were all crouched behind a collapsed concrete pillar.
'Hang on.' Jake said, 'That's the top four.'
'There's no way.' Troy said, peeking over the top, 'Ohh it is.'
'Hang on… The top four?'

Jake sighed, 'The four most powerful people in class B.'

'Ohh… I can't believe they are all together, they must be trying to take as many of us out at once.'

Jake didn't reply, instead he stood up and shot a fireball at the nearest one, setting him ablaze.

Really? I thought, *These are the top 4?*

The guy Jake hit was busy trying to extinguish himself when I leapt out from hiding and knocked him out.

'That was easy.' Troy said, also coming out of hiding.

The other 3 still hadn't noticed us, I swung my sword over my shoulder.

'Really, we just took out your teammate and you haven't even noticed?'

Suddenly, their attention switched to us 3, allowing Shanelle to make her escape, I just prayed she didn't panic and instead she went to save people.

Jake said, 'If we take these lot out, that should make it easier for everyone else right?'

I nodded, 'Troy, stay with us until we take another out, then go help Shanelle.'

He nodded. I pointed my sword at the girl in the middle, 'Hey.' I said, launching myself at her, Jake followed suit, blasting a ring of fire around us and fending off the over two, Troy leapt in the ring with me.

'She's the one with water powers.' He said, 'She's number one.'

I did not take this to mind as I ran at her, but I was ready when she blasted a jet of water at me. I split it down the middle with my sword, surface tension acts slightly different coming out of a person, it was wonderful. However, the sheer power of the jet was astounding, I was slowly slipping back.

'Aaargh!' I growled, summoning all my strength and turning the tide (get it, 'cos like, water?) and beginning to advance on her. I could see the frustration on her face, she was tiring quickly, she did not expect the battle to last this long.

I slashed, forcing her to pull her hands outwards, which was both a good and a bad thing, good because it left her wide open, bad because it put the fire out, allowing her friends to help her out.

I had to finish this quickly, I drove towards her and slashed again, catching her face as I moved the sword, then, in her daze, I ran forward and swept her off her feet with my sword. I glanced over at Troy, 'Can you tie her up or something?' He shrugged, 'Yeah sure.' Pulling a piece of rope out of his pockets.

I turned and faced the other two, who had now bunched together to try and fight Jake. I flicked my sword, 'I'll go and help shall I?'

I advanced on the other two, both had their attention on Jake so didn't notice me until I was stood next to him.

I planted my sword in the ground and stretched my arms, 'Shall we finish this?'

The other two glanced over to where the water girl was tied up, their eyes widened. 'Just how powerful are you?' One of them asked.

I laughed, 'I don't even have a power.'

They glanced at each other, 'WHAT?' They shouted getting to their knees, 'Please, just tie us up and get it over with.'

I burst out laughing, I couldn't believe what I was seeing, *this* was the future generation of crime-fighting heroes?

'Okay.' I said, pulling it out of the ground and slinging it other my shoulder.

'Jake, will you please...'

'Do I have to?' I shrugged, staring him in the eye, 'Fine.' He replied, trudging over to them.

As he got down on both knees to tie them up, they glanced at each other, leapt up, and grabbed Jake, taking his rope and tying him up.

I laughed again, 'What's so funny punk?' The girl said, 'We've got your teammate.'

'Well...' I said, catching my breath, 'There's a reason I didn't go in to tie you up, and it's not that I didn't have a rope.' I continued, pulling out the rope from my back pocket to prove it, 'It's because, if you had knocked my sword out of my hands, I'd have been defenceless, because I have no power. But because you were so positive, you'd win if you grabbed one of us you forgot one important detail.'

71

Jake set his hands alight.

'He can summon fire…'

He melted the ropes in an instant and then trapped his capturers in a ring of fire.

I high fived him, then turned to the two now trapped, 'Congratulations, you got caught.'

Jake went in again and this time they showed no resistance, after we had tied all 4 together, we stood in front of them, wondering what to do next.

'We should find Shanelle and Troy.' Jake said, I nodded.

'But where can they be?'

Jake shrugged.

'Why don't we go to H and see what we can do from there.'

'Yeah sure.' He replied, creating a ring of fire around our prisoners.

I looked at him, 'Can you keep that up?'

'Ohh yeah that's easy.' He said.

'Okay… Let's go.' And so we set off running towards the tallest tower, leaving behind 3 very frustrated faces and one that was still asleep.

We arrived at the tower in under 5 minutes, and we're met by one of Maddison's projections.

'What are you doing here?' It said.

'Yeah… we kinda cleared up all the enemies in our area so we came here to see where we are needed now.'

'Okay,' It replied, 'head on up.'

Unfortunately for us, the elevator was broken, so we had to run up 47 flights of stairs. We got to the top quickly enough, but heavily out of breath.

'What are you doing here?' Helena said, turning to us as we opened the door.

'Well…' I said, catching my breath, 'Me and Jake had defeated and captured the top four. They were the only enemies in our area, so we came here since you could probably tell us what to do next.'

'The top four were all in one place? And you two took them all out? How weak are they?'

I shrugged, 'Pretty weak, but very stupid.' I replied, chuckling.
'Okay,' Helena said, studying the battle ground, 'I'd say start by heading west, then once you've defeated the enemies there head North.'
We both nodded, then turned for the door.
'Where are you going? Just take the zip wire down.'
Jake turned around, his smile beaming, 'Zip wire?'
She pointed to what indeed appeared to be a zip wire that led off the top of the roof.
Jake, without hesitation, leapt off the roof and grabbed onto the zip wire.
I, with a lot of hesitation, followed him. It was actually amazing, we went flying straight down, having a couple close calls with buildings, and landed not too far away from where H told us the west side people were.
'Come on!' I shouted to Jake, running past him.
He smiled and caught up, 'There should be more enemies here, right?'
'Well, because there were only four against us, yes.'
'So... How many?'
'Like... Eight.'
He sighed, 'Yay...'
'But they should be weaker.' I said, swinging my sword over my shoulder, 'Come on!'
We saw Barukko and Alda soon enough, they already had four of them tied up, they were surrounded by another 4.
Jake and I crouched behind another fallen pillar (there appeared to be a lot of them) 'See, told you, eight.'
He shrugged, 'Okay, what's the plan?'
'This.' I said, stepping out into the open, above everyone else.
'Hey guys, wassup?' I said, planting my sword into the ground and leaning on it.
Barukko immediately understood and took advantage of their confusion, strengthening the shadows around one, knocking him out, and leaping at another. Knocking her out too.
I glanced at Jake, grinning, 'See?'
The 2 other enemies glanced around to find their friends knocked out.

'What? How?'

I rubbed my head, 'I feel like I'm hearing that a lot lately.' I muttered, 'Anyway! It's quite simple really, but I can't be bothered to explain it, so I'll allow you to surrender if you want.'

The girl scowled, 'We'll never give up!' She pulled a sword out of thin air.

'Ooo cool power!' I replied, pulling my sword out of the ground. 'Shall we finish this?' I said to Barukko.

He nodded and knocked them both out instantly with his darkness.

Alda stood there, dumbfounded, 'H...How?'

I laughed.

Jake stared at me, 'You're getting cocky you know.'

I smiled, 'I know. But when it comes to these dumbnuts over here I think I'm okay.'

Barukko turned to us after tying up the rest of them, 'So, where to?'

'Well Helena said to head North after we'd helped you so...' I pointed North.

He shrugged, and we took that as the go-ahead, setting off jogging North. All this travelling was making me tired, and really achy.

As we jogged, I had the time to properly see what we were training in, it was just loads of shells of buildings, like there'd been some sort of explosion that had blown out all the glass, and plenty of rubble, and the occasional fallen building but I like to think that was purposeful.

We arrived at the North to find that they weren't doing so well with the enemy, there were 7 enemies left standing and only 1 tied up and they were completely surrounded.

We stopped just round the corner of a building, I glanced around that corner.

'What are they doing?' I said.

Barukko looked, 'They're surrounded.'

'Jake, head to the roof, cover us, then we break them out of their situation, I'll distract, you two take them out.'

They nodded.

'Okay, you go round that side of the building I'll go round this side.'

I walked round the corner and planted my sword. 'Hey guys.'

They all turned to me.

'Who's this kid?' One said.

Sylvia shouted, 'What are you doing here? Why aren't you on the East side?'

'Because I sorted those lot out, and West side too.'

The group took a step back, 'You took out our top four? Single-handedly?'

I decided to go with it, 'Yep, all by myself.'

I saw the flash of a sniper scope up on one of the rooftops around me. I pointed to it with my sword, 'WHO'S THAT?' I shouted.

Thankfully Jake understood and a flurry of fireballs launched off the roof above me at the target, setting the opposing roof alight.

I turned back to the shocked group that stood below me, then looked behind them and found that Barukko and Alda had moved the 4 that were trapped away.

I rubbed the back of my head, 'Yeah, I may have lied about doing it all by myself.'

They all turned around to look at their group of prisoners, only to find them, well, not there. They turned back to me, scowling.

I swung my sword over my shoulder, 'Sorry not sorry.'

And with the most impeccable timing ever, Barukko and everyone else appeared behind me, all 8 of us, together, above the now cornered enemies.

I pointed my sword at the group below and charged.

I didn't even get to the bottom of the slope before Jess and Barukko launched themselves over my head and knocked out the enemy using their powers.

I got to the bottom, 'Could have left something for the rest of us.'

Barukko smiled a little bit, Jess turned away. I sighed.

A horn went off in the distance, we glanced at each other, confused. Then a voice blared out of some hidden speakers,

'Congrats everybody,' It was the Principal, 'can you all please head back to the entrance, thank you!'

We walked over and 10 minutes later there we all were, both class A and B, stood apart, but both at the entrance.

The Principal and Taper both walked through the doors.
'Alright everyone, we'll talk to you tomorrow in the morning, dismissed!'
I looked at Sylvia, *Is that it?*
She shrugged and began walking out, I went with her, the rest of the class following suit, except for 1.
'Hey shut it!' Screamed an all too familiar voice, I glanced around, and seeing that the rest of the class had come out with us, left him to it.
I walked back, alone staring into the distance where I could see CJ and Jess chatting, I was going to talk to CJ when I got back to the dorm, but he wasn't there, so I went to go play basketball instead, it was all I did really, that and sparring.

The Principal came in the morning, 'Hello everybody!'
He was met by a chorus of half-hearted replies.
He smiled, 'I've got something for you today!' He exclaimed, tapping the wall next to him. A holographic table popped up.
'Woah.' Half the class said.
'This... is your rankings, based on power, combat, knowledge, etcetera.'
I scanned the list.
1 – Barukko
2 – San
3 – Jessica
...
28 – Alfie
I put my head in my hands, *Ohhh No*
I looked up and saw Jess staring at me from across the room, she quickly turned away. I sighed, got up, and went to my room.
I was leant on the balcony when I heard my door open.
'Hey Alfie,' It was Sylvia, 'you okay?'

I turned back to the view, 'I don't know. I mean, twenty-eighth, last?'

She walked up beside me.

'I don't even know how I got in this school.' I muttered.

She studied me, 'There must have been something... Everyone out there looks at you as their leader.'

'Great, their 'leader' doesn't even have a power.'

Sylvia sighed, 'Not everything's about power you know.'

'But it is!' I complained, 'You know that combat rating that we get for non-power combat? That goes out the window when it comes to the end of year tests!'

I punched the concrete wall, cracking it, and walked inside.

Sylvia paused where I'd punched the wall, then followed me in.

'You'll be okay.' And with that, she left me alone.

10 - My Birthday is worse than Christmas this year, I think

A week later my birthday arrived, the 1st of September, I was the oldest in my dorm, but I didn't tell anyone about it, no point.

The morning and afternoon came and went, in the evening I video called my Mum when she got off work and we opened my presents, a new pair of shoes (black and white high tops), and a few small things.
Nothing really happened for a while, school was dull, hero training was okay, the rankings moved up and down, well, except for me.
The rankings updated every Saturday night at 7, so it became a weekly thing, get everyone sat around the screen, waiting for it to update. I was only there for everyone else. It just served as a bitter reminder for me.
Jess still hadn't gotten any better with me, but she seemed fine with CJ and Barukko, she and CJ were close as well...

Myself, the Ramirez triplets, Sam and Zoe discovered a basketball 'league' within school, so we competed in that, I dropped our first 50 bomb (50 points for those uneducated), we were pretty good actually. There was talk of like, an actual league starting with teams from across the country and we were pretty excited about that.

More time passed. Christmas was coming up and we were all pretty excited, 1st years had to stay in their dorms, so we decorated the whole building in one weekend, even Barukko, who hated lights, joined in.
We actually got the week before and the week after Christmas off, so you'll re-join the story on the second day of our holiday, when it snowed...

I awoke to Sam rapidly banging on my door, I opened it, yawning, 'Wassup?'

'IT'S SNOWING!' He yelled in my face.

I turned around and flung open the curtains, 'It certainly is.' I said. The sky was white, sheet white, I could hardly see 20ft out my window, 'This is one mighty snowstorm.'

He joined me at the window, 'It is!'

I laughed.

'What?' Sam asked.

'I just haven't had a white Christmas in a long, long time.'

He grinned, 'Neither have I.'

I got dressed and went downstairs, only to find it completely empty except for Jake, CJ and Jess, who were deep in conversation. Jake waved though.

'Don't like the snow?' I asked.

He shook his head, 'Too cold.'

I went out the back and found everyone, right before a snowball hit me in the face.

Gabby laughed, 'Sorry!'

I wiped my face, made a snowball and hit her right back. 'Not sorry!'

Barukko appeared next to me, 'I've got to say, I'm having fun.'

I stared at him, 'Are you suffering from hyperthermia?'

'Hey, don't joke,' Sylvia said, walking up to us, shivering. 'It can kill.'

I laughed, 'You'll be alright.'

I glanced back at Jess and CJ, 'They aren't coming out?'

Sylvia shook her head, Barukko was about to say something when he got hit in the face by one of Bianca's pinpoint snowballs.

'I'll get you for that!' He yelled, running off.

I scanned the area, 'It's like they're eight again.'

Sylvia chuckled, 'And we're the adults supervising.'

'And those 3 behind us think they're too grown up to have fun.'

She burst out laughing, 'Jake's just a wuss.'

I dodged a snowball and launched another one back.

'I wouldn't get this back at home.'

'Not many of us would, we all live so far away...'

I nodded, picking up a bunch of snow and stuffing it down Sylvia's back.

'IT IS SO COLD!' She screamed, I laughed until tears were coming out of my eyes, she had taken her coat off now, it was soaked.

'Here, take mine,' I apologized, then hit Tiago in the back of the head with a snowball.

I glanced behind me, Jess and CJ were gone.

It was one hell of a day.

The next day we awoke to find another layer of fresh snow, but we were all too tired to go out again so we had a normal day, but we actually agreed that over the course of 3 days (Christmas Eve, Day, and Boxing Day) everyone would organise a game and we'd play that game on one of those 3 days. We needed to do something to keep us all busy.

I made a custom charades game, which I thought was amazing (if I do say so myself) and I had no idea what anyone else had made.

Anyway 2 days before Christmas in the evening I was stood on my balcony staring at the melting snow, when I saw a rather odd predicament.

First, I saw CJ and Jess leave on a walk or something into the forest, (Okay, not that weird, but what happened next... Might just change your mind) but what followed was a dark group of human-like figures, darting between trees, heading in the same direction soon after.

Uh oh, this can't be good. I thought, I grabbed my sword. *Wait a minute Alf, should I just leave them alone?* I thought back to the shapes I'd seen in the trees, I realised that I'd also seen the glint of what appeared to be weapons. I swung my sword over my shoulder and headed for the elevator, casually heading my way to the door.

'Hang on Alfie.' Alex said, stopping me at the door, 'Where are you going?'

'Out.'

'Mhmm, I'm going with you.'

'Don't.'

'Nope!'

I glanced around, and saw Sylvia staring at me, I shot an aggravated look at her, then shrugged at Alex.

'Come on then.' I said. Alex caught up. We started walking in the direction CJ and Jess went.

'So, where are we going?' Alex asked.

'To check something out.'

'Is that why you've got your sword?' I nodded.

We continued walking for a solid 5 minutes when we heard a scream ahead of us. 'Jess?' I muttered. Alex set off running, I noticed the tripwire ahead of him that he hadn't seen. 'Wait!' Too late, he sprung the trap and got caught in a net, thankfully the ropes were rubbish, and I was able to cut him down.

He picked himself up and brushed off.

I scanned the surrounding area and then turned to him, 'Okay, I'm going to go on ahead, I need you to run back to dorm and grab Barukko and a couple others, keep going past here, watch out for traps.'

He nodded, turned, and ran back to the dorm.

I sighed and continued searching for Jess and CJ, *They must be in trouble.*

I moved as quickly as I could, looking out for traps, avoiding any I did find.

I continued searching for another 10 minutes before I heard voices up ahead.

It sounds like... laughter?

I leant against the back of a tree and glanced around the corner, there they were, 20 or so guys in black suits. *Wait, ninjas?*

I continued searching and right at the back, tied to a tree, I found Jess, she was bound to a tree by her hands and ankles, she was shivering. No sign of CJ...

I put my back to the tree again, *it'll be at least 10 minutes before everyone else gets here.*

I looked back round the tree, then I saw CJ, he came strutting out from behind a tree opposite me, a huge smile on his face.

'Well done guys!' He said, 'To think we actually infiltrated such a prestigious school so easily!' He threw his head back and laughed.

81

I hide behind the tree again, *He's a part of this? But how?*
He stood in front of Jess, 'Now where should we start?'
'Uhh, boss…' One of them interrupted, 'Shouldn't we just leave and do this later?'
He laughed again, 'No, no, let's give them a hint at what we're going to do…' He replied, ripping Jess's shirt off. She shrieked.
Okay that's it, I thought, stepping out into the open, sword glinting.
'Oh hi CJ!' I said.
The whole group turned around, 'How'd he find us?' One shouted.
CJ sneered, 'Alfie Jaeger, come to save the day all by himself.' I decided not to tell him about the reinforcements on the way, that never works in the movies.
I twirled my sword, trying to come up with a strategy, but what could I do in a 20 on 1 situation?
Well, I charged.
I lunged at one, catching him by surprise, and knocked him out, but now the rest were ready, weapons drawn, I scanned the crowd, katanas, Shurikens. *Yep, definitely ninja.*
I charged at another, deflecting his blade and sending him flying. Another lobbed a fireball at me, I sent it right back at him with my blade. I darted into the crowd, slashing, jabbing, deflecting, and knocking out anyone in my way.
I sent one guy flying into a tree and it grew around him, I paused for a second, *Wait, what?*
I turned around, there were 10 guys on the floor, and a dozen more stood in front of me, looking quite shocked.
I swung my sword over my shoulder, newfound confidence inside me. 'Come on then.'
One brave (or stupid) ninja stepped forward, raised both hands, and blasted a massive jet of water at me, *Uh Oh.*
I crossed my arms in front of me and closed my eyes, the last thing I saw was CJ's smile out of the corner of my eye.
CRACK
I opened my eyes, before me stood a huge ice sculpture of the water beam and the guy that it came from. I glanced around me, *who did that?*

I had hesitated for too long, everyone else was getting over their shock, I grabbed my sword and ducked under the ice, coming out of the other side to see a bunch of Shurikens flying at my face.

'Oops.' I said, smashing them all with my sword, returning them to sender, pinning him against a tree.

They all unanimously and simultaneously decided to charge at me 9 guys (excluding CJ, he just stood there) running at me, I thought I was doomed. I lifted my sword and planted my feet, a shockwave blasted the ground around me sending the front 4 guys into the air, I dashed towards them and slashed, hitting all of them.

I flicked the blood from my blade and twirled it, deflecting 2 more Shurikens.

I stood my ground, my eyes glowing with anger.

2 of them took one look at me and decided it wasn't worth it, one opened a portal and they left. Another panicked and ran slap bang into a very low branch, knocking him out.

'Just leave.' I growled.

CJ unsheathed his sword, 'Not gonna happen.'

I pointed my sword at them, and a lightning bolt struck me and channelled through the sword sending his two buddies flying, they didn't get back up.

Okay... That's weird.

I went with it, 'How 'bout now?'

His eyes glowed, he tensed his whole body up, gathering energy. I put myself between him and Jess hoping to absorb most of the shockwave.

BOOM

The shockwave erupted from his body, I held out my arms, eyes wide in fear. But something amazing happened, as the shockwave was about to hit my body it slowed, then stopped. I looked up and saw the surprise and fear in East's eyes. I saluted to him, then the shockwave reversed its direction and picked up speed, converging on him.

Blood fled from his body, he collapsed to his knees.

I walked over to him, sword in hand, 'End me.' He muttered.

I swung it over my shoulder, 'Na. I think I'll let you rot in a cell for a while. Then, if you come after me or her again, I'll kill you.'

He smiled, 'My Dad'll... kill... you.'

'I can't wait.'

He fell to the floor, he'd fainted.

I turned around and ran over to Jess, cutting her ropes and catching her.

She was crying, 'I'm sorry.' I said.

She shook her head weakly, 'No, its... my fault, his power...'

She fainted too; she must have been exhausted mentally, especially after suffering from CJ's power for so long.

'Alfie!' Yelled a voice in the distance.

I didn't move, 'Over here!' I shouted back.

Alex, Barukko and Sylvia walked out from behind a bunch of trees, 'Oh! There you are!' Sylvia said, running over.

Barukko stopped, looking around, 'How?' I locked eyes with him, 'Aah.'

'How is she?' Sylvia interrupted.

'Fine,' I said, taking off my coat and wrapping it around her, 'just tired from fighting his power.' I said, nodding at CJ.

'His power?' She asked.

'Emotional Manipulation.' Barukko said.

I nodded, 'He used his shockwave power to cover up his secondary power, Sylvia, is Jess's aura a lot clearer now?'

Sylvia stared at her, she gasped, 'How?'

I nodded at CJ.

'Ohhh.'

Alex turned to me, 'How'd you do this then?' he said, pointing to the guy who was part of a tree. I shrugged. I could feel my body weakening by the minute. It was weird, I was fighting to stay awake.

Sylvia frowned, 'Are you okay?'

'Yeah, just... tired.'

'I bet...' Barukko muttered.

'Is this it? Were you my reinforcements?'

Barukko smiled, 'Na, the principal and like 10 teachers are on their way, but poor Jake had to go get them, they'll be a long soon.'

84

And so they were, 2 minutes later they turned up to find us 5 all sat in a sort of semi-circle where the snow had been melted, facing the direction they were coming from.

The principal arrived first, 'What on Earth?' He took one look at me and seemed to understand immediately, 'Aah I see.'

The rest of the teachers arrived soon after, hesitated for a moment, shocked at what they were seeing, then going around, gathering everyone up and taking them off.

By this point I could hardly sit upright.

'What will happen to them?' Alex asked.

'Well, they'll be sent to prison eventually, for how long it depends...' Replied the principal.

'Depends on what?'

He stayed silent.

I yawned. The Principal took that as his cue, 'Ooh! Would you look at the time, you must be heading off back to your dorm, Jess will need a bit of sleep and she'll be fine in the morn...' He stopped because I had just passed out, still holding Jess.

Barukko later told me that they carried us back up to the dorm and the principal said he'd come to talk to us in the morning, but I suspected he wasn't telling me about something the Principal said.

Anyway, I woke up the next day with Jess sat on a chair next to me, studying my face.

'You're awake!' She shouted.

'Woah... Quiet down I just woke up.'

She smiled, 'Sorry.'

I sat up, staring at her, 'You okay?'

She rubbed her wrists, 'I'm the one who should be asking that, after all, you did take on twentyish guys by yourself just to save me.'

I chuckled, 'Just to save me.' I muttered.

'I know, and your... your...'

I sighed, 'I know... My err, power.' She nodded, 'Give me your hands.' I said.

She held her arms out, I grabbed both her wrists and focused. My hands emitted a warm light, and I felt my eyes light up. Jess's eyes widened in surprise. 'There.' I said, feeling dizzy.

She stared at her wrists, now completely healed. 'How... Are you okay?' She said, grabbing me.

'Yeah, just, still not used to it.' I said, grinning.

She laughed, 'I'm not surprised, you've only had it for two days, well, longer, but yeah.'

'What time is it?' I asked, looking out of the window.

'Three.'

'I've been out all day! What about lessons?'

'It's fine, the Principal gave us permission since you saved my life yesterday.'

'You're welcome.'

She laughed again, I looked at her, a tear ran down her face.

'Hey... I've always got you.'

'Yeah but I haven't had you once! In fact, I tried to kill you!'

I laughed, 'And? I don't care about that.' I said, hugging her. She buried her face in my shoulder, 'It's been a crazy couple of months so let's try to have a normal Christmas.' I whispered, 'Please.'

She smiled, 'Okay.'

We got up and went downstairs, I was still wearing my clothes from yesterday, but I couldn't care less. It was empty except for one person.

'Aah Alfie Jaeger.' Said the principal, who stood in front of the screen that showed our standings, 'Come, sit and talk with me.'

Jess and I sat on one side of the sofa, he sat on the other.

'Now, about yesterday, I've got to say I'm impressed with what you pulled off, especially since you had only just awakened your power.'

'Wait you knew about my power?'

He chuckled, 'What you think you got into this school by luck? No, I knew about your power, well, your potential. I didn't expect my power amplification to start the awakening, but I'm not surprised saving Jess released its full potential.'

I put my head in my hands, 'What exactly... is it?'

'Your power? Well, I guess we could call it God's power, or whatever you choose to name it.'

'God complex maybe.' Jess muttered.

'I like that.' The Principal said, 'Anyway there has been rumours of a power like yours for generations, a power so great that it could do anything, it would unite humanity.'

'No pressure.' I said.

'Yes… Anyway, I've made a rule change, from today until Boxing Day you can all go home, all of Class 1-A anyway. Just don't tell the others.'

I glanced at Jess, 'Like… now?'

'Yes now!'

I got up and pulled Jess up with me, we headed to the elevators.

'We shall talk more when you get back!' said the Principal, I nodded and headed for the elevator.

'Come on Jess! We've got to go! Have you got a bag?' She shook her head.

'So are you gonna go back home for Christmas?'

'Yeah I guess, I mean I'd rather go with you or Ba-'

'What do you mean "I guess"? Is there something wrong at home?'

She shook her head, 'Never mind.'

I packed as quickly as I could and then went round to Jess's room, 'Hey I'm done do you want me to walk to the station with you or…?'

She shook her head, 'Na I'll wait for everyone else they won't be long.' She said getting up, she walked over and kissed me on the cheek, 'See you after Christmas Alf.'

My face reddened and I nodded before turning and running off, 'Text me when you get there! Oh, and Merry Christmas!' I shouted as I got in the elevator.

I didn't stop running until I got to the station and was on the next train homebound. I pulled out my phone to text my mum, then hesitated, *Wait, I don't think she'll know I'm coming home, let's surprise her.*

I was so excited to be home for Christmas that I was bouncing on my chair the whole way home, and when I got off the train I ran the rest of the way, I had to be home by five.

I got there at ten to five and went inside, not turning any lights on or moving anything, I just sat down on the sofa in the dark and waited…

20 minutes later I heard the door unlock and the hallway light turned on, my Mum dropped her keys on the side and walked into the living room, sighing and turning the lights on. She saw me and dropped her bags, I laughed, 'Hiya!'

'What are you doing here?' She exclaimed, running over and hugging me.

This everyone, is my Mum, overwise known as Jackie and the best person ever (I may be slightly biased). She's slightly shorter than me, but otherwise looks pretty similar to me, she is a woman who knows a whole lot more than she lets on, it even surprises me sometimes.

'What are you doing here?' She repeated.

'Well… It's a long story.' I began a couple of months ago, at the fight that kicked it all off, then finished with me sat in her living room.

She covered her mouth, 'Oh my gosh Alfie.'

I rubbed the back of my head, and sat up, 'Yeah well there's something else you should know.'

She looked puzzled, 'What?'

Then set my hand alight.

She was so shocked she literally fell out of her chair. 'You have power over fire!'

'Well, yes and no.' I said, forming a water drop in my over hand, then a spark flew between two of my fingers.

Her jaw fell open, 'He told me you were the one, but I didn't believe him.'

I stared at her, 'What?'

She sighed, 'My power, I never really told you what it is, but it basically allows me to speak with dead relatives, on both your Dad's side and mine.'

Now my jaw dropped open, 'So that's who…'

She nodded, 'Most don't talk to me, but there's one on your Dad's, an ancient one, god-level warrior, who often talks to me about you. He first told me at your birth that he was special, I told your father of course, but that... Spooked him.'

I didn't push her; Dad was a touchy subject.

'Who is this relative?'

She shrugged, don't know, I just know that he was amazing... Anyway, are you hungry?' At the mention of food my stomach rumbled, 'I'll take that as a yes.' She said, walking to the kitchen and getting pans out of the cupboard. I got up and walked into my bedroom, I chucked my bag against the wardrobe and fell back on the bed.

I pulled out my phone, *One missed message from – Jess*

I clicked on the message and unlocked my phone, ***Jess – Hey Alf, I'm at Barukko's for Christmas, lemme know if you need anything.***

I sighed and closed my eyes before replying.

Me – Aight will do.

'Girl trouble?' My Mum asked, standing at the door.

I sighed, 'Yes and no, not really trouble.'

She nodded and let me be, only calling me when food was ready.

We ate together then went to bed early, we aren't really Christmas eve people, we always do stuff on Christmas day.

Anyway, I went to bed early and scrolled through my phone for a while, chatted with some of the lads on the group chat, then went to sleep feeling weirdly empty inside.

The next day I woke up early and walked into the hallway only to find my Mum already awake and making breakfast, 'How do you always wake up before me?' I said.

'Because you sleep like a log every night.' She said, ruffling my hair.

'Mhmm, what's for breakfast?'

'Sausage sandwiches.'

'Ooo lovely, how long will they be?'

'About... two minutes.' I nodded and plonked myself on the sofa. I reached for my phone but realised I'd left it in my

bedroom so instead I switched on the Tv, 'When's the football?'
She asked.
'I think around twelve, my god I haven't watched a game in a
while.'
Mum frowned, 'Why not?'
I shrugged.
Finally, she put a plate in front of me and I wolfed down the
entire contents in an amazingly short amount of time, 'My god
I've missed you're cooking.'
She chuckled, 'I never thought you'd say that!'
I laughed and put down the plate, 'Presents!'
'Hang on I haven't finished yet!'
'I don't care I wanna open them!'
She sighed and put her plate down, 'Fine... open the biggest one
first.'
'Mum there's literally one, it's the biggest, smallest, most box-
like, and least box-like.'
'Yeah alright stop being so sarcastic!'
I smiled and ripped open the wrapping, revealing a shoe box.
'You didn't get me a new pair did you?'
She smiled, 'Why don't you open it and find out?'
I slowly opened the box to reveal a pair of crimson red and
white basketball shoes, 'You did! You're the best!' I said.
'Oh it's really no problem.'
'Hang on let me go and get yours...' I said, darting off into my
room and coming back with a handful of presents. The biggest
one was the main one (of course, if it isn't you're doing it
wrong), the little ones were just like candles and stuff. She
opened the big one last, revealing a state-of-the-art coffee
machine (I know right?)
'Oh Alfie it's amazing.'
'It does a shed load of things that I don't really know about and
I imagine you'll literally use it for coffee and that's it but yeah!'
'Yeah, I will try and mix it up.'
I smiled and got up, 'Good. I'm going to go get changed into my
jeans and a shirt.'
'You only have one shirt.' She noted.

'Yeah alright. And then I'll come back out and I can whoop you at every game we play!'

I quickly got dressed and came back out, 'Mum do you only have like, that one dress?'

'Hey I like this dress.'

'I'm not saying it's bad just, you wear it a lot.'

'Yeah and I like this dress!'

I shrugged, 'Fair enough.'

We played our usual ridiculous amount of games throughout the day, I won most of them (of course) and by five o'clock we were both shattered.

'When do you have to go back to school?' Mum asked.

'Tomorrow... I'll probably leave in the morning, more trains then.'

She nodded, 'You hungry?'

'Not really.' I sighed, putting the basketball on, two teams I didn't really care about were playing but it was basketball, so I didn't care...

A while later my phone started vibrating in my pocket, Jess was calling me.

'Oh hey what's up.' I said, answering the call.

'Hey erm, you get the train from Central Manchester, don't you?'

'Yeah why?'

'Cos our we've got to switch over there on the way back to school and neither of us have been there before so... Can you meet us there?'

'Yeah sure I'm going there anyway tomorrow so what time?'

'Erm like... Hey Barukko what time do we get into Manchester?' I heard the muffled voice of Barukko in the background, then Jess relayed the information, 'We get in at ten past nine.'

'Alright, I'll meet you there... See ya!' I said, putting down the phone before I could say anything else.

'Who was that?' Mum asked.

'Jess... I'm going to meet up with her and Barukko at the train station.'

'Oh, do they live nearby?'

'No Barukko lives even further away from school than we do, they just have to transfer at Manchester and neither of them have been there before, so I'll have to leave like, quarter past eight, unless I jog… Na I'll go then.'

'Early morning then.'

'Yeah but it's still the holidays so I can lie in the morning after.' She laughed, 'What?' I asked.

'It's nothing, now then… More games?'

I got up, 'Honestly, I might go for a jog.'

She stared at me, 'I know you've got powers now but are you feeling okay?'

I laughed, 'Yes I'm feeling fine thanks! I'm gonna change then I'll have a shower when I get back.'

'Good, because you smell after exercise.'

I stuck my tongues out at her and went to get changed, I was out in 3 minutes, phone in pocket (one with zips so it doesn't fall out, I know, thinking ahead) and headphones on, I didn't really know where I was going, I just hadn't seen the place in a couple of months, so I went everywhere. An hour later I found myself in the city centre, it was already dark, but I didn't really mind that since the city was always busy.

Anyway, I stopped for a break down by the quay, I grabbed a drink and sat at one of the many cafes around the place. I watched the stream of couples enter and leave the restaurants and cafes, everyone was with someone else, except me of course, eventually it started to rain, *Did I do this?* I wondered, anyway it didn't bother me, I was sat under cover.

Zzz…Zzz…Zzz… Jess was calling again, *What's wrong now?* I picked up the phone, 'Hey.'

'Hey… You okay?'

'Yeah I'm alright why?'

'I don't know you just ended the call before I had the chance to talk to you earlier.'

'Yeah… Sorry about that… Anyway, how's Christmas been up there?'

She sighed, 'It's been alright, Barukko seems… weird but otherwise it's been okay, how about you?'

'It's been okay, haven't really done much.'

'Oh… Okay well erm, Alf-'

'Oop hang on Jess I've just gotta move.' I said as I glanced around and saw a couple of waiters looking at me, I'd already paid so I got up and walked out into the rain, 'Sorry Jess what's up?'

'It's… Nothing, where are you?'

'I'm currently in the centre of Manchester stood out in the rain.'

'Oh my god are you okay? Do you want me to come down now?'

'Woah there… I'm fine, I just went for a jog when you called me and now I'm standing out in the rain, it doesn't bother me anyway.'

'Okay… Well look, erm…' I heard Barukko's voice in the background, 'Hang on…'

I presumed she covered the mic with her hand, but that doesn't do anything nowadays, 'Yeah hand on babe I'll be right down.' I heard her say.

'Right okay, what was I saying?'

'Babe?' I cut in.

There was a pause, 'You heard that?'

'Yep.'

'Dammit, I was hoping to tell you tomorrow but yeah, we're dating.'

'Oh good for you!' I said, trying to sound happy.

'Yeah thanks, so anyway I've got to go I'll see you tomorrow yeah?'

'Yeah see you.' I replied before ending the call, I stared at the sky, rain streaming down on my face, I gathered my composure and set off back home again, jogging the direct route back, ten minutes later I was in the middle of a park when I came across some old friends…

'Hey! You there stop!' A guy ran up to me and shoved a gun in my face.

'Ugh, seriously I'm not in the mood for this.' I muttered.

'Hey… Wait, Alfie? Hey guys this is the kid I used to rob all the time back in the day!'

'Oh great.'

The other two walked over, I could tell they were struggling to keep the fire in their hands lit, either they were very weak or very wet, or both.

'Hahaha really, it's a throwback.' One said, laughing.

'First off,' I said, 'I'm not in the mood for this, second, I have no idea who you are.'

'I robbed you like six times as a kid what are you on about?'

I shrugged, 'Well it won't be the same.' I said.

'Why? You're still powerless.'

'Okay I'm done.' I muttered, blasting the guy with the gun with lightning and then turning to the other two, who proceeded to lob fire at me, only to have it extinguished by the rain.

I laughed, 'You guys are stupid, two fire users rob a guy in the rain!'

The other guy ran up to me and put the gun against my head, 'SHUT UP!'

I sighed and summoned a lightning bolt on me, blasting myself and the guy, I then blasted the other two guys with lightning bolts, frazzling them, and left, I just presumed the police would show up at some point.

Anyway, I got back soaked, didn't say anything to my Mum and got in the shower, not knowing whether they were tears or just shower water that were running down my face.

I got out, got changed and went to bed...

I woke up the next morning, packed my stuff, ate breakfast (lovely as always) and said bye.
'Okay I'm going to go now Mum.' I said.
She hugged me, 'Okay Alf, be safe okay?'
I nodded, deciding to not mention the fact that the attack that's on the news was me, and so I'd be fine.
'See ya later!' I shouted, jogging around the corner.
'Alright then.' I muttered to myself, 'Let's go back.'
I made my way through the maze of streets towards the train station, past the park where I'd been last night, it was still cordoned off.
'Really? It's not that big of a deal.' I muttered.
'What?' An officer said behind me. I jumped, 'Kid, they think that those three lightning bolts were the three largest in recorded history.'
My jaw dropped, 'What?'
He nodded, 'Whoever did it must be one powerful guy.'
'Yeah... He must.' I said before quickly exiting, *Three most powerful lightning bolts in recorded history? Mad. I cannot believe I was the one to do that.*
I carried on walking, choosing to avoid the park entirely and walk down the docks, I was idly strolling when I realised that I was on a schedule, I pulled out my phone, ten to nine, 'Oh sugar I'd better get a move on.' I muttered before setting off, jogging towards the train station I wondered what would happen if I arrived late, *Would they wait or just try and figure it out themselves? Actually, I imagine they'd call me first, then depending on how far away I was they'd make their decisions, but I'll get there in time anyway, so it'll be fine.*
I got to the train station slightly out of breath, and on time, I glanced up at the board, *09:02, Lovely.* I scanned the board, finding the train that was coming in at ten past, platform 25, *Great, the other side of the station.*
I ran through the maze of tunnels and corridors making my way to the platform, I got there just as the train was pulling in.

95

I stopped by the stairs and waited for them to come out, but as it turns out half the train was getting off at Manchester, so it wasn't that easy.

The platform eventually cleared out and I saw Barukko and Jess looking completely bewildered in the middle of the platform.

'Hey! Over here!' I shouted. Jess saw me and ran over, tackling me in a hug, 'Should you be doing that with me now you've got a boyfriend?' I said jokingly.

'Oh yeah good point.' She muttered, pulling away before Barukko caught up.

'Hey man wassup.' I said.

'Nothing much, you?'

'Na, never… Anyway, we've got like ten minutes to make it to the next platform so let's go.'

We chatted about what we'd done over the break whilst we walked, well, Jess did most of the talking, Barukko just kinda nodded and held her hand.

We boarded the train and grabbed seats, we didn't say as much on the train, Jess and Barukko talked a bit but that was all.

Right as we got off the train and I was about to suggest a race back to school Jess sprung a question on me, 'Hey Alf.'

I put my hands behind my head, 'Yeah?'

'Was it you on the news this morning?'

I glanced back, acting like I had little idea about what she was on about, 'Huh?'

'On the news, you know, about the lightning bolts?'

'Oh you mean the three most powerful lightning bolts in recorded history? Yeah, that was me.'

Barukko grunted, Jess's jaw dropped, 'What? Why did you even do it?'

'These three guys tried to rob me, one of them had a gun and I wasn't in the mood.'

'You know they'll have heart problems for the rest of their lives?' Barukko said.

'Hey look I'm surprised they didn't die, besides who cares they were just criminals.'

'That's ruthless.' He said.

I shrugged, 'It doesn't bother me, if they do it again I might just kill them.'

'Alfie!' Jess complained.

I ignored her, 'Hey wanna race back?'

'Not really.'

I sighed and stuck my headphones on, walking back the rest of the way pretty much in silence... until Jess got cold.

She tapped my arm, 'Hey erm, Alfie could you do something about this wind?'

I took my headphones off, 'Huh? Oh yeah I mean... I could try.'

I stopped and closed my eyes, concentrating on the wind and forcing it to divert around us, it seemed easier than stopping it entirely.

'Did it work?'

'I think so.' I said, putting my headphones back on.

'Thanks...' She nodded.

We made it back to dorm slightly warmer than we would have been without my magic (if I do say so myself) and walked in on Talia having a rant.

'-And he would have been mine if it wasn't for that meddling WITCH who had to go and get save...' She stopped when she saw us, and blushed.

I dumped my bag on the floor and leant against the wall, 'Oh no please carry on, don't let us stop your unwinding.'

'No...No, it's err, quite alright.'

'You sure?'

She nodded and ran for the elevator.

Jess turned to me, 'What was that about?'

I decided not to say anything.

Tiago turned to us from across the room, 'Hey Alfie have you seen the scoreboard?'

'No why?'

'They updated it over Christmas.'

All 3 of us turned to it and did the exact same thing, started from the bottom, *Wait, I'm not there.*

I continued going up, 20th, 15th, 10th, still no me.

5th, nope, 4th, nope, 3rd – Alfie Jaeger.

Jess turned to me and hugged me, 'Oh my gosh!'

I didn't say anything, absolutely dumbfounded. *How?*

'I knew you were powerful, but...'

'San's going to be fuming.' I finally said.

Everyone laughed, I glanced around the room, 'Where's everyone else?'

'Not everyone has gotten here yet.' Tiago replied.

'Okay.' I said, picking up my bag and heading for the elevator, 'Back in a min!'

'Alf wait up!' Jess shouted, running to get in the elevator before the doors closed, 'You could have waited for me!'

I stared at her as she leant against the wall, 'What?' She asked.

I looked away, 'Nothing...'

I got out of the elevator and walked into my room, Jess followed me in, 'Look, Alf... Erm...'

I sighed and turned to her, 'Jess... It's fine... You do what you want to do, it's your life... You know?' I said, before shoving my stuff in my wardrobe.

She sighed and walked out of the room.

I sat down on the bed and noticed a note stuck to my computer:

Can you come to see me when you get this?

- **Principal**

I thought about showing it to Jess but decided against it, I plucked the note off the screen and stuck it in my pocket before leaving.

'Hey where are you going?' Maddison called.

I pulled the note out my pocket, 'Principal's.'

'Do you want me to come with you?'

'Na I'm alright thanks.' I said, shoving the door open and making my way to the Principal's.

I arrived at his office and knocked on the door, 'Who is it?' he shouted.

'It's Alfie... Jaeger.'

'Oh come in!' he said, I opened the door and he gestured to sit down across from him.

His office was this huge space, with floor-to-ceiling windows on one wall and a series of awards and photographs on the wall opposite him. I looked at the pictures on the wall for a second and then sat down.

'You'll be on there at the end of this year, and possibly in the hall as well.' He said, gesturing to the wall behind me.

I nodded, 'Anyway, I'm assuming you wanted to talk to me about my power.'

He nodded, 'Yes, now as I'm guessing you already know, a power of your… magnitude is going to be incredibly draining on your body; however, this will only get easier the more you use it.' I nodded again. 'Another thing, I think you should keep this power a secret from the public for as long as possible.'

'Because it'll make me a target, as of now I'm a weak kid with a very powerful future, if the bad guys get wind of me, I'll be targeted now.' I guessed.

The principal nodded, 'Exactly.'

'Okay, what happens if I hit three guys with the three most powerful lightning bolts in history, but no one knows it was you?'

'That was you?' I nodded, 'I saw the footage, that was unbelievable, the most powerful lightning user in the world can't do that.'

'I know.'

'I'm presuming you've seen the scoreboard by now?'

'Yeah.'

'It may be slightly wrong, you are actually the most powerful child in that class, you might even be the most powerful student in the school if I'm speaking honestly, but we can't show that, a jump from last in the class to first? That would fire off some questions.'

'Yeah, Sir… You know when you told me I didn't get into this school by luck? So you already knew of my power?'

He smiled, 'Kind of… I knew of your potential.'

That didn't really answer my question, in fact… It was almost an identical answer to earlier, but I took it anyway.

'Is that all?' I asked.

He nodded, 'Alfie, just be careful, and keep practising, if you do it right, you can be great.' He said as I left.

I stopped at the door, 'Thanks.' I replied, then left.

I walked back to the dorm to find Barukko stood outside, staring into the distance.

'Hey.' I said, walking up next to him.

He blinked, 'Oh, Hi.'

'What's up?'

He sighed, 'Not much.'

I didn't really want to talk to him, so I turned around and was about to walk off when he said. 'Alfie?'

'Yeah?'

'Do you like Jess?'

I didn't even pause to look at him, 'Look mate, you two are together and as far as I can tell that's how it'll be, I won't do anything about that.' I finished, walking away and into dorm. I walked in and scanned the room, there were at least 20 of us downstairs now.

'Hey AJ!' Called Alex, 'Come look at this.' He said, signalling to the tool station that had been set up in the corner of the room.

'Okay, what is this mess then?'

He laughed, 'It's not a mess yet! But it will be.'

'So it's like a tool station.'

He nodded, 'So I can make those new shoes of yours even better.'

'Hey they can't be improved... wait, how do you know about them?' He nodded at my feet, I sighed, 'Yeah okay, just don't ruin them!'

Gabriella pointed at them, 'Are they new?'

'Yep.' I said, walking up to her.

'Cool.'

'You had a good Christmas?'

'Meh, it's been alright, didn't do much.'

'I don't think many of us did.'

'Well we are teenagers.'

I laughed, 'We are indeed.'

'Awe I need a boyfriend!' Queenie cried out of nowhere. Tiago looked up from across the room, I caught his eye and chuckled. Jess looked up, 'What was that about?'

I ignored her and stared at Tiago.

100

Gabriella looked over to where I was looking, 'My god he makes it obvious doesn't he?'

'It's a miracle she hasn't noticed.' I muttered.

I caught Sylvia's eye and pointed to Tiago, then Queenie. She looked confused for a moment, then caught on and looked at them both. She shrugged.

I nodded, 'Maybe wait.' I silently mouthed to Tiago.

He looked disappointed, then nodded and sat back down.

'What are you doing?' Gabby asked.

'Detective work.'

'And?'

'Yeah no, not now.'

Jess looked at us, 'What are you two talking about?'

I shrugged, then went to talk to Jake who was staring at Sylvia. 'What is going on today?' I said, Jake snapped out of it and looked away.

'I don't know...' Jess complained.

Jake sat down and looked at me, I looked him in the eye, and he knew I knew immediately. He sighed and fell back into the chair.

I sat down next to him and picked up a controller, 'You're the one guy I can't help.'

He looked at me, 'Why?'

'Well 'cos I can't ask her, that kind of gives it away.' I said, grinning.

'Yeah, good point.' He replied, picking up the other controller, and for once I let him win...

'Haha yes!' He shouted, as he beat me by an *astounding* 10 points. 'I win, you lose, you're trash.'

'You know I'm up twenty-three to one, right?'

I glanced around the room and saw Sylvia staring at Jake, smiling.

Hmm, okay.

I smiled, 'What are we doing about all our games then?' I shouted.

Everyone looked up, 'Oh yeah.'

'Why don't we just start tomorrow, and do it over the course of three days like we said?'

Sam stood up, 'Alright then!'

The mood in the room seemed to have improved, after all we had something to look forward to.

Later that night after most of us had gone up, Tiago, Jake, Sam, Zoe and I were sat around the games console. Playing and chatting, when I decided to switch the topic, see what I could grind out of them now everyone wasn't around.

'Right okay people,' I said, 'today I've noticed a lot of, surprising things, mainly with you know, girlfriends, and boyfriends in Zoe's case.'

Jake glanced at me, frowning.

'So come on, spit it out.' I said.

Jake sighed, 'Fine.' Sam and Zoe stared at him.

'You know that if she wants to know, she'll know.'

He nodded.

'Wait… Syl?' Sam asked.

He nodded.

Zoe smiled, 'That's a tough one.'

'I know right.'

'And we can't ask her about it like we normally do.'

Zoe looked at me, 'What do you mean by that?'

'Well, like with this guy other here,' I said, nodding to Tiago, 'I just ask her, but well, I can't because that may tip her off.'

'Wait what do you mean 'with Tiago'.' Zoe asked.

I stared at him, 'Q' He muttered, falling back into his chair.

'And Sylvia said?'

'Not yet.' I replied.

They both nodded their heads.

'So, what about you two?' I said, grinning.

'You haven't already had Sylvia take a look at us, have you?'

I shook my head, 'Not yet anyway.'

'There's no point anyway.' Zoe said, ruffling Sam's head.

It slowly dawned on the rest of us, we all sat up at the same time. 'Wait what?' Jake shouted.

I laughed, 'Since when?'

'Ohh about two months ago.' Sam said.

My jaw dropped, 'And you didn't tell us!'

'You four are the only ones who know.'

'You know I'm telling Jess…' My voice trailed off.

Zoe nodded, not seeming to pick up on what I said, Sam glanced at me though, worried, 'In fact.'

And with impeccable timing, **DING…** The elevator doors opened and Jess ran out, tackling Zoe in a hug.

'Oh my gosh!' She shouted, 'How come you didn't tell me!'

'I didn't tell anyone!'

She looked up, 'What are you doing here?'

'I was here first.'

She shrugged, 'Whatever, I'm off back up then, I'll talk to you in the morning.'

I turned back to Zoe and Sam, 'So this has been going on for two whole months, and none of us noticed, not even Sylvia?'

Zoe shook her head.

'You guys are good.'

'Yeah, we're the best at everything.' Sam said.

'You've lost the plot over Christmas haven't you?' I asked, jokingly.

Zoe giggled, 'Yes he has, now it's late, we will be off now.'

I nodded, 'I'll go too.'

We headed for the elevator.

'I'm gonna ask her.' Jake said.

'When?' I turned around.

He shrugged, 'New Year's.'

Zoe smiled, 'That's a good time.'

I went upstairs and onto my balcony.

I leant against the balcony and stared at the night sky for a while, wondering what would've happened if I'd have asked Jess to come with me for Christmas. Eventually I shook the thought out of my head, *I can't think like that, it'll destroy me if I constantly think about "what if".*

Now I'm going to confess something to you all. I may have fallen in love with Jess on the 23rd of December that year, but that's not important. Then I thought about what Jake said. *New Year's Eve. Not a bad idea.*

Anyway, I said goodnight (to myself) and I hopped into bed.

103

I went to sleep that night with plenty of ideas running through my mind.

12 – The contest with lots of smaller contests and no overall winner!

I woke up the next morning to a rapid banging at my door. It opened before I'd even gotten out of bed.
'Oh hi Jess.' I muttered.
'I've got a problem.'
'You don't have a game.' I suggested.
She stopped, 'Yeah...'
'Can't you do Barukko's?'
'Hmm, never thought of that.'
'Okay, now I'm off back to sleep.'
'It's seven o'clock!'
'Exactly.'
I went back to bed and went back to sleep for another two hours, it was great.
Anyway, I got up and showered before heading downstairs.
The doors slid open to reveal a completely normal scene, absolute carnage.
I grabbed a bowl of cereal, and after dodging one of Bianca's projectiles, sat down at one of the tables with Alex and Alexandra.
'What's up?' I said to Alex.
'Nothing much.' He said.
His sister turned to us, 'The next three days are going to be, interesting.'
I stared at my bowl, 'They certainly are.'

Zoe and Sam came down at the same time,
I had like a flashback, I realised that they came down together nearly every day.
So it was obvious, we just weren't looking.
I finished my cereal quickly; I had no idea what was in store for today...
I looked around and realised Barukko wasn't here.
'Hey has anyone seen Barukko?' I shouted.
No one said anything.

I glanced at Jess, she shrugged, I decided to go get him, I walked for the elevator doors and as I did, they opened. And Barukko walked out.

'Speak of the devil!' Jake said.

We all laughed.

Barukko looked confused, 'What?'

'Don't worry about it.' I replied.

'Is everyone here?' Sylvia asked.

'Everyone but San.' Helena replied.

'Eh, sod him.' Sylvia said, 'Okay we'll start then, who wants to go first?'

No one said anything, then...

'Ah, yeah sure why not.' Barukko said, scratching his nose.

I turned to him. 'Really?'

He shrugged, 'Why not?'

He turned and walked towards the centre of the room. 'Okay everyone I hope you've brought you're running shoes! 'Cos we've got a scavenger hunt!'

Excited conversation erupted from everyone.

'Alright everyone let the guy speak.' I interrupted.

'It will be done in pairs, and you will each have a bucket,' he pointed outside. 'In this building and across the street in the sports courts there are over 60 black orbs like these.' He said, holding up a black ball about the size of a tennis ball. 'In your pairs, one person, and only one, will go and find one of these balls, bring it back, then the other will go and find one. There will be a 5-minute time limit and whoever has the most at the end wins. The use of power IS allowed and stealing from each other's buckets are not allowed, everything else is. You've got two minutes to choose your partner then select a bucket outside, then I'll set you all off and the time will start.'

Helena stuck her hand up, 'There's an odd number of us.'

He shrugged, 'There can be one three then.'

Me and Jess instinctively locked eyes and went outside. We didn't care if we weren't on the best terms at the time, we just wanted to win.

'Is there a strategy to this or not?' Jess said as we stood by our bucket.

'I've got an idea off the bat.' I whispered it in her ear.

'YES!'

'Yeah? Okay, I'll try that. It might tire me out a bit, but it'll allow me to find some more and make it easier for us.

She nodded.

A minute later everyone else was gathered outside and were raring to go.

'Okay…3…2…1…GO!'

I tensed, then immediately teleported like 30 metres away and summoned a Stone box around everyone else.

'HAHA yes it worked!' Jess screamed.

Barukko laughed, 'I never thought that'd happen.'

I turned and set off to the sports courts, finding 5 or 6 more before picking up one at the entrance to the whole thing. I sprinted back to find that they were still trapped in the box. I put the ball in the bucket and Jess set off.

'I can't believe it worked.' I said, gasping for breath.

'They're not going to be happy with you.' He chuckled.

I shrugged.

The stone had just begun to crack when Jess got back with another ball. She put it in the bucket, and I set off sprinting, I had just picked up another orb when I heard a huge **BANG.** *Uh Oh…*

I sprinted back before anyone could catch me and put it in the bucket, we were 3 ahead before anyone else had even found 1.

'Alfie Jaeger!' Someone screamed, I just laughed, I was winning, and they weren't.

Jess got back just as everyone else was finding orbs.

'I've got another idea.' I whispered it in her ear when she got back. I then went and got another one. Jess set off then stood in the middle of the path, waiting for someone to come round the corner.

I turned away and everyone else stared at me, Barukko caught on and also turned around.

Suddenly there was a blinding flash and then I heard the clatter of another orb in the bucket. I set off running.

'Hey that's cheating!' I heard someone complain.

Barukko shrugged, 'I didn't see it… TWO MINUTES GONE!'

It was getting harder to find orbs now, there were a few left in the courts and god knows how many in the dorm. I grabbed one and made haste back to our bucket. I put it in and Jess grabbed me.

'Build a box around their buckets.' She said.

I laughed, concentrated, **_BOOM._**

'Alfie, I swear to god!' Gabriella cried.

I laughed, 'Sorry not sorry!'

This idea was actually better than mine because they didn't work together this time, it took some a whole lot longer for some teams to destroy their part of the box, and Barukko didn't let them go until they did.

The game ended with us having 17 orbs and the second-highest had 7 (Queenie, Shanelle, and Helena).

Barukko called the game to an end and Jess and I both collapsed to the ground exhausted, just as everyone else was.

'It's not fair.' Sam complained, Zoe laid on the ground next to him, 'He's basically a god.'

Jess snorted, 'He's not a god, he's just powerful.' She said.

'What do you mean by that?'

'Well, we wouldn't be here.' She whispered, 'Somewhere like the Bahamas would be nice.'

'Hmm, I wonder,' I held out my hand to her and concentrated, a one-dollar bill appeared in my hand.

'Wha-? How? Did you steal it or make it?'

'I have no idea. I mean you can't use it here anyway but keep it.'

She took it from me, 'Thanks...'

I laid down on the cold ground, 'Can we go back inside now?'

Barukko smiled, 'Yeah, you can.'

All the balls vanished from the buckets.

'Oh, cool!' Jess said.

I laughed and walked inside, 'Come on it's cold!'

We all sat down in the various chairs and sofas, I don't think there's ever been this many down here at one time, Jess sat on Barukko on the sofa, I glanced around the room; Sam was sat with Zoe in his arms.

Okay how did we not notice this?

Jake kept glancing at Sylvia and Tiago was chatting to Syl and Queenie.

'Wow, they're all on it today?'

'What?' Gabby asked next to me, I pointed to the lads around the room.

'They are on it.' She confirmed, then went back to watching the Tv.

'Hey who's next?' I called...

We played games for the next 12 hours, only stopping for food and pee breaks. I spent most of the time talking and playing with Gabriella and Jake. By 8 o'clock that night we were all shattered, we'd run, shouted, and drank (no alcohol you dirty minded people) ourselves to death.

We were all sprawled out on the sofas, chairs and floor by now. Sylvia yawned, 'Okay I'm shattered.'

I smiled, 'I think... everyone is.'

I looked around the room and no one moved, well except Barukko and Jess. He smiled, all his attention on her.

I looked at Gabriella, 'I'm gonna go up, need a load of sleep for tomorrow.' She nodded and got up. I yawned and wandered to the elevator, Gabriella joining me, 'You coming up too?'

She shrugged, 'Actually I want to talk to you.'

I nodded and sat down on the bed, she plonked herself in the chair opposite me, in quite un-Gabriella fashion.

'I'm so tired.' She yawned.

I smiled, 'I can tell.'

DING...

Sylvia - You should probably tell Gabby to sleep with you there's gonna be a prank.

I sighed, 'Look at this.' I showed Gabby the text.

'What the hell?'

I shook my head, 'I know right? I mean I think it's part of the prank, they'll want you to be in here so they can get us both.'

She thought about it for a sec. 'Yeah, you're probably right... So what are we going to do about it?'

I sighed and closed my eyes, putting my hands behind my head, 'What do you want to do?' She shrugged, Alfie got an idea, 'Well, I mean we could just reverse prank them.'

She looked at me, 'What do you mean?'

'Hang on...' I summoned my cloak and pulled out a couple of wooden shurikens, 'Take these.' I put up a shield, 'Okay, now toss one of those slowly at me, and get ready to catch.'

'What...? Okay.'

She threw one at me, I saw her eyes widen when I didn't move... Then all of a sudden it bounced back, a direct course back to her hand.

'What?'

I grinned, 'You like it?'

'What... Is it?'

'A reflection shield, instead of just stopping whatever is thrown at me it redirects it right back to where it came from.'

'That's so cool!'

I shrugged, 'I know... Now then, we just need to wait.'

'So what shall we do?'

'I don't know.' I said, getting up and walking to the balcony, 'What do you wanna do?'

She walked outside with me, I leant against the wall, 'You know Alfie, you don't act like the most powerful kid in the world.'

I frowned, 'What do you mean?'

'Well... You're so laid back; I'd expect you to never stop you know? Do everything you can?'

I smiled, 'But I don't need to do much, there's a world of heroes out there, they don't need me yet.'

'Yeah I guess you're right...'

I pulled out one of those shurikens from earlier and tossed it away, before using the wind to bring it back.

'You did that so casually!'

I smiled, 'Yeah and...?'

'Well I couldn't do that.'

'Yeah but you don't have the power,' I did it again, 'It's not the same thing as... I don't know, making a half-court shot.'

'Yeah I guess.'

I spun around and looked at her, 'What's up?'

She looked at me, 'What?'

'I don't know you seem, disappointed almost.'

'I have no idea what you're on about.' She said, moving next to me.

I nudged her shoulder, 'Hey what if we're still up at one in the morning and it turns out that they actually were hoping to prank you?' I chuckled.

'Well then, we've got an all-nighter.'

I smiled and walked inside, 'Alright then, you'd better prepare because it is going to be awful!'

She smiled and followed me in...

An hour later we were still waiting, and she'd beaten me at three different board games...

'Okay they're gonna be a while.' I said, yawning.

'Yeah probably.'

'I'm gonna have a shower then, I don't really mind what you do to be honest if you want to go to sleep in your room and I'll just prank them anyway it'll be fine.'

She yawned, 'Maybe I'll go have a shower, get changed, then come back.'

I shrugged, 'Okay... See you in a bit then.' She winked at me and left, I got in the shower and changed, sticking on some shorts and the baggiest t-shirt I had (I don't own any pyjama tops), then sat on the floor, resting my head against the bed.

Soon enough I had a knock at the door, 'Come in!' I said.

Gabby's head popped through, she was covering her eyes, 'You decent?'

I laughed, 'Yeah I am.' She smiled and skipped into the room, 'You know I've never seen you like this.' I said as she sat down next to me.

'What do you mean?'

'You always act really tough when we're around everyone, and now you seem more... Carefree.'

She shrugged, 'Yeah I guess... So, what do you wanna do?'

'I don't want to play any more board games against you, you're annoyingly good at them.'

'Yeah well, that's not my fault.'

'Do you want to watch something then?'

She glanced around the room, 'You don't have a Tv...'

I kicked the chair out of the way.

'Huh?'

'The Pc.' I sighed.

'Ohhh, yeah sure.'

I got up and switched the Pc on, grabbing a remote as well before sitting on the bed, I tossed her the remote, 'You choose.'

She sat down on the bed next to me, 'Okay! Don't complain if you don't like it though!'

I didn't need to complain, she put on one of my favourites, about this team of drivers who steal a bank.

About halfway through the film Gabby started nodding off, 'You okay?'

She put her head on my shoulder and I put my arm around her, 'Yeah I might fall asleep though, wake me up when they come.'

'Okay.' I muttered, and sure enough, she went to sleep...

I sighed and continued watching the film, waiting for this damn prank, *If it gets to one and nothing's happened I'm off to sleep.*

Half an hour later the film finished and I put on the next one in the series, Gabby started shivering so I covered her in a blanket, and I as well.

Finally, the time came, it must have been ten past twelve when they finally knocked, I woke Gabby and grabbed the air horn from my desk drawer.

'Why do you have that?' She whispered.

'It comes in handy more times than you'd think.'

'Wait if you have the barrier why do you even need it?'

'So no one else finds out about my barrier, thinking ahead.' I said, tapping my head.

She smiled, 'Okay.'

They knocked again, I did my best to sound like I'd just woken up, 'Yeah... Hang on.' I said.

Then I swung open the door, sounded the air horn and put up a reflection barrier all at the same time.

I can't even describe the sound it makes but it was loud. I couldn't stop laughing, I was stood in front of Sam and Jake, with Tiago and Sylvia filming. Sam and Jake were covered in the cream pie they were gonna chuck in my face.

Gabriella cracked a smile too even though she was still basically asleep.

'You've got to send me that video!' I wheezed, 'You actually thought we'd fall for it!'

'Wait so Gabriella was actually sleeping with you?' asked Tiago. I shook my head, 'Na… I mean she did fall asleep but that was never the plan.'

Jake looked confused, but then shook his head and went back to eating some of the cream cake that hadn't been in his face.

'Yep, now I'm off back to bed.' I said, turning around.

Gabriella kissed me on the cheek, 'Thanks for tonight.' She said before walking to the elevators.

'Uhh, yeah no problem.' I said, watching her leave.

Sylvia's eyes flicked between us two, 'What exactly just happened?'

I shrugged, 'Not that sure… Oh well! I'm off to sleep, if anyone else wakes me I'll blast them with a lightning bolt.' I threatened, walking back into my room and falling onto the bed, lights out.

13 – A slight detour for something far more important...! And then back to the regular schedule...

I woke up after another dreamless sleep wondering whether I could turn my dreams on and off.

'Ugh, what time is it?' I hit my phone, 'Half seven, I'm not getting up, my whole body aches.' I muttered, I'm still not 100% sure who I was talking to.

'Hmm... I wonder.' I said, still talking to myself, suddenly my whole body lit up like a glowstick and when the light died? I felt a whole lot better.

'Huh, that's... Amazing.' I said, feeling like I should get up all of a sudden.

I showered and changed, putting on basically the same outfit I always wear. I went out onto the balcony, finding Jess out here on hers.

'Hey, I'm about to go down you coming?' She said.

'Yeah but I'm going to try a different approach.' I said, swinging my legs over the wall. 'You coming?'

She looked at me, 'What are you? Oh no, you're gonna jump off, please don't.'

'No, I'm going to take a controlled descent down, worst case scenario I break my legs, you'll be fine I'll save you if anything happens.'

She sighed, 'Fine.' She wrapped her arms around me, and I took a step off the ledge, we fell, slowly, to the bottom. 'That was weirdly amazing.' She said.

I grinned, 'I know right?'

We walked in through the back door, 'Where on Earth did you come from? I was the first one down here and I never saw you come down.' Natalia said.

'You never saw us come down the elevator.' I replied

Her eyes widened, 'You didn't.'

'I did.'

'I didn't even know you could!'

'Neither did I until about a minute ago.'

Jake spat out his drink, 'You mean you did that for the first time, WITH HER?'

I smiled, 'Yep.'

'You've got some cojones bro.' Tiago said, standing next to Jake.

'Uh, thanks?'

Jess smiled, grabbing some food, 'It's a compliment.'

I nicked a piece of Sam's toast. 'Cool.'

There was a knock at the door, 'It's a bit early for anyone to be here isn't it?'

Jess shrugged, I walked over and opened the door. 'Hello Alfie.'

'Oh, hey Principal, what's up?' I said, moving out of the way so he could come in.

'I have news!' He exclaimed, walking past me, 'Where is everyone?'

I rubbed the back of my head, 'Still asleep, we had a busy day.'

He shrugged, 'You'll just have to tell everyone else when they come down. So anyway, the news... You are aware of the global sports festival for kids your age and a couple years above, yes?'

We nodded.

'Well, I'm not supposed to tell you this yet but this year we are hosting it.'

'What?' Gabriella shouted, 'There's no way!'

He smiled, 'Yes way, and also, I've brought the team sheet forms that you'll have to fill in, so you can start and prepare early. But don't tell anyone!'

We crowded around the sheets he'd put down on the table, I didn't care much for the individual sports, but the team ones...

'Now... please bear in mind that you will be competing against the best in the world, but you are part of that best... Oh, and it's in three and a half months.'

I smiled, 'Thanks Sir.'

'Ohh it's no problem at all, after all, you are my class.' He said, winking and leaving us to do our thing. I grabbed all the good team sports and read through them.

'Wait, we need eight for both basketballs?'

Zoe, Sam and Gabriella looked up, 'Eight?'

'Yep, and we've only got six. And if we're gonna do this thing properly we're going to need someone naturally tall for controlling the paint.'

Jess turned to me, 'Troy.'

I nodded, 'Yeah... isn't he naturally like Eight and a half feet tall?'

She nodded.

'Great. Now for our eighth...'

Jess stuck her hand up, 'I can play!'

I looked at her, 'You can?'

'I mean, I haven't played in a while, but yeah.'

'Well, we've got three months to get you up to scratch... Wait, manager?'

Bianca popped up, 'We need a manager?'

Helena came out of nowhere, 'Did someone say manager?'

'Yeah, but for the basketball team.'

She grinned, 'That's fine, give me a day, tops and I'll know everything there is, do you have any tapes of games?'

'Weirdly enough yes I do.' I muttered, 'I can send you them if you want.'

Natalia stood next to me, 'So there's eight and a manager, we're sorted.'

'Well, if Troy wants to.'

'If Troy wants to what?' Troy said, walking out the elevator.

'Be our centre for basketball.' I caught him up to speed on what the Principal said.

'Yeah I'm down.' He said.

'You are? Both power and non-power?'

He nodded.

'Can you actually play?' asked Zoe.

'Kinda.'

'Does he need to be able to play? Of course we'll teach him the basics and stuff, but complex dribbles and anything further than mid-range doesn't matter, you're what? Eight-foot seven at natural height?

'Eight-foot eight.'

'Sick!' Sam cried, 'Can you dunk?'

I laughed, 'He can probably reach the hoop without jumping! Of course he can dunk!'

Jess grabbed my arm, 'Wait, they aren't single-sex, are they?'

'Na, all the team sports are unisex, if you're the best, you're the best.' I guessed.

I looked at the football sheets, same kind of thing, starting eleven, 4 subs, a manager, I decided to discuss this when everyone else came down.

Sylvia walked up to us, 'Shall we postpone the games till later then? This looks important.'

I nodded, 'Please.' I looked down at my feet, realising I had my basketball shoes on. 'Hey anyone got a basketball nearby?'

Gabriella looked up, 'Hoops?' She said, grinning.

I nodded, 'You coming?' I asked Jess.

'Yeah, I need to get practising!'

I had a quick word with Alex before I went out, then ran to the court.

We put in 3 hours of practice, playing 4 on 4, doing drills, repetition, before realising that everyone else would have woken up by now and that we should go back in.

'My hands are numb!' Gabriella complained, I grabbed her hands and heated them, 'That's so much better.' She said. 'Come on, we've gotta grab team spots.'

We went inside to see carnage; everyone was shouting at each other over team spots. Sylvia was trying to control the carnage but was having no luck.

'HEY! EVERYONE CALM DOWN... AND SIT DOWN!' I shouted, everyone did what I said immediately.

'Impressive.' Gabriella said.

'Thanks... Alright then, I'm presuming you all know what's going on?' Everyone nodded. 'Alright then, since we can't do this orderly, I'll do it, one by one. It'll take a while, but we'll do it properly. Now, I'll start with the team sports, we've already sorted out the basketball team, but the football, netball and hockey teams are still empty...' This went on for a long time. It took us over 2 hours to go through all the sports, but we got it done, with very few compromises, I did a great job.

I ended up on both the football and basketball teams, (captain of both thanks), and was also doing trio, duo, and singles combat. Anyone could do that no matter the number.

The basketball team consisted of:
Me, Jess, Gabriella, Natalia, Bianca, Zoe, Troy, and Sam.

The football team consisted of:
Me, Troy, Jess, Paris, Gabriella, Tiago, Natalia, Queenie, Bianca, Barukko, Zoe, Sam, Alex, Alexandra, San, and Jake.

The trio team was me, Jess and Barukko.
The duo team was me and Gabriella.
And of course the singles team was me

'All right then!' I said, collapsing back onto the sofa, 'That is all of them!'
Jess looked at me, 'Well done.'
I nodded.
Sylvia got up, 'Games?'
Everyone kind of half-heartedly nodded.
'Jess do you want to do mine? it'll probably descend into carnage anyway.'
'Are you not going to do it?'
'I'll help but I need a brain reset after sorting all that out.' I muttered.

You know what, I was right, it did descend into carnage, organised carnage, but carnage nonetheless.
It was entertaining though.
We stopped again at eight, we hadn't got through as many as we wanted but we'd actually done most of them the day before, so it wasn't much of a problem. I went to bed early, like 9, but I could *not* sleep, I was still awake at 1 in the morning.

I sighed and swung my legs off the bed. I stuck on my clothes and shoes, grabbed a basketball and went outside. It was freezing but I didn't really care, I was just shooting, my mind blank. About half an hour later I heard the dorm door open and footsteps.

Sylvia walked round the corner.

'Hey.' I said, sinking a three.

She yawned, 'Why are you up?'

'Can't sleep.'

She nodded 'Too much to think about?'

I passed the ball to her, 'Yep.'

'I hear you.'

I looked at her, 'What's up with you?'

'I shouldn't talk about it...'

'Jake...' I guessed.

She didn't say anything.

'He really is into you, you know?'

She sighed, 'I know, it's just, I don't know if I'm ready.'

I caught the ball and stopped. 'Okay then, tell me, what happens when you see him?'

She thought about it, and stared up at his window, 'I get this... warm feeling in my chest, and my stomach ties itself in a knot... I lose my train of thought for a second...' She turned to me, 'Oh my god.'

I smiled.

'I should go tell him!'

'I'd wait if I were you.'

'Why?'

'He's got a plan apparently.' I shrugged and went back to shooting.

She smiled, 'Thanks Alfie.' Hugged me, then went back inside. (I know, I'm a great matchmaker)

I looked up at Jake's window, smiled, then turned back to shooting, I was out there for another hour before anyone else came down, I was surprised to see who came down though...

First, there was a pair, Jess and Barukko, they were just talking, and I didn't listen in to what they were talking about, even when they came outside for a walk, I was weirdly happy for them, as I should be, I guess. They didn't even notice me playing they were that invested in their conversation.

The next person to come down didn't surprise me, Gabriella came creeping down 30 seconds later, following them out the door, she paused when she heard me playing basketball though.

'Gabriella.' I said, 'Why are you following those two around then?'

'Why are you awake at half two in the morning.'

I shrugged, 'Couldn't sleep.' I said, shooting another shot.

She studied me, 'You okay?'

'Yeah, I might just... I'm thinking...'

'About what?'

I smiled, 'I can't tell you.'

'Why not?' She complained.

'Cos its important.'

She caught the ball. 'Okay.' She said, pouting her lips.

I dunked the ball, 'Trust me you don't want to know, yet.'

She held out her arms, 'Okay...'

I hugged her.

'You should go to sleep.'

'I know.'

I picked her up and carried her inside, leaving her in her bed, she had fallen asleep on the way up.

I didn't go to sleep for another hour. But once I did go to sleep, I slept like a baby.

For once I didn't wake up to someone banging on my door... or any noise at all in fact, I thought everyone had died.

I stretched and rubbed my eyes, 'Is everyone ok? I haven't been woken up.' I muttered.

I checked my phone, **08:07**.

It's peaceful. I thought.

I got up, showered, and dressed. I got in the elevator, still, no one had disturbed me.

I went downstairs, there were a few of us, but not many. 'What is going on?' I said as I exited the elevator.

Alda looked up, 'Everyone is still asleep, everyone's shattered from everything over the past couple of days.'

I yawned, 'I can understand why.' I muttered, grabbing breakfast and heading outside, all ball in hand. 'I really should play football.' I said to myself, heading to the basketball court. I decided to ignore my own words and started to shoot. 20 minutes later I heard someone come outside.

'You're out here alone, again?'

'Hey, yeah I am, it's kinda nice though.'

'I should get you some headphones.'

'Well, you did forget to get me a Christmas present so...' I smirked.

'Yeah alright!'

'Yeah I know, I'm not bothered anyway, just messing with you.' I replied, hitting a triple.

'You're good, you could go pro you know.'

'Yeah, but I'm not here to go pro, am I?'

She hugged me from behind, 'No, you're not.'

I turned around, 'You okay?'

'Yeah, but I'm not the one playing ball by himself all the time, and at two in the morning.'

'I'm sorry.'

'Don't apologize to me, apologize to your sleep schedule, that's the one in trouble.'

I smiled, 'Yeah that's fair.'

'Now come on, one versus one me.'

'Powers?'

'Mmm, na. Let's do this properly.' she said, I tossed her the ball. 'You start.'

I was going easy on her, but then she went 5 points up and she started trash-talking me, and well, I won't take that, especially not classmates, and *especially* not Gabby.

The score ended 100 – 67.

'You could've gone easy on me!' She complained, leaning against me.

'You started trash talking me five points up!' I argued.

She smiled, 'Yeah... I did, didn't I?'

'Yep, and you know I don't take that.' I chuckled.

'That was fun though.' She sighed.

'Why do you want to go again?'

She laughed, 'No I am much too tired for that, I'm off inside.'

'Pull me up!' I asked.

She laughed, pulling me up eventually, and we walked inside together.

It was nearly silent.

I threw myself onto one of the sofas, 'Okay what is going on today?'

Jake yawned, 'We're just tired, that's all.'

'No, even we shouldn't be this tired... Wait where's Barukko... and Jess?'

Zoe and Sylvia perked up, 'Oh, actually I have no idea.' Zoe said.

'I bet he's not paying attention.' I said.

'What do you mean?' Gabriella asked.

'Hang on, it might get a little cold but stick with me.' I said, sending a breeze through the back door and out the front.

'What are you doing?'

'Look, it's getting brighter, no more vibrant.' Gabriella said, I frowned, not believing that I was actually right, and she motioned for me to turn around. Immediately the room seemed a lot more, colourful, everyone perked up as well, seemed more, awake. Everyone looked around, I dropped the wind and the room dulled again.

'You're right, what on Earth?' Sylvia muttered

'Dammit, he's not paying attention.'

'You're right.' Gabriella said, standing next to me.

'Okay, we need to find Barukko.' I said.

So there we were, me, Sylvia, Gabriella and Zoe, stood in the elevator going up one floor.

The doors slid opened and I knocked on Barukko's door. No answer. 'You don't think he's with?'

Gabriella shook her head, 'There's no way.' She muttered as we got back in the elevator.

We went up to the fifth floor, the darkness was still here. I walked up to her door and knocked, after a solid 10 seconds it opened. And who was there?

Barukko, shirtless...

'Oh there is a way!' I hollered, laughing.

Barukko stared at us, confused. 'What?'

I continued laughing, 'Whatever you're doing in there, just err, tone it down a bit and control your darkness 'cos you're making this whole building fall asleep.'

His eyes widened; he took a look out onto the hallway. 'Oh, so I am, sorry.'

'Barukko, come back.' Jess's voice mumbled behind him, she was stood by the bed, peering at us. Sylvia's and Gabby's eyes widened. I burst out laughing again, Zoe held her hands over her mouth, trying to contain herself, I was nearly crying.

I patted him on the shoulder, 'Okay bro, you go back to your girl, we'll leave u alone now.' I said, wheezing. I steered the girls to the elevator and hit the button to got to the bottom, the darkness was already clearing. The doors closed and I and Zoe burst out laughing again.

'That was… the most… amazing 3 minutes ever! You should've seen your faces!' I shouted.

The elevator doors opened and I walked out to find everyone staring at me.

I cleared my throat, 'Problem solved!' I wheezed.

Maddison chuckled, 'What happened up there?'

I struggled for breath, 'Basically… these two were adamant that Jess wasn't with Barukko, and guess what?'

'She was with Barukko?' Maddie guessed.

'Yep.'

Zoe grinned.

Sylvia and Gabriella just looked astounded.

I patted them both on the shoulder, 'Don't worry, it'll happen to you lot too at some point.'

They blinked, 'That's… not the problem.'

I laughed, 'Sure…'

I sat back down, 'What do you think they were…?' Gabriella asked

I shrugged, 'I don't really want to know, but since I was asleep in the room next to them and I heard, well, nothing. I'm guessing not much.' I whispered back.

She put her head against me, 'Good point.'

'Hey, do we actually have any games left?' I called out.

No one said anything, 'Is that really all of them, sick...'

'Ball?' Sam asked.

'I'm good.' We all chorused.

He sank back down in his chair, Zoe hugged him.

'Yeah, Alfie just whooped me at a one vs one sooo...'

'Didn't he go easy on you?' Zoe asked.

She sighed, 'He did but then I trash-talked him so...'

Zoe nodded, 'Okay that's understandable.

'What was the score anyway?' Troy asked.

'One hundred to sixty-seven.'

Sam spat out his drink, all over Zoe, 'What? How hard was he trying?'

I laughed at Zoe, Gabby smiled, 'Not that hard, there were a few times where he could have dunked over me and he didn't.'

Zoe laughed from the kitchen, 'Oh well at least he didn't posterize you.'

(Posterizing is where you just jump over someone and dunk the ball, that's for you none basketball fans)

'They would've been good too.' I complained.

Everyone chuckled.

The rest of the day went by smoothly, Barukko and Jess came down later on, I gave them a round of applause when the doors opened. Syl and Gabby grilled Jess. Barukko looked the tensest and relaxed I'd ever seen him. (It was a weird look just go with my description all right?)

The next day went past pretty quick, there was more prep for New Year's, fireworks and stuff, but otherwise it was pretty quiet.

14 - The rest of our lives starts now

I was downstairs on New Year's Eve morning when I had the best idea ever. 'Hey why don't we do it on the roof?'
Everyone looked up, 'What?'
'Why don't we have the party on the roof.'
Jake jumped onto his feet, 'That's an amazing idea!'.
'Grab a couple of patio heaters, camping chairs, and loads of blankets, it'll be great.'
Everyone suddenly started shouting.
'Yeah alright!' I interrupted, 'But we'd better start now, leave the blankets and food till last because they'll get cold, but we should move stuff up now.
It took us an hour to move all the tables and chairs onto the roof (bear in mind there's 28 of us), I controlled the weather so that it wasn't windy, it was perfect.
Jess hugged me, 'This is brilliant!'
'I know right?' I replied, staring out into the distance.
I and Gabby bagsied the best seats, we had one for everyone, but some of us would just need one.
We changed the plan, we'd be dressed up "nice" for 5 until 10, then we'd dress warm and wait for 12.

Anyway, at about half four I was in my room getting dressed when I got a knock at the door, 'Who is it?'
'Gabriella!'
'Come in.' I said, getting my shirt stuck over my head.
'What are you doing?' She asked.
'Yeah alright gimme a sec.' My muffled voice said as I pulled the shirt down, 'There... Wow, you look good.'
'Aww thanks.'
She was wearing this one-piece dress that stopped just above the knees, she had a belt looping around her waist, (don't really know why) and had white trainers on. Her brown, wavy hair flowed over her right shoulder.
'I mean seriously...'
She blushed, 'Yeah okay stop it!'

I smiled, 'You ready?'

We played games, ate, sang (I tried to avoid that bit), and had an amazing time. Come 10 and we were all more than happy to change, and then we were all sat in some sort of semi-circle after. Gabriella sat with me for most of it...

It was 2 minutes to 12 when I had an idea, I grabbed Alex's camera. 'Guys, we don't have long, I know it's cold but I think we can grab a timed picture of all of us with the fireworks going off behind!'

Alex stood upright immediately, I could see the gears in his head working, 'He's right, as long as we time it so that it goes off at twelve it'll work!'

Everyone got up excitedly and moved to the edge of the building, with 10 seconds till twelve Alex set off the camera and sprinted to us. Gabriella was stood next to me, but she was more taking the picture with her sisters which didn't bother me. I stood in the middle, arms crossed, feet apart, a confident grin on my face. The fireworks exploded behind us and the camera went off... Best... Photo.... Ever!

I put my arm around Gabriella and kissed the top of her head, staring at the fireworks...

I finally glanced around, the first two I see, Jake and Sylvia, holding hands in the corner. I chose to let them be and pulled Gabriella over to everyone else.

We all talked and sang for another couple of hours, it was great.

Later on, we were all huddled in our chairs again, Gabriella and I sat together again.

'Hey Alex let me see the photo!' I called over to him.

He waddled over and handed me the camera, I stared at it, 'Look at that.'

'Woah.' She replied. 'Best idea ever.'

I laughed, 'Yeah it sure was, I hope you all know we're doing this every year now.'

Everyone agreed. And I didn't want to go to sleep for once.

At around 3 in the morning we all just kind of dumped the stuff on the top floor and went to bed. I pulled Gabriella into my room, 'Do you want to sleep with me tonight?'
She smiled and put her arms around me, 'Sure why not?'

I woke up at 9 the next morning with Gabriella still asleep in my arms. I didn't want to wake her, so I stuck my headphones on and stared at the ceiling, thinking...
I noticed a couple of things that morning:
1. Gabriella looks cute while she sleeps (To be honest I think most girls do)
2. I need to redecorate my room.
3. I need a Tv for when Gabriella is asleep.
4. Gabriella really doesn't like to be moved whilst she's asleep.
It was an intuitive hour of doing nothing.

Gabriella finally woke up and tilted her head back to look at me.
'Hey.' I said, smiling.
She exhaled, 'Hi.' She mumbled.
'Did you enjoy your sleep?'
'It was very comfortable.' She said, 'What time is it?'
'Like, half ten.'
She stretched, still not moving off me. 'Okay...'
'Can I get up?'
She shook her head, 'I'm warm.'
'I'm only going to my computer.'
She looked up at me again, 'Take me with you and I'll let you.'
I sighed, 'You're such a baby.' I said, picking her up.
'Yep, I'm your baby.' She mumbled.
I didn't reply as I sat down in the chair and turning the Pc on, I took a quick glance at the wall behind me then turned my attention to the screen in front of me.
'I forget how quick this thing is.' I said when it loaded up immediately.
'It should be, it's like a two-grand masterpiece.'
'How is half-a-sleep you more intelligent?'
'Wha-?'

127

I smiled, 'Nothing.'

I watched a couple videos of old basketball players, the best, MJ, Steph, James, Ball. The old players were the best, no powers, just skill.

After an hour she was fully awake and starting to get bored, 'Can we go down now?'

'You can go down whenever you want.'

'But I want you to come with me!' She complained.

'Why are you being so... sappy today?'

She hugged me, 'I don't know.'

I ran my hand through her hair and sighed, 'Fine, come then.' I said, picking her up.

'Yayyy.'

I carried her all the way downstairs and sat down on one of the sofas.

'Hey everyone.'

I was met by a bunch of tired, half-hearted hellos.

'Have you only just gotten up?' Jake asked, sat across from me.

I shook my head, 'But she has.'

Sylvia came and sat down next to him, he put his arm around her. 'A lot has happened recently huh?'

I smiled, 'There sure has.'

I glanced around the room, Barukko, Bianca, Jess and Natalia were sat in one corner, Alex was tinkering with something, Sam and Zoe were chatting to Tiago.

'He's still had no luck?'

'Huh, oh, Tiago, no... not yet.'

I nodded, I looked at Sylvia, she was staring into space.

'I don't think it's going to happen...'

'Why not?' Jake asked.

'I don't know why, it's just... she's not interested, not just in him... in anyone.'

I nodded, 'I get that.'

Gabriella looked at me, 'You do?'

'Well, I was the same at one point.'

'Why?'

'You go through too many bad ones, then you try and avoid them for a while.'

'When was this?'

'Oh like, right up until I got here, I'd been in one for what? Two and a half years?'

'What made you change your mind?' Jake asked, Gabby stared at me.

'No it was not you… Well actually, I don't know… I don't think I ever thought, 'You know what, I'm ready'… It just happened. You know?'

She stared at me, 'No, I have no idea.'

Sylvia spoke, 'You know I kind of do.'

Jake looked at her, 'You do?'

She nodded, 'Yeah, I went through a period like that, not for as long as you though.'

'Well, I'm glad you're not in one now.' Jake said.

Sylvia stared into the distance. *There's something you aren't telling us.* I thought. Jess launched a basketball at me from across the room. Something in my head told me it was flying at me, like an alarm. I caught it, one-handed, without looking.

'How'd you do that?' Jess demanded.

'Why'd you do it?' I asked in return.

'Barukko told me to.'

'Hey!' He complained.

'You're a bad influence on her.' I said, pointing my finger at him and laughing.

'No, but seriously, how'd you do that?' She called.

I shrugged, 'Not a clue, just…' I tapped my head, not really answering the question.

I lobbed the ball back at her, I would've hit her in the head if it wasn't for Barukko, who put up a wall of darkness at the last second.

I can't say whether I was happy about that or disappointed…

Later on (after Gabby finally agreed to spend half an hour without me) I went to see Alex.

'Hey er, I need you to do some work on my old boots (or cleats for you Americans, whatever) and my basketball shoes mate.'

He nodded, 'Alright.'

'Can you keep it to the minimum visually on the shoes though?'

He smiled, 'Yeah, what do you want doing to them?'

'Huh, oh err, whatever you want on the boots I don't really mind, they're wrecked anyway. And for the shoes... Just could do with increase grip and spring, also I don't know how many times I'll play in a day so could you make them like really good on your feet. Please.'

He nodded, 'That's easy stuff so yeah... And you said do whatever on the boots? What position do you play?'

'Oh,' The question caught me by surprise, 'Err, Midfield, attacking or central.'

'Nice, good position that.'

'I just asked a lot are you sure you're okay with it?'

Alex laughed, 'A lot? You should've heard what Sam asked for!'

'Oh god, I don't want to know.'

He pulled out a massive list from one of the drawers, 'Here.'

My jaw dropped, 'Is half of what he said even possible?'

'Some, no... some, I have no idea... most, surprisingly yes.'

I laughed, 'Alright thanks man I owe you one.'

I went to the roof and took a deep breath.

Last year was mad. I thought to myself. *This year might be even crazier.*

I held out my hand, sparks flew between my fingers, *But I'll keep going, no matter what.*

'You'd better.' Said a voice next to me.

I jumped, 'Who are you?'

The man that stood next to me was this, short, muscular guy, with long, stuck up sliver hair and a staff over his shoulder. He was wearing some kind of ancient, Chinese armour.

He laughed, 'You're telling me you don't recognise your own ancestors?'

I frowned, 'No! Wait are you the one my Mum talks to?'

'Yes.'

'So you're the great warrior.'

He nodded.

'Cool, why are you here?'

He shrugged, 'You must have summoned me.'

'Why?'

130

'I don't know! Do you want some advice?'

I shrugged, 'Not really.' I leant against the wall.

'I'll give you some anyway whilst I'm here… the road ahead is perilous, perhaps worse than mine, but you must not stray off the path.'

'Why? Because if I do I'll die?

No reply, I turned to only find that he had disappeared.

'Hmm, well… Nice talk… And a cheery one too…'

The wind picked up again, I climbed up onto the wall and stood up, the view was even better than it was from my room, I overlooked the whole park from here, I could even see the walls of the training areas.

I was stood staring when a leaf was blown into my face by the wind.

'Pwehpwah.' Is the best way I can describe the incredibly heroic noise I made. I grabbed the leaf and tossed it into the wind. Revealing white cloak-like clothing on me.

'Wha-?' I grabbed the sleeve, rolling it over, there were markings on the underside. 'I don't remember putting this on this morning.' I muttered.

I checked the pockets, in one there was an envelope, unsealed. I pulled the paper out from within and read it.

Alfie Jaeger,

This is a gift, from me to you, it will also serve as a reminder, to never give up.
No matter how hard it gets.

Sincerely, Your, Great-Great something Grandfather.

'Jeezus.' I muttered. I created a mirror for the first time, *Huh, cool.* I examined the back of it, more markings. 'White and red, not normally my style but it works.'

Now that I could see the cloak, I began to understand how amazing it was. From the high neck to the bottom by my ankles, it looked amazing. Red like trimming in all the right places. And my initials appeared in the same red on the centre of my back.

'Okay!' I said, hopping on the spot in excitement, 'I'm liking this!'

I put my hands in the pockets, feeling something metallic in my right hand I grabbed it and pulled it out.

'A Shuriken?'

I spun it up in the air and caught it again, 'Alright...' I launched it at the mirror and it went straight through, cracking the mirror into a million pieces.

I put my hand back in the pocket, my hand wrapped around a handle. 'What?'

I pulled out a knife, midnight black, not even 10 inches in length. *I thought throwing stars were in there.* I put my hand back in and pulled out nunchucks. 'I don't even like nunchucks!' I complained. *Wait, can I like, choose?* I thought about another Shuriken, put the nunchucks in my left pocket and put my hand back in the right. I pulled out a Shuriken. 'Oh yes!'

I tossed it up, caught it, and threw it at the only thing level with me, the entry to the roof.

I hit the brick 5 centimetres from Jess's face.

'Oh sugar!' I shouted, jogging over, 'I'm sorry I didn't hit you did I?'

'No I'm fine.' She replied.

I sighed, 'Good. What're you doing up here?'

She sighed 'Just wanted a breather.'

I laughed, 'From what? I haven't seen you happier when you're with him.'

She looked at me, a weird... sadness in her eyes, 'What are you doing up here? And where did this cloak come from?' She asked, studying me.

'It looks good doesn't it?'

She walked around me, 'I normally would say you don't suit white and red on one piece of clothing, but yeah you do... So how'd you get this?'

I passed her the envelope, she read the letter, 'Wait, he's been dead for, centuries, at least if he's your great-great something grandfather, how?'

I shrugged, 'I saw him, and talked to him.'

She looked up at me, 'What?'

'I was stood up there, and a voice appeared next to me, I could see and hear him, I think I can like... summon him.'

'What'd he say?'

I shrugged, 'Nothing much.'

I checked my pockets, the shurikens and the nunchucks were gone. *Nice.*

I put my arms behind my head and smiled.

'What are the markings?'

I shrugged.

'Look Chinese.'

'They may be, I'll ask H at some point.'

'So are you just gonna wear that downstairs or...?'

I closed my eyes for a moment, then opened them again, the cloak was gone.

'Nice.'

'How did you?'

'Not a clue...' I turned around and walked up to the ledge, getting up on it. 'Up here, the air feels, amazing. I feel free, and powerful...'

She joined me, 'You are powerful.'

'I know...' I said, stepping off the edge.

'ALFIE!' She screamed.

I twisted round onto my back as I fell, laughing as the wind rushed through my hair. Right as I was about to hit the ground I teleported.

'Alfie!' Jess screamed again, staring down at the ground and seeing nothing.

'Boo.' I said behind her.

I actually scared her so badly she fell off the ledge.

'Woah...' I said, grabbing her and pulling her in, 'Just 'cos I jumped off doesn't mean everyone can go doing it.'

'You scared me!' She said, literally shaking.

I smiled, 'I'm sorry. Shall we go back?'

She nodded, not letting go of me. I picked her up and pulled her away from the edge before putting her back down.

'I can't be seen carrying you around can I? I said to Jess.

'Why 'cos you're dating Gabriella?'

'I wouldn't call it dating just...'

'I mean you did sleep with her last night.'

'Yeah I guess I did... I mean apparently, you're not happy with Barukko already, maybe I should stay away from relationships!' I said, walking back down.

'What was that scream?' Alexandra asked.

'Oh it was nothing.' I replied, 'Just having a bit of fun that's all.'

'Were you scaring Jess again?' Sylvia asked, knowing full well I had.

'Yep.'

'Alfie!' She complained.

'What? I wouldn't be complaining if I were her, her best friend is so powerful he's got to jump off a roof to scare her.'

Sam spat his drink all over Zoe again. 'WHY DO YOU KEEP DOING THAT?' she complained.

He ignored her for the time being, 'You did what?'

I shrugged, 'I jumped off a roof.'

Sylvia looked like she was about to faint.

'He has a point though.' Jess mumbled.

'What?' Sylvia replied.

'He has a point, I should consider myself lucky that my best friend is so powerful that he has to jump off a roof to scare me.'

Sylvia looked horrified, 'Well... I guess there are two ways of looking at this...'

Sam grinned at me. 'You are mad.'

'Na, just creative!' I joked.

We didn't really do anything the rest of the day, everyone was too tired to be bothered to do anything, we all just sat around and slept.

The next day however, we all felt like we had to do something.

'Basketball?' Sam offered.

I shook my head, 'I'd rather do combat training.'

No one offered to go with me, even Gabriella, so I went to the clearing in the woods, alone, to practise.

When I got into the woods, I summoned my cloak and it appeared on my body. Once I finally got to a clearing I created a dummy to practise on and went through the basics, around 50 kicks in a voice said behind me, 'I can help you with that you know.'

I turned, 'Hey, err... Grandpa?'

'Grandfather will do.'

I nodded, 'How can you help?'

'Well, once I became this... form that appears before you, I found I had a lot of time on my hands, so I decided to learn every type of martial art that I hadn't already learnt, and so I did, and I mastered them all. And I can teach you.'

'You can?'

He nodded.

'Okay great. Where do we start?'

'Where do you wish to start?'

I shrugged, 'Taekwondo?'

'Which form? WTF or ITF?'

'WTF. More kicking.'

He nodded, 'Okay, we'll start with the basics, I don't care if you claim you already know the basics to some martial arts, until you prove to me you can, I won't believe you.'

I nodded, and begun with the basics, I trained for 5 hours straight, I learnt all the patterns, individual moves, you name it. About 4 hours in he said something that surprised me, 'You're actually very impressive, you are memorising every move and pattern after only seeing it once... And doing it to an impressive standard immediately.'

'T...Thanks?'

We got back to training, by the time I was done, I'd gone all the way up to the fifth-degree black belt, and I don't even think that's possible if you do it properly

When I called that I was done I collapsed to the floor, Grandfather laughed, 'I'll tell you what boy, I have never seen a child progress at such an incredible rate.'

I smiled, 'Thanks.' I was still wearing the cloak, it felt so light, sometimes I forgot it was there.

There was a moment's silence, then he asked, 'Why do you want to master all the martial arts? You've been told you literally have the most powerful power ever, why now?'

135

I thought for a moment, 'Because it opens up everything, it allows me to control my body and my emotions, and when you're the most powerful kid ever, what's wrong with giving yourself a few more attacking and defensive options, and well, it is what I'm used to.'

He smiled, 'Good answer... Now I'll see you again...?'

I shrugged, 'Whenever I have a lot of free time.'

He seemed pleased enough with that answer, and so he disappeared.

I got up, put my hands on the back of my head, and walked back to the dorm in silence.

I walked in without realising I was still wearing my cloak.

'What the hell are you wearing?' Maddison demanded.

Everyone looked over at me.

I rubbed the back of my head, 'It's new...'

The Ramirez lot looked at me in approval, 'It suits you.' Gabriella said.

'Is it magic?' Helena asked.

'Er, yeah it is.'

Barukko lobbed a tennis ball at me from behind. I pulled out a Shuriken and impaled it to the wall without looking.

'What is wrong with you recently?' I asked smiling.

Barukko shrugged, 'I wanna see if you're untouchable.'

I walked over to him and patted him on the shoulder. 'Here, see? I'm touchable.'

'That's what she said!' Sam called from across the room.

'Does that even make sense?'

'Not really.' H replied.

'Where did the Shuriken come from?' Natalia asked.

'That's how this is magic. The pockets... I can basically summon whatever weapon I want in my right pocket... And get rid of it with my left.'

'Seriously? Can you pull out, like, an assault rifle?' Alex asked.

'I don't think the pockets are big enough.'

'Just try, please.'

I sighed and stuck my hand in my pocket, surely enough there was something in there.

'Wait.' I said, pulling it out.

I pulled out this, almost compact version of an M4 Carbine, that seemed to unfold as I pulled it out of my pocket.

Alex laughed, 'That's amazing. Can I have it?'

'Erm, no, let's not mess with rifles.'

'That's a good idea.' Sylvia said, walking past.

I put the gun back in the other pocket and promised that I wouldn't bring another one out unless I absolutely had to.

'Oh yeah, Helena, do you know what these writings are?'

She stared at them, 'They look Chinese, but ancient, the ones that are lost in time. The few that I can't understand.'

I sighed, 'Great, thanks.'

'You'll have to ask your grandfather.' Jess shouted from one of the sofas.

'Have you seen this coat Jess?' Gabriella asked.

'Yeah... He got it from his grandfather.'

'Well, great-great something grandfather, but yeah... It's a long story.'

'Wait,' Helena said, bringing the topic of conversation back, 'You'll have to ask your Grandfather? But no one alive speaks that language!'

I smiled, 'I never said he was alive.'

Everyone stopped and looked at me, everyone's face said the same thing, *UH WHAT?*

I laughed, 'I can basically summon the guy, but I just spent the past 5 hours combat training with him, so I could do without seeing him for a while.'

'Ohh, so that's what you were doing this whole time.' Jess said.

'Yep.' I made the coat disappear and went and sat down across from her. 'I am starving.'

'Here.' Jess said offering up her can of crisps.

'Thanks.'

Everyone turned to the coat hook by the door, 'Wait, where'd the cloak go?' Alex asked.

I held out my hand, made it reappear, then disappear.

No one said anything. I didn't bother turning around, I already knew what their reaction was going to be. I had my eye on Barukko, who was stood to the right of me, he was looking at me, almost with resentment.

'You good bro?' I asked.
He nodded, then went to talk to Bianca.

I went to bed that night thinking about why I could pick up martial arts so easily, I did not reach an answer.

The next day went by amazingly quick, but I guess nothing really happened, Barukko didn't even try to throw anything at me.

15 – School starts again, with one small difference…

Anyway the fourth of January finally arrived, that morning we were all sat around in the common area, even San was here, and he was never around nowadays.

'What do you think we'll be doing today then?' Jess asked.

I shrugged, 'Not a clue, at this school? It could be anything.'

Jake came over, 'Yeah I mean for all we know we could be learning to snowboard!'

I laughed, 'Well I mean it's a possibility.'

There was a knock at the door.

'I'll get it!' Queenie shouted even though no one else had moved.

She opened the door, 'Hey Pr… You're not the principal.' We all looked over immediately.

BANG…

Queenie went flying across the room, Tiago caught her but his back smashed against the wall.

'What the?' Me, Jess, San and Barukko all stood up immediately as 7 guys in black clothing rushed in and grabbed Sylvia and Natalia, before rushing out again.

We were all too dumbfounded to move, but Bianca came to her senses the quickest and ran out the door, Barukko chased after her. I ran after him with Jess and San close behind.

I stopped at the path, 'Which way?'

San ran past me, looking beyond excited, 'This way come on!'

I ran after him, and sure enough, he was right, we rounded the corner and I saw Barukko and Bianca chasing the guys.

'Are they the ninjas?' Jess asked, running next to me.

I shook my head, 'Did you see the way they hit Q? That was pure power, not a ninja thing. And look in the direction they're heading!'

Jess glanced around, 'There's no way this is training!'

'Well why haven't they used their powers yet? If it wasn't they wouldn't know to not use them because of Natalia!'

She thought for a sec, 'You're right!'

'I know!' I said, summoning my cloak, 'Now watch this!'

I teleported in front of them and faced them. 'Hi.' I smashed my hands into the ground and a massive stone wall erupted in between us, blocking their path. I then teleported past the wall, putting myself between them and the wall.

'Hey guys.' I said.

'Alfie? A little help!' Sylvia shouted.

Barukko and Bianca finally caught up.

I held my hand out to stop them, Barukko stopped immediately, Bianca looked fuming but stopped.

'Was this really necessary guys? All this for a training session?' The shortest guy took his mask off.

'You figured it out already huh?'

Bianca's jaw dropped, 'A TRAINING SESSION?'

I laughed, 'It was so obvious, they weren't using their powers because they'd grabbed Nat and they were running straight for the training areas.'

She thought about it for a second, 'Oh yeah.'

Jess finally caught up, 'You stopped them too easily.' She panted.

'I know but they had grabbed Nat, so that became their downfall really, they should've dropped Nat and ran with just Syl, it would've given them an advantage.'

'You did well to stop us though, the lead guy said as the rest took off their masks.'

'Who are you guys anyway?' Jess asked.

'Oh we're second years.'

'Cool.' I said, 'Do we still have to go to the training area then or...?'

He laughed, 'Yeah, you do, you just don't get the epic build-up now.'

'What if I did it?' Barukko said.

We all stared at him, 'Uh what?' I said.

'I could just take Syl and beat you there.'

'That's great but we literally have twenty-six other kids, one of which is the perfect counter to yours, you'd never make it.'

He didn't say anything, but I saw his whole body tense up. He launched himself at the second years, catching them all by surprise, then he stopped.

'What?'

He looked behind him to see me, grabbing him by the hood, 'See, told you you'd never make it.'

His body relaxed, 'Fine.'

I let go of him and set off walking to the training area, Gabriella caught up. 'Come on then!'

Everyone followed me to the arena, the second year that I'd talked to caught up with me, 'Hey...'

I glanced at him, 'What's up?'

He held out his hand, 'The name's Brandon.'

I shook his hand, 'Alfie... Jaeger.'

'You're powerful.'

'Oh, wow, you get straight down to the point.' I muttered.

'Like, I've never seen anyone teleport, then be able to create such a massive wall. What exactly is your power?'

I held out my hand, doing the usual trick with the sparks. 'It's a long story.'

'Can you fit it in like, 5 minutes?'

'I can try...' I took a deep breath, Gabriella looked like she was about to laugh, 'Basically, I never knew my Dad so my Mum raised me, for the first fifteen and a bit years of my life I was powerless, went to a powerless school and everything, first fourteen years of my life sucked but we'll skip past that bit. Decided to try for the entrance exam anyway, tried really hard, got in, by some miracle. Placed last on the scoreboard for four months, then, just before Christmas, Jess back there got kidnapped... oh yeah, backtrack a bit, we didn't know at the time but Jess was under the influence of this guy's power, which was emotional manipulation, and the just before Christmas they went for a walk in the woods and I happened to see them go, then I saw a group of ninjas following them, so I decided to check them out. I followed them into the forest, found Jess strapped to a tree, jumped in to save her, my power awakened at some point in that battle, and saved her successfully, knocking out all 20-odd guys in the process, they're all in jail now, and have been finding more and more out about this power ever since.' I took in another deep breath. 'That was impressive.' Gabby admitted.

Brandon stared at me for a minute, 'Wait... I think I get it? But I still don't know what your power is.'

Jess stepped in, 'Well, it doesn't actually have a name, but we... I call it God Complex, because it basically allows him to do whatever he wants, control the weather, teleport, build massive structures, even make money, but that one has issues.'

'What do you call it?' He asked me.

'I call it God Complex because she calls it God Complex.' I said.

'So you can do whatever you like?'

'Yeah, but I'm like, seven years behind everyone, at least, so, at first the simple things tired me out really easily, but now I can do two or three things before I feel dizzy.'

'And you've only had it what? Two weeks?'

'Pretty much yeah.'

'That's incredible.'

I rubbed the back of my head with my other hand, 'Yeah...'

The training area came into view, Brandon turned to Jess, 'So... what's your power.'

'Light... Light Manipulation.'

'So do you just like bend it or...?'

'No I can create it. What about you?'

'Me? Oh, density manipulation.'

'So you can make yourself as solid as a rock or as soft as a sponge?'

'More like I can make myself really light or heavy.'

Isn't that the same thing? I thought.

I nodded, 'So you can break your opponent's hand or take no damage from a hit?'

'Well, in a simple way yeah. But because my muscles are built for my specific density now, I have trouble moving when I get heavier, and when I become lighter...'

'You move too much.' Jess guessed.

He nodded, 'Oh yeah.' He said, changing the topic, 'I haven't introduced you all! We've got Jessie, Morgan, Olive, Zachary but we just call him Zac, Benjamin and Abigail.' All the guys nodded; the girls waved at me.

I smiled, 'Hey.'

Gabby looked at me, 'Don't be getting any ideas.'

'I'm not.' I said, turning back around.

'Why you guys?' I asked Brandon.

He shrugged, 'We *are* all top ten in our class but I don't think there was a specific reason.'

'You're all top ten? Any of you top three?'

'Nope!'

I smiled, almost embarrassed, 'What're you then?'

'Fourth.'

'That's cool, the top three must be powerful then.'

He scratched his nose, 'Yeah they really are!'

We finally arrived at the training area, we all walked in to find the Principal, looking rather concerned.

'I'd thought you'd gotten lost!' He said to Brandon.

Brandon laughed and scratched his nose, 'Yeah… Erm, this kid stopped us like, almost immediately.'

'Couldn't you use your powers?'

'They grabbed Nat.' I said.

He nodded, 'That's unfortunate… Anyway, as I'm presuming you all know by now this is a training session, and we will be doing a hostage rescue, just without the build-up now. So, who will be the hostages today?'

The screen behind him lit up and a wheel with all our names on appeared, like he'd prepared for them to not get here with the hostages.

'There will be two hostages!' He called.

The wheel spun, spinning… spinning… spinning… **Helena**.

I groaned, 'Great.' She walked over and stood next to Sir, Jess looked at me and smiled.

'And now for the final hostage.'

Spinning… spinning…spinning… spinning… **Alfie**.

This time everyone, (including myself) groaned. 'Great.'

Even Jess looked annoyed now, 'Looks like it's my turn to save you.'

'Well, yeah I guess, I mean there's no real danger but, yeah.'

The Principal looked slightly bothered, but when he saw me staring at him he composed himself.

'Ahem, okay everyone, Alfie and Helena come with me, everyone else, I'll brief you through the speakers.'

He led us through a winding maze of corridors and then we came back outside on top of a mountain, a snowy mountain, perfect for snowboarding.

'What the?'

Helena didn't say anything but I could tell she was memorising her surroundings.

He led us into an underground bunker of sorts, 'Sir, is there any problem with us escaping on our own?'

Helena glanced at me, Sir smiled, 'Well, I guess not, if this were a real scenario there would be someone stopping you but if you could overpower them…'

I locked eyes with H, *So that's a yes.*

We finally stopped outside a vault door, he opened it and motioned for us to walk in. We walked in, WILLINGLY, and the door shut behind us, 'Well, we walked into that one didn't we?'

Suddenly these chains lashed out of the ground and wrapped around our ankles and wrists, pulling us onto the steel chairs in the centre of the vault and strapping us to them, back-to-back. Then, parts of the wall spun around, revealing wall-mounted machine guns, 'Oh great.'

I could hear the muffled voice of the principal through the loudspeakers, but the walls were so thick I couldn't tell what he was saying.

'We've got a problem.' H said.

'Why, they should easily beat seven guys.'

'It's not just seven guys, I think both over first-year classes are here.'

'What? How are they supposed to get through sixty-odd kids to get to us?'

She shrugged.

'At least there's no punishment.' I muttered.

'Oh there probably is, and those are probably real machine guns, I've heard before that after Christmas they just throw us in the deep end. Maybe they weren't kidding.'

I exhaled, 'Any way of escaping? I imagine I can't teleport out of here without being shot by these guns so…'

'Actually, having you here is a huge advantage, you're probably the only kid who can get us out of here.'

'So that's why he looked so bothered when my name popped up.'

Helena continued, 'I memorised most of our surroundings on the walk up here, but first we need to stop these machine guns, what I need you to do is to build the strongest and thickest stone box around us that you can, then dig a hole about two metres straight down from where we are, then summon a massive lightning bolt to hit about one kilometre in that direction.' She nodded with her head, 'Then...'

'Hang on...' I interrupted, 'Let me do this first, then we can decide what to do after because those are three big things.' She nodded.

I closed my eyes, not showing any signs of doing anything, then I summoned the biggest, strongest box I could around us, I could hear the machine guns through the walls, they were trying to destroy the box.

'Hurry!' Helena shouted.

I was a little dizzy, but I managed to dig a hole easily enough, we dropped down and the chains snapped as we dropped. That didn't really bother me. Helena stood up but I remained seated, just in case I passed out from this next thing.

I concentrated, then we felt this huge rumble through the ground, the machine guns stopped.

'Nice, now come on.' Helena said, climbing out of the hole now that the box had crumbled to pieces.

'Just gimme a min.' I said, laying on the floor after climbing out the hole, my whole world was spinning...

I sat there for around two minutes whilst Helena examined the door.

'There's no way to open it!' She exclaimed.

I stood up, still a bit wobbly, 'We don't need to open it.'

I grabbed her arm and teleported to the other side of the door.

'Woah.' I said.

'All the powers are building up, you need to be careful.'

'I'll be alright.' I replied, summoning my cloak, my sword also appearing on my back. *That's new.*

We set off sprinting in the direction we came.

'It's so dark!'

I stopped, 'What?'

'Wait, you're telling me you can see perfectly fine?'

'Yep.'

'Can you carry me? I can't see anything and we need to head outside, I can direct you.'

'Yeah alright.' I said, picking her up and putting her on my back.

'Straight on.' She said.

She led me through the maze of corridors almost perfectly, we were outside in almost 2 minutes.

I took in our surroundings, the snow glistened all around us, the random little groups of trees standing out against the white background. There was a lot of smoke coming from the other side of the mountain but all the noise was on our side, 'Was that me?' I asked.

Helena shrugged, 'Yeah probably.'

I pulled some binoculars out of my pocket, 'Here.' I passed them to Helena.

I heard someone behind us, I spun around and hit him with a shuriken, he didn't move.

'Did you kill him?'

'I hope not, that was meant to have a narcotic on it.' I went over and checked, 'He's still alive!' Helena had started making her way down the mountain, 'Hey wait up.'

I caught up with her, 'Can you blast something explosive at the guard station?'

'Huh, oh yeah.' I summoned a massive fireball above my head and blasted it at the guard station, now people noticed us. 20 or so guys turned to us and started blasting their various powers and guns at us. Some started running to us. I put up a force field and turned to H, 'What do we do now?'

'You can take all these guys, right?'

I sighed, 'Yeah but not whilst protecting you, unless...'

'Unless what?'

'It won't be great but I can put you in a hole in the ground, you'd be safe.'

She sighed, 'Sure why not.'

I smiled, 'Cool.'

I put it here in a hole and covered it, leaving a small hole for air.

I put down the force field and surprised everyone by revealing there was now only one of us.

'Sup?' I said, pulling my sword off my back right as the first guy jumped at me, I sent him flying into another one. I launched a duo of narcotic shurikens at two guys, knocking them out, this one guy literally swooped down to attack me, I brought him down with a bolt of lightning. I pulled out a bow and collapsed another guard tower with an explosive arrow

Shot two more guys with, hopefully, narcotic arrows, but now there were 6 guys nearly on top of me, I put my bow back in my pocket and pulled my sword out of the ground, 'Come on then!' I set my sword on fire. They all hesitated. 'Fine, I'll do it myself.' I summoned a massive wave and it exploded outwards, soaking everyone, I then charged at the first guy, slamming the flat of my sword into him and sending him flying. I then hit the next guy with an ice blast, freezing him, before the other four guys stopped, turned, and started running. I summoned a bola and wrapped it around one guy's body, I built a stone cage around the other and hit the last two with lightning bolts. I opened up the hole Helena was in and she looked around, 'What? Did you kill them all?'

'I hope not, it took me longer than I expected because I couldn't kill them so...'

'That's amazing.'

'You want the binoculars again?'

She shook her head, 'No it's okay, I know where we need to go.'

'How far?'

'Like, two kilometres down the mountain.'

We ran down to the guard station and found a pile of skis and snowboards that were now littered across the ground.

'Oh nice! Grab what you need and let's go.' She gingerly grabbed the skis, 'You ski?' I asked.

'Yes.'

'Cool.' I said, strapping the snowboard to my foot, 'Lead the way!'

I have never had so much fun whilst trying not to be killed. We sped down the mountain, flying over accidental ramps and some purpose made ones, I hit a couple of guys with shurikens

147

but I missed most, it's not as easy as you think to hit someone at 40 mph.

We made it down the mountain in 5 minutes. I didn't actually know where everyone was so when I hit a ramp going 50 and pulled off a laid-out backflip OVER EVERYONE I couldn't stop laughing. I had to spin round off the landing and head down a hill without falling over though, which isn't easy when you're laughing uncontrollably.

'Hahaha... Hey... Everyone...' I said, laughing as I got off the board.

Jake pointed up, 'Was that you?'

I nodded, 'I didn't actually know where you all were, I didn't mean to flex on you all like that.'

Gabby hugged me, 'Glad you're back anyway.'

'Did you lot even try to come and get me?'

Jess smiled, 'They wanted to but I told them to wait fifteen minutes to see if you'd escape.'

I sighed, 'Okay, do you guys know exactly what's going on up the mountain?'

'We know there are at least ten guys up there.' Barukko said.

I laughed, 'Ten guys! There are both other first-year classes and those second years up there!'

'That's at least sixty guys.' Jess complained.

'Well... not now.'

'What did you do?' Jess asked.

'He took out like, thirty guys.' Helena said.

I rubbed the back of my head, 'Yeah...'

'And he took out their power plant with a lightning bolt.'

Zoe stared at me, 'That was you! That was the biggest lightning bolt I'd ever seen.'

'I never saw it.'

'You didn't kill anyone did you?' Jess asked, concerned.

'I don't think so.'

'You don't think so?' Sylvia shouted.

'Look, I just took out thirty guys, it is not easy to do that without killing anyone, I didn't aim for any vitals and only used narcotics so as long as no one has an allergic reaction we'll be fine.'

'You're amazing.' Jess said, hugging me, Gabby frowned at us.

'Yeah alright… now, shall we get moving?' Everyone nodded.
'H? You seem to know the way…' I gestured for her to lead on. I
swung my sword over my shoulder, 'Come on then…' My voice
died. Everyone stopped as the ridges of the crater we were in
was suddenly ringed with enemies.
'Sugar.' I grabbed Jess instinctively and teleported out to the
top of a nearby tower.
I glanced down and saw that a couple of us had gotten out, I
watched the some that couldn't escape run at the enemies and
get shot down by blow darts, presumably narcotic.
'What should we do?' Jess asked, staring at me.
'I don't know, I've probably got a teleport and another big
attack before I collapse.' I said, leaning against the wall.
'Are you okay?' She asked.
I nodded, 'There's a small chance that I'll spontaneously
combust but I'll be fine.'
'Really?'
I shrugged, 'Hey look, Barukko and Bianca are over there, oh
and Shanelle.'
'Can we teleport over to them?'
'I think so, but maybe don't ask me to do it again.'
I grabbed her arm, 'Ready?'
She nodded, and suddenly we appeared next to Barukko and
the rest.
'Hey.' I said letting go of Jess as she went and stood next to
Barukko.
'So what's the plan?' I asked.
'Well it depends on how much you've got left in the tank.'
Barukko said.
'Not much, one big move really and that's it.'
He sighed, 'Okay, we're going to have to round everyone up so
you can hit them all at once.'
'How?' Bianca asked, 'I only have so much ammo.'
'Actually with me here you might have unlimited.' I said.
'Oh yeah.'
'But still…' Shanelle interrupted.
'Well what if we did the opposite, what if we got them to crowd
around you two.' I said to Barukko and Jess.

'And then you hit them from behind...' Jess finished.

I nodded, 'With me and Bianca we can probably hit what, ten or fifteen of them before they notice, then the four of us can finish them off, hopefully without me having to use a super attack that may cause me to spontaneously combust...' Everyone nodded, 'Shanelle, once we attract all of their attention try and free the others.' She nodded. 'Barukko, can you take her down, I'll take Bianca.' He nodded, I locked eyes with Jess, winked at her, then they were gone.

'Right okay, Bianca take these.' I said, pulling a lot of narcotic arrows out of my pocket, 'Careful, they've got narcotics on them.' She took them gingerly and put them in her quiver, replacing the others. I put my hand in my pocket and pulled out 10 shurikens, putting five in each hand. I glanced over the edge, they'd already taken out one but now they were surrounded, they'd put their backs up against the wall, leaving us with a clear shot.

'You ready, I go left you go right?' She nodded, I grabbed her arm and we teleported down there. We didn't say anything, we just went into action, we took down 20 guys in 4 seconds between us, this was before anyone had noticed. The last lot finally reacted by turning to us, but Jess and Barukko pounced on them.

Shanelle freed the rest of us, I high fived Jess, 'Alright!'

I was about to turn around when heard a small, **_Thwang_**.

A bow! Was my instant reaction as I saw an arrow heading straight at my face, I caught it and fired it straight back with my own bow. The shooter fell out of their position, presumably knocked out, and hit the ground with a dull **_thud_**.

Brandon and 5 of his mates appeared above us, all tightly clustered. 'So, you took out my sixty other comrades, what a shame.'

'You've lost Brandon.'

'No, we've got the high ground.'

I smiled, 'You know that never works.' I said.

The sky rumbled and tore open as a lightning bolt emerged from the heavens.

'No Alfie don't!' Jess screamed as the lightning bolt electrified the air, smashing into the 6 above us.

I promptly collapsed.

I had dreams for the first time in a while.

I 'awoke' in a destroyed urban area, not a training centre, I was flat on my back, I got up and looked around, at the centre of all this destruction was a guy in a black suit. And stood before him were Jess and Barukko, with a sweep of his hand a beam covered them both, when he moved past, they were gone. I screamed and screamed and screamed, then I blacked out.

I 'awoke' again, in the same scene, but now I was on my feet, stood in front of this guy, I screamed in rage and blasted him with a bolt of I-don't-even-know-what, a gold beam of power. When I stopped, he was gone, I promptly collapsed to my knees, and blacked out...

I woke up again to rain, it felt strange, it hadn't actually rained in a while so I'd almost forgotten what it felt like, it was only a few drops mind you, almost more like crying...

I snapped open my eyes to find that it wasn't actually raining, 'Alfie!' Jess cried, wrapping her arms around me and sobbing into my chest, 'It's only a training session! I thought you were going to die!'

I laughed weakly, 'I'm sorry, I don't like to fail...'

'But... you don't have to push yourself so hard.' She said, not letting go of me.

'I know, I'm sorry.' I sat up and looked around, 'Oh hey everyone.' I muttered.

Everyone, and I mean everyone, was crowded around me, even the ones I'd knocked out.

'How long was I out?'

'Like, five minutes.' Barukko said.

'How is everyone else awake?'

'We had some reversals for the narcotics.'

I nodded weakly, trying to get up, 'Nope, okay I'm gonna have to sit down for a while.'

Jess pulled away, 'It's okay,' I whispered, glancing at Barukko, who did *not* seem very happy with Jess.

'That was one amazing lightning bolt!' Brandon exclaimed; his white hair stuck up in every direction.

I smiled, 'It nearly killed me, but thanks.'

He smiled and finally the Principal decided to show up, 'Alright everyone thank you for coming today, your individual teachers will go over it with you tomorrow, you are all dismissed, and thank you to our second years for helping out, even if you did get stopped and frazzled by one child.'

Brandon scratched his nose, 'Yeah... let's not tell anyone about that.' He said as he turned away.

'Are you alright my boy?' He asked, turning to me, 'I feel like we find each other in this situation a lot.'

I smiled, 'Yeah, we do... But I'm fine, can't stand up right now but I'm fine.'

He nodded, Jess muttered, 'You're not fine, you're much too warm for your own health.'

'So I was close to spontaneously combusting? Huh...'

Sir nodded, 'Yes, but now you've come this close, you'll be able to go further, every time you nearly experience death, you'll become exponentially stronger.'

'But if I die, then that's a different matter.'

He paused for a moment, as if wishing to say something else then deciding against it, 'Yes, that's a different matter.'

'Can we go now?' I said to Jess, 'I can just teleport...'

'No, we're walking, you're in no state to release any power.'

Sir chuckled, 'You don't know anything about him if you think he can't release any more power.' He sat down on a crumbled pillar, 'Even now he is releasing power, not by his knowing, mind you before you tell him off. But his body is healing him, his power is helping him regain his power. It is constantly at work, it's what keeps him alive really. Every time he uses a large amount of said power, it's almost like tearing a muscle from working out, it comes back stronger, it makes his body stronger, literally and power-wise.'

Jess looked up, her eyes bloodshot, 'Is that supposed to make me feel better about him nearly dying once a month?'

He shrugged, 'It is only information, it can make you feel however you wish… However, you'll probably find that he'll be able to carry you home pretty soon, if not now.'

I picked Jess up, and stood up, he was right. 'H…How?' I muttered, putting Jess back down.

He chuckled again, 'When you're not using large amounts of power, glucose and the ability kind, such as when you're sleeping and relaxing, all the power sat inside you gets to work on rebuilding the parts of your body that need rebuilding. It'll only get quicker the more powerful you get… It's been what? Fifteen minutes since you passed out? Eventually you'll be able to play a full game of football by the time you wake up, but that will take time to get there.'

I nodded and started walking towards the exit.

'Alfie, you're power is beyond great, and it will take you further than you thought possible, you and everyone else…'

I continued walking, I scanned the area for Gabby but she was nowhere to be found. We were halfway back to dorms when Jess said, 'Can we go and sit in the park? Under a tree or something?'

I nodded and veered left, straight into the park where once I'd found a suitable tree to sit under, I sat down. Jess finally looked up at me.

'You're powerful you know that.' I smiled, 'But really stupid at times.'

I laughed a little, 'I know, I'm sorry.'

She wasn't done, 'But… I get this feeling that we aren't fully understanding what Sir is saying, I have a feeling that… me, and you, and some others, we're going to have to go further than anyone else has ever gone, ever.'

I wasn't fully understanding what she was on about, but I nodded anyway.

'But… I don't want anything to happen to us…'

I put my forehead against hers, 'Jessica, nothing will ever change between you and me, for the worse anyway, I can promise you that.'

'Pinky promise?' She asked, holding up her pinkie.

I smiled, 'Pinkie promise… And if anything…'

'No…' She stopped me.

'But…' She got up and walked off, 'Jess! Jess please!'

I didn't move, no point, I'd annoyed her, if only I'd have kept my mouth shut…

I felt a water drop splash on my arm, then my face.

Huh, rain. I didn't bother to change it, it felt about right round about now. I sat there for another minute before deciding to walk back to dorm. I took my time, letting the rain soak my whole body, soaking in everything, "Being in the present" as they say. I got about 50 metres from the dorm when I saw Jess lying on the floor, one of my black hoodies on with the hood up, hair tucked in. I walked up next to her, her eyes were bloodshot again from crying, maybe she was still crying, I couldn't tell in the rain. I didn't say anything, I just laid down next to her, I was soaked but I didn't care. I stared across at her, wanting to say something. We laid there together for a long 10 minutes.

Finally, Jess rolled over and stared at me, 'You're powerful, but stupid at times.'

I turned over and smiled, 'Shall we go in?'

She nodded, I pulled her up and carried her in.

'What? You're both soaking!' Sylvia cried as I walked through the door, 'What were you doing?'

'Laying in the rain.'

'Nice.' Sam said.

Sylvia glared at him, 'Go and dry off!'

I sighed, 'Alright mum.' I replied, heating up my whole body and holding Jess close, drying her off too. Once I was dry I sat down.

'Thanks Alf.' She said as she dried.

I ran my hand through my hair, 'That's gonna be wet for a while.'

She pulled her (my) jumper off, shook it a couple of times, then put it back on!

I sighed and put my head back. Sylvia walked past chuckling. She winked at me.

'Hey anyone got a tennis ball?' I asked, Sam lobbed one over. I immediately launched it at Barukko's head, who was staring at us from across the room.

'Oww… Who did that?' He complained, I stuck my hand up, 'Why… okay fair.' He said, returning his attention to the Tv, Sam even made the effort to get up, walk over, and high five me. 'You shouldn't applaud that.' Zoe chided.

Sam smiled, 'Why not? He just hit Barukko in the head with a tennis ball from across the room without the girl next to him noticing, I'd clap that if I were you.'

'Thanks man.'

'No problem dude.'

I winced, 'Please don't call me that.'

'Okay dude.' He said smiling.

I sighed, 'We're the next generation of heroes huh?'

Tiago laughed, 'Yep.'

'Anyone know what time it is?'

Sylvia glanced at her phone, 'Half twelve why?'

I sighed, 'I'm hungry.'

Tiago laughed, 'It's only just after lunch, do you want me to grab you something?'

I nodded, 'Pass me the remote, will you?' I asked Jake, switching the Tv channel to something more interesting.

BuhDING…

Everyone looked over at the scoreboard. Tiago got up and walked over, 'It's Monday why would it…?'

'What? What is it?' Sylvia asked.

'There's been a change.' He announced, signalling to me to come over. I moved Jess's legs off me and laid her back down on the sofa before going to see what had happened, everyone was crowded around it by now.

'I don't get it…' Sam said, 'What's changed?'

'Look who's number one.' Tiago answered.

Everyone's heads angled upwards, 'Ohh.'

1 – Alfie Jaeger

'Well that's not a surprise is it?' Sam said as we all sat back down. Tiago patted me on the back as he walked past. I nodded and sat back down next to Jess, who then proceeded to put her legs on me.

'We don't have anything that we need to do, do we?'

'Like what?' Sylvia asked.

I shrugged, 'Anything.'

She shook her head and walked off.

'Why?' Tiago asked.

'Gunna go train when Jess wakes up.'

'You've just taken the top spot and you're going to go train?'

I smiled, 'Yeah...'

16 – I beat up an old guy (he started it)

An hour later I was so bored I woke Jess up, 'Hey…'
She stretched, 'Hiya.'
'I'm going to go train in like, five-ten minutes okay?'
She stretched again, 'Fine…'
Once she'd woken up I left her to Sylvia and went to the roof. I
opened the door and summoned the jacket, (I'm calling it a
jacket now), my Grandfather was already on the roof.
I frowned, 'What are you doing here?'
He shrugged, 'I have only been here a minute, you must have
summoned me ahead of time.' I nodded, 'Are you ready to
become a master of taekwondo?' he asked. I nodded and
summoned a dummy. For 3 hours he worked me, pointing out
the smallest mistakes in my technique, he was a whole lot
harsher today. If my toe was in the wrong place he'd make me
do it again. It'd taken me half the time it actually took me if he
wasn't so strict.
'Trust me you'll thank me for this.' He said.
I put my hands to my hips, 'Will I?'
He smiled, 'Yes, now, spar with me.'
'How? You don't have a physical body.'
'Why don't you make yourself like me?'
'A spirit? How?'
'Imagine your soul leaving your body, but not death, because
you can return at will, imagine that, and then you can fight me.
You may want to lay down too.'
'Why?'
'Because when you leave the body, you'll collapse if you're
stood up.' I nodded, laid down and closed my eyes. 'Imagine
your soul leaving the body…' he said, and I did, then suddenly, I
felt, weird, like I couldn't feel the ground anymore, or the
coldness of the January air. I opened my eyes and stood up,
well, floated up.
'What? Why can't I feel the floor?'
'Ah!' he exclaimed, walking other and touching my arm,
suddenly I felt gravity again, and the floor, 'Yes now you're in
this form I can affect you.'

I nodded, 'But what happens if someone comes up and sees me lying there?'

'You can do something about that too, imagine yourself walking through a door and seeing this scenario, you on the floor but also you stood up, in your spirit form. There's no knowing that it's worked until someone comes and checks on you but if they don't then there's no need for it.'

I nodded, and took my stance, 'Shall we get going then?'

He laughed and took a different stance, one that I didn't know. 'Alright boy! But let it be known that I am not just going to use Taekwondo against you, but I'll only use one or two.'

I let him come at me, blocking and deflecting any attacks, studying his style, learning to use it and combat it. I noticed that his kicks involved a long start, but hit with more power, maybe I could use that start though... I was on constant defence, he gave me no chance to break out, *I should've attacked first!* But then, an opening, when he went for some sort of triple spin kick, he left himself open, he had all his weight on one foot. I struck out with my right leg and hooked my foot around his planted leg, using my momentum to sweep him off his feet (well, foot). I then, (with help from my power) swung back around and smashed him into the ground with an axe kick. Well, he went straight through the floor, but close enough.

I paused, resetting myself and taking a breath when all of a sudden he emerged from the floor, a metre from me. 'Alright then!' He lunged at me and did some weird move that I didn't know and before I knew it I was in leg-lock.

'Really, Brazilian jiu-jitsu?'

He laughed, 'So you know of it?'

'OF COURSE I DO. I also know I can't get out of it, unless...' I put my hand flat against the ground and launched us up in the air, he was caught by surprise and loosed his grip on me, allowing me to free myself and hit him with my usual triple tornado kick, while in mid-air. This time he came into contact with the floor and hit the ledge on the opposite side of the building.

'How? Aagh!' He collapsed back to his knees after getting up. 'You only hit me once how is there so much pain in three...'

I smiled, 'That's right old man, you're getting slow.'

'But we were in mid-air, you shouldn't have been...! How fast are you?'

'Fast enough.' I growled, moving my hands into the shape of claws and summoning a load of electricity, 'Now, catch this.' I hurled bolts of electricity at him, again and again, I pounded him, pounding and pounding I hurled bolts at him till I could no more, I collapsed, 'We're done.'

He got up, 'Oh no we're not.' He replied, 'You're still in your spirit form!' The door opened on the other side of the roof. 'Alfie?' Jess said, 'Are these power outages you?' She saw my real body, 'Alfie!' then saw my spirit one, 'Wait, what?'

'Oh hey Jess.' I waved, 'I'll explain later first I've got to-' **BANG** I flew backwards and off the roof. 'Alfie!' Jess shouted.

I flew back up, coughing, 'I'm okay, just got to deal with this guy first.' I said, cracking my knuckles. He laughed, 'Good luck stopping this one!' He bellowed, his eyes glowing with rage, he thrust his hand into the air and a massive ball of energy appeared, it then condensed into a sphere the size of a football and he lowered his arm, pointing it straight at me. 'Bye.' He growled, launching the sphere of death at me.

Right as it was about to hit me I thought, *Hmm, I wonder...*

I channelled all of my energy into my right foot and swung around, catching the ball on my foot and redirecting it back at my Grandfather, his eyes widened as I clasped my hands together and pooled together all my energy, and added it to the sphere already hurtling to his face.

'See ya.' I said, falling back into my real body as the sphere engulfed him. When I woke up he was gone, and Jess was looking very confused.

'What... on... earth?'

I sat up and rubbed the back of my head, 'It's a long story.' And so I proceeded to tell her the whole story, training, spirit, bla bla.

The one thing she took from the whole thing?

'You redirected a ball of pure energy and hurled it at your own Grandpa?'

'Well when you put it that way it sounds bad!'

Anyway, it was another week before I summoned him again, he didn't even mention it, he was probably too embarrassed because he was beaten by his own grandson after training for a couple hundred years.

The build-up to the sports festival was quick, we practised for every event, I kept on with combat training despite complaints from Jess and Gabriella, and then it was announced, 2 months before the competition was due to start it was announced. It was on every news channel in minutes, 'Super Schola to host sports festival!' Since we already knew we just ignored it and kept practising.

Actually, on the morning it was announced there were 3 separate knocks on the door, (it was a Sunday so that wasn't normal) the first was class 1-B, well, the number 1 and 2 girl and guy, respectively, to be precise.

'We really wanna be on your sports teams!' They said simultaneously, 'Just us two! The girl said, staring at me.

'Actually we decided our teams ages-' I covered Sam's mouth.

'Sorry, we've already done the teams.'

'But they announced the thing an hour ago!'

I shrugged, 'We're organised... Oh and be sure to tell 1-C that too.'

They both pouted and turned around.

I closed the door, 'Why'd you shut Sam up?' Tiago asked.

'Because we can't let them know that we already knew.' Jess answered, I nodded.

The second knock came an hour later...

I opened it, 'Oh hey Brandon.'

He smiled, 'Hey, erm I've got a question to ask of you.'

'Sure go ahead.'

'Will you be on our trio team please?' He begged.

Jess and Barukko stood up immediately, I put my hand out at them.

'Who's this?' I asked, motioning to the girl and glancing behind me, Jess looked like she was about to punch Alda who was sat next to her.

'Oh this is our number one, Harlequin.'

'Harlequin huh? Yeah I'm good thanks...' Their faces dropped, 'Not that I've got anything against you but I've already got a team thanks.'

'B...B...But... We're stronger!' he complained.

I shrugged, 'I guess we'll see, sorry guys.' I said, closing the door.

I sighed and leant against the door, Jess smiled and sat back down, Barukko returned his attention to the Tv.

The next knock came 10 minutes later, I was getting pretty fed up by this point.

'Someone else get it!' I said.

Barukko got up and opened the door, 'Who are you?' He asked. I glanced over, *Third years?* Was my immediate thought, these two held themselves highly, you could tell that easily.

'Are you the one with the amazing power?'

Barukko shook his head, 'That's him over there.' He said, jutting his thumb at me.

The guy walked up to me, who hadn't bothered to move off the sofa.

'Will you join up with the two most power-'

'Na.' I interrupted.

'W...What?' He stammered, glancing at the girl, 'Why?'

'Cos I got my team,' I said, 'And we'll win, go play with your third I'm sure he's good enough.'

He huffed and stormed out.

Jess smiled, 'You could have won that thing easily with those two you know.'

'Yeah but what's the fun in an easy win?' I said, smiling, 'Now we are going to win this thing, or at least beat the rest of this school, that's for sure.'

Barukko nodded, 'You're right about that.'

'Wait, are you saying fighting with us is a disadvantage?' Jess asked.

I shrugged, 'I mean you kinda said it yourself so...' I shut up because Jess was looking at me like she wanted to kill me. She huffed, 'That's right.'

Zoe laughed across from me, 'Complete control huh?'

I smiled.

'And he sure does know it.' Jess said, getting up and grabbing some food.

'That's going to kill you!' I said, she just shrugged and shovelled it into her mouth.

We kept on training until the day came...

And the day couldn't come quickly enough, but here it was, the 5th of May, the start of the month-long festival that would showcase the best and brightest, and me.

The day before we'd all been given these headbands with the school initials on them, **SS**, engraved in a steel plate on a black stretch of cloth, these were necessary since we didn't have a uniform.

Anyway, the morning before the opening ceremony, which everyone was forced to attend, we were all gathered in the communal area preparing for the long two hours ahead.

'Hey Alf?'

'Mhmm.'

'Are you going to wear your cloak for the ceremony or not?'

I shrugged and put on the cloak, 'I don't know, should I?' Talia, Maddison, Sylvia, Gabriella and Jess nodded, 'It looks that good huh?'

'It's not that the cloak itself looks good, like if you put it on Jake, it wouldn't work, but with you, it looks powerful.' Maddison said.

'Huh, thanks.'

'Don't let it go to your head.' Jess said, she was wearing this white and gold outfit, everything, and I mean everything, was white with hints of gold. She dragged me over to the mirror and pulled out her phone, 'This is for the socials!' She said, snapping like twenty pictures of us.

'Really?'

'What? They'll go viral after you become famous from this event.'

I sighed, 'At least we look good.'

'I know!' She replied, winking.

'Hey AJ come here.' Maddison said, 'Pass me your headband.' I gave it to her, she took the metal plate off and pulled a white one with red letters on the sides and attached the plate to that, 'Here.' She handed it back.

I examined it, the letters were my initials, **AJ**.

'It looks amazing.' I said, putting it on, 'Thank you.'

She nodded and turned her attention to Tiago, who was having some sort of a nightmare now that he had to dress somewhat properly.

I turned back to Barukko and Jess, 'You guys ready to go?' They nodded.

Two minutes later there was a knock at the door, 10 o'clock.

Queenie got the door (quite reluctantly, she seemed to have a phobia after the training incident), 'Hi Principal.'

He walked into the room, 'Hello everybody! Are you ready to go?'

We all nodded, 'Just about.' Tiago muttered.

'Good, now as you know you'll be one of the last ones out from our school because you're first years.'

We nodded.

'But that doesn't mean you won't get any attention, well not if you want it, you can always make an entrance, especially you three.' He said nodding to us.

Alda grumbled, 'I mean we kinda said we'd kick back for the start but if they want to...' I smiled and patted her on the back before following the Principal out the door.

'Let's go!' He called, I walked to the arena alongside the Principal, 'So, what are you going to do to attract everyone then?'

The question caught me by surprise, 'Honestly, I haven't thought about it, I always thought no one would care.'

He laughed, 'No one cares unless you give them a reason to, you make an entrance, you make a name. Then people care...'

I nodded, 'So I should make an entrance?'

'Yes.' He chuckled.

I glanced at Jess, who'd just caught up to us, 'Are you being a bad influence on him sir?'

'Well, not really, oh yes Alfie, there's one thing I forgot to tell you, when your year goes out they're going to call out your name, because you are the highest ranked in your year, so, yes, make an entrance.'

My face went as white as a sheet, 'They're going to call me out?'

'Yep.'

'Ooh great…'

'Oh… and you two,' he said to Jess and Barukko, 'You're not going to get called out but you're going to want to make yourselves known.'

They nodded, and we walked the rest of the way in silence, when the arena came into view, I squeezed Jess's arm.

'The arena,' He said, 'Capable of holding two hundred thousand people and with millions more watching worldwide, an entrance here will be heard…' he announced.

No one said anything, but we all had the same thought, *200,000?*

I put the cloak away, Jess frowned, 'Why'd you do that?'

'You'll see.'

We got to our entrance underneath the arena.

'Okay everyone, this is where we depart, when you go down there'll be someone there to put you in your starting position, you won't be the first down there, you won't be the last, but there will be other schools, so be nice.'

We all nodded and walked down to the waiting area, where a guy met us and took us to our square waiting area, pretty close to the exit.

'Seriously? No furniture or anything? Just the floor?' Sam complained, Jess and Gabby stared at me, I sighed.

'Fine.' I muttered and suddenly loads of sofas appeared before us. Gabriella smiled, took my hand and pulled me onto one of them. 'You're welcome.' I shouted. A couple of kids glanced over and grumbled.

(Honestly, I didn't even know if I could summon furniture and to this day I have no idea how I did it)

'Don't attract attention.' Jason hissed at me.

'Why not, I'm gonna do it when I get out there why not start now?'

More and more groups filled in until the place was nearly full, there had been a couple of arguments between groups but we kept to ourselves, until the group below us arrived…

'Hey how come these lot get sofas?' The first guy in complained.

I raised my hand, 'That was me.'

'So what, your power is woodworking?' he laughed, 'Who's your number one?'

I kept my hand raised.

He stopped laughing, glared at me, 'You can't be serious?' Jess got up.

'Don't...' I said.

She walked over to the edge of our box, 'Listen here you little punk...'

I teleported over and put my arm across her, 'I said don't. We'll beat him at some point don't worry about that.' I pulled her away and the various screens across the massive room lit up. The man on the screens, the Principal of course.

I sat back down and put my arm around Gabby.

'Hello everybody!' He called, 'And welcome... to Super Schola's Sports Festival!'

I heard the roar of the crowds from down here.

'I am the Principal of this fine school, and allow me to say, let the games begin!'

The exit door opened and everyone stood up. I made our seating disappear, much to the surprise of that guy I really wanted to beat up.

'You ready?' I called to everyone.

'Yeah!' They called back.

I squeezed Gabriella's hand one last time before revealing myself to the world and let go.

We moved forward bit by bit, edging ever closer to the light. And then I was there, stood, by myself, just in front of everyone else, waiting for the call.

'And now, THE FIRST YEARS AND THEIR NUMBER ONE...' I glanced back at Jess.

'Go for it.' She mouthed.

'ALFIE JAEGER!'

I nodded and jogged out to a huge cheer, it was indescribable, I took five steps into the sunlight and launched myself into the air, twisting and flipping onto the ground, I rightened up and summoned a massive lightning bolt, the air electrified and my hair stood up as it hurtled down and blasted me, I summoned my cloak while the bolt hit me and when the lightning stopped it looked like I'd transformed, my hair stood up and I stood with this aura of power, I looked at one of the screens out of the corner of my eye, I looked powerful. I smiled. The noise was even more unbelievable than before.

I had arrived, and the whole world knew it.

Jess and Barukko came out next, leaping out and landing next to me, leaving massive light and dark patches like blast marks where they landed.

Barukko kissed Jess. Another roar.

'You shouldn't have done that.' She giggled.

'I love you.' He replied.

I cleared my throat as everyone else caught up and we got moving, we had to do a full lap of the arena before we got to our area, where we'd line up in power order and wait.

I glanced up at the screen and saw the entrance, momentarily clear of people, the blast marks from my bolt and Jess and Barukko's landings were still there. We'd left our mark alright. I genuinely felt like a celebrity, I waved occasionally to the people in the stands, but the whole time I never stopped smiling...

'This is amazing.' I said.

'The atmosphere, the weather, the people, the place!' Jess agreed.

I laughed, 'We'll win everything.'

'You'll win everything.' She said.

We arrived at our place and took our positions, now all we had to do was wait, and wait, and wait.

An hour later everyone had come out and the Principal made a big speech, such an honour, can't wait for the games, bla de bla...

Then we made our way out again, this time in reverse order.

'Hey guys shall we go out with a bang?' Jess said about halfway round the track.

Barukko and I shrugged, 'Sure why not?'

'Right as we get to the exit, we all spread out, say five metres apart or something, and we all simultaneously imprint our initial on the floor, A J B, like ten metres in length, In our colours, on the floor.'

I grinned, 'That sounds mad.'

'But what order, and how do we know when?' Barukko said.

'Like Jess said, A J B.'

'And I'll call it.' She said.

'We keep in line with you.' I said to Jess, she nodded.

So as we got close to the exit we backed off from the rest of the group and spread out. I could feel everyone watching us.

We kept in line, then twenty metres from the door Jess shouted, 'Now!' And we all instantaneously stamped out feet, **A J B**.

The noise was deafening, I walked inside and looked back, to see the blazing red of the **A**, the blinding white of the **J**, and the nightmare black of the **B** imprinted on the ground. I laughed and turned around, everyone was staring at us, no, everyone was glaring at us, we'd stolen the show and they knew it.

Later that evening it was on every news channel, just a picture of us three stood in the middle of our letters. I actually saved that picture, and another one taken from the top of the exit. Those went on the wall...

I went downstairs and found that half of us have already gone to sleep.

I yawned, 'What's the sport on tomorrow?'

'Basketball, power.' San said in a weirdly cheery mood.

'Hey Alex?'

'Yep.' He said, tossing my shoes to me, 'Try them on.'

I put them on, they felt impossibly light, 'These are amazing.'

He smiled, 'I know right, the mods you asked for are some of the best I've ever done so you'll fly in those things.'

I nodded; 'These are fantastic.'

Jess came over, 'Let me see...'

'Aha! No, not yet anyway.'

She pouted, 'Why?'

Alex chuckled, 'You'll see.'

I went up to bed soon after, Jess came with me.

'Where you sleeping tonight?' I asked her.

I'm at mine, it's easier to sleep without Barukko.'

'That makes no sense.'

She grinned, 'I know, I mean if I go to sleep first it's fine... But if he goes to sleep first I feel like I'm suffocating in his darkness...'

I nodded, 'We'd better win...'

She chuckled, 'We will...'

And with that, the day that the world was introduced to **AJB** was over.

18 – Basketball!!!

The next morning we woke early, we were downstairs and ready to go by 8.

'We're gonna get off!' I said, 'We've got to be there earlier than everyone else because we're playing but I expect you all to be there!' I said.

'We will!' Sylvia said.

Together the nine of us walked to the arena, our kits in bags over our shoulders.

We got to the arena in 10, and put our kits on, 'I don't get it.' Jess said, 'Why can't I see the shoes?'

'You'll see.'

Anyway one of the organisers went over the rules with us, 32 minutes, 8 minutes a quarter, until the semi-finals, then 12 minutes a quarter. All powers were allowed but you could not just block the hoop by putting someone on top of it or something, it had to be accessible at all times, if not you got a technical foul and the opposing team was given two free throws.

We didn't know who or when we'd be playing but we were given a box under the arena and told to wait there.

I summoned a couple of balls and we just started to toss them between each other, not really paying attention, but warming up. A lot of people were looking at us, probably because of me and Jess.

Eventually someone walked over, 'So these are the big shots that took the stage yesterday?' he looked around, 'Where's the third?'

'Who are you?' I asked.

'You don't need to know that.' he said. Mr GetLost was this tall, muscular guy that had the look in his eyes that told you that he wanted to kill you. His red spiky hair screamed maniac too.

'You don't look so bad.' He said.

I teleported him to the other side of the room and left him there, 'Yeah whatever.' I muttered before teleporting back, summoning a ball and pinging him in the head with it.

'OW!' I heard from across the room.

Sam high-fived me, 'Nice.'

He turned around and glared at me, I laughed.

The screens lit up and the Principal's face came into view.

'Hello!' The roar from the crowds was the same as last time, I stared at the ceiling, 'And welcome to our first event! Power-based basketball!' He paused for a moment, 'The matches for the first round have been decided beforehand.' The matches popped up on the screen.

I scanned down the list, **Super Schola Year 1-A Vs King Henry Year 1-B**.

'So were up against King Henry's B-team huh, never heard of them.' Zoe said.

I nodded and re-laced my shoes. 'We're what? Twelfth game on?'

Jess sighed, 'Yeah…' And sunk back onto the sofa. I sighed and sat down next to her.

'And it could be while if we win this one too.' Gabriella said.

'So, anyone got any hidden talents?'

'I can burp whenever I want.' Sam said.

'I told you that's not a talent!' Zoe complained, 'Or hidden!'

I laughed, 'You're not wrong.'

'I'm never wrong.'

'That answer there is wrong.' Helena butted in.

'See?' I said.

Helena smiled, and I glanced around the room, everyone seemed in good spirits, well, they were just about to play sports. There were four courts in the arena above us, and every single one of them were full, pretty much at all times.

Half an hour later the first batch of games were done and once the teams came down, we were sent up to court two and told to warm up.

We were given two minutes to warm up.

The refs quickly came on and introduced themselves, I didn't catch their names. Anyway we got Troy up for the toss and got ready, I had no idea what to expect, this was power basketball after all.

171

The ref tossed the ball up and Troy just enlarged his hand and caught it, wrapping his fingers around the ball. He brought it down and handed it to me, who just leapt and teleported to the hoop, 2-0, we'd scored within two seconds.

'Well this will be interesting.' I said to Jess as I jogged past.

The other team's powers were pretty weak, wind, telekinesis and size reduction were trash, very weak versions which did nothing, basically pointless. One girl could create the occasional portal, another girl had something similar to Bianca, and their centre had multiple arms, the best was their point guard though, he seemed to have superhuman agility, so he just darted through us all when we were locked down on defence. Finally the ref blew for half-time, we were all shattered.

'How do we stop that point guard?' Zoe said, panting.

'We don't,' H said, turning to us. 'Don't even try, your ten points up and your destroying them, try and intercept any passes coming his way and his positioning is awful so there isn't many, the rest you can easily deal with. Now get out there!'

We nodded and walked back on court, the ref tossed me the ball and we got to work, the game ended quickly and we won by twenty-seven points, 95-68. I ended up on, 38 points, 6 rebounds and 8 assists, I think.

'Good game guys.' I said at the end when we were all walking back, 'Onto the next round!'

Me and this guy bumped shoulders, he fell over, 'Ow…'

'Oh sorry mate.' I said, offering a hand, 'Didn't see you there.'

The guy stared at me like I was stupid, I mean he was 7ft tall and about 4ft wide, and pure muscle, but I didn't see him. He swatted my hand away and got up, lumbering past me and joining his teammates. There was a look in his eyes when he glanced back, anger? No, fear, not a clue why though.

'You okay?' Gabriella asked.

'Yeah… I'm fine, come on.' I said, putting my arm over her shoulder and walking back to our area. It was another four hours before our next match, we had lunch about an hour before the game, that's how long it took.

Anyway, just after two in the afternoon, the next round of matchups were announced, we were to play against this school called **Moc szkoła**, not a clue what it means but I think it's Polish. Anyway another hour later and we were up, we made our way onto court two again and got ready, another two-minute warm-up and then got ready to play.

'Hey, Alfie?' Helena said from courtside.

'Yeah?'

'Can you alter your vision to see their powers by any chance?' Jess looked at Helena, 'Will that work?'

I shrugged and closed my eyes, when I opened them again I couldn't *see* their power exactly, I just kinda looked at them and knew.

'A very bad form of omnipresence, wolf anatomy and tiger anatomy,' (those two were obvious), 'water manipulation, and superhuman reflexes and stamina.' I said, 'Did we like not get a memo or something?'

Nat glanced at me, 'What do you mean?'

'Well, both teams we've played against have had a powerless player.'

Gabriella shrugged and shot the ball. Jess turned to me, 'Their loss.'

I smiled, 'Yeah, now let's win this thing yeah?'

The ref told us to get in our positions.

'Hey Troy, can I go for the toss?'

He glanced at Helena, who shrugged, 'Yeah sure why not?' He said.

I went up and stared at the other guy, the wolf anatomy one. He glared at me, 'Can't wait to beat you to the toss.' He laughed.

I smiled, 'Sure.'

The ref tossed the ball up and I teleported, grabbed the ball and teleported again, dunking the ball in their basket.

I think I broke a world record, I got something like 0.18 of a second or something. I jogged back past Wolf, 'Nice one.'

He growled again.

This game was a lot more problematic, the two superhuman's lead their team, one never stopped running and the other grabbed any ball within touching distance, we had to completely change the whole way we played to get around them.

We were up by 5 at halftime, 'You'll win this.' Helena confirmed, 'As long as you don't do anything stupid you'll be fine.'

I glanced over at the other team, 'It's fine, look.'

Everyone looked over, they were all arguing between themselves, we got back on the field and the other side lost all ability to play basketball, missed pass, or no passes, we just grabbed the ball and got the easy two points, we won by a bigger margin than the last game, that's how badly they fell apart.

I bent over and clutched my knees when the game ended, Jess came over from the bench and studied my shoes.

'You'll... see...' I said, gasping for air.

She stamped her foot and walked off.

The final score ended 87-53, for those who care, and I got a triple-double actually, 11 steals, 28 points, 10 rebounds and 8 assists for anyone making a stat sheet.

We walked back and when we got inside I realised just how many teams had gone, it must have been half empty.

'What round is next?' Sam asked, thinking the same as me.

'Round of 32.' Helena said, he nodded.

'Still 32 teams left?' I asked, 'That means...'

'There were 128 teams at the start.'

'That's lucky to get exactly 128.' Bianca said, I nodded.

'Anyway, let's not get bogged down about how lucky they are, we need to pay attention, in like, half an hour they'll announce the next round, it's only going to get harder.'

Everyone nodded and Jess glanced at me, 'I'm going to find out what those shoes are about.'

I chuckled, 'Yes you will if we make it to where we should be.'

'The finals?'

I smiled, 'Well...'

'Win it?'

'Basically.' She crossed her arms, 'Why are you looking so glum? I thought we were going to win this thing?'

'We are, I just don't want to wait that long.'

Everyone smiled, 'Well, there's not much you can do about that.' I said.

The screens showed the matchups again half an hour later.
Super Schola 2-B Vs Super Schola 1-A.
'So we can finally play the second and third years?' Sam said, 'Might get some actual competition now.'
Gabriella cracked her knuckles, Helena winced, 'Probably not.'
'Anyway we're the first game!' Jess interrupted, 'Let's go!'
She dragged me outside and we did our 2-minute warm-up.
'Powers?' Helena asked.
'Acid generation, angel anatomy, animal powers, not sure what animals, vortex breath, density control on objects, electricity manipulation, ice manipulation and jet propulsion.'
'Wow so no real basketball helping ones, just more, movement problems for us...' Nat said.
I nodded, but since we can play and our powers are better, we'll be fine, you ready?'
Everyone nodded, 'Alfie you going for toss?' I nodded and grabbed Gabriella.
'Hey you're going need to be ready for this so I'm gonna teleport you above the hoop and teleport the ball to you okay?'
She paused, taking it all in, then nodded.
I went for the toss and vortex girl waited by the hoop. The ref tossed the ball and I did exactly what I said, teleported Gabby to the hoop with the ball and teleported myself to the 3-point line, vortex girl turned her attention to me whilst Gabby slammed the ball into the hoop.
I high-fived her and we got back for defence.
The game didn't go as well as expected, we made a bunch of stupid mistakes on both ends of the court and we were down by 11 by halftime.
'You are so much better than these guys!' Helena shouted, 'You're just being idiots, go back to basics, play the simple game, you can make mistakes on defence but you've got to outscore them!'
'A good offence beats a good defence.' I muttered.
'Exactly! Now get out there and play your game!'

We slowly brought the game back, but we were still down by 2 with 20 seconds left, I had the ball in my hand and I was making my way up the court, I had Jess in front of me ready for the blind-3 as we called it (just where the defence couldn't see me making the shot, because of Jess's light).

But I made the call, 'ALL GO!'

Everyone panicked for a second but understood, we'd practised it but never pulled it off in a game.

"All go" is our last call strategy, where, quite literally, we all used our powers, Jess lit up to block anyone from blocking me, Sam would paralyse the vortex girl, Troy would cover both of the animal boys and Nat and Zoe would distract acid and density, they couldn't do much without the ball.

The clock counted down, the stadium got louder, 2 seconds left, 'GO!'

The plan set into motion and I stopped just short of Jess, pulled up and released, a 30footer, the buzzer went and the ball was still in the air, do or die time.

I held my arm out, **SWOOSH.**

The game was over, we had won.

The opposing team fell to their knees, I turned around and walked back to centre court, my arm still out. Everyone leapt on me.

'That actually worked!' Zoe shouted.

'Of course it did!' I laughed.

I glanced over at the other team, most were still laying on the floor. *Wow, it affected them that badly huh?*

I turned back and saw Jess studying my shoes, 'No.'

'I wasn't!'

'You were!' I shouted, laughing, 'I told you, we win…' I turned to everyone, 'Now come on, we've still got four more games to win!'

Everyone cheered as we walked off the court and back to the waiting area. By the time the next matches were decided, the room was practically empty.

'Okay!' The Principal said through the screen, 'The last sixteen! It's getting to the best of the best now!' The crowd roared, 'Anyway, the next match-ups are...'

The matches popped up on the screen.

We were at the bottom of the list, **Super Schola 1-A Vs Campeão Escola 2-A**.

The Ramirez trio groaned.

'What is it?' I asked.

'Champion school, it's the best school in the whole of Brazil.' Gabriella said.

'That's fine, we're the best school in the whole of this country.' She shrugged, 'I mean, yeah...'

'We'll be fine.' Jess said, 'We're better, probably.'

'It's a good job we haven't come up against their third years, they've won both basketball competitions every year they've competed.'

'Oh, great, so they're the ones to beat. Who came second?' I asked.

'The guys were about to play.'

I threw my head back and groaned, 'Oh great! Well, we've got half an hour till our game so enjoy!'

'It might be our last.' Zoe muttered.

I ignored that and spun a ball on my finger.

Half an hour later we braced ourselves and got ready, I re-laced my shoes and we all walked up to the court, we were the first there, the ref gave us the two-minute warm-up and then we got ready to play.

'Powers?' Helena asked.

I looked at them, 'Err kinetic absorption, marksmanship, that guy has an eye in the back of his head, poison generation, cyborg, size reduction to self, telekinesis and wall-crawling.'

'How is wall-crawling going to help?' Jess asked. I shrugged. Natalia looked over at Bianca, 'Oh no... That's her...'

'Who?' I asked, looking over.

'Brianna. She's been Bianca's greatest rival since forever, they've got the same power so it's only natural.'

I nodded, 'Okay...'

'Is she going to be okay?' Helena asked, 'Because I can easily start Zoe.'

Gabby nodded, 'She'll be fine, just keep an eye on her, if she starts to get angry, pull her off.'

The ref called for us to get ready and we all gathered round, Troy took the toss this time but lost, the telekinesis guy just grabbed it off the bat and carried it to the point guard.

The game got off to a bad start, we were still figuring out how to beat their powers when they went eight points up.

'Come on guys!' Helena shouted, 'Play the simple game!'

And we did, and we started to turn it around, by the end of the half we were only down by one.

'Okay guys, you improved well, massively, but you need to be careful, don't start getting cocky or you'll just lose it again.'

We all nodded and got back on the court, we started with the ball and I saw a lane to the hoop down the left side of the court, I went for it, a guy stepped in to block and I faked a pass behind the back, going around him and leaping, straight over three-eye guy and windmilling it into the basket.

'Yeah!' I shouted, jogging back down the court.

H subbed me off.

'Why!' I complained.

'I said to stick to the basics, and you didn't!'

She kept me off for the whole third quarter, we did fine though, we were five up at the start of the fourth.

I finally got back on the court and did, well, pretty average, 7 points and 2 assists in the fourth.

We won though, 74-64.

'Haha nice!' I said, high fiving everyone when the game ended, 'That wasn't that hard was it?' I said, turning to Nat. She shrugged. I said it wasn't hard, we were all drenched in sweat, we'd worked our butts off, but we'd won so I didn't mind.

We walked back when I heard a familiar voice, 'ALFIE!'

I spun around, 'Sylvia...? Hey guys look!' I pointed to our classmates, who were on the bottom row of the stands, just outside one of the courts.

I waved, 'Hey guys!'

Everyone waved back, 'Don't let us distract you!' Talia shouted.

I stuck my thumb up and turned around, walking into the waiting area...

19 - The Finals!

I could count the number of teams left on my hands.
We walked down and the room was silent, everyone left was chatting, but since there were so few of us it was nothing. Because of our convo with Sylvia and Talia we'd missed the Principal, and the fixtures were already up on the screen.
'Oh yay...' I heard Jess say.
'What... Ohh...' I looked at the screen, we were up against our own third years...
We turned around and walked back on the court, Helena opened her mouth.
'Yeah, I know...' I interrupted, 'Web creation, vision, superhuman touch, sound manipulation, psychometry, plant manipulation, wind control and necromancy. None of those really help with playing do they?'
'Well, except touch and wind no not really.' Zoe said.
'Yeah well it doesn't matter, just play your game and you'll be fine.'

It turns out we'd be less than fine, we got outplayed on every level, we were down by twenty-five points at halftime.
'Well, that's it for us...' Jess said glumly.
'No it's not!' I shouted, 'We are not stopping now, we either go out in the final, or we don't go out at all. You hear me?!' Everyone nodded, 'Good, now we're gonna mix up the game a bit, play a bit less than just the basics, these guys can actually play basketball, so we've just got to outplay them!'
Helena nodded and told us what to do, then we went back out on court and took over the game, we climbed back up till we were up by 1 with twenty seconds left...
'Come on!' I shouted, 'Lockdown!'
They had the ball and were passing it around, looking for an opening...
10...9...8... Still passing the ball, then, Gabby slipped after running around a screen, a lane opened...7...6... He ran to the hoop...5...4... He leapt up ready to lay it in...3... **BANG!** Troy swiped the ball out from his hands and I set off running, leaving

everyone in the dust, he launched the ball to me...2...1... I caught it and slammed it into the hoop, hanging off it just to rub it in...0...

We went wild, I dropped down from the hoop and ran all the way across the court to Troy, I jumped on him.

'That was amazing!' I shouted, 'Block of the century.'

Everyone else piled on and we all laughed, 'We're through to the semis!' Sam shouted. We all went over to the rest of the class where everyone congratulated Troy, he looked so embarrassed I thought he was going to pass out.

'Come on guys! We've got to get back!' I said, jogging back to the waiting area.

'The final four!' the Principal shouted, 'And one of our own! Congratulations to the teams that have made it this far and commiserations to those that fell.'

The next round matchups appeared on the screen.

Super Schola 1-A vs King James 3-B

We got out on court and were told about the timings again, 12-minute quarters now instead of 8.

'Teleportation, superspeed, wings, spider anatomy, shoe manipulation, ice breath, dragon anatomy and flight.' I rattled off.

'Great, they all help to play basketball.' Sam groaned.

'But that probably means they can't play.' Helena said.

I shrugged, 'We'll find out! Teleport toss?' I said.

Troy and Helena both nodded.

Now I'm going to confess, I'm basically going to skip this game because it was a runaway! 130-68!

I dropped, 53 points, 15 assists and 10 rebounds. We ran rampant, I think I got like 4 posters and it was just incredible, the most fun I'd had in a long time.

When the game ended the whole arena was silent, the other game had finished two minutes ago so everyone was watching us. The horn blew and we just burst out laughing, the semi-finals and they played like it was the first 128.

Half their team was in tears and the other half walked off; it was a sight to behold.

Anyway, we didn't go into the waiting room this time, instead we were given a ten-minute break because they had to set up the last court, right in the middle of the arena.

We didn't really say much, the rest of the class offered encouragement but it was nerve-wracking, we were in the final, up against the team that had won it every time, **Campeão Escola 3-A.**

I sighed, 'Force field generation, multiple arms, that's obvious, illusions, superhuman strength...' *Wait, that's the guy I knocked over earlier.* '... superspeed, telepathy, unbreakable bones and weakness detection.'

'Wonderful, they can all play ball and have good powers.' Jess noted. I coughed, 'Yes I know we're the same!'

The ref called us all to get into position and I walked up to the toss, the guy I'd knocked over earlier was also there, 'Sup lightweight.' I said.

He glared at me but didn't say a word.

The ref tossed the ball up but instead of going for the ball feather boy went for me, I mean it didn't matter since I teleported before he even moved but I bopped him on the head with the ball and teleported again, dunking the ball in the hoop. 2-0.

After that the game was inseparable, we traded leads, if we got a block, they got a block, if they hit a three, we hit a three.

We were tied up, thirty seconds on the clock, they just scored two and I had the ball in my hand. I dribbled up court, 'Be careful Alfie! The time!' Helena called.

I kept bouncing the ball, waiting, waiting, two seconds left on the shot clock, *GO!* I sprinted, crossed over, broke feather boy's ankles, pulled up and sunk the three. The whole stadium went berserk, but the game wasn't over, feather boy grabbed the ball of the floor and began sprinting down the court with it, but I knew the game wasn't over...5...4...***SNATCH***... Suddenly the ball wasn't in his hands, it was in mine, I took the ball back up court where Jess was waiting...3...2...1...

'Oop!' I called and Jess leapt, I tossed the ball up and she caught it in both hands, slamming it down and hanging off the hoop with two hands too...

0...

'YEAH!' I screamed, I walked to midcourt and pointed to the shoes, I looked up at the screens and saw that they'd done as I suggested, they were zoomed in on the shoes, which had transformed entirely...

'Jess!' I shouted, pointing to the screens.

She glanced at the screens, then my shoes, 'Are they even the same shoes?'

I laughed, 'Yeah!'

The shoes had completely changed, becoming this flowing, ever-changing red. They looked amazing, and powerful.

The Principal walked towards us.

'Oh Principal, hi!' I said.

He smiled, 'Hello my boy! I just wanted to congratulate you on your amazing victory before the ceremony.'

'Thank you!'

He motioned for us all to follow, 'Come on!'

He led us back to the court in the middle, where there was now a podium with a very shiny golden trophy sat on it.

Sam looked around, 'Where did that come from?'

I laughed, 'Who cares?'

The other team walked back out looking *slightly* miffed and accepted their SECOND-PLACE medals.

(You don't think I'm a sore winner do you?)

The Principal then turned to me, 'And now, the winners of the Global Sports Festival Power Basketball tournament!' he held out the trophy and I took it gladfully with both hands, I looked around at us in our semi-circle shape.

'We deserved this.' I said, raising the trophy and hearing the roar of the crowd, it was unbelievable.

I passed the cup to Gabriella who was stood next to me. I could hear Sylvia shouting at everyone to look behind them, I caught her eye and put my finger to my lips, she stopped shouting after that.

When Sam grabbed the trophy he glanced around and saw what was happening behind us, 'Uh Alfie, did you do this?'

I laughed, 'I can't believe you only just noticed it!'

Everyone else turned around and was met by a massive roar again, I caught the Principal's eye and he smiled. Behind all of us, glowing on the ground was everyone's first initial. **N B T J A G S Z H**, all glowing a powerful blue colour.

Jess grabbed my arm, 'It's amazing!'

I laughed, 'I know.'

I looked around again and I finally noticed all the photographers in front of us, it was weird, I genuinely felt like I'd just won a major trophy, even though we had just beaten a bunch of 16-year-olds.

'You know you're going to have to do very well to beat this next year.' She said.

I laughed, 'Oh god didn't think about that…! Maybe you can pull it out the bag next year.'

She shook her head, 'Nope!'

I passed the trophy to Zoe who called Sam over. I stared at Jess, 'You good?'

She smiled, 'Yeah!'

'Onto the next one then?' I asked, she nodded.

'Of course.'

The Principal came over, 'Alfie the press would like to talk to you.'

I stared at him, 'The press?'

'Yes, this is a global sports tournament after all.'

I glanced at Jess and she shrugged, I went with the Principal off to the side. Where there indeed were a lot of press.

'Okay everyone, you know who this kid is, he is only fifteen so don't pound him please!'

I stepped forward and everyone started shouting at me, 'Alright everyone!' I interrupted, 'One at a time,' I picked this random guy at the front, 'Yeah go ahead.'

'Hi Alfie, so, this is your first year at the school, and you've already won a tournament! Congrats! What are your thoughts on the win?'

'Well, we worked hard for this. Six of us had been playing basketball all year, but Troy and Jess only joined us for the tournament and were relatively new to the game, but we worked hard and got what we worked for.'

Everyone started shouting at me.

'Er yeah, you at in the middle.' I said to this woman.

'Hi there, you've already made a huge impression on this competition and it's been heard all around the world.' I smiled, 'But was it the right choice?'

I hesitated, 'What do you mean?'

'Well, would it not be better, at your age, to kind of, sit back and let your abilities develop a bit more before revealing yourself?'

I laughed, 'What? Look, I mean no disrespect but I am one of the most powerful kids in the world, probably the strongest of my age, I think I'll be okay, anyway, we made the choice to come out and I'm sticking to it.'

'But what if it does backfire?' Another man said.

'Well we'll deal with it.'

'How?'

I shrugged, 'It depends on how it backfires. Now can we please get back to the sports!'

I picked a girl at the back.

'Uh, Hi, are you planning on taking part in any other competitions, and if so, what?'

I smiled, 'Of course I am, the other basketball, the football and all three battle formats.'

'Do you plan on winning them all?' She asked.

'Of course, I wouldn't be entering if I wasn't.'

'And who are your teammates for the combat?' Another guy asked.

I smiled, 'You'll find out...' I replied, turned away, and walked back to the Principal.

'You handled that well.' He said,

I shrugged, 'I just told the truth, if they've got a problem with that then fudge them.'

He smiled, 'Indeed.' He signalled for Helena to come over, 'You're done now, you can take the trophy and head home.'

'Really? Okay.'

I walked back to the group and put my arm around Gabby, telling them all that we can go.

'But shouldn't we just take a walk around the stadium?' Zoe said.

Jess shrugged, 'Why not?'

'Sign some autographs...' I said jokingly.

'I know you're kidding but you may have to.' Gabby said.

'Yeah whatever!' I said, putting on my cloak.

'Aren't you warm?' Jess said.

'That's why I put it on, this thing is magical in more ways than one you know.'

She felt the inside of it, 'Oh! It's so cold!'

'I know.' I laughed, walking to the track on the outside of the stadium.

We had a quick word with the rest of our class but it was so loud we could hardly hear each other, we all agreed to talk back at dorm.

We walked back to the waiting area and sat down for a moment.

'This is mad.' I said.

'I know, and we've still got the next one to win too.'

Everyone smiled, I got back up and Sam passed me the trophy, 'Let's go then.'

We walked outside to a significantly smaller and much more surprising cheer. There was a small crowd on both sides screaming at us for autographs, specifically from me (hehe).

Gabby burst out laughing, 'You weren't wrong.'

I smiled and walked over, doing what I'd seen every celebrity do on the Tv, pics, autographs and a couple of high-fives before moving on and catching up to everyone else.

'Famous at fifteen aye?' Sam said.

I slapped him in the head, 'Shut up! And I'm sixteen!'

'Oww!' He complained.

'He didn't hit you that hard.' Zoe said.

'You're supposed to help me out!'

I laughed, 'She's supposed to do what she wants.'

She fist-bumped me, 'You've got that right.'

Jess looked at me, 'Hold up... Wait a minute... You're sixteen?'

I frowned, 'Well... Yeah.'

'Since when?'

'September.'

She stared at me, 'You're the oldest in the class and no one knows?'

I rubbed the back of my head, 'Yeah but only by like, three weeks.'

'Yeah but still! How come you didn't tell anyone?'

I shrugged, 'Didn't feel that important.'

'Alf it was your sixteenth! It's very important!'

'Yeah in Sparta you'd be a man.' Sam added.

We all stared at him, even Zoe, 'How... Never mind... But anyway, it's been and gone now and it didn't bother me so...'

'Hmph!' She exclaimed, crossing her arms and scrunching her nose.

I ignored her, 'So then, what's next?'

Zoe laughed, 'We only just won! Can't you celebrate a victory?'

'Been there, done that, got the t-shirt, we move onto the next thing, and win that.'

'That's a mad mentality.' Sam said.

Jess glared at me.

'Fine...' I said, smiling.

'Complete control huh?' Zoe said.

I nodded as she pulled me to dorm, 'Complete control.'

She pulled me all the way back to dorm and threw open the door where everyone was waiting.

'Hiya!' she shouted, everyone cheered.

I quickly followed, only because she still had hold of my arm, 'Hey everyone.'

Jess finally let go of me and I handed the trophy to her, going off to the corner to talk to Barukko.

'Good win.' He said.

'Thanks,' I said, sitting down next to him, 'time to move on to the next one.'

'It's not even been two hours.'

I shrugged, 'It's just how I want to work, becoming the best ain't gonna take a day off.'

'Says the guy that had a two-week break over the holidays.'

'...Okay fair enough maybe it does take a few days off when needs be.'

He laughed, 'So you'll work hard until the Principal or Jess tells you to stop.'

'Hey, I defy Jess sometimes...'

'Sometimes.'

I stuck my arms behind my head, 'Yeah okay... I work hard most of the time, barring a fair amount of reasons.'

He laughed again, Jess came over and he put his arm around her, 'Good win Babe.'

I heard a massive crash from the kitchen, then an 'Uh oh.'

'Oh god that sounds like Sylvia.' I muttered, getting up to see what she'd done.

I crossed the room, 'Syl what have you done?'

She chucked a bunch of glass in the bin, 'Oh nothing.'

'Mhmm.' I opened the bin and looked inside, 'Did you smash a window?'

She smiled, embarrassed, 'Na just a couple of glasses.'

'How many?'

'Five or six.'

My jaw dropped, 'How'd you break five!'

'Well they were on the counter, then they just weren't.'

'So you knocked them off.' She nodded cautiously. I laughed, 'Were you going at a hundred miles an hour again?' She nodded. 'Slow down every once in a while, it makes life last longer.' She nodded, 'I'm off upstairs for a min, I'll be back soon.'

The doors closed I breathed a sigh of relief. I put my hands to my face and didn't pull them away until the doors had opened at the top.

I walked into my bedroom and got straight in the shower, just soaking in the running water, calming myself down.

It has been a hell of a day.

Suddenly the world went dark, and I awoke again in the destroyed city I'd been in before, I was lying on the ground and

I only just got up to see Jess and Barukko get blasted to nothing, I screamed in rage again, I screamed and screamed till I could no more, then my vision went black again, I awoke in a house, on my knees, knelt over a picture of Jess smashed on the floor with a length of rope in my hand...

My vision went black again and I awoke in front of Jess and Barukko, I screamed in rage and blasted the guy to dust.

I opened my eyes again, back in the shower like nothing had happened, I hadn't even moved. I climbed out of the shower, put on some fresh clothes and threw myself onto the bed.

What was that vision just then? Especially the new part. Was I about to?

I shook my head, there was no way.

I heard the door open, I didn't bother moving, I closed my eyes.

'Hey... You okay?' I didn't say anything, she sat down by my head, 'What's wrong?'

I exhaled, 'I had a vision.'

'About what?'

I shrugged, 'About us, and Barukko.'

'Something good?'

'No... ... ... It was more like two visions, alternate endings to a story almost. In one, you and Barukko got blown to dust and I couldn't do anything, in the other...'

'You saved us.'

'Well, killed him before he killed you.'

She ran her hand through my hair, I opened my eyes. She looked into them, 'It's scared you.' I didn't say anything. 'We'll be okay, I've got you.' She smiled, 'My body aches.'

I laughed, 'You've just played a day of sports what do you expect?'

'Can you do the healing thing?'

'In the morning.'

She looked at me, 'Why not now?'

'God you're needy.'

On reflection that wasn't the best answer to that question.

'What? What do you mean?' She demanded, getting up.

'No wait that came out wrong!'

'Did it! Did it really?'

189

She stormed out and slammed the door.

'Fuh… Great!' I walked out to the balcony and gripped the wall, cracking it. 'Ah sheesh! It is not going well for me today!'

'No kidding.' A voice said next to me.

'Oh I summoned you this time did I?'

He smiled, 'No actually I think this one was me.'

I sighed, putting my hands to my face, 'What do you want?'

'You should really go and get that girl.'

'And you're telling me this why?'

'Because that girl that's just stormed out, you don't know just how important she is.'

'I do know, I do.'

'Boy you know nothing.' He growled, 'Herself, and some others, they're so much more important to you, to your story… than you think.'

I stared at him, 'What do you mean by that?'

He shrugged, 'You'll know… eventually… probably…'

I groaned, 'My best friend is mad at me and now I've got to deal with your riddles.'

He chuckled, 'There are worse problems to have.'

I made the cloak disappear and leaned against the wall, 'Did you ever have a long-term relationship?'

'Kid, I'm your ancestor.'

'That doesn't really answer the question.'

He sighed, 'You know, in all the stories they never mention the normal stuff, but yes…'

'Was it… worth it?'

He smiled, 'You find the right girl? And yes, it can be taxing at times, but yes.'

'Taxing huh? You've got that right and I'm not even dating her.'

'Oh you don't know the half of it, there can be periods where she doesn't talk to you for weeks. Speaking of women, yours is stood out there thinking about storming in here, do what you want with that information.' He said, disappearing instantly.

I walked to the door and threw it open,

'Alfie!'

I hugged her, 'I'm sorry.'

I had caught her by surprise, she slowly wrapped her arms around me, 'No, I was in the wrong, I shouldn't have just demanded you throw around your power like that.'

'Did Syl tell you to say that?'

She smiled, 'Yeah… kinda.'

I laughed. 'It's okay.'

'But it's not!'

I chuckled, 'Jess, your best friend is one of the most powerful people in the world, it's okay, I should've just done it.'

She sniffled.

'Hey… It's okay.' I picked her up and carried her into my room, 'It's been a long day.'

'But still…'

I put my forehead against hers.

'Alf…'

'Don't tell Barukko or he'll beat me up.'

She laughed.

'You should get some sleep.'

She nodded and got up, I heard her through the wall… I hit my head against the pillow and was asleep quicker than you could say "dreamless".

20 – Not much to say here... It doesn't go well...

I woke up the next morning to my door opening.
'Oh hey, I was just about to wake you.'
'Mhmm, how are you feeling?'
'Yeah fine actually, my body doesn't ache at all which is weird...'
She stared at me, I stretched, doing my best poker face. 'Hmm, anyway yeah it's only seven so you've got ages before we have to do anything.'
I nodded, leaning against the wall, 'Please tell me they're not doing something I'm in today, I think I might combust if I use my powers like that for another day.'
She smiled, 'No I think they alternate team and solo sports, I think it's like tennis today or something.'
'Oh thank god.'
Jess chuckled, 'Come on, go shower and change, I'll meet you downstairs.'
I nodded and got up leaving Jess and going in the shower, putting on the usual clothes and heading downstairs.
'Hey Alfie!' Alex said running past me.
'Oh hey.'
Everyone seemed pretty relaxed today, except for Alex who was the most hyper I'd ever seen the kid.
I yawned and walked around to Sam, who was eating like, 5 croissants. 'NO!' he said, 'You can't have any of my croissants!'
I smiled, 'Why not?' I asked, grabbing one and walking away.
'Hey no!' He shouted, whacking my arm.
'Hey! I nearly dropped my croissant!'
He laughed, 'Okay you can keep it.'
I frowned, 'Really?'
He couldn't stop laughing, 'Yeah.'
I shrugged and walked off.

Later on we all went to the arena to watch the tennis, *yay*, but to be fair we had to, Paris, Alex and Alexandra were playing.
'I didn't know Alex was a tennis kid.' I said to Barukko.
He shrugged, 'Neither did I but apparently he is.'

Anyway, there we were, in our class section of the stands when the crowd above us saw us, or well, me.

I heard a scream then a bunch of voices shouting, 'Alfie! AJ! AJ! Alfie!' I turned around to be a pretty large group of girls shouting at me, 'The cloak!' They shouted, I sighed and put on the cloak, more screams.

Jess noticed that Barukko and I weren't watching the matches and turned around to see what we were looking at. I watched her face go through a flurry of emotion when she saw the large crowd now gathered above us. She walked over, much to the joy of some and the disappointment of others.

'AJB!' They started shouting.

I smiled and nodded, 'Looks like we've got fans.'

Barukko and Jess laughed, 'Looks like it. Lot of girls there too.' Barukko pointed out.

Jess glared at both of us, 'What?' I said.

'Alright, alright come here.' Barukko said, turning back to the game and putting his arm around Jess, much to the disappointment of both the boys and the girls, I turned around moments later.

'Are we done now?' I asked.

They both nodded and I waved back to them, then put up an invisibility shield so they couldn't see us.

'God, I don't want to be famous.' Barukko said.

I laughed, 'Well, bit late for that!'

'Well at least for the next month.' Jess said.

'And then in a year's time.' I continued, 'And then in another year and then if you do become a hero, you'll be famous all the time!'

He smiled, 'Okay maybe this isn't the job for me.'

I laughed.

That day went pretty quick, I mean everyone was out by lunch so we all got to leave but it went surprisingly quick, don't really remember much about it either.

The next day we had power-less basketball...

193

The less said the better, we got knocked out in the first round, played awfully, got outplayed by a team that no one's heard of...

'What the hell just happened?' I questioned, walking out of the stadium.

'Not a clue.' Jess said, refusing to look at me.

I looked around at everyone, not one person met my eyes, not even H.

'Aargh!' I shouted, punching a hole straight through a tree, the following shockwave blowing down the one after that.

Jess stared at me, 'How'd you just...?'

'I have no idea.' I said, pulling my hand out of the tree.

Another group who'd just been knocked out walked past, they noticed me and laughed.

I glanced up and glared at them, that shut them up.

'Come on Alfie.' Gabby said, 'Let's get back to dorm...'

I nodded and set off walking, keeping my hands in my pockets.

We arrived back at dorm in no time, everyone commiserated us then quickly dispersed, probably sensing the power I was accidentally emitting.

I went up to my room, slipping away when no one noticed, and got in the shower.

What the hell was that Alfie? We go from champions to losers in a game!

I let the water soak my clothes which I was still in, *Why the hell am I still wearing my clothes?*

I sighed and closed my eyes, leaning against the wall.

'Hey Alf.' A voice said.

I opened my eyes and saw Jess stood at the bathroom door, 'Oh hey.'

'You okay?'

'Do I look okay?'

She smiled, 'I mean you are in the shower with your clothes on.'

I chuckled, 'Yeah that's a fair point... Hang on... Did you know I had my clothes on when you came in here?'

She blushed, 'I was like, ninety percent sure, you normally just dump your clothes on the bed and I couldn't see them anywhere else sooo, I also saw that you'd taken your shoes off so I just guessed.'

I smiled, 'You know me too well.'

She took a step towards me, 'Well… You are my best friend, and we win together-'

'We lose together… We live together.' I said, finishing off the old class motto, 'I haven't heard that in a while…'

She pulled off her shoes and hugged me, clearly not caring about not getting wet as she was now in the shower with me, 'I know… I'd almost forgotten about it.'

I put my head against hers, 'I'm sorry about today.'

'What are you sorry about? You're the only one who kept going! We should be apologising to you.'

I smiled, 'I know but I still couldn't win.'

'Alf… You can't win against eight guys on your own, you know that right?'

'I can in a fight.'

She laughed, 'But that's not the same thing!'

I glanced up, I thought I'd heard my door open, but no one appeared so I just shrugged and leant against the wall again.

'Well let's not do so badly at football next okay?'

She laughed, 'Yeah alright, I mean we actually have a group of pretty talented footballers.'

'We do! Although there is like fifteen of us so that's a good thing, we really can't just depend on a couple of players.'

She shrugged, 'I mean…'

'Yeah okay maybe we can, I mean I am pretty good…'

'Not just you!' She shouted.

'Err, Alfie?' A voice said behind Jess.

I looked up, Gabriella and Barukko were stood at the door.

'Ohh sugar…' I said.

Jess's smile faltered and she looked behind her, Gabriella had already run off, Barukko quickly followed.

Jess ran out of the shower chasing Barukko, I shut off the shower and quickly followed, I ran out of my room but stopped at the elevator Barukko and Gabby had already gone down, Jess was stood at the top in tears.

I raised my body temperature to dry my clothes, 'Jess…'

She wiped her eyes, 'It's not your fault.'

I hugged her from behind, 'I'm sorry.'

She sobbed, 'At least I've still got you right?'

'Always.'

The elevator started coming back up and I pulled away from Jess, just in case, we watched the number slowly rise, then the doors opened.

Sylvia walked out, 'What the hell were you two doing? And why are you soaked through?'

I opened my mouth but Jess spoke first, 'We were in the shower, fully clothed, both of us, but together.'

'How come Alfie's dry then?'

'I raised my body temperature, Jess can too... She just hasn't.'

Sylvia nodded, 'So you were being idiots and now you've wrecked your relationships.'

Jess nodded, I stared at the ceiling, *Was it really a relationship? Even after we'd slept together I was always closer to Jess...*

Sylvia stared at me, I knew she could tell what I was thinking, she sighed, 'Well at least you've got each other...'

Jess nodded, I didn't move, *What the hell is wrong with me, she had a boyfriend who is also my best friend why didn't I stop her?*

I sighed and turned around, walking into my room and onto the balcony, I felt Jess's and Sylvia's eyes follow me out.

I gripped the wall and leant out over the balcony, watching the birds fly between trees, up and over, round and under, twisting and turning, dipping in and out of the leaves.

I summoned the elements, fire, water, earth, electricity, and laid them out, each in its own ball, on the wall. And by sheer luck a gust of wind caught it and pushed them all together, they combined spontaneously and formed this gold orb.

'What is this?'

I picked it up and instantly felt the power it held, it was like having the power of a black hole in something as small as a ping pong ball.

'Woah...' I tossed it up and caught it, it was ridiculously volatile, yet it didn't explode with me messing with it, *It must need an ignition, like my power...*

'What's that?'

'Aargh!' Jess scared the living daylights out of me, causing me to drop the tiny ball of power, thankfully I caught it again, well... Most of it.

'Oh sugar.' I thrust my hand out and summoned the wind, forcing the tiny, raindrop sized, ball of power as far away as possible before it hit the ground, it got about 300 metres away before exploding.

'What was that?'

'Aah poop.' I said as it imploded. I threw up a shield around the dorms, it must have been nearly half a mile long and I threw it up like it was nothing.

'WHAT... IS... THAT?'

'Hang on...'

BOOM! It exploded, clearing all the trees within a 200-metre radius, a shockwave blasted the shield, thankfully the shield was strong enough.

'Jeezus!' I laughed.

Jess stared at me, 'What the hell?'

I grabbed her arm, 'Come on.' I teleported us to the centre of the explosion, I crouched down and grabbed a handful of dirt, it was burnt to a crisp.

'That was something I'd just discovered.'

'How much did you use to cause this explosion?'

'First of all, this was accidental, you scared the hell out of me, secondly, about the size of a raindrop.'

Her jaw dropped, 'What?'

I sat down, 'I know right?'

'Why did you sit down?'

'Well you know this massive explosion I just caused? I imagine someone is going to have some questions about it... Unless...'

'Unless what?'

I summoned a load of earth and condensed it, feeding it with my power until it couldn't hold anymore.

'You might want to come here.' I said, she moved and sat next to me, 'Watch this.'

I slammed the condensed earth into the ground and waited, I could feel my power spreading, then all of a sudden plants began to grow, trees, shrubs, flowers, all of it began to grow instantly, the trees kept on growing and growing until they were 100 feet tall.

'Woah…'

I stood up, 'My god this is amazing.'

Jess stood up next to me, 'How did you do that? These trees are beyond tall!'

I smiled, 'I know right? Now I'm going to have to answer a completely different set of questions.'

She laughed, 'Yes you are.'

I heard the sound of a helicopter in the distance, I glanced up, *No sign of it, it could just be passing by*.

5 minutes later I heard the sound of a lot of footsteps walking in our direction, 'They're coming…' I said to Jess, she nodded.

Soon enough a group of five teachers and the Principal walked into the small clearing that we were in.

'Why… Is it always you two?' The Principal sighed, 'Well at least I know everyone is okay at least.'

'I mean I did put up shields around the dorms so they were bound to be.'

He nodded, 'I wondered where those came from.' He nodded to the woman to his left, 'This is Rocky, but don't call her that call her "Miss", she'll just ask a couple questions whilst we investigate the surrounding area.'

'There's no need to, I know exactly what did it and also how this area is exactly as it is now.'

He nodded, 'I know, but we've got to do it anyway, legally.'

'Right then,' Rocky said turning to us, 'What did this?'

'Erm, it's hard to explain,' I said, summoning the elements and making it into the golden orb thing, 'this is what did it, but only a droplet size.'

She went to poke it, 'What is it?'

I quenched it before she could touch it, 'I would not touch it if I were you, this the size of a tennis ball could blow up everything within… About 200 miles.'

'What is it?'

'God element.' Jess butted in, 'That's what we're calling it.'

I nodded, kinda liking the name.

'Okay… And how did the forest end up like this?'

'Oh yeah, that was me too.'

'W…What?' She stammered, 'How powerful are you?'

I smiled, 'You don't want to know.'

She walked away muttering something under her breath, I exhaled and stood up, 'Hell of a day.'

Jess stared in the direction of our dorm, 'Yeah…'

'Hey… You okay?'

'Yeah… I'm just thinking about Barukko…'

'It'll be alright.' I said, offering her my hand. She took it and I pulled her up.

'Hey Sir! Can we go?'

The Principal walked out of the woods behind us, scaring the life out of Jess, 'Yes you can go, try not to blow anything else up please.'

I smiled, 'No promises… I'll do my best.' I finished after seeing the look on his face, 'Come on Jess.' I said, offering out my arm. She took it and we teleported to the front door of our dorm.

'After you.' I said.

'Erm, no, I don't know what's going to happen when we walk in there!'

I laughed and shrugged, 'It was worth a shot.'

I threw open the door and was quite surprised. No one was shouting at us, just at each other.

I glanced back at Jess, who looked just as confused, 'Hey!' I shouted, everyone ignored me, 'HEY!' Still no reply, no one even noticed we were here.

I stamped my foot and literally froze everyone but Helena, who seemed to be the only one trying to stop this thing, I sighed, 'Helena, what the hell is happening?'

'You two have accidentally started a war.' She said, 'On this side, we have the ones defending you two,' She pointed to Sylvia, Sam, Zoe and most of the others, 'And on this side we have everyone who currently doesn't like you.' She signalled to Barukko, the Ramirez triplets, Talia, Ajax and San.

'Wait, why does San care?'

'Oh he doesn't, he just knows there's a fight and joined in.'

I sighed and unfroze him, 'Do you even know why they're fighting?'

He shook his head, grinning, 'Nope! But I know it's because of you two!'

'Go upstairs.' I said.

He frowned, but did as I said, trudging to the elevator.

I unfroze Jake and Q next because I know they can't last out in the cold very long, especially Jake, 'Sorry about that.' I said.

He smiled, embarrassed, 'It's alright, it's the best way to get us under control and at least you remembered that we couldn't last that long.'

I patted him on the back, 'It's alright, can you erm, just head upstairs for like, an hour or so? I'm sending most others up too... Just till we've sorted this thing out.' He nodded, 'Queenie you too please.' She nodded as well and they both got in the elevator.

I unfroze Talia and Ajax next, 'I presume you heard me talking to Jake and Q?'

They both nodded and headed for the elevator looking rather sheepish.

I defrosted basically everyone else at once, except from Syl, Barukko and the Ramirez lot, and sent them up to their rooms.

Next, I defrosted Syl, 'My god that was cold.' She complained.

'Did you start this?' I asked her.

She shook her head, I looked at Helena, who pointed at Nat.

I nodded, 'Okay, just step back, in case these lot go mad.' She nodded and stood behind the kitchen's island. Jess basically hid behind me, waiting for these four to defrost.

Instantly the ice around them melted and they stood there, mildly bewildered, before coming to their senses, 'Now before you say anything! If any one of you start another fight... I'll refreeze you and leave you on the roof to defrost naturally. You hear me?'

Everyone nodded gingerly, I sat down and Jess came and sat next to me, Barukko and Gabriella glared at me from the opposite end of the room.

Where do I even start? I thought.

Jess started for me, 'Barukko...'

He completely ignored her, putting his arm around Bianca instead, whether out of spite or whatever, it seemed to destroy

200

her. She got up and ran to the elevator in tears, I pulled out my phone and texted Zoe.

Me – *Hey can you check on Jess please, I've got to try and sort this out, she's just gone to her room, thanks.*
Zoe – *Yeah sure*

I put the phone away and sighed, I glanced at Helena sat across from me, she shrugged, 'Look... And I'm saying this to everyone, I'm not saying we drop the matter, or forgive us or whatever, because I'm not. But do not! Do not! Bring the rest of the class into this, I'm not having it interrupt lessons or this sports festival, this problem is between us, in this building. Out there, that problem does not exist... Okay?' Everyone nodded begrudgingly.

'Good.'

Helena looked at me, a level of respect in her eyes that I'd never seen before.

'I will also be telling everyone else this... And telling them to report anything to me! So don't try it. Any objections?'

No one said anything so I took that as a no and got up, me and Sylvia went to the elevator, 'You go and see Jess if you want, I'll come up in a min I'm just going to brief everyone on what's happened.'

She nodded and hit the button for the top floor, the button for floor 1 already lit up.

The doors opened and I got out, 'See you in a couple of minutes.' I said, knocking on everyone's doors.

Once everyone on the floor had gathered, I briefed them on what we'd agreed.

'So basically guys, the issue stays in this building, outside... The issue doesn't exist, and if you hear anyone talking about it outside, I want you to tell me okay? I'm not allowing this to interrupt our school stuff.'

They all nodded and I moved up the floors, telling them all what I'd told the first lot.

Finally, I'd finished briefing the rest of floor 5 and knocked on Jess's door. Sylvia opened it, 'Hey.'

'Hey,' I said, entering, 'How is she?' I whispered.

She shook her head, 'Could be worse, but not much.'

I looked around the room, Zoe, Maddison and Queenie were all in here as well. I went and sat down next to her, 'Hey.' She sobbed and put her head on my shoulder, 'It okay.' I whispered, putting my arm around her.

'How is it? I've lost everyone.'

'How have you lost everyone? There are five people in this room looking after you.'

She glanced up, as if noticing that there were indeed more people in here, 'Yeah okay...'

I kissed the top of her head, 'You'll be okay, it may feel like it is but it's not the end of the world.'

Jess wiped her eyes, I glanced at Syl for reassurance, making sure I was doing the right thing by saying this, she gave me a thumbs up and went back to studying Jess.

She sobbed again then went quiet, I glanced at Zoe. 'Has she gone to sleep?' I whispered.

She knelt down and looked at her, she nearly burst out laughing, 'Yep.'

I sighed and looked at her, 'Poor girl must be shattered.'

They all nodded and Sylvia tapped her phone, 'I'll text you.'

I nodded and laid down on the bed, Jess cradled in my arm next to me. Syl turned the light out as she left, leaving me in total darkness.

My phone buzzed in my pocket, I grabbed it.

Syl – Is Jess OK?

Me – Yeah she's fast asleep next to me

Syl – Okay... What do you think is going to happen next?

Me – Idk, I think they'll get over it eventually... It may just be a little tense for a while, especially between Barukko, Gabby and us two, I imagine the other two sisters will get over it pretty soon.

Syl – And what about you?

Me - ?

Syl – How quickly are you going to get over it?

Me – I guess I already am, I've got to set an example and I guess it never really bothered me in the first place, I think me and Barukko should get back to normal quicker than him and Jess...

Syl -Yeah… Okay well text me if u need anything
Me – OK thanks

I put the phone down and put my other arm around Jess, going to sleep soon after.

I woke up the next morning to silence, the sun shined through the open curtains, Jess was still asleep next to me.

I checked my phone, 10:21, I sighed, *Glad I don't have a solo sport today, in fact, I only have one, and that's in the last week of the festival.*

I looked at Jess, who was sleeping peacefully, I didn't want to wake her, especially with what happened yesterday, so I switched on my phone and didn't move her…

20 minutes later I got a text.

Syl – Hey you two okay?

Me – Yeah I'm fine, Jess is still asleep

Syl – What? She never sleeps this long!

At that moment Jess chose to roll onto me, I smiled.

Me – Yeah ik It's mad but I don't want to wake her either so I'm just kinda sat here

Syl – Haha, most others are awake, not much is happening, quite a lot of tension I think…

Me – Yeah I bet, what sport is it today?

Syl – Erm, doubles tennis I think, the Pendrakon twins are competing but after yesterday they said that they don't mind if we stay here, I was planning on going down anyway tho

Me – Yeah I might, depends on when Jess wakes up and if she wants to

Syl – You don't have to spend every minute with her, she's capable of looking after herself

Me – I know that, but that's not the problem…

Syl – Yeah I know…

I put the phone down after that because Jess began to stir.

'Hey… You enjoyed your sleep?' I whispered.

She stretched and yawned, 'Mhmm.'

'Good.'

'Alf?'

'Yeah?'

'What how long have I been asleep for?'

'Like... twelve and a half hours.'

'What? I never sleep that long.' She mumbled.

'I know, but then again you did have a stressful day.'

'Yeah... I didn't say anything stupid last night, did I?'

I smiled, 'Na you didn't, you just went to sleep on my shoulder and hardly moved.'

She moved up, putting her head closer to mine, 'Good... I am going to get up... Just not right now...'

I chuckled, 'Okay Jess.' I put my arms around her.

She breathed a deep sigh of... Relief? And snuggled against my chest, 'Alf what sport is it today?'

'Doubles tennis don't worry.'

21 – Tennis is dull until it gets exciting (words of wisdom from me)

An hour later Jess decided that she was going to get up and went in the shower, I crossed into my room and found a note on my door.

That's it... We're done. Was all it said.

'I thought that was obvious?' I said to myself, burning the note in my hand before getting in the shower. I quickly got changed and knocked on Jess's door, covering my eyes I said, 'You decent?' As I popped my head through the door (not literally).

'Not yet! But come in I can't have you stood there with the door open!'

I stepped in and spun around to face the door...

'Okay I'm good.' She said.

I turned around and looked at her, 'What?' She asked.

'You look good.'

'Yeah well hang on.' She said, jumping over the balcony to mine, then coming back, 'Ta-da!'

'You do look good.'

I stared at her, green high-tops, black leggings, and MY green jacket.

She blushed, 'I know, I'm wearing your jacket.'

'Oh I know!' I shouted, 'Because I can no longer wear it!'

She laughed and pulled me out the door, 'Come on we might as well go and watch the tennis.'

I sighed as we got in the elevator, 'Do we have to?'

'Yeah! You're our number one you've got to set an example.'

'Fine...' I had a flashback to Zoe "Complete control huh?".

Complete control, I agreed.

She continued to drag me out of the building, 'Hang on can I get some food first?' I asked.

She rolled her eyes, 'Yeah sure, can you get me some please as well?'

I nodded and grabbed two cans of crisps, I held them in my hands, *I don't want to carry these.*

'Hurry up!'

'Yeah hang on...' I walked around the corner before having an idea, I closed my eyes, 'What are you doing?'

'Just... Watch...'

Suddenly I tossed the cans into an empty space, when I opened my eyes they weren't there.

'Where'd they just go?'

'I think into dimensional storage...'

'You think?'

I shrugged, 'I guess we'll find out when we get hungry!'

She laughed and grabbed my hand, 'Come on! We might be missing their game!'

'Yeah alright wait up and I'll teleport us.'

She stopped outside and held her arms out, I picked her up and teleported to the stadium, putting her down when we arrived and walking to our box, 'Hey everyone!' Jess said, letting go of my hand and skipping down to sit next to Sylvia.

'Hey.' I said.

We were met by a chorus of bored "hi's" and "hello's".

'Have those two played yet?'

Sam nodded as I sat down between him and Jess, 'Yeah they're through to the quarter-finals, I think they're up next actually!'

'Oh nice!'

I glanced around, Nat was here but the other three weren't. Zoe noticed me looking around, 'They aren't here... In fact, I haven't seen them all day.'

I shrugged, 'Oh well, I guess they'll miss the twins winning the tournament... Actually is this power or non-power?'

'Power.' Sam said, filling his mouth with crisps.

Jess stared at me, I sighed and pulled out the cans of crisps easily, 'Nice!' Jess said, ripping open the top of one of the cans, 'They haven't changed a bit.'

Paris and Troy stared at me from behind, 'How on Earth did you just pull those out of thin air?' Paris said in bewilderment.

'Dimensional storage.' I said, 'You want some?' I said, offering the crisps, 'Not you.' I said to Sam, who was already eating his own.

Half an hour and one boring match later the twins came on, we all cheered, trying to sound excited, then prepared for a probably boring game of tennis.

'Are those custom tennis rackets?' I asked.

'Yep, Alex made them himself, they do a ridiculous amount of things it's actually amazing.'

'That's cool.'

Now... I don't know much about tennis, but I know that those two obliterated their opponents, I don't think they lost a... Set? And they definitely did not lose the game, they worked amazingly together.

'Wooo!' Sylvia shouted as they won the game, they both walked over, drenched in sweat.

I leant over the wall, 'Well done guys.' I high-fived Alex.

'Thanks.' Alexandra said.

'So are you two going to win this or not? Because I've just seen you play and if you lose, you're not allowed in the dorm.'

They smiled, 'Yeah we'll win.' Alex said.

'Good.' I replied, sitting back down. Jess stared at me, 'What?' I asked.

'You just did a leader thing.'

'Yeah and?'

'That was really cool of you.'

I put my arm around her, 'Thanks I guess.'

She put her head on my shoulder and closed her eyes, 'Alfie what happens with the Trios team, and the doubles in fact?'

'Well the duos I already got changed, the trios I didn't change, I presumed you still wanted to be with me.'

'But didn't you get over offers for the trios from over teams? Like those third years?' Jess asked.

'Well... Yeah actually I had an offer from the number one-third year but I thought that was a bit unfair.'

'Wait... You had an offer from the top kid in the school and you said no?' Jess asked.

'Well, actually I've done it twice now!' I laughed.

'You're bonkers.' Zoe muttered.

'I know!'

Jess smiled and yawned.

'How are you still tired?'

She shrugged and got up, moving across a seat and sitting on my lap and resting her head on my chest, 'I don't know… Wake me up when they play again…'

She tried to sleep for a solid 5 minutes before deciding it was too bright, 'It's too bright!' She complained, 'Unless I do this!'

She wiggled her way into my jumper, WHICH I WAS WEARING, and went to sleep.

I chuckled, 'Not if you do that…' I muttered, wrapping my arms around her waist. I looked around the stand and saw 3 or 4 girls clutching their chests. Queenie looked like she was about to die.

'It's so comfy.' She whispered.

'I bet it is.' I said, 'After all you're in my hoodie with me.'

I was glad I'd put on a baggy hoodie that day.

Two or so long hours later the twins still hadn't played another game and finally there was some movement from under my hoodie, and no it wasn't me, I glanced under and saw Jess waking.

Oh thank god, she might look cute but I am going numb!

'Hey… Have you had a good nap?'

She nodded and stretched within the confines of the hoodie.

'You gonna emerge from the womb soon?'

Tiago nearly burst out laughing, I smiled.

'NO! It's so warm and cosy.'

I sighed, throwing my head back, 'WHY?' I mouthed.

Tiago compressed his laugh into a chuckle. 'You should consider yourself lucky.'

'Yeah!' Jess said, 'What he said!'

'Yeah but I'm going numb.'

'Can't you just teleport out?' he asked.

'Yeah but then I'd feel bad.'

He laughed again, 'At least I don't have that problem!'

I glanced at Q, who was glancing over in our direction, *Hmm, maybe you will…*

Jess went back to sleep (much to my despair) and it was another hour before I could wake her up for the twin's next game.

'Hey...'
She opened her eyes, 'Why'd you wake me?'
'It's game time.'
'How long?'
'Like, fifteen minutes.'
She nodded and stretched, 'I'm staying here for like, five minutes then, and only then will I get out of your hoodie.'
Sylvia smiled, I put my head back and sighed, 'WHY?' I mouthed. Sam patted me on the back, then stood up, then sat down, then stood up.
I stared at him, 'I am so going to kill you.' I said to him.
'Why?' He said, laughing, and sitting back down again.
'If you do it again, I will blast you.' I smiled.
He stood up, 'Yeah okay.' I stuck my hand out and zapped him with a little electricity, 'OWW!'
Zoe laughed, 'You were asking for it, he did warn you.'
I fist-bumped her, 'Are you sure you're my girlfriend?' Sam asked.
'Bit of tough love never hurt anyone.' I said, laughing.
'You two are mean.'
'You're a pain in my backside.' We both said, 'So don't complain.'
'Okay what on Earth?' He sat back down.
Me and Zoe secretly fist-bumped behind him.
'Alright then! Who actually thinks the twins can go all the way?' Everyone stuck their hand up, even Jess, 'That's good I like our confidence!'
Jess finally got out of my jumper, 'Hello everyone.'
'She's emerged! Huzzah!' Jake shouted, we all laughed, the twins walked out the tunnel, the whole stadium cheered, even Jess moved back to her seat to watch the game.
'How good actually are these two? Like could I beat them or are they like, top one hundred or what?'

Paris leant forward, 'Well it depends on the rules, one versus one no power, you'll get whooped, one versus one using power… I'd say you stand a very good chance, you using marksmanship and just teleport to the ball and realistically, you can't lose, in fact I'd say you could probably two versus one if you had powers.'

'Sooo… They won't win?'

He shrugged, 'It depends, I say you could enter every power tournament and easily win with your powers.'

I put my arms behind my head, 'Huh…'

'No.' Jess said.

'What?'

'You were thinking about entering next year, you aren't because you've got to let someone else win something.'

'Well… He doesn't.' Sam said, Zoe, Jess and Sylvia glared at him. I laughed, 'Unfortunately I think the girls will beat me up if I do.'

'Total control.' Zoe agreed.

I smiled and the match began…

As far as I can tell, (and from what Paris told me) it was a pretty close game, back and forth points, deuces and all that stuff. But thankfully they came out on top, beating, apparently, 4th in the world to get to the semi-finals.

'Hey well-done guys.' I said, leaning back over the wall, 'One step closer, and to beat fourth in the world?'

They glanced at each other, 'They were fourth in the world?'

Paris leant over the wall too, 'Yeah, for high-school kids at least.'

'Huh… Nice!' Alex shouted.

I laughed and sat back down.

'Hey Paris, I didn't know you liked tennis this much.'

'Well I didn't originally, I was forced to take it up in school and well I kinda just got used to it, still play it out of school sometimes.'

'But if you enjoy it so much why didn't you go to a school that had tennis courts?'

'That's most of the reason why I came to this school, my parents wanted me to go to this fancy private school down south but I wanted to come here.'

'Wait... You're a private school kid?'

'I was yeah.'

'Huh...'

'You know I could have been.' Jess said.

We all stared at her, then laughed, 'Yeah right! You'd hate it!' I said.

'Yeah but still...'

'And you'd never have met us, so I'd say it was the right choice.'

'Although it would have been a peaceful life!' She joked.

I put my arm around her, 'That is very true...'

Jess stared at me, 'Can I go back to sleep now?'

'No their next match is only like... half an hour away, you shouldn't go to sleep now anyway you won't sleep tonight.'

She pouted, 'Okay...'

I ruffled her hair and pulled out my phone, I opened the socials and scrolled through for a while, noticing that there were a lot of posts containing me and Jess sat in the stands...

'Hey look guys they have more interest in us than the tennis.' I said, passing the phone to Jess.

'What do you mean?' Tiago asked.

'Just look at the phone when it comes to you.' I said, watching the phone get passed around the class.

'Ohh yeah.' He said, 'I mean it's mostly you two and about the fact that Jess and Barukko were dating and now you've got your arm around her but yeah.'

I smiled, 'Yeah but still.'

Sam grabbed the phone and refreshed, 'My god do they not have anything else to talk about? There must be another twenty posts about us!'

'Okay that's enough.' I said, throwing up an invisibility shield, 'I imagine that's all they ask any of us about next time we talk to the media.'

'I hate the media.' Sam said.

'And you haven't even had to talk to them!' I said, 'They seemed rather interested in me making a show at the opening ceremony.'

'Yeah I know I saw it on the news, you seemed to handle it well though.'

I shrugged, 'Yeah I guess… Hey do we always have the same stand?'
Sylvia glanced at me, 'Yeah I think so why?'
'Just wondering…'
'Uh-huh.'

Half an hour later (like I said) the twins came back on for the semi-finals. Right before the game started, I noticed a couple more newcomers enter and sit at the back, I didn't bother saying hi.

The twins got on the court and into their positions, ready to play.
'COME ON GUYS!' I shouted, 'YOU CAN DO THIS!'
Alex stuck his thumb out and tossed the ball into the air, rocketing it into the far corner, 20-0. The stadium went mad.
'That must have been a hundred maybe two hundred miles an hour!' Sam shouted.
I laughed, 'That was amazing… Hey Paris, how good are these girls anyway?'
He shrugged, 'They're basically unknown, a bit like our two, but I think the twins will win.'
And they did, I wouldn't say they blew it out of the park, but they did pretty well, only losing 1 set out of 4.

'Onto the finals!' I shouted as they walked over after the game.
They both smiled, 'We will win this thing!'
I fist-bumped him, 'You'd better.'
Jess hugged Alexandra and whispered something in her ear, she seemed full of confidence right after.
'What'd you say to her?' I asked once they'd walked away.
She winked at me but didn't tell me anything, giving me no hints at all.

The final couldn't come quick enough, normally I hated tennis but now our twins were in it I couldn't wait.
I leant over the railings in anticipation, 'Come on twins.' I muttered as they took their places.

The match kicked off with their opponent's serve, Alex rallied it back, the game had begun. They shared points, sets coming down to the wire every time. We got to the final set, 2-2. We got down to the last point, advantage them, the twins were behind and looked like they were about to lose the game.

'COME ON YOU TWO!' I shouted, 'YOU'D BETTER NOT LOSE ON ME NOW!'

Jess smiled, 'You're really into this.'

'Of course, I can't have our lot lose after our shambolic basketball performance.' Alex glanced over and gave me the same thumbs-up as before, I sighed, 'Okay were good.'

Zoe frowned, 'How on Earth do you know?'

I pointed to the game, Alex smashed the ball out of the air and out of their reach, deuce.

I didn't move, the rest of the arena went crazy.

I dropped the invisibility shield and stood up, walked to the railing, stuck my hand out and give Alex a thumbs down.

He nodded and laughed.

Jess glared at me, 'Why'd you do that?'

I spun around and put my back to the game, I already knew what was going to happen. I watched Barukko out of the corner of my eye, he was staring at me, wondering why I gave him the thumbs down, I slowly watched the realization dawn on him, then he sat back, completely relaxed.

Jess glanced behind her, 'HOW ARE YOU TWO SO RELAXED?'

I heard two hits of the tennis ball, the serve and the return... Then... Silence...

'I told you... We're good...'

The crowd went berserk, they'd come from 2-1 down to win the match.

Everyone but Barukko stared at me, even the Ramirez three, 'How?'

'There's two denominations of the thumbs down.' I said.

Jess frowned, 'Thumbs down meaning bad, and thumbs down meaning-'

'Kill.' Helena finished, 'That's why you had complete confidence in them. The media would eat that up if they saw it.'

'I think they will have.'

Barukko laughed (much to Gabriella's annoyance), 'You dropped the shield?' I nodded, 'That is unbelievably... Brave!'

'Or stupid.' Jess offered.

I laughed and ruffled her hair, 'It worked didn't it?'

She frowned, 'Yeah but that's not the point.'

'Of course it is! The whole point in me doing that was to give them confidence!'

She shrugged.

I waited till they'd been given the trophy and celebrated a little before teleporting down there.

'Well done!' I said, jogging up and high-fiving them both, 'That was amazing.'

Alex laughed, 'Thanks but you helped massively.'

'What are you on about you two were the ones playing tennis.'

'Yeah but you're little moves had this huge effect on us confidence-wise.' Alexandra nodded at the lunatic next to her.

I smiled, 'That is wonderful! Do you mind telling Jess that later though?'

He laughed, 'Yeah sure.'

The Principal walked over and I backed off, 'Congratulations!' He said, glancing at me, who definitely should not have been there. I continued backing off until I was back at the stand.

'Oh yeah Jess, Alex needs to tell you something about me later.' I said, grinning.

She rolled her eyes and leant over the railing, 'Really?'

I kissed her, 'Yep!'

She blushed and became very flustered all of a sudden, I hoped the media were interviewing the twins, I smiled then leant against the wall, watching the Principal walk towards me, 'The press want to speak to you.'

'Why?'

He shrugged, 'I don't know.'

'Have they spoken to the twins yet?'

'They have spoken to Alexandra but not Alex.'

'Tell them to talk to the winners first and then I'll talk.'

He nodded and walked back, I turned to Jess, 'You're so nice, letting the media tear apart the twins before getting to you? Such a leader.'

I laughed, 'I'm just giving them the recognition they deserve, I wasn't even in the tournament and they want to speak to me, everyone else must really hate me by now.'

'Yeah we do!' Sam called, followed by, 'OW! What'd you do that for?'

'Thanks Zoe!'

'No problem, anytime.' She shouted.

I turned around and teleported to the middle, next to Alexandra.

'How'd the press go?'

She shrugged, 'Fine, they asked me more about what you were doing than about our win.'

I sighed, 'I'm sorry, they ask all the wrong questions.'

She laughed, 'It's okay! We got the trophy and that's all that matters to us.'

'I mean... Alex seems to be loving the media though.' I said, watching him talk to them.

'Yeah, but that's him, I'm happy with this.' She said, holding up the trophy.

'And so you should be,' I patted her on the back, 'anyway, it looks like Alex is just about finish so I'd better go over and prepare for a grilling.'

She laughed, 'Yeah... I guess you had.' She said before turning away and walking to meet the rest of the class.

I went and stood next to the Principal, 'How's he doing?'

'Surprisingly well actually, I mean you handle them pretty well but he... He really... Vibes with them.'

I nodded, trying not to mention the fact that he just talked about "vibes". Anyway, Alex finished up and walked past us, high-fiving me and walking to join his sister.

'Hello everyone.' I said, walking over, 'Let's not shout over each other this time please. Yeah you go.'

'Hey Alfie, you're actions from the stands we're a little, baffling to us, can you explain them?'

'Well, I was just giving them encouragement really, especially at the end when the game was coming to an end.'

'And can you explain the thumbs down? Were you unhappy with something or...?

I smiled, 'There are two denominations of the thumbs down, isn't there? One's a lot older than the other, the more common one is the sign of displeasure... And the other was used by the emperors of Rome in the Coliseum games.'

'The sign for kill?' Another reporter asked.

'Well yeah, not kill in the literal form, more like, "finish them" ... But yeah... Anything else?'

'Yes erm, you're relationship with Jessica Verose, it's a peculiar one don't you think?'

I frowned, 'What do you mean?'

'Well a couple of days ago it was her and Barukko Knox, now it's her and you, what's the reason behind that?'

I chuckled and scratched the back of my head, 'Yeah I'm sorry but I'm not going into that, and if you're suggesting that Jess is some sort of player or something, that's definitely not it... Yeah... That's all thanks everyone!' I said, walking away.

I jogged back to the class and leapt back over, 'What'd they ask?' Jess asked.

'What we expected, stuff about my actions then a little bit about you.'

She scowled, 'What did they ask about me?'

'Just a bit about how you were with Barukko and now you're with me.' I yawned.

'And what did you tell them?'

'Oh nothing really, just avoided the question, I'm not telling them anything about our personal lives.'

She smiled, 'Good. Now can you carry me home?'

I smiled with a pained look on my face, 'Yeah sure.' I replied, putting my arm under her and lifting her up, she wrapped her arms around my neck and put her head against mine.

'Thanks Alf.'

'It's okay.'

We walked back together, avoiding the potential crowds by teleporting back to the main path down to the dorms and meeting up with the rest of the class who'd left before us.

'Does anyone know what the sport tomorrow is?'

'I think it's like, swimming or something.' Sylvia said.

'Does anyone even like swimming anymore?'

We all shook our heads, 'Lovely, a day in then tomorrow.'

'I'm going to sleep all day.' Jess mumbled.

I laughed, 'As much as I'd like that, I highly doubt it, you've slept too much today I imagine you'll be pretty wired tomorrow.'

'Oh great, a wired Jessica Verose, what a joy.' Sylvia said.

'Hey!' Jess complained.

'I'll put you down.' I warned, jokingly. She shut up after that though.

We got back to dorm in no time...

'Hey, I think we need a trophy shelf.'

Maddison looked at me, 'What do you mean?'

'Well, we've already won two trophies and it's been what? Five days?'

'Four.' Helena said.

'Exactly, and what's to say we don't win more? I think we've got a very nice chance of winning at least one of the football tournaments, if not both of them.'

'And you're in all three fighting tournaments, there's three more!' Jess pointed out.

'I'll get right onto it then!' Alex said, running over to his workbench.

'You know I could just...' I held out my hand and summoned literal gold.

Zoe stared at me, 'You can do that?'

'Yeah. I just tend to avoid doing it.'

Jess grabbed my hand and pulled me onto the sofa, 'Just let him do it.'

I destroyed the gold, 'Alright.'

She put her head on my lap whilst I sat on the arm of the chair, 'Hey I think football is after swimming so I want you all at practise tomorrow!'

Everyone playing groaned, 'Come on AJ you know we hate unscheduled practises!' Tiago complained.

'Do you want to win or not?' I asked.

'We'll be there.' Zoe said, I nodded.

'That means no all-day sleeping for you.' I whispered to Jess.

She closed her eyes, 'I know… Besides I wouldn't be able to sleep the whole time anyway, like you said.'

I stroked her hair, 'I doubt you'll sleep like that for a long time.' I said, without realising that she'd gone to sleep. I had to like, wriggle over the arm of the sofa to sit down, just so she wouldn't wake up, I ended up picking her up and sitting her on me though, her head against my shoulder.

'I feel like this happens a lot.' Tiago said, sitting down next to me.

'Oh it does, and it will, for a long time!' I complained.

He laughed, 'Look bro you're the one who chose to have her, it's your fault, not ours.'

I smiled, 'I know…'

Queenie came and sat down across from us, much to both our surprise, she looked like she was worlds away, in some alternate reality almost, 'She looks happy.' He commented.

'She could be dreaming about anything right now.' I joked.

She chose that moment to snap out of her daydream, 'So, what about you T? You got your eye on anyone?'

We glanced at each other, *Was she having a convo with us in her head?* I wondered.

Tiago swallowed, clearly nervous, (and if I could pick up on it anyone could… Apart from Queenie apparently) 'N…No…' He shook his head.

'No?' She asked, 'Fair enough, neither to be honest.' She said, turning her attention to the TV, Tiago's face dropped. I saw that out of the corner of my eye (but only because I was watching the TV) that her eyes kept flickering to Tiago, trying to gauge his reaction, *Haha they do like each other!* I thought, *Just they're both too scared to admit it. This may be interesting to see unfold, I mean, they could go out tomorrow, or next year…*

I closed my eyes and I may or may not have fallen asleep, I woke up 6 hours later with Jess eating a pizza whilst sat on me. I opened my eyes and looked at her, I watched her munch on the pizza in her hand, not even noticing that I'd awoken. I rolled my eyes and glanced behind me Talia was cleaning up whilst just sat at the table, watching everything happen.

'Hey you're getting good at that.' I said to her.

Jess nearly choked on her pizza, she put it down, 'You're awake!'

'Thanks Alfie, it's actually getting pretty easy to multitask like this.'

'But you're not multitasking.' Jess said, I shot her a warning.

'Not in the literal sense, but I'm controlling every one of these objects separately, so I am multitasking.'

I nudged Jess, 'Ow…' She turned to Talia, 'Oh okay that's cool, I guess.'

I rolled my eyes and glanced across the room, I locked eyes with Sylvia, who shrugged. I decided to pocket that conversation until later. I kissed Jess on the head, 'I'm going to go outside for a bit.'

She got up, letting me go, 'Okay, don't be long.'

I nodded and teleported upstairs, putting my football boots on and teleported to the football field opposite the dorm, every year had their own football field, but we never had any problems with other teams, a lot of us played we just never ran into each other… Until today.

I jogged onto the football pitch and stopped, noticing that our second years (who shouldn't actually be on this pitch anyway) were on the pitch, not the first years. And who jogged over, our favourite resident second year (or at least my favourite second year) Brandon.

'Oh hey… You don't mind us using the pitch, do you? Another second-year team were using ours.'

I shook my head, 'Na as long as I can practise with you guys.'

'What it's just you?'

I nodded, 'Yeah we're getting our practice in tomorrow, I just got bored.'

He laughed, 'Yeah okay that's fine.'

I stuck my ball in my dimensional storage, 'Okay cool.'

'How'd you do that?'

'Heads!' A couple of lads shouted as a ball came flying to us, I teleported under the ball and trapped it between my legs, 'How'd you do that?'

'Practice!' I shouted back, 'You should try it!'

That got a few laughs. I jogged back with Brandon and he introduced me, they all knew who I was to be fair, the only guy's name I can remember is this kid called Leo, and he could score anything on his right foot, and almost anything on his left. We trained for 4 straight hours, playing an 8-a-side game for 2. They put us and Leo on the same team when we swapped around an hour in but ended up swapping us again after half an hour because we were just unstoppable.

As long as I got the ball to his feet, he put it in, I whipped it around players, over players, left foot, right foot, whatever.

At the end when we all decided to call it quits Leo, myself and Brandon had a chat.

'I'd ask you to join us but I know what you're like.' Brandon said.

'Well, I'd ask the same for Leo but I imagine you want to play with your lot.'

Leo laughed, 'Yeah you're right but um,' He glanced at Brandon, 'Look, in the summer the football team we enter a tournament, it's basically a non-professional world cup for all ages, the school has a team, we take our best players and compete. And I'm captain... Would you like to...?

'I'd love to!' Especially if us two get to tear up the field together that'd be great.'

He smiled and held his hand out, 'Alright then it's a deal, Brandon will text you the details at some point.'

I nodded and shook his hand before going to exit the pitch.

I walked towards the exit and noticed that Jess was stood at the gate, MY hoodie on, sleeves over her hands and hood up.

'Hey, how long have you been out here?' I said, pulling down her hood.

'Not too long, like an hour.'

'What? Why didn't you say anything?' I said, hugging her.

'You looked happy, as happy as when we'd won the basketball, so I left you be.'

'You at least could have played or something.'

She shook her head, 'I was alright, it was fun watching you play.'

I kissed the top of her head, 'You're amazing.'

'Says the guy who can do it all… Alf?'

'Yeah.' I said, hopping over the gate and walking towards the dorm.

'What were you talking about at the end?'

'Huh? You mean in the summer? Just this football tournament in the summer.'

'What about it?'

'Well I don't really know that much about it but they asked me to play so I said yeah.'

She looked at me, 'But what about us?'

I laughed, 'It's not going to take six weeks!'

She smiled, 'Yeah okay.'

'What time even is it?'

'Oh, it's like half eleven.'

I stared at her, 'You should've gone to bed instead of watching me!'

She yawned, 'Yeah whatever.'

I sighed and picked her up, 'Go to sleep.'

'Does that mean I'm with you tonight?'

'Yeah, if you want.'

She smiled and nestled against me, 'Okay.'

She was asleep like that…

I teleported up to my room and put Jess in the bed, I got changed then got into bed as well, Jess immediately rolled onto me.

I exhaled and wrapped my arms around her, going to sleep as well.

I woke up the next morning at around the same time as the previous morning, 10:07 to be exact, *What is happening? This late two days straight?*

I glanced down at Jess, who was watching some random show on my Pc, 'Hey…' I whispered.

She looked up at me, 'Hiya, you okay?'

I ruffled her hair, 'Yeah I'm good. How'd you sleep?'

'Like a log.'

I smiled, 'You always do.'

She crawled up and put her head on the pillow next to mine, 'What are we going to do today?'

'Well, training.'

'Yeah but apart from that?'

'I don't know… What do you want to do?'

She kissed me, 'Stay right here.'

'I can do that.' I replied, moving her hair behind her ear and kissing her.

She giggled, 'What?' I asked.

'It's just the way you look at me.'

'What do you mean?' I said, laughing.

'I've never seen anyone look at me the way you look at me.'

'I bet you have, you just won't remember.'

She stared at me, confused, then the realisation dawned on her, a tear formed in her eye.

I kissed her, 'You know who I'm on about don't you?' She nodded.

'I love you.' She buried her face in my chest, 'You're the best Alf.'

I wrapped my arms around her and held her.

We laid there for another hour, talking and stuff, before finally deciding to get out of bed and actually do something.

'I'm gonna go in the shower, I'll meet you downstairs in like, ten minutes?'

She nodded, 'And make sure to wear something suitable for football!'

'It's you that needs to remember not me!' I shouted as she skipped out of the room.

I hopped in the shower and then back out again, I stared at my wardrobe, 'What on Earth should I wear?'

I ended up putting on the same kind of clothes I used to put on as a kid, football shirt, shorts, shin pads (of course), long socks and boots in my hand.

'This is a throwback; I never normally train like this.' I muttered to myself.

Knock Knock Knock

'Who is it?'

'Who else would it be?' Jess's voice rang through the door.

'Why'd you bother knocking then?'

She opened the door, 'I don't know… I just did.'

I spun around and looked at her, 'Is that… one of my football shirts?'

She twirled around, 'Yep.'

'Well at least you picked a good one.' I muttered, staring at her. She wore the football shirt, shorts, shin-pads and long socks (I think those were my old ones too), she also had her hair in a ponytail.

'What is it?'

'It's just that I've never seen you with a ponytail.'

'Well it's needed if I'm playing football so…'

'Hey I've not got a problem with it it's just unusual, that's all.'

'So you coming or not?'

I smiled and walked over, grabbing her hand and teleporting us downstairs.

'You could have warned me first.' She grumbled.

I laughed, 'Do you want food or not, cos otherwise we can go out to the football field…'

She sprinted to the kitchen, I chuckled and followed her, at a much slower pace, and made some cereal (I know, exciting) before sitting down across from Sylvia and Zoe, they were both staring at Jess.

I frowned, 'What is it?'

'She's… Glowing…'

'Literally or…?'

'Literally and figuratively, and I don't think she's intentionally glowing, she's just so happy she's glowing.' Zoe muttered.

Sylvia turned to me, 'What exactly did you do to her?'

I laughed, 'I didn't do anything! In fact, I'm surprised she isn't tired.'

'Why?'

'She was up late watching me train…'

We all turned and watched her, she was glowing, she turned around and saw us three, she glanced behind her, no one there, 'Err, what is it?'

We all turned around without saying a word.

'Erm, guys, what is it? Guys?' She asked, walking up to me, 'Alfie!'

'Jess you're glowing.'

'Aw thanks.'

'Well, yes in that sense but also in the literal sense.'

'Huh?'

'You're literally glowing.' Zoe said with a mouth full of food.

'Oh sugar erm, I didn't know, I don't even know if I can turn it off!'

'Hey it's okay! It's because you're happy.' I said.

She stopped, 'Really?'

'Yeah… Now calm down.'

She smiled and sat down next to me.

'Seriously what did you do last night?' Zoe asked her.

She smiled, 'Nothing I just watched Alfie train till like, half eleven then fell asleep whilst he was carrying me.'

Sylvia and Zoe sighed, 'Why don't ours carry us?'

I laughed, 'Maybe you should ask them that and not me! Where are they anyway? They aren't training already?'

'Yeah but they've only been out… Twenty minutes or so?'

I nodded and finished my cereal, getting up, loading the dishwasher (I'm a responsible guy), then leaning over the back of the sofa I kissed Jess on the head, 'Come out soon yeah?'

She nodded and watched me leave, I stuck my boots on then jogged onto the pitch, immediately picking up a stray ball.

'Come on guys really?' I joked.

'Yeah alright, just cos you're one of our best players.' Sam complained.

'Speaking of our best players, I wonder if San is going to train with us today?'

'I'm right here.' He growled, behind me.

'Oh so you are, come on then.' I said, joining the rest of the lads.

We practised from lunchtime until 7 o'clock, SEVEN HOURS of almost constant playing, practising both power and non-power, practising power play is really interesting because it is more about combination plays more than anything else, like me using gusts of wind to bend the ball to impossible angles to feed San, or Jess lighting up so that the attackers will miss their shots, or at least gave Troy an easy save.

By the end of training we were all shattered, looking back I now realise that I could have just used superhuman stamina but oh well.

'I love this game, but god it's tiring.' I gasped.

Jess smiled, 'It really is.'

'I'm hungry!' Sam complained.

'You're always hungry.' We all said, causing a few laughs.

I leant on my hands, 'Okay I think we can call it a day, we shouldn't injure ourselves training before the big day!'

'Even though you can heal us.' Queenie said.

'Even though I can heal you!' I repeated.

Jess laughed, 'Can you carry me back?'

I groaned, much to Jess's disappointment, 'Yeah I can.' Her smiled reappeared.

'Can you carry us all back?' Jake pleaded.

'I am not strong enough for that!' I said.

'What if you used superstrength?' Alex suggested.

I paused, '...Yeah but that's just lazy.' I picked Jess up, 'You lot coming or not?'

They all groaned and got to their feet, following me in.

I paused in the middle of the room, 'Do you wanna go up or stay down here?'

She looked at me, thinking, 'Go up.' I nodded and teleported upstairs, 'Why didn't you just take the elevator?'

'Cos its slower, a waste of electricity, and harder than teleporting.'

225

She sighed, 'You're weird.'

'No that makes perfect sense.'

She thought about it, then shrugged, 'Whatever, I'm tired.'

'That sounds like excuses to me.' I said, putting her down on the bed.

'Okay, then why didn't you just teleport us into your room?'

'I did I just didn't put you down.'

'Huh? Really?' She asked, I rubbed the back of my head, 'Why?'

'Well because I'm in no rush to let you go.'

She stared at me for a second, 'Are you being romantic?'

I frowned, 'Am I?'

She pulled me down and kissed me, 'I don't care whether you were doing it intentionally or not.'

I kissed her back, 'Good, 'cos I wasn't.'

She laughed and wrapped her arms around my neck, 'Whatever, now sleep.'

I picked her up and put her on top of me, 'Yes ma'am.'

And sure enough, I was out in under two minutes (I think).

The next morning I woke up with Jess sat by my head, 'Good morning sleepyhead, I was just about to wake you.'

I stretched and wrapped my arms around her waist, 'What time is it?'

'Half seven.'

'Ugh, did you have to wake me up this early?'

She laughed and ruffled my hair, 'Yeah, I did, now come on get up we've got football to play.' She said, tossing the kit on the bed, 'And put this on.'

'Oh yeah the school kit...' I opened my eyes and studied Jess, 'You look good in it.'

She got up and threw open my curtains, 'I know, now get up!'

'Okay fine... I'm getting in the shower.'

'Good, I'll see you downstairs in ten minutes.'

'Okay.' *Jeez when did she get so bossy?*

I showered, changed, and was downstairs in seven minutes (yes I was keeping track of time bossy Jess kind of terrifies me).

'Good you made it.' She said as I appeared in the kitchen. I grabbed a bowl of cereal and sat down with Jake and Sam.

'What's with her?' Jake asked.

I sighed, 'I have no idea she's really bossy today for some reason, I'm thinking she might even be able to control San today.'

She winked at me, 'Thanks AJ.'

'How did she even hear me?' I whispered, they both shrugged, terrified.

She walked over and sat next to me, 'Make sure you eat up!'

Okay there is something wrong. I stared at her, switching between all the visions I had to see what on Earth was happening.

She panicked a little, 'Alfie what are you doing?'

Finally, I found it, I switched to my "power reading" vision and found that when I looked at her, well, you'll see.

I knew it! Okay let's mess with them.

I winked at Sam and Jake, hoping they'd understand that I knew something.

'Oh it's nothing I'm just not sure about you in that outfit.'

Now that got literally EVERYBODY'S attention, it was almost funny.

The fake Jess was slow to react, 'W...What do you mean?'

'Hmm, I'm just not sure...'

Sylvia glared at me, 'Alfie what?'

I shot her a look, hoping she'd understand.

'Syl back me up here!' Fake Jess said.

'No I think she agrees.' I replied, 'Also you're acting really bossy today, I'm not a massive fan of this side of you.'

Everyone else was shocked into silence.

'H...How dare you!'

I shrugged, 'I mean, I'm just giving my honest opinion. And you aren't even that good at football.'

At this point I was genuinely surprised the real Jess hadn't popped out from upstairs to argue with me, but I kept ongoing.

'I mean... Can you even do twenty keep-ups?' I started raising my voice.

'Of course I can!'

Zoe opened her mouth but Sylvia stopped her, 'And you're hair in a ponytail again? Can't you do something different? Spice it up a little?' I said, my voice still getting louder.

'I should slap you right now!'

I toned down my voice again, becoming scarily calm, 'Go on then... Do it.'

Darius finally spoke, 'Yo Alfie, maybe calm yourself...'

'I said do it!... Oh wait... You can't can you, not because you don't want to, you can't.'

Everyone stared at me, 'Wait, what?' Darius said.

I went to punch her, 'Alfie no!' Queenie and Zoe shouted, but as my fist made contact, instead of being met by a solid mass, it passed straight through.

The fake Jess stared at me, 'How... How'd you know?'

I sat back down and ate another spoonful of cereal, 'Can I have my girlfriend back now please?'

The projection disappeared, 'How on Earth did you know?' Sam asked.

'Just wait till the girls get here, then I'll explain.'

And soon enough they did, Maddison and Jess, both looking quite annoyed, arrived in the elevator, 'There my girl is!' I said. She smiled and sat next to me, 'Seriously how'd you know?'

'I didn't.'

Now when I say that started a war, I mean it started a *war*. Suddenly everyone was shouting at me, Jess just stared at me in disbelief, Zoe shouted at me for trying to punch my girlfriend, and well I couldn't be bothered to deal with everyone shouting at me.

'Of course I knew! I knew! It's so obvious, A. You were not acting like yourself, B. You were way too slow to react, and C. When I switched to power vision it told me you were a projection.'

Everyone calmed down, 'You little Joker!' Jess shouted, 'I thought you'd actually just tried to punch me!' She said, nearly slapping me on the arm.

Why'd she not hit me? I switched to power vision, took one look at Jess and sighed, then looked at Maddison, she was real alright.

I stuck my hand out and generated a ball of electricity, 'Can I have my girlfriend back?' I growled.

Fake Jess V.2 stared at me, 'Erm Alf what are you doing?'

'Stop me, just try and stop me.'

The second projection disappeared and the real Jess ran out of the elevator and tackled me in a hug, 'You're amazing!'

'There's the girl I know!' I said, wrapping my arms around her.

Maddison shook her head in disbelief, 'But I did it so much better since I was in the room, how'd you know?'

'You didn't hit me on the arm.' I said, kissing Jess on the head, 'It was the fact that you'd missed that tipped me off.'

She sighed, 'I'm so stupid.'

I laughed, 'It was an impressive attempt though I'll give you that.'

'Thanks.'

'I so thought we had you.'

'Hang on a minute though, so it was you when I was still in bed, but then after that it was a projection?'

'Yeah.'

'Okay cool... Can I finish my cereal in peace now?'

'No, because you've got the real me to deal with now.'

I put my arm around her, 'There are worse things to deal with.'

She started to eat her cereal, 'Yeah I know I'm the best!' She said with a mouth full of cereal.

'Oh god eat with your mouth closed please!' Sam said, sat directly across from her.

I laughed, 'She doesn't do it all the time!'

'No only when she's talking, which is all the time!' He said.

I laughed, Jess glared at me and my bowl of cereal suddenly became very interesting.

I quickly finished my bowl and then found that I had no idea what to do next, I stood in the middle of the room, just staring into space.

'Alfie? Alfie... Earth to Alfie come in!' Alex said, waving his hand in front of my face.

I snapped back to reality, 'Oh hey what's up.'

'You look lost.'

I frowned, 'What?'

'You look lost.'

'Well, I'm just kind of waiting so I guess I am...'

'Well you can always find me.' Jess whispered, wrapping her arms around me from behind.

'Is that meant to be romantic?' I asked, looking over my shoulder.

'Mmm, maybe.'

I spun around, 'Thanks.' I muttered, kissing her forehead, '...Hey when do we have to go for football?'

'We're supposed to be there for half eight but we were planning on going in... eight minutes.' Helena said, walking through the back door.

'Well it looks like we're all here... Except for one...'

'No I'm here.' San said, waving his arm in the air.

'Oh, we're all here.' I said, *Why is he in such a good mood?*

San noticed me staring at him, 'What?' He growled.

I looked away, 'Nothing... Now then, shall we go?'

Everyone playing nodded and got up, I was first out the door, Jess right behind me. We got to the stadium for 8 o'clock, I don't know why we went half an hour early, because once we got there we still had to wait, but we did.

Anyway, half an hour later the screen lit up, showing a video of the crowd, it cut to the Principal, who did the usual "hello and welcome" blabbing on. Then he announced that due to the high amount of teams, the competition would take place over two days (although it always did) and that the first-round fixtures were now announced.

We were up against **All Souls**, which was a pretty awful name, and they were pretty awful footballers.

Matches were only 45 minutes long, but we still beat them 27-0, I think out of all of our goals, San and I `combined scored or assisted in 20 of them, it was almost a joke by the end, we had our full-backs trying to hit 40-yard long shots, they just gave up. Anyway, when the whistle blew for the game to end the opposing team walked off in shame, they didn't even bother shaking our hands, I mean, I don't blame them to be fair.

Jess walked up to me after the game, 'Do these shoes do anything special then?'

I glanced down at them, 'Erm, no, actually not a thing appearance-wise.'

She pouted, 'Okay…'

I laughed and put my arm around her, 'Come on we've got to clear the field.'

'Hey Alfie?'

'Mhmm?'

'Don't you think it's weird, how powerful you are?'

The question caught me off-guard, 'I don't get what you mean.'

'Well you know, in the stories, if there's ever an overpowered hero, there's always some downfall to him.'

I thought about it, '…Yeah but this isn't the stories. So maybe I don't.'

'Yeah but surely God wouldn't allow someone as powerful as you to exist.'

'God!' I said, sitting down, 'When has God ever had any relevance in this, I might as well be God.'

Queenie looked at us, 'What are you two talking about?'

'Whether Alfie has a downfall or not.'

Sam leant over, 'What do you mean "has a downfall or not"?'

'Well in the stories, every massively overpowered character has some, weakness, but Alfie seemingly doesn't.'

Tiago shrugged, 'Maybe he's meant to be the next God.'

'What is it with everyone and God? There is no way a God exists and I'm like this.' I said, staring at the sparks flickering between my fingers. *Do I have a weakness?*

'Hey you okay?' Jess asked, putting her hand over mine.

'Huh? Oh yeah, I'm good.'

'You sure?'

I looked away and nodded, Jess sighed and gently put my head on her lap and stroked my hair, I closed my eyes, I knew everyone was staring at me. I may or may not have fallen asleep, or well at least I think I did as I don't really remember waiting another 4 hours for the next game, neither do I remember the announcements for the next games. The next thing I actually do remember is stepping onto the pitch and yawning, much to the disgust of the other team, who seemed to forget who I was...

The ref called the captains forward and we shook hands, or well, he shook my hand, 'Better not fall asleep Captain, don't want to let the team down.'

I yawned, 'Yeah whatever just wait till I've got the ball at my feet.' I muttered.

We kicked off and San passed the ball to me, I then proceeded to smash the ball up the field, towards goal, San stared at me, 'WHY'D YOU DO THAT?'

I held my hand out as the ball began descending towards the net, 'Kaboom.' I replied, sending a fireball flying towards the keeper, forcing him to dive out the way, even though it petered out before it even reached him.

The ball it the back of the net, 1-0.

The opposing captain scoffed, 'What the hell was that cheap tactic?'

I stretched, 'It's called, winning, maybe try it some time.'

He growled, *He doesn't like me.* I thought.

I continued to mess with him for the next half an hour, before getting him sent off in the 33rd minute, Tiago threaded the ball through to me, where I proceeded to nutmeg the guy, not once, not twice, but four times in a row, in the end the guy just kicked me, I fell to the ground in pain.

'Aargh!' I shouted, slightly exaggerating the injury, 'My leg!'

Now my leg was actually bleeding, but the opposing captain did not care, he stood over me, glowering, 'Who's winning now boy.'

The ref ran over, showing him a red card, even in power football, you can't just kick someone with your studs up, 'I think I am.' I said as Jess knelt down next to me.

'Hey you okay?'

I nodded, 'Yeah just give me a min.' I held my hand out over my leg and healed it, much to the surprise of the other guy.

'What? I got sent off for an injury you healed just like that?'

I laughed, 'Yep, I can heal basically any injury as long as it doesn't kill me instantly, now bye.' I said, summoning a gust of wind that blew him off the field, the crowd roared.

Jess smiled and pulled me up, 'Love you.'

'Love you too, now let's win this.' I said, fist-bumping her.

The game resumed with a freekick which I dinked onto San's left foot, which he neatly tucked away.

'Alright!' I said, high ten-ing him.

The game ended 16-2, we scored 6 in the last 10 minutes when they had 10 players.

'Good win guys!' I said once the ref blew the whistle, making my way off the pitch with everyone else.

'Hey Alf, is it my turn to sleep?' Jess asked.

I looked at her, but she did her puppy-dog eyes thing (that mildly annoys me because it's so cute) and well... I couldn't really say no. I picked her up and she nestled her head against my neck, 'Thanks Alf.'

'You're always welcome Jess.' I whispered, kissing her cheek.

Zoe stared at us, 'Can you two stop showing the rest of us up?'

I smiled, 'What do you mean?'

She formed a square with her hands and put us in it, 'Just this... You're making us look bad!'

San scoffed, 'Maybe that's your fault, not theirs.'

Zoe and Sam glared at him, 'What?' They demanded.

'Well, maybe if you two were... Better... Then you wouldn't be complaining.'

I sat down, 'He's got a point.'

They ignored me, 'Listen you little punk, what do you know about being in a relationship?'

He sighed, 'A lot more than you do apparently.'

'I bet you've never even had a girlfriend!' Zoe shouted.

'Guys!' I complained.

'Oh yeah? What do you know about my life, what?' No reply, 'That's what I thought, you know nothing about me.'

'It's not like you know anything about us either!'

He groaned, 'Oh please, you've been going out since October, you've slept together what? Five-ish times, you haven't met Sam's parents but he's met yours, you've kissed but *you* don't know if you're ready for it yet.'

'San enough.' I said.

Zoe growled, 'Listen here, just because you know some facts about us doesn't mean you know everything!'

He scoffed, 'Yeah okay.'

Zoe charged at him.

'Enough!' I shouted, freezing them both and causing some laughs from nearby teams. I put Jess down and walked over to them, 'Listen you two, I don't care how much you know about each other, we are here to play football, and that is what I expect you to do, sort this out after we win this thing, Do you understand?'

Neither said anything because they were both frozen.

'...Good.' I said, unfreezing them and sitting down, Zoe turned away and sat on the other side of the square with Sam.

I rubbed my head and sighed, 'What's going on with them?' Jess mumbled.

'Just squabbling over nothing.' I replied.

She sighed and went back to sleep, 'Okay.'

I picked her up and laid her on top of me, 'I'll wake you in a bit...' I whispered, but she was already asleep.

Another 4 hours later and it was time for the next set of games to be announced, we were playing **Great West High.** Which was basically this fancy school from way down south. Anyway, our game was at least 2 hours away so we decided to have lunch.

I woke Jess, 'Is it game time?' She asked immediately.

I laughed, 'No but it is lunchtime so I figured you'd want waking.'

She nodded, 'Thanks.'

I passed her a sandwich, 'You know I'm kinda getting bored of sandwiches after fifteen years of eating them.'

Jess nodded, 'I know what you mean, but we don't have anything else.'

'Unless...'

'There's no way.'

I held out my hand and tried to summon a pizza, trying the same thing I do when I summon the elements, and suddenly, with a **Poof!** There it was, one steaming hot Margherita pizza, 'HAHA yes!'

Everyone looked over, 'Where'd you get that!' Tiago asked.

Jess and I both took a piece and bit into it, 'Oh my god this is amazing.' I said, Jess agreed, 'Hang on guys.' I said, walking around and giving everyone pizzas, much to the annoyance of the other teams, 'I think this might be my favourite power.' I stated.

Everyone else agreed, but were too busy stuffing their faces to say anything...

Another hour later and it was finally our turn, our last for the day.

We took to the field and I shook hands with their captain, a short, pink-haired girl who looked like she was going to be a problem, and I was right...

They had kick off and well, they passed it to their captain who had super speed, she just ran past us and put it in the net.

'Oh great! Here we go.' I grumbled as we kicked off again. Their team was pretty awful except for the girl, so we dominated really, the game ended 10-6 to us, the captain scored all 6.

Everyone looked exhausted as we walked off the pitch, but I
don't blame them, we'd played three games in a day, and it was
getting late…

We walked back to the dorm together, we hadn't said anything
about the game, not even when walking off the field, we'd all
silently agreed to talk about it in the morning.

Halfway down the path I picked Jess up as she started to lag
behind, 'Come on you little baby.' I said.

'I'm not a baby.' She mumbled.

'I thought you were my baby.' I said, smiling.

She put her arms around my neck, 'I am.' She grinned.

I sighed, 'Okay then… But if you're this tired you're going to bed
when we get back and I'm not.'

She yawned, 'Okay.'

'I'll meet you guys back at dorm.' I said to everyone, teleporting
straight back to the dorm. I put Jess down in her bed and
covered her in the duvet, then went back downstairs.

'Why do we have to wait so long between matches?' I
complained, walking out the elevator doors (yes I teleported to
the bottom, where the elevator was, don't question my
methods).

'Hey look it's good for some of us, just because you're body
recovers from fatigue in five minutes doesn't mean all of ours
do!' Nat argued.

I smiled and rubbed the back of my head, 'Anyway… Have they
announced who we're playing tomorrow or not?'

'Yeah you just missed it, it's this team from Argentina, they won
it a couple of years back I think most of their players have
graduated by now.' Zoe said.

'Oh yeah, I forget most other teams are mixed ages.'

She nodded, 'I guess it must only be their third years that were
part of that winning squad, if any of them still play.'

'That's fine, we'll beat them anyway.'

Everyone nodded half-heartedly and soon enough the rest of
the class began trickling back into their rooms.

'Where's Jess?' Sylvia asked whilst looking around the room.

'She's asleep, playing tired her out.' I explained, staring at the
Tv.

'Who's room?'

'Why does it matter?' She shrugged, 'She's in hers, can't have her in mine all the time.' I muttered.

She nodded and went in the elevator, Jake joined her. I glanced around the rest of the room, it was business as normal, Sam and Barukko were playing video games whilst most of us had our attention on the various TVs around the room, Darius was cooking again in the kitchen, it smelled amazing as always. A couple hours passed and after beating the lads at virtual combat, I went up to bed.

I changed and fell back onto my bed, *Lights out.* I thought, closing my eyes and entering another dull, dreamless sleep. Or so I thought…

24 – I really hate dreams, there is just no point…

I arrived in the abyss or at least the very depths of space, there seemed to be twinkling lights in every direction, but they were so dim it was hard to tell whether I was imagining them or not. 'Where… Where am I?' I asked myself.

'The centre of my universe.' A voice said next to me. The person this voice belonged to looked like an athlete at the top of their game, muscles covering his whole body, a short, black beard and wavy black hair, he was wearing just a loincloth, something I didn't really want to see. But I felt a massive amount of power, I looked at him, it was emulating from him, his power was incomprehensible, it made mine look like a drop of water if his was an ocean. It nearly blew me away.

'Okay and who are you?'

He smiled, 'I'll leave that up to you to decide.'

'Okay… And which universe is this?'

'Universe Three-Zero-Four-Seven.' I looked at him, confused. 'It's the universe you reside in, you're currently in the middle of it.'

'Wait… We're in the middle of a supermassive black hole? How is that possible?'

He shrugged, 'Anything is possible my child, you especially should know that.'

'Okay… And why am I here?'

'I just wanted to introduce myself. You'll need me soon enough. Good-bye.'

'Wait!' I shouted, 'You haven't really answered anything!' But it was too late, I was already waking up, 'HEY! Answer me!'

I was literally zooming away at this point, going faster and faster, heading towards one of the lights that I saw earlier, it was getting brighter and brighter, bigger and bigger, faster and faster.

Well this is just great.

Suddenly the one light exploded into millions of other lights, I kept going until I hit one of those lights and the milky way came into view.

Am I going to hit the Earth going a billion miles an hour? I kept flying towards Earth, *This isn't good! AAAH!*

THWUMP, I sat up in my bed, sweating and panting heavily.

My door burst open and Jess ran in, 'Are you okay?'

She saw me and embraced me in a hug, 'What's wrong, did you dream?'

I tried to calm my breathing and nodded, putting my face in her shoulder.

'What happened?'

I didn't say anything, I was still breathing heavily, I'm not even sure what scared me so much.

She hugged me tighter and sat down on the bed, 'It's okay, you're with me now.'

I gripped her arm and began to calm down, 'I...I...'

'What is it?'

'I think I met God...'

She was silent for a moment, 'What happened in the dream?'

I explained the dream to her, right up to the point where I'd woken up.

She finally pulled away, a worried look in her eyes, 'I mean... it makes sense.'

'But why would he just want to introduce himself?'

I rubbed my eyes, 'How am I supposed to know, maybe it's because I'm so powerful or... I don't know.'

'I mean we don't even know if it's God or not...'

I shrugged and fell back on my pillow, 'I don't know!'

She smiled softly and laid on my chest, 'You'll be okay Alf.'

I ran my hand through her hair, 'I know...'

'Do you wanna get up or...? It's only seven so we can stay here if you want.'

I smiled, 'I think I should get up.'

She looked up at me, 'You sure?'

I put my hands behind my head, 'Yeah...'

'Cos you look pretty happy right here.'

'I am... But I can't stay here forever can I?'

'I wish we could.'

'So do I... But we've got some games to play.'

She nodded and stood up, I kissed her and got in the shower, changed and went downstairs for some breakfast, a plate of pancakes which I summoned whilst in the elevator.

The doors opened and I walked out, surprising everyone by having a mouth full of pancakes, 'Where'd you get those?' Sylvia asked.

'Wait, don't tell me!' Jess said, I nodded and summoned some in my other hand, putting the plate in front of her and sitting on the table, 'You're amazing.' She said.

'I know.' I replied, another mouth full of pancakes.

Sylvia stared at me, 'How…?'

'I think I can summon any food I know how to cook, so pancakes and pizzas and stuff like that.'

Darius glared at me, 'Look don't worry, I can't make the stuff you do, I wouldn't even know where to start.' He shrugged and turned back to his cooking, I wondered if he ever stopped.

'Hey Alfie, what are on these pancakes?'

'Erm, lemon and sugar I think.'

'I wondered why they tasted so amazing.' She said, wolfing another one down.

'They're so boring.' Sam complained from the other side of the room.

'Look they're the best flavour.'

'It's just so bland.'

'You're bland.'

'What'd you say?' He said, marching over, 'Never call me bland!'

I laughed, 'Why, is it like the real-life version of being called "chicken"?' Jess nearly choked on her food.

Sam turned to her, 'Listen here Jessica, do not laugh at me.'

'Hey, don't talk to her like that.' I warned.

He scoffed and walked away, I glared at him and zapped him in the back with a bit of electricity.

Zoe stood up, 'What was that for!?'

I sighed, 'I don't mind people having a go at me but no one argues with Jess.'

'You didn't need to zap him!'

'Oh please it was ten volts, he hardly felt it.'

'I'll show you volts.' Zoe growled.

'Let's not.' I said.

'Why? You scared?'

'No, it's because I don't want our first-choice winger to be incapacitated.' I said, my voice remaining emotionless.

She grunted and moved to the opposite side of the room.

'You shouldn't have done that.'

'Why not?'

'You shouldn't have to protect me.'

'But I will, and I'm in a bad mood enough as it is today, so I won't take anything from anyone.'

She sighed and finished her pancakes before wrapping her arms around my waist, 'You sure you're okay?'

'Yeah I'll be fine.'

She put her head on my lap and sighed, 'You shouldn't sit on the table.'

'You're currently the one stopping me from getting off the table.'

She smiled, 'Fair point.'

'How long have we got till we've got to go?' I called.

'An hour.' Helena replied behind me, 'So don't go doing anything stupid.'

'Who me?' She glared at me, 'Fine, *I promise*.' I said mockingly. Jess got up and pulled me outside...

'What is going on with you today?'

I scratched the back of my head, 'What do you mean?'

'You just seem really... Moody!'

'Do I?'

She nodded, 'And you can't just do whatever you want all the time, you've got to be nice.'

'When has anyone ever won anything by being nice.'

She stared at me, 'What?'

'When has anyone got anywhere or won anything worthwhile by being nice? Do you think the World Government was formed because we were being nice? You think the best sports teams have won stuff by being nice?'

'But there's a line Alfie! Those are your teammates in there! Your friends!'

I sighed and put my hands to my face, 'I know, I know! I don't know what's going on.' I opened my eyes and saw Jess studying me, worried.

'Will you be okay?'

'Gods I don't know, I think I should be fine once I step on the pitch...'

'Well then shall we go? I don't care if we're very early it should give you time to clear your head and calm down.'

I nodded and she stuck her head inside, I presumed that she told everyone we were heading to the arena to cool off. Then grabbed my hand and set off walking to the stadium.

'Alf?'

'What's up?'

'Can you put me on your shoulders?'

'Yeah sure why not.' I said, crouching down.

'If you turn around I'll kill you.' She warned.

'You're wearing shorts anyway! But that's fine.' I said as she climbed on.

'Come on! Giddy-up.'

I sighed and set off walking again, 'Woah... I can see so much from up here!'

'Well, you are like nine feet tall.'

She ignored me, 'I can already see the stadium.'

'Cool.'

She sighed and leant on my head, 'Alfie what if it was God?'

'There's no way it was God.'

'Then who was it?'

'What if it wasn't anyone, what if it was just a dream?'

'But you don't just have dreams.'

I thought about it, then shrugged, 'I don't know... Maybe we'll find out one day.'

'Yeah...'

I squeezed her leg and we walked in silence for the rest of the walk, Jess kept trying to snag twigs from the branches above her head, thankfully she didn't fall off.

We got into the stadium when fans had only just started to trickle in, so we were allowed to go up onto the floor and talk to some of the newcomers. It wasn't the most exciting but it was cool to meet some people, and it took my mind off of things.

Anyway, eventually they kicked us off the field and sent us back down to the waiting area.

'You feeling better now?'

'Yeah I am actually.' I said, putting my hands behind my head, 'Just want to play some football.'

She nodded and sat down next to me, closing her eyes she said, 'This should be easy shouldn't it.'

I laughed, 'With our powers? Yeah.'

'Well, you and San alone could probably win this thing.'

I shrugged, 'Depends on what my limit is for the number of times I can teleport a game.'

She laughed, 'Yeah.'

Eventually, everyone else arrived and in good spirits too, clearly up for winning this thing. An hour later it was our time to play and we walked up to the pitch.

'Right then guys!' I said as we all crowded around, 'I think there are only four games till the final, it will be a long day, but we can do this!'

Everyone nodded and we dispersed, getting into our positions and ready for the game, the referee called the captains forward, we shook hands, 'I heard you guys won this thing a while back.'

He smiled slyly, 'Yeah, and we don't plan on losing.'

'That's a shame.' I said, turning around and walking back, we had kick-off.

I felt him glaring at the back of my head as I walked back, I got in position and we kicked off, the ball ended up at my feet and I dinked one behind the backline, San latched onto it but the keeper made the save, the game had started off quick.

It was a massively back and forth game, both teams having huge amounts of attacking talent and there was only so much a good defence could do. It was the 42nd minute and the score was 10-11 to them, I had the ball on the left side just outside the box when I was brought down, free kick.

San and I stood over the ball, 'I should take this, but I want you to run behind from the left side of the wall, if the keeper saves it he'll just tap it down or over, I want you to chase it.'

He nodded and walked off.

I stood over the ball and looked past the wall into the top right-hand corner of the goal, *There!*

I activated my marksmanship and smashed the ball, whipping it from right to left and curling it into the corner, just out of the keeper's reach.

I didn't have time to celebrate, I teleported and grabbed the ball, putting it down on the halfway line and telling everyone to get ready, momentum was everything in football, and it was on our side. They kicked off again and I don't think we've ever dominated a game so much without touching the ball, we pressed and pressed until we'd basically got them locked down in their own box, then their goalkeeper hit a wonder-ball up the field to their striker, I thought it was all over, 44:27, *No, it's never over till we give up.* The defenders had stopped running, everyone thought it was a 1v1, but I had other plans, I teleported right in front of the striker and swept the ball from his feet, hitting it long in a desperate attempt to avoid penalties. Zoe latched onto the ball in the corner and whipped it into the box, no one was there. San retrieved the ball on the other side and crossed it back in, I was there this time, having just teleported in, but I was too far in front of the ball, with my back to goal I had one option. I jumped like I was going for a back-flip and went attempted a last-ditch attempt at a bicycle kick, I made contact with the ball but it was flying wide of the post. But then suddenly Sam, who I thought was on the other side of the pitch, materialised at the post, onside because of the woman on the line, and tapped it in. 44:39. It took us 12 seconds to stop an attack and score the winning goal.

'WHY DID YOU TRY A BICYCLE KICK?' He shouted at me.

'Hey it worked.' I laughed.

'He's bonkers that's why!' Zoe shouted.

We all jogged back but there was no point, as soon as they kicked off the ref blew the whistle. We'd won by a small mistake and some brilliant positioning, but who was I to complain.

Jess ran and tackled me in a hug, 'I cannot believe you tried a bicycle kick for the win!'

I laughed, 'It was a last-ditch attempt alright!'

'Onto the next one then?'

'Definitely.'

We all walked off the pitch, ready to wait another 2 long, dull hours before our next game...

Most of us slept the whole time, but Jess didn't, 'What's up?' I asked her.

'Huh? Oh nothing.'

I stared at her, 'You sure because most of us have been sleeping and you... Have not, which isn't like you.'

She sighed, 'I know I'm just thinking.'

I moved over to her and put my arm around her, 'What about?'

'Just your dream… And… Stuff.'

'Forget about the dream… It must have just simply been a dream, nothing else.'

She put her head on my shoulder, 'Alfie what will you do after school?'

'What?'

'I mean, you're going to be the most powerful guy in the world by the time you leave school right? So what next?'

I chuckled, 'Oh god I haven't really thought that far…! But I don't know, I mean, I could run the world I guess.'

'What run for World President?'

'Yeah why not? The election is three years after we leave school so I don't see why not.'

She smiled, 'Alfie Jaeger, World President.'

'I know sounds cool right? I mean, I may be too busy saving the world to actually run but it's an option.'

'So it all depends on how corrupted the world is huh?'

'Yep.'

'Okay… When's our next game?'

I glanced up at the screen, 'About two minutes, once the next game finishes.'

She nodded and stretched, 'I suppose we'd better wake the rest of them then.'

I nodded and zapped everyone with a tiny amount of electricity, just enough to wake them up, 'You could have done it the normal way.' Jess muttered.

'Yeah… But what's the fun in that.'

'You're so powerful it's ridiculous.' She muttered under her breath.

'I know right?' I replied anyway, 'Now then everyone! Our game's in roughly a minute, so up on your feet come on or I'll blast you all with water!'

'Can you blast me anyway?' Sam muttered.

'Sure!' I held my hand out and did as he asked, soaking him in freezing water.

'My God that's cold!' He complained.

246

'You asked for it, anyone else want some?'
No one said a word and instead started making their way up to the pitch.
'You go on ahead.' I said to Jess, 'I'll dry Sam off.'
I walked over and held out my hand, 'Do you want me to dry you off or are you just going to stay soaked?'
He glanced at my hand, 'How are you gonna dry me?'
'I'm just going to blast you with fire, it won't burn you it'll just feel warm.'
He shook his head, 'I'll pass.'
'Alrighty then.' I said, jogging out onto the field with Sam in tow.
We were playing this team from Brazil, a country known for its footballers, but apparently this school hadn't gotten the memo. Brazilians are (generally) world-class skillers, their flair unrivalled, apparently not these kids. They just played tiki-taka the whole time, no more than three touches per player, the kind of things you do in training, they never even got in the box…
We smashed them to pieces with our creativity in attack, between myself getting forward and Bianca's passes from deep, they couldn't keep up. The game ended 9-0, they had like, 68% possession I think I heard on the news later. I couldn't believe it.
I high-fived everyone after the whistle went, 'Good job guys! One step closer.'
Everyone nodded and we walked off the field, the other team had already left. It made me wonder how some teams make it this far in competitions.
We walked back inside and I summoned another round of food to eat before our next round, more pizza because I couldn't quite figure out how to summon burgers, I could get the bread, just not the actual meat, which is kind of important.
'Alfie, I'm so glad I was born in the same year as you.' Jake said, munching on a ridiculously large piece of pizza.
'What would you do without me!' I laughed.
He smiled and shrugged, then continued eating.

After eating I decided to sleep off the food, (ugh that's an old person sentence). I slumped down on one of the sofas, solidifying the air to keep my feet up, and with Jess sat next to me I went to sleep. An hour-ish later Jess woke me and told me that our next game was against this German team that was impossible to spell and sounded really aggressive (but it is German what do you expect).

'Oh great, we've got to defend against an all-out-attack team? Lovely…'

Jess stared at me, 'How do you know?'

'They're German.' I sighed, 'That's the only way they play.'

She nodded, seeming to understand, 'So how do we beat them?'

'We score more than they do.' San and I said simultaneously and then grinned.

'I mean… Yeah.'

'Okay then, let's do this!' I shouted, 'What is it now? Three wins now till the final?'

Everyone nodded, determined looks on their faces.

'Alright then, let's win this!' I shouted, everyone going to their places. I went up to the ref and shook hands with him and the opposing captain, who stared at me silently. *Not very friendly, how German…*

I stared him down which seemed to surprise him, which was exactly what I wanted, the guy had that kind of stare that made you want to dig a hole and hide, I bet you someone standing up to him touched a nerve.

Anyway, they got kick off and started exactly as I said. All-out attack…

Immediately 5 players ran forward off kick off, their only remaining midfielder hit the ball wide, which was immediately intercepted by Tiago, who passed it to Bianca who pinged it to me, we'd eliminated 5 players in two passes, I took out their last midfielder with a pass to Zoe on the right, who dinked it into San who hit the header over the bar. We'd failed in scoring but we had done `what we'd set out to do, shock them. They were used to scoring off the start, and we had prevented that.

It was a goal-fest, goal after goal, shot after shot. But we scored more, the game ended 20-17 to us, 37 goals in 45 minutes, absolute madness. But we'd won, we were all shattered from running back and forth constantly, but we'd won, so I didn't care.

I bent over once the ref blew the final whistle, gasping for breath.

'Alf… Use your… Super stamina…' Jess panted.

I nodded and attempted to use it, I instantly felt better, still tired but not out of breath, I had to be careful not to use full-blown super stamina, using super anything at full power took a whole lot out of me. I kissed Jess, imparting some of that super stamina on her, (again, not a clue how I did that either).

'Thanks.' She said after I'd pulled away, looking into my eyes.

I nodded, 'No problem, now come on, once we get down you can go to sleep if you want.'

She nodded, 'Good, I need a sleep.'

I laughed, 'You've been sleeping more and more recently.'

'Says you.'

I shrugged and entered the waiting area. Everyone was silent, which was weird, even though there weren't many teams left there was always some noise, but as we walked down there wasn't.

'Erm, what's going on?'

'Apparently those guys were tipped to win this thing.' Queenie whispered.

'Nice!' Sam shouted.

I smiled and leant back into the sofa and closing my eyes.

'Alfie how can you just go to sleep after being told we beat the guys tipped to win this?'

I shrugged and put my feet up.

'It's because he's so powerful, it must be.' Sam said.

'No, I think it's because competition brings out the real him.' Jess said, sitting down next to me.

'What do you mean?' Sam said, I didn't move, pretending to be asleep, I heard a lot of movement coming towards us, I guess I was a hot topic.

'This level of calmness that you're seeing, that's him, at the epitome of concentration, I mean he's not there yet, I doubt you'll see it at this tournament though, I've only seen him do it once, back at primary school, he was in a fight with one of the most powerful kids at school, and he had an unshakeable level of calmness in that fight, bear in mind he had no power at this point, just the sword in his hand. But he was completely calm, he forgot all about everyone else, it was just him and his opponent. That's how I know he hasn't hit that epitome yet, he still reacts, acts with emotion.'

'What? How many people have actually seen this?'

'Oh there mustn't be more than ten, and I doubt that many remember.'

'Actually, in that fight you were just on about I hadn't hit my peak.' I muttered.

'Alfie! You're still awake!'

I nodded, 'As far as I'm aware one guy has seen me at the top, and he's dead.' I said, unmoving.

'That... Is... Unbelievable.' Sam said.

'Terrifying.' Queenie argued.

'Wait Wait Wait... So no one alive knows you at your peak?' San demanded.

I didn't move, keeping my hands behind my head.

'Why not?' Jess asked.

I didn't reply, so Barukko tried to, 'It must be too powerful or something, too terrifying, I don't know, or too hard to reach.'

'Power is created from a need, not a desire.' Sam said.

Zoe laughed, 'Where'd you come up with that?'

'He's not wrong.' I finally said, 'If I could do it when I wanted, I'd do it all the time. Although where he got that old-man quote from is beyond me.'

Sam laughed back, 'Hah!'

I sighed and put my arms back behind my head, I could feel Jess studying me, 'So... this calmness you have now, where are you at?'

'I have no idea; I don't think it's a scale or anything.'

'Hang on so... When you're at your peak is it like when you're in the flow state?' Jake asked.

'Kind of, it's more powerful.'
'How?'
I shrugged and didn't say anything else.
'Great, so we haven't actually seen the most powerful kid at school try yet?'
I liked that idea.

An hour later Jess woke me up because we had our next game, 'Come on Alf, we've got the quarter-finals now there's no time for sleeping!'
'Weren't you asleep as well?'
'Water under the bridge!'
'I don't think it's meant to be used like that.'
She shrugged, 'Oh well, anyway come on we've got to go.'
I stood up, 'Come on then.' I walked away and up the ramp and into the sunlight. Everyone else was already on the field so I joined them, 'Who are we playing?'
Helena shook her head, 'Doesn't matter, now we just go out there and play our game okay?'
I frowned but nodded, 'Come on guys, let's go out and do this!'
'You're not calm now?' Sam asked.
I shook my head as I walked over to the ref, 'Sleep resets it I think, or just extended periods of time.'
He nodded and turned around, I smiled and shook hands with the ref and the other captain, 'Good luck.' He said.
I smiled, 'You're the one who needs luck.'
We got ready for kick-off, I put my hands on my hips as San stood over the ball, 'Come on guys, we can do this!'
San kicked the ball to me and I controlled it looking up and finding a pass, I swung for the ball, but it wasn't there.
'Huh?'
I glanced behind me and saw their striker with the ball at his feet, charging the defence. He knocked it past Jess and flew past (not literally), then smashed it into the top right-hand corner. Bianca looked at me, 'What... Just happened?'
'I don't know...'
They did that three more times and we still didn't know what was happening.

251

'Come on guys! Mix it up a bit!' Jess shouted.

It was too late, we'd never gone 4-Nil down before, we had all but lost. Yet Jess continued to work hard, learnt how to stop that mad attack and launched some of our own. She played her socks off, the rest of us did not, whenever I received the ball I just passed it off immediately, I just was not feeling it. the game ended 10-2, we'd played miserably and like we couldn't be bothered, and we'd paid the price.

The whistle blew and Jess collapsed to the floor in tears. We all looked over, too ashamed to say anything. Helena shouted at us all, but she wasn't getting through. I glanced around, the other team were huddled around, a team. We were spread out all over our half, staring at the ground or Jess.

I shouted at the sky and made my way to the exit, before glancing back at Jess, she hadn't moved.

I sighed and walked over, 'Come on Jess.' I said, 'We've got to clear the pitch.'

She glared at me, I looked at her, sighed and walked away, she didn't want to talk to me.

I met Barukko and Zoe at the exit, 'What's wrong with her?' Zoe asked.

I looked back, 'She doesn't want to talk to us for a while.' I replied, putting on my cloak and walking out the exit. They both hesitated then followed me out, leaving the crowds behind.

We walked out and were met by a few fans, but I didn't want to speak to them, I kept my eyes on the path ahead of me, I saw these two girls out of the corner of my eye who were holding some kind of equipment, but as I said, I didn't want to speak to them.

I continued walking, the crowd built up a little so I opened up a portal and we all jumped through it, appearing just outside of dorm.

I sighed and slumped against the wall once we got inside,

'Argh.' I slammed my fist against the wall, cracking it, 'Ah sugar.'

Sam smiled, 'What'd you hurt your hand?'

'No, but I cracked the wall.' I replied, staring at where I'd hit it.

His jaw dropped, 'What?!'

I sighed, 'Yeah well... I'll be upstairs if anyone needs me.'

Zoe looked up and nodded, I fell forward, acting like I was going to fall flat on my face, Zoe reacted but it didn't matter. I teleported up to my room and fell on the bed.

'Ugh.' I moaned, 'That was... Worse than awful... Shameful.' I muttered.

What the hell happened that last game? We just... Stopped playing!

I clenched my hands, 'Oh boy that was awful.' My grandfather said behind me.

'Oh great, you.'

He laughed, 'Kid I haven't seen a performance that disappointing since Brazil lost in the world cup!'

'When was this?' I said, keeping my face against the bed.

'Oh about a hundred years ago... Anyway... Why am I here?'

'I don't know, I imagine my subconscious wants some advice again.'

'No combat training?'

I shook my head, 'But actually there may be sometime next week, I've got a break before the fighting competitions. So we'll probably get some practice in then.'

'Ooo! Power or non-power?'

'Both.'

'Okay then, I'll see you next week.'

I stuck my hand up and waved, not knowing whether he'd left already or not.

'Oh, by the way, your girlfriend has returned.'

'Okay... Thanks?'

No reply, he'd definitely left.

I sighed and got up, I walked out onto the balcony and saw Jess walking back inside from hers, I watched her go in, *Should I follow?* I stared across into her room, then decided to go talk to her, I jumped over the balcony and slid open the door, the shower was running.

Should I? There's no way she got undressed in the time between her leaving the balcony and getting in the shower, she must be dressed. So I decided to risk it and prayed that she was dressed, I walked in, 'Hey.'

She didn't say anything, just stared at her socks, which were already soaked, and sobbed. I took my shoes off and walked in. 'I'm sorry.' I whispered, putting my arms around her. She still didn't move; it was like she hadn't even noticed. I pulled her in and held her, letting the water soak over us, 'Why are we always in this scenario after we lose.' I chuckled, pointing my head to the sky and letting the water hit my face. Jess bumped her head against my chest.

'I know, we let you down… I'm sorry…'

She sat on the floor, I stared at her for a moment then joined her, 'Jessica…'

She looked at me, her eyes bloodshot. *Wow, this loss hit you hard huh?*

She put her head on my lap, I stroked her hair off of her face, 'We'll do better in the next one.'

She nodded and closed her eyes, wrapping her arms around my waist. I sighed and sat with her for another five minutes before turning the shower off, 'Can we move to the bed?'

She nodded and sat up, I heated my body temperature and dried my clothes and Jess's, but they were stiff, so I took off my t-shirt and Jess put on her pyjamas and climbed into bed, holding her arms out with her eyes closed out I swapped my shorts out and hugged her, 'I love you.'

She snuggled against my chest and looked up at me, I smiled and ruffled her hair. She smiled and went to sleep, I was tired too, I guess two days of football does that to you, even me, who healed in about 5 minutes. I closed my eyes and had another dreamless sleep.

The next morning I woke up to find Jess sat three inches from my face, studying me.

'Ah Alfie you're awake!' She exclaimed, pulling away.

I smiled, pulling her back and kissing her, '…What are you so scared of?'

She blushed, 'I don't know! I just didn't know that you were awake that's all.'

I laughed, 'Well I am now.' She smiled sheepishly. I kissed her again, she put her arms around my neck, 'Alf… Do you ever think that we moved really quick?'

'No… I think we moved at the pace we both felt right, even if we didn't talk about it. I mean it's not like we had just met right? We've known each other for years.'

'Yeah, I guess you've got a point.'

I stroked her face, 'Why, do you want to slow down?'

'Huh? No definitely not I love where we're at! I just wonder what everyone else thinks.'

'Who cares though? It's me and you, yes everyone outside that door is our friend, but in here it's me and you.'

She smiled and cuddled up to me, 'That's so romantic.'

(If I'm honest… I have no idea how to be romantic I just do it accidentally… a lot…)

I put my arm around her and fell back, pulling her with me, 'What do you want to do today?'

'Just stay here till we go back to sleep.'

I smiled, 'I doubt you'll be able to last that long! Your attention span cannot last.'

'Hey! That's mean.' She said, putting her face above mine.

I kissed her again, 'Na it's just honest.'

She smiled, 'Hey Alf?'

'Mhmm?'

'I love you too.'

She kissed me, and we held each other for a long time. In fact, we hardly moved the whole day.

The next day I woke up with Jess curled up in my arm, I smiled and stared out the window at the clear, blue sky. 'We've had a good couple weeks for weather.' I muttered. I got out of bed without disturbing Jess and went out onto the balcony, the park was busy today, 'Guess the sport in the stadium today isn't that popular.' I held out my hand and tried to summon a hot chocolate, **Poof.** 'Huh... Nice.'

I took a sip, it tasted like every hot chocolate I'd ever had, just not right, *Huh, well guess even I can't get everything perfect but this is nice...* I thought, standing on the balcony on a warm summer's day, a slight breeze running through my hair, *This is like, the perfect day.*

Zzz...Zzz...Zzz... My phone vibrated on the table, I picked it up and answered, 'Oh hey Syl what's up?'

'You know powerless football is today right?'

I glanced at Jess who was still asleep, 'It is? Oh sugar okay, what time is it?'

'Half seven...'

'Okay I'll wake Jess and be down soon, thanks!' I said putting the phone down. I sat on the bed and shook Jess a little, 'Hey come on, it's time to get our revenge.'

'Huh? What about revenge?' She mumbled, her face against the pillow.

'We forgot about football, we have to win this one right?'

She sat up and nodded, I laughed.

'What?'

'You're hair's all over the place, it's cute.'

She looked at me and smiled, 'Yeah well it's shower time, so go on, I'll see you in ten.'

I nodded and teleported to my room. I got in the shower and changed into my kit, grabbing my boots and heading downstairs I glanced out the window again, 'The perfect day for football.' I muttered, getting in the elevator...

'Good you're here.' Helena said, handing me a football, 'Do thirty keep-ups.'

'Why?'

'Just do it.'

256

I shrugged and dropped the ball on my foot, and then proceeded to do fifty just to prove a point before picking up the ball, 'Okay… Now what?'

She smiled and turned to Bianca, who did not look happy, 'He didn't use a power there did he?' She asked Sylvia.

'No, that was all skill.'

'How on Earth did you have the time to be able to do what you do?'

I paused, trying to understand that sentence, *It has way too many similar syllables in it.* I thought.

'You forget that I lived the first fourteen years of my life with no power, all I did was practise.' I finally answered.

Helena laughed, 'I told you!'

Bianca shrugged and sat down, I smiled and grabbed a buttered croissant then sat next to Jess. She was staring into the depths of her cereal.

'Hey you okay?'

She nodded, then ate another spoonful, 'I guess.'

I put my arm around her, 'We won't lose.'

'Damn right we won't!' Helena shouted, 'Not after our previous performance.'

I smiled, 'See? We'll be fine.'

She looked at me and smiled, 'Yeah, maybe you're right.'

I finished eating then got up, 'Is everyone ready?'

We all nodded and set off for the stadium, adamant that we would not have a repeat of last time.

'Hey Alfie?' Helena called back to me.

'Yeah?'

'Don't injure yourself, we're going to need you today.'

'Why does it matter, he can just heal himself anyway.' Sam said.

'Oh yeah good point.'

'How can you forget that!' I laughed.

Helena shrugged, embarrassed, and kept walking, we arrived at the stadium and found a lot less teams than last time…

'Woah, there can't be more than fifty teams here!' Jake shouted.

'Yeah alright calm down, but you're not wrong there aren't many.' I replied.

'Oh well, looks like we might be able to get this done in a day.'
Jess said, and we will go back with another trophy.'
Everyone nodded and an official walked up to us, well, I
guessed he was an official, he looked more like an office worker
with his brushed-over hairstyle, 'You're late.'
'No we're not.' I said.
'No, *you're* late.'
'Erm... What?'
He sighed, 'Come with me.'
I glanced back at everyone, they just shrugged and watched me
walk away.
'Okay so... What's happening?'
The official sighed, 'Have you really not been told?'
'Been told what?'
'About the exhibition matches.'
'Hang on! What exhibition matches?'
'The exhibition matches against the top three heroes to
promote the festival.'
My jaw dropped, 'WHAT? Why am I fighting them?'
'To promote the festival of course!'
'The festival doesn't need promoting, and why not at the start
of the festival!?'
He chuckled, 'Well the number one of every year from your
school is going to fight one of them so you'd better suck it up!'
I put my hands behind my head, 'Ugh fine.'
He led me through a maze of corridors and into an executive
box. Where the number 1 of years 2 and 3 were waiting. They
both stared at me as I walked through the door.
'Hey guys!' I said smiling. Neither said a word, 'Good talk!' I
threw myself into one of the chairs. The official turned and left.
Finally, the guy spoke, 'How can you be so relaxed? We're
about to fight the most powerful heroes in the world.'
'Because all the pressure is on them, we're the underdogs here,
we don't need to succeed.'
He shrugged, 'Says you, you're only a first-year.'
I turned to the girl, 'What about you?'
She glared at me, 'What?'
'Well, how are you feeling?'

'Okay I guess, I mean we are about to fight one of the most powerful people on the Earth.'
I put my feet up, 'Yeah I see you're point...'

5 minutes later another official walked in, he was wearing the exact same as the last guy – a grey suit and black tie. The only reason I could tell the difference is because this guy was blond, 'Right, now that you're all here I can explain what's happening... As you know each one of you will fight one of the top three heroes, you can choose to fight who you want to fight, but discuss that later, you will fight till one of you are knocked out, or the time limit is up, there is a ten-minute time limit, your year gets a week off after the festival if you last the five minutes.'
'What if you knock out the hero?' I asked.
They all stared at me like "*you can't be serious?*"
'Well, I don't know they haven't planned for that.'
'Well, I'm sure you can come up with something. Anyway carry on.'
He cleared his throat, 'Ahem, anyway do not worry I know the two boys have football today, you're games will be played last to give you the most time to recover, if you win, again, your games will be played last to give you the most time to recover.'
We both nodded, 'Okay that is all, any questions?'
I stuck my hand up, 'Yeah erm, do we all fight at once on separate stages or?'
'Yes, whoever fights "The One" will fight last though.'
I nodded and he looked at the other two who didn't say anything. He nodded and left.
'I'll fight "The One".' I said.
The other two stared at me, 'Are you bonkers? You'll be killed!' They said.
'Well you two both wanted me on your fight teams, right? So clearly I am strong enough, and also I seem to be the only one with the balls to try so unless you have any objections.'
Neither said anything, they just stared at their feet.
'Okay then! Now that's sorted.' I got up and walked to the window.

259

'Jaeger, did you really mean it when you asked what we'd get if we beat them.' The boy questioned.

'Yeah… I imagine they'll at least start by going easy on us, I want to beat them whilst they're unaware.'

'What if they don't start easy?' Harlequin said.

I shrugged, 'I'll beat him anyway.'

'But don't you think that'll have some kind of effect of crime? If the number one hero gets beaten by a first-year?'

'Well, I'm hoping it will scare them, they're already scared of "The One" right? If a first-year beats him? They should poop themselves.'

She put her head in her hands, 'But there's no way we can beat them!' The boy cried.

'Look, whatever your name is.'

'It's Cadmus.'

Really? Who names their kid "Cadmus"?

'Look Cadmus, who cares if we win or lose? But we might as well try right?'

He looked out the window, 'Yeah I guess…'

'Come on… Let's put on a show.'

He looked at me, 'You're mad'.

'Na… Just a believer in my abilities.'

Another 10 minutes later the same official as before walked in, 'I'm presuming you've all chosen who you are going to fight?' We all nodded.

'Okay, so who's fighting last?'

'I am…'

He stared at me, 'Really?' I nodded, 'Okay, please come with me, someone will come to collect you two shortly.' He said.

I followed him to another box, he opened the door and I walked in, there they were… The top 3 heroes in the world. "The One" was stood by the window he had his usual blue and red suit on, red boots, and stripes down the arms and back, the rest was blue. The number 2 heroine was sat on one of the chairs with her feet up, she wore a blood-red outfit that covered her whole body, but stopped at the neck, plain and simple. The number 3 hero was stood with his back against the window next to Cirillo, he wore a sky-blue outfit, a proper superhero one, with a cape and everything.

They all turned to me when I walked in. "The One" laughed, 'See! I told you the kid had guts!'

The other two shook their heads, I frowned, 'Erm, what?'

'Oh nothing... Anyway, kid so you're the one who's fighting me?' I nodded, 'Nice to meet you kid, can I call you Alfie?'

'Yeah you can.'

'Okay then call me Cirillo.'

Oh yeah, I forgot his actual name was completely fancy, I really hate some of these posh names they make no sense whatsoever.

Standing before me was Cirillo, aka "The One". He was and had been the number 1 hero for a couple years by that point, and he was crazy powerful, his powers consisted of every superhuman variant possible, superspeed, superreflex, superstrength... You name it, he's got it. He wasn't the brightest, but my god was he powerful, leagues above 2nd and 3rd. He wore a blinding white outfit, kind of like Jess's...

'Erm yeah, anyway can I ask you something before the fight?'

'What is it?'

'Don't go easy on us, any of you, please, let's make this interesting.' They all stared at me, then laughed. I put my arms behind my head, completely calm.

Cirillo stopped and looked me dead in the eye, 'Wait... You're serious?'

'Yeah.'

He smiled, 'Okay then... I promise I won't go easy on you.' He held out his hand. I shook it and the official walked towards me. 'Okay kid it's time to go.'

I nodded and winked at Cirillo as I left.

The official lead me down to the field and into the waiting room where the other 2 were waiting, 'Wait by the door, the heroes will come out first then you three will be announced in age order.'

We all nodded and the guy walked off, Jess ran over, 'Alfie! We were all told to go to our stand! What's happening?'

I smiled, 'Just go to the stand... You'll see.'

261

'But I won't get there in time!'

I grabbed her arm and teleported to the stand, immediately teleporting back to the waiting area, avoiding any and all questions they could've asked me.

'That was quick.' Cadmus said.

I shrugged, 'That's teleporting for you.' He chuckled and wiped the sweat off his face, 'What's wrong you scared?'

'Aren't you?' He asked.

'Na... We'll be alright.'

'I can't believe how... Okay you are with this...'

I shrugged and heard the roar of the crowd, 'Well... I guess there's no going back now.'

The other two heroes were announced, the roar of the crowd getting louder every time – it was deafening when Cirillo arrived - then it was our turn. Cadmus went out first, attention on the challenge in front of him, not the crowd around him. Anyway there was a big cheer, then came Harlequin, as soon as she entered the spotlight her entire personality changed, she became bright and cheery, carefree, so much different from what she'd like in private, but to be fair she was up against a massive challenge.

Then it was my turn, I heard my name get announced then walked into the sunlight as soon as I heard the crowd reach its peak I hit myself with a thunderbolt and put on the cloak as usual. *They go mad every time.* I thought, smiling.

I jumped down and stood next to the other two, 'Show-off.' Harlequin grumbled.

'I told you to put on a show.' I replied.

The announcer went over the rules then called over the first fighters, Harlequin walked into the arena and smiled, but behind those eyes were a look of fear, she did not want to do this.

'This isn't a good idea.' I muttered.

'What? You were all about this a moment ago!'

'Not me... Her, she's dead scared.'

'She is?'

I nodded, 'Hopefully she'll be okay once the fighting starts, what's her power anyway?'

'Combo fighter…'

'Okay… And what does that do?'

'The more consecutive times she hits an opponent, the harder she hits, and the more she gets hit by an opponent, the less it hurts.'

'That's an amazing power!'

'Yeah, but when you're up against someone who can solidify air, the odds of you getting consecutive hits without missing or punching solid air drastically increases.'

I nodded… The fight started and Harlequin darted at her opponent, hoping to catch him off guard. It worked, kind of, she hit him, once, twice, 3, 4, 5 times before he reacted, he leapt back and solidified the air in front of her, stopping her from rushing in. She tried to run around, another wall, she tried to run around that one, another wall. Before she knew it, she was boxed in. The guy smiled, 'And now! Airhead-' (I know… Terrible name, and yes he did refer to himself in the first person) 'will unleash his ultimate move! Unbreakable box!'

The walls began moving in, trapping her in a space so small she could hardly move. Then, he tensed up, 'Harlequin run towards him!' I shouted.

She glanced at me but seemed to understand, she noticed that the wall facing Air Head had disappeared and as soon as he took off towards her, she squeezed out and unleashed her power, hitting him 10, no 20, no 30 times, uppercutting him on the last hit and sending him into the air.

'Yes!' I shouted.

'No…' Cadmus muttered, 'Once he's in the air he's unstoppable, he can now move in any direction by solidifying the air beneath his feet.

And to prove his point, the fight was over in a minute, he jumped around, waiting for an opening, and when he saw one he took it, hitting her at full force to the face and sending her sprawling. She lasted 2 minutes and 12 seconds…

'Harlequin!' I shouted, teleporting into the arena. The announcer called the match and announced Air Head as the winner. I held out my hand and healed Harlequin's head injury, 'He did this much damage with a punch?'

263

Cadmus nodded, 'And he's only number three...'

Harlequin came round after I'd healed her, 'Ugh... What happened?'

'He hit you hard.' I admitted.

'So I lost?'

'Yep.'

She hung her head, 'Ugh!'

Cadmus smiled, 'Yeah... But now it's my turn.'

'Hey, what is your power?'

He smiled, 'Imitation, I can instantly memorise and copy any technique, I can also copy powers, but that's only for about five minutes after the power is used.'

I nodded, 'Good luck.'

He nodded and climbed into the arena, ready to fight "The Princess of war". The number 2 heroine, she had the power to summon and use any weapon to perfection, that's where she got the name, it was an interesting matchup that for sure.

As soon as the match started the Princess charged him, summoning a broadsword, so he copied it, summoning a broadsword and countering, they exchanged jabs, slashing and countering, the match went on for a good 5 minutes like this, but then experience kicked in, even when Cadmus was armed with all her techniques he couldn't keep up, and when he did strike she just predicted and counterattacked. 5:27. That's how long he lasted before collapsing.

I brought him off and healed him to a point where he could stand before taking my place.

I swung my sword off of my back and planted it into the ground before leaning on it, 'So are we going to do this or what?'

Cirillo laughed, 'You are one confident kid I'll give you that.'

I smiled, 'Thanks.'

The match began and I didn't move, I chose to let Cirillo make the first move, which really could've gone either way.

He decided to launch himself at me, I looked him dead in the eye and smiled, much to his surprise, right before teleporting next to him and knocking him to the ground. The arena was silent. 'Ah sugar, I didn't kill you did I?'

He laughed and struggled to his feet, 'I must admit, I did not expect that, but neither did you!' He punched me, hoping to catch me off guard whilst he was so close to me, well he tried to punch me. I caught his fist.

'How… Are you using superstrength?' I asked.

'No.'

'What?'

I saw him tense and then I got sent flying, *So there is the superstrength…*

BANG! I slammed into the opposite wall, 'Ow.'

I got to my feet and smiled, 'This will be fun,' I summoned electricity in both hands and started hurling lightning at him, it was all he could do to dodge it, I wasn't allowing him to get any closer, as long as I kept my shots on target…

'Gotchu.'

BOOM!

Now I was on the other side of the arena in the wall, 'Okay now you're annoying me.' I muttered, spitting the blood out of my mouth and climbing out of the wall. I spread my feet and lowered my stance, 'Let's do this.'

He flew towards me and broke the sound barrier by doing so, I spun around and caught his charge, redirecting him into the wall behind me and using that momentum to take me with him, hitting him another 3 times before he hit the wall.

BOOM!

Parts of the wall crumbled around me, I stepped back, 'Is that all you've got?'

I began gathering energy around my hands and feet, ready to discharge the instant I hit him, he ran at me again, when he got within punching distance he went for my jaw, I shoved his fist aside with my left and uppercut him with my right, discharging my power as soon as I hit him, almost like he got hit twice. He lifted off his feet, only 2 maybe 3 inches, but that was enough. *How strong is this guy?* I thought. *Oh well, he's in trouble now.*

Triple kick, temple, jaw, chest, instantaneous death for an average guy.

BANG BANG BANG!

I think I broke the sound barrier 3 separate times.

'See you.'

THWOOM! He flew into the wall, I took a deep breath, the world was fading around me.

'Will you just give up?'

'I'm only just getting going!' He shouted, charging me again. I summoned a staff and began twirling it around, using it in both defence and attack, whenever he tried to hit me I diverted or blocked with one end and attacked with the other, but I couldn't hit him, I think he was actually using his superreflex now.

'Now this is a fight!' He laughed, 'I haven't had this much fun in a while!'

I summoned a tidal wave and forced him to the wall, giving myself a bit of time.

'Alright then… I guess it's time to take this seriously.' I said, running my hands through my hair and taking off the school headband.

I put all my weight on my toes and waited for the moment he started running to me. As soon as I did I teleported in front of him and kicked upwards, using his own momentum against him.

BOOM!

Another sonic boom and a huge shockwave afterwards, **CRACK!** The sound of every bone in a man's body breaking was one of the worst things I'd ever heard, I nearly threw up at the sound of it. Cirillo collapsed to the ground.

I walked back to my sword and leant on it. The roar of the crowd slowly came back to me, and so did the sight of them, I realised something
in that moment. Millions of people saw me near the peak of my calmness, but still…

No one alive had seen me at the top of *that* mountain.

I smiled as the medical team rushed Cirillo away, 'Well that was fun.'

I heard a slow clapping behind me, I turned around to see the Principal with a huge smile on his face, 'Well done!' He said.

I rubbed the back of my head, 'It was easier than I thought actually.'

266

He burst out laughing, which was a sight I never thought I'd see, 'You know what this means right? The most powerful hero in the world is a sixteen-year-old boy.'

'Do you think I'll ever lose again?'

'I imagine you will, but not because you're not strong enough, more like because you're too strong, the opponent will use your own power against you, or by a technicality.'

I nodded and leant back on my sword, 'Alfie!' A voice shouted behind me.

Jess ran up behind me and tackled me in a hug, 'What on Earth was that!'

I laughed, 'Sorry about that.'

'Why didn't you tell me?'

'Because I didn't know about it until about ten minutes before I actually did it.'

She turned to the Principal, 'You didn't tell him?'

'Nope... He had no clue.'

She stared at me, I just laughed and rubbed the back of my head, 'Oh well!'

'Wait... But there's no way you can play today! Your body must be wrecked from all the powers you used.'

'Jessica, how many powers did you see him use?'

'Well, three.'

We both stared at her.

'WAIT! You're telling me you beat him by using martial arts and your own freaking strength!'

'Yeah kind of...'

'But why? You could've won so much easier if you'd have used fire! Or even a massive lightning bolt... Or I don't know!'

I grinned, 'Yeah but what's the fun in that? I learnt a lot off of fighting him hand to hand.'

'Yeah, but you did the most damage with your feet.' She grumbled, 'Also... What the hell was that? You like, bent reality or something.'

I laughed, 'What?'

'She's not wrong, something about that kick... It was unbelievable.'

'...Huh... Cool...'

Jess slipped her hand into mine, 'You okay?'

'Yeah I'm fine.'

'Well, we're going to get you checked out anyway.'

I groaned, 'Why? I've only got a couple of bruises.'

'Yeah but you just fought the number one hero.'

'And won, I'd like to point out, does that mean I'm like, a certified hero now?'

The Principal scratched his nose, 'I mean, yes?'

'Nice.' I said, swinging my sword over my shoulder

'Alfie put the sword away, you've flexed enough today come on.'

I sighed and rolled my eyes, making my sword disappear I glanced around at the crowd, who seemed to be in complete shock and awe. I smiled.

'What?' Jess asked, seeing my face.

'Nothing... Just thinking about how I like it here.'

'Oh don't get soppy now you're the king of the world, come on let's go get you checked up.'

'But I'm king of the world.' I replied, doing my best to act innocent and badass at the same time.

'Even kings get looked after.'

I smiled, 'Fine, let's go then.' I replied, right before she dragged me to the welfare area.

A nurse sat me down on one of the beds and did a pretty extensive check up on me, x-rays, CT scans, all that weird stuff, she kept looking even though I kept telling her there was nothing wrong...

'But how? You just fought Cirillo yet there isn't one thing wrong with you.'

'Did you see what I did to him?' The nurse shook her head, 'Yeah I would look at his x-rays if you want to see why I'm fine.'

She frowned and got up, leaving to go, presumably, see Cirillo's x-rays.

'You okay Alf?' Jess asked.

'Yeah I'm fine why?'

'I don't know, it was just, in the fight, you literally had this aura of power around you.'

'What'd it look like?'

268

'It was just a flowing, red aura, looked pretty cool.'

I nodded, 'So are we going to win today or what?'

'Huh?'

'Football.'

'Oh yeah, I mean, you shouldn't play that much-'

'I told you I'm fine.' I growled.

She stared at me, 'Fine.'

The nurse walked back into the room shaking and sat down, very, very carefully, 'Who the hell are you? Are you some kind of monster?'

'Hey!' Jess shouted before I cut her off.

'No... I'm just powerful.'

She looked like she was swallowing a stone but nodded, 'Yeah you're good to go...'

I hopped off the bed, 'Lovely, come on Jess... Oh, is Cirillo awake?'

'Nope.' The nurse replied, turning her back to me.

'Okay then I guess we just go straight back.' I said, turning to Jess. She nodded and we walked out of the infirmary and back to the waiting area, where the rest of the team were waiting... As we walked down the row to our area every single pair of eyes we passed turned to us, some with envy, hatred, awe, amazement, all of them, were on me. I glanced around the room, the whole place was staring at me, I put my arms behind my head as we walked, just showing everyone that I was fine...

'WHAT ON EARTH WAS THAT?' Sam shouted as we sat down.

I laughed, 'Just a fight.'

'Just a fight? You whooped the number one hero whilst using basically no powers, you're a freaking god!'

I shrugged, 'I mean, I'm not, I just spent fourteen years practising how to fight without powers, then got powers, and had my physical ability rapidly improve, so my combat power increased in leaps and bounds rather than baby steps.'

'So... You used superstrength?'

'No... It's just that when my powers you know... Turned on, my physical attributes increased a lot easier, like... Now I can carry Jess around easily, but before... Maybe not.'

'Hey, what are you trying to say?'

269

'I'm trying to say that I was weak before... Even with all my practise.'

Everyone was silent for a moment, then, '...Oh well, it doesn't matter since you've got powers so who cares?' Zoe said.

I smiled, 'Yeah... So! Who are we playing first?'

Helena looked me dead in the eyes, 'The same team we just lost to.'

Silence throughout the team, I realised I had to say something, 'That's fine, we promised we wouldn't lose right? So we won't who cares what happened last time?' Jess avoided my eyes, I looked around at everyone, they were all staring at the floor, 'Oh come on guys! You can't all give up on me now!'

San looked up, 'He's right, we're here to win, if not, we might as well go home now.'

I nodded, mildly surprised that he was the one who spoke up, and sat back, 'You know what? He's completely right, if you aren't planning on walking onto that field and expecting a win, you can leave, right now... No hard feelings, but I don't want you on that pitch.' Not one person moved, 'Okay then.'

Helena sighed, 'He's right guys... If we go into this game thinking we're going to lose we stand no chance of winning.'

I caught her eye and sent her a silent message, *Thank you.*

Everyone started looking up, but the mood was still pretty glum...

An hour and a half later it was our turn to get redemption.

We stepped onto the field and I turned to everyone, 'Look... Guys we all know what happened last time, but now it is just ability, and we are better than anyone, so let's go out and prove it okay?'

San nodded confidently whilst everyone just kinda, looked everywhere but at me.

I sighed and walked over to the referee, shaking hands with him and the opposing captain, 'Good luck.' He said.

I smiled and turned around, 'Hey San we got kick-off.'

'Really? Okay.'

He stood over the ball and waited, the ref blew his whistle and the match got underway, San passed the ball to me and I looked up, they didn't know what to do without their powers, they tried the normal tactic but when the guy ran at me I just knocked it past him, I ran up the field and looked up, it was just me and San, I glanced back, people were moving up but not quick enough.

I sighed, 'Fine, I guess we'll do it.'

I nutmegged one then laid it off to San who dinked the ball over the backline where I latched onto it and smashed it into the net.

'Haha nice!' I said, high-fiving San. Everyone stared at us, 'See? We can do this come on!'

That goal won us the game, it told everyone that we could beat them, and we did, I think we played the best game of football I ever played in that game. We outplayed them in every area of the pitch, 45 minutes of total dominance. We got our revenge alright. When the whistle blew for the game to end, we were up 15-1. The captain of their team walked past me as I gasped for breath, 'Good luck.' I said, he glared at me like he wanted to kill me, I winked back, knowing full well he couldn't.

Jess ran over and tackled me to the floor with a hug, 'You were right! We did win!'

'Of course we did, I said we were going to, didn't I?'

She laughed and pulled me up, 'That was great.'

I put my arm around her and steered her back towards the waiting area, 'It really was.'

We walked back and sat down, I turned to everyone, 'See? It wasn't that hard!'

'Yeah well I need food!' Sam replied.

'You always need food.' I muttered, 'In fact, it's getting old.'

He pulled this stupid face until I gave him some pancakes, which shut him up for the time being...

'They'll announce the next matches in like five minutes.' Helena said.

We all nodded.

The next couple rounds went by like a breeze. We won by clear margins in all three games, 12-1, 14-4 and 11-1. And now before us were the semi-finals, we were stood on the field

271

crowded around Helena, 'Look guys, we're one win away from the finals, let's get out there and win this yeah?'

We all nodded and dispersed, I went up and did the usual shaking of the hands before getting ready, they kicked off and well, it was a tight game, there wasn't a single goal for 20 minutes, which was basically unheard of in this competition. Finally, the break came when they awarded me a freekick on the right-hand side on the edge of their box.

I turned to San, 'This isn't the best side for me but I think I can hit it in.'

'Yeah but the keeper's definitely just going to run to this corner...'

'So... What? Are you saying that I should hit this into the far corner?'

He shrugged, 'I'm saying that it's an option, and I'll be down there to head it in if it misses so...'

I nodded, 'Alright then, we'll do that.'

He nodded and ran to the opposite side, I stood over the ball and took 4 steps back, legs spread apart, breathe in, and out, and in, and go. I ran up to the ball and struck it, dead centre, a knuckleball, *Damnit!* I thought turning away, *There's no way that's going in.*

Then... A roar... I spun around, 'What?'

Barukko jumped on me, 'That was ridiculous!'

'Wait... It went in?'

He stared at me, 'That was the best goal I've ever seen you score and you didn't even see it?' I shook my head and he laughed, 'I guess that's payback for stealing my girl!'

I smiled sheepishly, 'Yeah...'

How can he act so calm about that? I wondered.

We walked back and they kicked off again, the game went another 25 minutes without another goal... Yep, that's right... I won the game with a goal I never saw... Wonderful...

Also, it turns out that it was the first and only 1-0 win of the tournament that year so yeah, cool.

Anyway... We'd gotten to the final, we hadn't reached where we wanted to be yet though, there was still a game to play. Half an hour later they called us back onto the field for the final.

We were ready to play, my boots were still warm from the last game, 'Alright guys! You know what we're here to do, let's go and do it.'

Everyone nodded and went to their positions, Helena pulled me aside, 'Hey Alfie.'

'What's up?'

'Whatever happens... Win this.'

I smiled, said, 'Roger that.' And went over to the referee, shaking hands and looking the opposition captain dead in the eye, 'We're winning this.' I said.

He grunted and turned away, *Weird guy...*

We had kick-off, so San stood over the ball and when the ref blew his whistle, passed it to me...

The game went 5 minutes without a goal, and once one was scored, it wasn't what we wanted. A floated cross into the box was missed by both our defenders and allowed their striker to latch onto it and tap it into the net, 1-0.

'Come on guys! We can still win this!'

We played our hearts out but couldn't score a goal... 10 minutes later Zoe was brought down in the box, penalty.

Myself, San and Zoe were stood over the ball, 'Zoe should take it, she won it...'

She put her hands up, 'Oh no... I don't want that responsibility, one of you two can take it.' She said, walking away.

'You take it.' I said.

He nodded and stepped back, I walked away and continued walking, Jess glanced at me, 'What are you doing?'

I smiled and kept on walking, waiting for the shout of San's celebration.

'Yes!'

I laughed, 'That's why.'

She shook her head, 'You're unbelievable.'

I put my arms behind my head, 'I know right?'

The game was back and forth from then on, but no goals, the ref blew the whistle for full time, 1-1.

'So what happens now? Penalties or extra time?'

H looked at me, 'Penalties.'

I facepalmed and groaned, 'Are you serious?'

She nodded, 'But I don't know what order!'

'Do we have to do a certain order or can we just make it up as we go?'

'I've got to announce the first five now.'

I nodded and turned to San, 'Do we just do our best five first?'

He nodded, 'But one of us two need to go fifth.'

'Okay but who?'

We couldn't decide so we decided to do it the fairest way possible, 'Rock Paper Scissors Shoot!'

I made my hand into a fist... He held his out flat, 'Damn! So what now?'

'I'm going first.'

I sighed and nodded, San stepped up to the penalty, looking the keeper dead in the eye he tucked it into the bottom left corner, sending the keeper right.

Their captain stepped up and blasted it into the net, no saving it.

Now Barukko, calm as ever, he slotted it past.

Next was their striker, who smashed it past Troy.

Now Bianca, who placed it into the top corner, where no keeper in the world could stop it.

Another one of their players stepped up, and slipped as he hit it, sending it over the bar, cheers erupted from our side, one step closer.

Sam walked over to the ball, smashed it, down the middle, saved. The keeper managed to stick his leg out and tap it over the bar!

'Aargh!' He shouted, walking back.

I patted him on the back as another player stepped up and slotted it away. 3 All.

Now... My turn... I stepped up to the ball and took a couple steps back, feet apart, go.

One Two Three and hit. I dinked the ball (or a Panenka for those that know) down the middle, the most ballsy thing a person can do in football. The keeper had already dived, goal.

We went mad, 'Alfie you dirty boy!' San shouted.

We all stopped and stared at him, 'Yeah alright San calm down.' I said laughing, he glared at me.

I walked past their fifth penalty taker, I looked straight at him and saw the fear in his eyes, I smiled.

I turned around and watched him step up, I watched him run at it and dink the ball, I watched Troy stand still and catch the ball. Silence...

I burst out laughing and the rest of the team went mad, we all sprinted to Troy. As I ran past the kid I patted him on the back, 'Oh well I guess it isn't for everyone.' I said, going to join the team.

We all jumped on top of Troy, 'This is amazing!' Jess shouted. I pulled her out of the pile and kissed her, 'Told you we'd win.' She smiled, Sam ran over and jumped on me, 'You are one ballsy son of a gun! To Panenka it in the final!' He scoffed. I smiled and high-fived him.

Everyone gathered around, 'We deserved this!' I shouted, 'Be proud of yourselves!'

Everyone smiled, Jess hugged me. The Principal walked over, 'Ahem, it's time for the trophy.'

I smiled and followed him, my arm around Jess, he led us over to a stand where the trophy sat. He picked it up and handed it to me, 'Captain.' He said, nodding.

I gladly took it and raised it above my head, everyone cheered. I laughed and kissed the trophy before passing it onto San.

After the initial celebrations with the team I was stood off to the side, talking to the Principal before I was due to talk to the press (again), 'You've become a real leader for them you know.' 'I have?'

He nodded, 'They all look up to you, even San, who hardly looks up to anyone.'

I looked at San, who was talking to the media, 'Yeah I guess.' 'Even if you don't realise it, they do, just keep doing what you're doing, it's great.'

I nodded and began walking over to take over from San, 'Thanks.'

San pulled away and fist-bumped me as I walked past.

'Hey everyone.' I said, standing in front of the dozens of mics, 'Okay, erm, yeah let's just keep this simple, one at a time please.'

A woman at the front spoke up, 'Alfie, we see you win this competition after going out disastrously in the quarter-finals of the previous football competition, surely this is the best redemption?'

I smiled, 'Yeah it really was, especially after beating them in this competition, it was the best revenge we could have asked for really.'

An old guy in the back raised his hand, 'Alfie, you're really starting to look like a leader in front of your classmates, is this something you always planned on being or...?'

I rubbed the back of my head, 'Does anyone ever plan on being the leader? I didn't really anyway, I always planned to lead by example but whether I was ever classed as the "leader" or not, that didn't bother me.'

'So... You were perfectly happy leading in the shadows, never being recognised?'

'Yeah... The important part was that the team, class, whatever, did well.'

A young guy raised his hand, 'Alfie you've already won two trophies in this tournament, are you planning on winning anymore?'

I laughed, 'Of course! I'm only in the next three fighting tournaments and that's it, but I plan on winning them all.'

'You seem confident.'

'Of course, did you see my fight earlier?'

Another woman spoke, 'Speaking of the fight earlier, how come you were able to play so much football after a fight with the number one hero?'

'Well I won, didn't I? I was pretty much unscathed, just a couple bruises that I healed myself.'

'And what of "The One"?'

'Yeah... That's all today folks, thanks!' I said and quickly exited, walking back to the Principal.

'It's like you've trained them.' He said chuckling.

'What?' I asked, confused.

'I mean that you've got them under control, they're raising their hands and everything.'

I smiled, 'Yeah.'

'Anyway… You're done for the day so you can go.'

'Okay cool, see you later.' I said, walking out of the emptying stadium.

I walked out to a pretty large crowd, I smiled, high-fived some people, then at the end of the crowd those girls from before stopped me.

'Alfie Jaeger, please, just listen to what we've got to say.'

I stopped, 'Okay…'

'Right, okay… Look, we're engineers, inventors, and we have built a device that can gauge somebody's power level.'

I frowned, 'Really? How does it work?'

She pulled a pair of glasses out of her bag, 'Put these on.'

I grabbed them and put them on, 'Woah…' The glasses looked like something out of a film, dials and bars everywhere, 'Okay. So what am I looking at?'

'They probably look quite confusing right now, but if you say "Power reading mode", it should change…'

'Power reading mode.' I said, the view changed, loads of charts popped up, a graph of attack, speed, health, creativity, strength and defence on the right, and some random facts on the left about like, height and weight and stuff.

'Wait, so I can see how strong someone is?'

They nodded, so if you look at just one of us, you can see our "attributes" as we call them.'

I looked at the girl with the crazy, mad scientist hair on the right and the graph changed, health and creativity flew all the way into their respective corners whilst all the other stats went back into the middle, 'How… Does it measure these?'

'Through a series of incredibly complicated algorithms that take a long time to explain.'

I nodded, 'Okay these are cool… Why are you showing them to me?'

'Because we want you to work with us, we can't pay you or anything but you'll always be the first to receive any products or updates that we do.'

'Okay… Do you want my number or…?'

The girl on the left nodded, 'Yeah that'd be great.'

'Okay err,' I pulled out my phone, 'here.'

They took my number and smiled, 'Okay we'll be in touch.'

'Cool.' I said, teleporting back to dorm and bumping into Jess.

'Oh hey, I was just coming to look for you!' She said, 'What took you so long?'

'Yeah erm, I met these two girls, inventors, and they showed me this piece of amazing gear that showed people's power levels.'

'Okay and...?'

'Well they asked if I'd help, like test it and stuff.'

'Well what'd you say?'

'*Well,* I said yeah if it works how they say it does I then it'd be amazing.'

She nodded, 'Okay cool, now come on inside everyone's waiting.'

I smiled and followed her in, I was welcomed to the sight of a new trophy shelf and by a big cheer, 'That looks amazing!' I said.

The trophy shelf sat in the corner of the room, a wooden base with hints of gold on the supports and on the corners, sat upon it were the trophies we'd won.

Alex beamed, 'I know right?'

Zzz... I pulled out my phone, **Unknown number has added you to a group.**

Hi Alfie, it's Alexia, the girl from earlier, the other girl in this gc is Phoebe, just making sure this is working.

I sighed, **Me – Yeah It's working.**

Phoebe – Cool.

Was that really necessary? I thought, putting the phone away and joining everyone else, 'Well everyone... I'd just like to say well done today, we deserved what we got and we got revenge on the side, we did well!'

Everyone cheered, and spread out, I sat down on one of the sofas and switched on the news, they were showing the fights from this morning.

'Hey Alfie have you seen these headlines?' Sam asked.

'What?' I replied, reading the screen, **FRAUD?** It read, 'Are you serious? Who are they accusing of being a fraud?'

'I think "The One" because he lost.'

I sighed, 'Sometimes I really hate the media.'

Jess put her head against me, 'We all do.' I switched the channel and put my arm around her, 'Thanks Alf... For today...'

I looked at her, 'What do you mean?'

'Well... If it wasn't for you, and San, we may never have gotten past the first round.'

I smiled, 'What are you on about, I had complete confidence in you guys.'

'That's what I mean, that confidence, it pushes us forwards.'

I frowned, 'Okay... Thanks, I guess?'

She chuckled and closed her eyes, 'I'm going to sleep.'

'If you're going to sleep why don't you go to bed?'

'Well because Darius is cooking for us all and I don't want to miss it.'

'He is?' I asked, craning my neck around to see if he was in the kitchen. He was, and he looked busy, 'Okay that's fair.'

She smiled and knelt her head against me, I picked her up and put her on top of me, her head now against my chest, 'Better?'

She nodded and went to sleep. I wrapped my arms around her, Sylvia came and sat down next to us, 'You two look cute together.'

'I'd be worried if we looked anything different.' I replied, Sylvia chuckled.

'How's it going?'

'Oh yeah fine... All of it, Jake, school, you know.'

I nodded, 'Are you in the volleyball team?' She nodded, 'I think that's next...'

'Yeah, I think it is, I can't wait.'

'Yeah I bet, I have literally never seen a game in my life.'

Jess mumbled something under her breath, Sylvia frowned, 'What?'

'I think she's dreaming.'

'About what?'

'God knows unless she says something clearly I've got no clue.'

She laughed, 'And even then...'

'And even then I still have no clue.' I agreed.

A couple of hours later Darius announced that the food was going to be ready in 5 minutes, so I woke Jess up.

'Food?'

'Nearly.' I said, 'Five mins.'

She nodded and stretched, 'It smells amazing.'

'It really does.' Sylvia said getting up.

'Are we going to move the tables together?' Jake suggested.

Syl shrugged, 'Yeah why not, someone help me out.'

I flicked my fingers and a gust of wind pushed the tables together, 'Oh cool.' Jake muttered.

I laughed and stood up, picking Jess up and forcing her to stand up by putting her down, 'I can't wait.' I said, Jess hopped on the spot in excitement, or she needed the toilet.

I went to grab a chair when Sylvia and Maddison stopped me, 'Ah no. Top three at the head of the table.' Maddison said, pointing to the end, I sighed and sat at the head of the table.

Jess smiled and grabbed my hand, 'Don't look so unhappy about having to sit at the head of the table.'

'Yeah but I feel like a dad!' I complained, making everyone else laugh.

Even Barukko smiled, 'Alfie if you were our Dad we'd all be dead.'

'Yeah alright.'

'...Hey Barukko, are you Japanese or Chinese?' Bianca asked.

We all stared at her, Barukko scoffed, 'Uh, what?'

'Are you Japanese or Chinese?'

'Yeah I heard the question but I'm asking where this has come from?'

She shrugged, 'Just wondering.'

'Mhmm, well anyway I'm Japanese.'

'Why'd you come here then? Long way from home don't you think?' Jason asked.

'Well I don't live in Japan, both my parents are Japanese and I've got family in Japan, but we live in England.'

He nodded, 'Okay, any more random questions to ask anyone whilst we're waiting?' Jess slapped my arm whilst drinking, 'What?'

'Yeah Alfie, what happened to your Dad?' Jake asked.

Jess spat her drink all over me and Barukko, we all stared at him, Sylvia clamped her hand over his mouth, 'Ignore that question.'

'And what about Jessica's parents?' Sam asked.

Me, Barukko and Jess shot to our feet, eyes blazing, 'Not... Another... Word...' I growled.

Sylvia and Zoe dragged the boys away, 'Have you no limit?' Zoe shouted.

Jess fell into my arms, 'Shhh... It's okay.' I whispered, rubbing her back, 'I know...'

Barukko looked at me, 'What was that?'

I shrugged, 'Not a clue, I know I asked for random questions but.' I sat back down and held Jess, everyone else studied the table, 'I'm sorry everyone, I don't know what that was about.' I stroked Jess's hair, she kept on sobbing, Darius brought over the food and I messaged Syl and Zoe to get down.

The elevator dinged and the pair walked out without the boys, I sat Jess back on the chair but she clung onto my hand, they both knelt next to her and apologised, she nodded and we all got to eating, but it was silent, I glanced at Barukko, 'Do something.' I quietly mouthed.

He shrugged, 'You know I'm the worst at that.'

I cleared my throat, 'Ahem, so the battles are next week, do all the teams have a game plan or what?'

Bianca looked up, 'Yeah we've got a game plan, but we're not telling you it.'

I shrugged, 'That's fair, we don't actually have a plan to be honest.'

'You don't?'

Barukko shook his head, 'Na... But we don't really need one.'

Natalia stared at us, 'You don't need one?'

He laughed, 'Well, we do have Jaeger here!' He said, clapping me on the back.

I grimaced, 'Yeah...'

I glanced at Jess, who hadn't even looked at her food, never mind eaten it.

I sighed, ate another spoonful of whatever amazing food Darius had cooked, and picked her up. Looking at Sylvia I mouthed, 'What's up with her?'

She stared at her, then shrugged, 'Just sad...'

I nodded and cradled her, Barukko glanced at us, 'Is she okay?'

I shook my head, 'Never seen her quite like this though.'

He nodded, Zoe and Sylvia looked over, an apologetic look in their eyes. I kissed Jess on her head, 'Are you going to talk to me?' She bumped her head against my chest, 'I'll take that as a no then.'

Once everyone finished I took Jess up to bed, 'Are you staying with me?' She nodded. I let out a pained smile and walked into my room, putting her down on the bed I got changed in the bathroom and climbed into bed, Jess putting her head on my shoulder and closed her eyes, I quickly followed suit.

The next morning I woke up to find Jess rolling around in her sleep, 'Huh... That's weird.' I said, yawning, 'She'll be fine.'

I watched her for a minute, stopping her from falling off the bed a couple of times, before getting up. I walked out onto the balcony and stared at the morning sky, it was early, the sun was only just breaking out of the horizon, the sky had turned amazing shades of red, 'Sometimes you forget how amazing the world is...'

I leant against the wall and watched the world go by, listening to Jess talking in her dreams, the birds chirping and the leaves in the trees rustling, it was a peaceful start.

That was very quickly broken...

I heard Jess scream behind me, I whipped around and saw her sat up, wide awake. Eyes wide and breathing heavily, I ran over and knelt on the edge of the bed, 'Hey what's wrong?'

She stared at the end of the bed, a tear ran down her face, 'Hey... Come on don't cry.' I said, pulling her towards me, 'What happened?'

She sobbed and grabbed onto my arm, I wrapped my arms tightly around her, 'It's okay... You're with me now, here.'

She sobbed again, 'It... It was... My p-p-parents.'

I kissed her head, 'Okay... I'm sorry...'

'B-but I saw them, with me, and you.'

I looked at her, 'What?'

'In the d-dream, we were all together, l-like a f-f-family.'

'But that isn't possible is it?' I whispered softly.

She shook her head, 'There's no way.'

I put my head back against the pillow, 'I know...' *But with my powers, is there a way?*

She stared at me, 'You're thinking of something crazy aren't you?' She sniffled.

I shrugged, 'It doesn't matter.'

She fell onto the pillow next to me, 'I'm going back to sleep.'

I got back up, 'Okay, I'm not but I won't go anywhere.'

She nodded and closed her eyes.

I waited a while then got up, heading back outside I leant against the wall and held my hand out, letting electricity flicker between my fingers, *Is it really possible?* I shook my head, *There isn't any way I could, there are just some things you can't do, right?* I shook my head again and watched the sunrise for a bit, before getting bored.

I went back inside and got changed, I kissed Jess's forehead and left a note, saying I went out and wouldn't be long. I swung my sword over my shoulder and put my cloak on before heading outside.

I jogged into the woods and found a good spot to train before summoning my wonderful grandfather.

'Wassup kiddo.'

I rolled my eyes, 'Please don't say that again.'

He laughed, 'Alright, so... I'm guessing since we're out here because you want to train?'

I swung my sword off my back and impaled it into the ground, 'Well I wouldn't call you for a nice chat...'

He laughed, 'I'm going to work you extra hard for that! Now come on, let's get started.'

We trained for 5 hours before I collapsed to my knees, 'Okay... I'm done.'

He nodded and sat down across from me, 'You've done well.'

'Yeah well I'm starving, I haven't eaten anything today!' I complained.

'Kids these days.' He muttered, 'Anyway, I'll be off then!'

I saluted casually, 'See you.'

He nodded then disappeared, I sighed and fell back onto the grass, hearing footsteps behind me, 'What do you want?'

'I was wondering where you were.' Barukko said behind me.

'Oh it'

'Oh, it's you, what's up?'

'Nothing really, just seeing what you were doing.' He said, feigning interest.

I glanced at him, 'You're being nosey, aren't you? Anyway, I was just training.'

'By yourself?'

'Na with my grandfather...' He shrugged and sat down next to me, 'Oh quick FYI I know Jess sent you, you couldn't really care less about what I was doing could you?'

He laughed, 'That obvious huh? Yeah, Jess did send me, she seems to forget how powerful you are.'

'I know right? I mean five or six months ago I'd understand but now...?'

We sat and watched the clouds float past, talking about what we were like before we came here, and about how bonkers the world is at times. We were there for another hour before Jess called us...

'Where are you two! Barukko I sent you to get him not join him!'

'Yeah... Sorry about that...'

'And you! Alfie Jaeger, you said you'd be back soon. It's been six hours!'

I laughed, 'Sorry but I was training!'

'Training shmaining, you could have at least texted me!'

I shrugged, 'Yeah okay that's fair.'

'Head back will you?'

I nodded and ended the call.

'Jeez, what a kid.' Barukko said.

I laughed, 'I know right?' I said, getting up and offering Barukko a hand, he took it and I swung my sword over my shoulder. And putting my arms behind my head, we walked back together, into the forest.

'It's about time!' Jess shouted at us as we walked through the back door.

I leant back a bit, 'Yeah alright calm down.'

She pouted and jumped onto a sofa, me and Barukko glanced at each other and shrugged, 'I'm hungry!' I said loud enough for Jess to hear, 'I wonder what food I'll make?'

And you'd never guess who jumped up and shouted pancakes...

I sighed, and turned around, grinning. She stared at me, 'You planned that didn't you?'

'Yep!' I replied enthusiastically.

She facepalmed and sat back down, probably thinking she wouldn't get pancakes. However, being the amazing boyfriend that I am, I gave her some.

'Here.' I said, passing her a plate and sitting next to her.

She smiled and stuffed her face, before remembering her manners (nice priorities), 'Thanks Alf.' She mumbled.

I ruffled her hair, 'No problem.'

She glared at me but continued to eat her pancakes.

'Hey Barukko want some pancakes?' I called, but he was already gone, 'I swear that guy is like a ninja or something.'

'Who's like a ninja?' He asked, popping up behind me.

BANG!

I may have hit him with a lightning bolt.

'Ah sugar sorry!' I said, jumping up and helping him to his feet.

He grimaced, 'It's alright, I think.'

He stood up and I glanced at the wall, it had a massive crack in it, *That's going to need fixing...*

Jess laughed, 'Really Alf, the guy only scared you!'

'Yeah but... Well, I don't know, I just blasted him he'll be fine... Probably.'

'Thanks Alfie.' He mumbled.

'No problem B.'

'I told you to not call me that.'

'It's growing on me,' Jess said, 'I might start using it!' She joked.

I smiled but Barukko didn't look half pleased, 'Oh cheer up! You can have pancakes!'

'I'll take some pancakes.' He grumbled, making me laugh.

'Alright then,' I said whilst handing him a plate, 'hey what sport is it today?'

'God knows.' Zoe replied.

'No he doesn't, he just asked the question.' Jess said.

'I told you I'm not God.'

'Jess seems to think you are.' Barukko replied.

'Yeah well she should, I'm her boyfriend, but still she shouldn't say it like that.'

'Hey look you haven't actually asked me yet!' She shouted.

I glanced at Barukko, he shrugged, we're both clueless when it comes to this stuff. Jess caught the looks on our faces and rolled her eyes, sitting back down. We finished our pancakes then Barukko turned to me, 'You wanna fight?'

'Na, I'd rather wait till the tournament, only want to whoop you when it matters.'

Jess snorted.

'What?'

'I love the confidence Alf.'

'Err, thanks...? Okay what now? We've got ages till our next competition.'

'Can I get a hug?'

'Why?'

She shrugged, 'I want a hug.' She said, holding her arms out, I sighed and picked her up.

'You're such a baby.'

'Mhmm.' She mumbled, I chuckled and walked outside before sitting down, 'Woah it's actually pretty warm today.'

'Well it is May, it should be warm most of the time.' I said.

'Yeah but still, it's like picnic weather.'

I fell back onto the grass, Jess looked at me, 'What?' I asked. She shrugged and ran her hand through my hair, 'Can we sit out here for a while?'

'Yeah why not?'

Jake and Sylvia walked outside and sat down next to us, they were so engrossed in whatever they were talking about they didn't even notice us sat there. We both stared at them, waiting for them to notice.

'Ahem.' I said, eventually, making Sylvia jump.

'Ah! What are you two doing here?'

'Seriously, you didn't notice us already here when you arrived?'

'Nope!'

Jess facepalmed and I laughed, 'Well then!'

Slowly more and more people filtered outside until the majority of the class was out here enjoying the sun.

'It's kind of like a group picnic!' Jess said, still sat on me.

'Yeah it is... It's nice.'

'Hey, do we have a barbecue?'

'Yeah it's over there why?'

Jess turned to everyone, 'Hey do we have the stuff for a barbecue?'

Darius sat up, 'Yeah why?'

She smiled and everyone else realised what she was on about, 'That's a great idea!' Jake shouted.

Jess leapt up (much to my relief) and ran over to the barbecue, 'How do you light this thing?'

'It's a charcoal one.' I said.

'Really, didn't those things go out of date forever ago?'

'Apparently they make the food taste better.' Jake replied.

'Well, there's charcoal in it...'

'I'll get a lighter!' He shouted, running inside.

'No wait!' We all called, too late, he'd gone inside.

'Oh well.' Jess said, poking the charcoal, 'He's not the WOAH!'

I'd watched it happen, Jessica poked one of the coals and it burst into flames, the rest catching fire quickly.

'Hey are you okay?' Zoe asked, running over.

She nodded, Me and Barukko locked eyes, 'Did you do that?' He silently mouthed.

I shook my head, 'Did she...?'

We both shrugged, promising we'd discuss it later, and I went over to Jess.

'Hey how'd you do that?'

'Do what?'

'Set the charcoal on fire...'

She stared at me, 'I didn't... Did I?'

I shrugged, 'I doubt it, could have just been a fluke, but it doesn't matter.'

She stared at me, 'Yeah...'

I pulled her away and let Darius get to work, I hoped he was cooking up another Jamaican masterclass, or a British one, this was a barbecue after all.

An hour and a bit later Darius had cooked up enough food to feed 20-ish hungry kids.

'I don't know how you do this.' I said.

He laughed, 'What do you mean?'

'Well,' I gestured to the table, 'How do you make enough food for thirty kids in just over an hour?'

'Magic.'

'Alfie's magic and he can't do that!' Jake shouted.

'Yeah alright.' I replied, getting up and brushing the grass off me, 'Am I sitting at the head again?'

Sylvia nodded, making Jess laugh, 'You know that's your spot forever right?'

'Yep.' I sighed whilst sitting down.

'Oh cheer up. You've got me next to you.' Jess said.

'Yeah but last time you were on me!' She stared at me, 'Sugar sorry.'

She laughed, 'I'm just messing, but I'm still going to sit with you!'

I smiled and wrapped my arms around her, 'Nothing wrong with that.'

'Aww, Alf.'

'What?'

She rolled her eyes, 'Never mind, now am I eating here or...?

'Do what you want.'

She smiled and grabbed a burger, eating it whilst hardly even moving, I laughed and grabbed a burger too.

We laughed and talked the whole afternoon, I kept that thought about Jess's power in the back of my mind the whole time, I could tell Barukko was too.

Later that night when most of us had gone to bed, I talked to him about it.

'So... What do you think?' I asked, sitting down next to him.

'I have no idea, I mean… She already has her ability developed right? So of course it will get stronger, but fire?'

'I know that's what I thought, to undergo a complete change at fifteen…'

'Yeah but you did five months ago.'

'Yeah but that's different.'

He rubbed his face, 'Yeah it is… Have you tried your power-vision on her?'

'No I haven't… But will it come up because it was only tiny?'

He shrugged, 'Not a clue, but it's worth a shot.'

I nodded, said bye to everyone still awake and headed upstairs, where Jess was already asleep.

I opened my door and found Jess asleep on the bed, I studied her as she laid there then remembered what Barukko said to me.

"Have you tried your power-vision on her?"

No, I haven't, but I will now…

I knelt down beside her and switched to power-vision… Nope… Nothing at all…

I sighed and stood up, changed then went to sleep next to her, it was another dreamless night, I was almost getting bored of sleeping (that's a lie it's great).

27 – Fight Night, but over a couple of weeks!!!

Anyway, the next week and a bit went by quickly. The girls did well in their volleyball tournament but didn't win anything. We all kept on training for the fighting tournaments, I trained with my grandfather, and then the day came for the trio's tournament...

I woke up and got changed right before Jess knocked on my door.

'You decent?' She said, poking her head around the door.

'Yeah I am.'

She walked in and stood in the middle of the room, 'It's a wonderful day to beat some people up.'

I laughed, 'When you put it like that it makes it sound like were the bad guys!'

'Well, we are to some people.'

'Yeah and when we step in that arena, everyone but me, you and Barukko are the bad guys.'

'Damn right, now shall we get going?'

'Can we have breakfast first?'

'Alfie we need to be going! Grab a croissant on the way out.'

'Ugh fine.'

She smiled and grabbed my hand, dragging me out of the room. I could tell she was excited, she was bouncing up and down in the elevator, and hardly waited for me as I grabbed some food.

'Come on!'

'Yeah alright! See you all later.' I said to everyone before Jess dragged me outside to where Barukko was waiting.

'Took you long enough.' He said.

'See?!'

I chomped on my croissant and shrugged, 'Shall we go then?'

They both nodded and we set off, me with my croissant hanging out of my mouth, and Jess and Barukko looking at me weirdly...

We arrived at the stadium to a huge crowd, and I mean, a HUGE crowd.

'Why are there so many people?'

'Well the fights are huge, especially with you here, apparently they're expecting their highest viewing numbers ever.' Jess said.
'Yeah look over there.' Barukko said, pointing past the crowds to our left, 'They're setting up screens.'
'My god yeah. Reminds me of the pictures of the World Cup back in the day.'
Jess stared at me, 'You're weird, these people are here to watch fights and it reminds you of the World Cup?'
'Yep! Now come on.' I said, carrying on walking into the waiting area.

We sat down and I glanced around, 'There is a whole lotta people in here.'
'I know, it'll be interesting to see how many go through from the battle royal.' Jess said, Barukko nodded.
'But we need to be careful, we can't afford to get cocky.'
'Meh, we probably can.' I replied.
'Just don't kill anyone.' He complained.
'I won't! Purposefully anyway.' He glared at me, 'Okay I'll do my best!'

Soon after the screens lit up and the Principal's face appeared, he introduced himself as always and welcomed everyone, before getting into the rules.
'The first round will be a battle royal, there will be two battle royals, sixty-four teams will go through from each battle, before entering a bracket-style tournament in which only one team will emerge victorious! Now without further ado… Let the fighting begin!'
The doors to the field rose open and the first set of teams were called up, this included us, so we stood up and got ready.
'You guys ready for this?' I asked.
'You know a lot of teams will either target us or run away right?' Jess said.
'Of course! We're probably favourites to win this thing, I bet most the third-years will target us, it'll be fun!'
'You two are bonkers.' Barukko grumbled, before walking into the sunlight.

'Aren't you two nervous?' Jess asked.

'Nope!' I said, sticking my hands in my pockets, 'We're visible now, shall I do the cloak thingy?'

They shrugged, so I did the cloak thingy, I blasted myself with lightning and put on the cloak. Which got a massive roar from the crowd.

'You're such a show-off.' Barukko (again) complained.

'And you're stood next to me! You're also part of this team so show off a little!'

He facepalmed which made me and Jess laugh, causing a few teams to glare at us. They were nervous.

'So... What's the plan?'

'Just... Knock out everyone who comes at us, or actively fight, either one.' Jess explained.

'Great, so defend or attack... Barukko?'

'GO!' A voice shouted from the speakers, Jess and Barukko immediately left me, not answering the question.

'Oh sugar.' I said, ducking under a fireball, 'Okay fudge it.' I muttered after getting swarmed by just about everyone.

I summoned a tidal wave and blasted everyone around me away, then blasted them with a lightning bolt whilst they were still soaked.

'Woah! Alfie Jaeger just took out eight teams in one fell swoop!' *Only eight? Great.* I thought.

It turned out that the battle royal really wasn't that hard, it was just tiring, you know how annoying it is to take out like a 100 people all firing their random powers at you? No, ok you don't, but it's so tiring, especially since I had to pull my punches so I didn't kill them.

I electrocuted, lit on fire, kicked, punched, shot, dodged, blocked and fired at every attack and person who came my way. It was a massacre (can it be a massacre if no one dies?).

The battle royal was over in 5 minutes, the siren sounded and I stood, panting, alone in a sea of unconscious bodies, it looked like something out of a horror movie. Jess and Barukko picked their way through the bodies (that sounds really bad) and met up with me.

'You had some fun didn't you?' Jess laughed.

'Look...' I gasped, 'It's not easy trying not to kill this many people.'

Barukko chuckled, 'That is one hell of a problem to have.'

I grinned, 'I know right?'

'So... How many did you take out?'

I looked around, 'A lot?'

'I mean, you're not wrong.' Jess replied, 'So what now?'

I watched everyone else on the field, 'I mean, everyone else who's not unconscious is walking back so I guess we follow them.' I said, walking inside.

I found out later that I'd knocked out 103 people in that battle royal, so yeah, do what you wish with that information.

Anyway, the second battle royal came and went, it took a lot longer than ours did but they didn't have a guy that knocked out over a 100 people. But before I knew it was time for the round of 128, and who were our first opponents?

The Ramirez sisters.

'Oh they don't like us...' I said, as we all stared at the screen.

'They are definitely going to try and kill us.' Jess agreed.

'I'm alright.' (You already know who said that)

'You're on our team, they need to beat you to win.'

'Oh yeah.'

I facepalmed, 'It's fine anyway, we are the most powerful kids in the year.'

They both nodded and we made our way onto the field, ten fights took place at a time, all three teammates would fight at the same time, and the last team standing wins, but you could literally be the last person left on your team and still win.

Anyway, we climbed into the concrete arena and looked around, it was a flat space, no wider or longer than 25 metres.

'It's not very big is it?'

'I think they get bigger the further you get in the competition.' Jess explained.

I nodded and the other three climbed into the arena they all glared at us.

'So... Who wants to take them on?'

Barukko looked at me, 'What?'

'Well… There's no point in all three of us fighting, we might as well save two of us.'

'You're confident.'

'Why shouldn't I be?'

He shrugged, 'Okay then, why don't you go first?'

I smiled, 'Alrighty then… Let's do this!' I shouted as the horn sounded to signal the start of the match.

Jess and Barukko stepped back as I blasted the triplets with a lightning bolt, sending them all flying into the walls.

'Erm, should I take it easy on them?' I asked.

They both looked past me, saw the fury in their eyes, and shook their heads.

I grinned, 'Nice.'

I turned back around and electrified my hands, letting Gabriella run at me, I planted my feet and waited. She ran straight at me, swiping at my legs to try and knock me off balance. I teleported behind her and tapped her on the neck, knocking her out.

I turned to Bianca, who was just loading a cannonball into a cannon, yep, A CANNON.

I stood there and watched her load it, then fire, I reacted instantly, spinning around and catching the ball on my foot, redirecting it back at the canon, blowing it up and knocking Bianca out with the explosion from the canon, which sent her into the wall again.

Natalia tried to copy my lightning and blast me with it, I held my hand out and absorbed it, 'Really… That's the best you've got?' I swung my sword off my back and planted it in the ground, I then proceeded to lean on it, 'Come here… Come on I've got to tell you something!'

'Err Alf?'

I didn't move, Nat walked towards me consciously, 'Come on, I need to whisper something to you.'

She walked right up next to me, I put my mouth to her ear, 'You idiot.' I whispered, putting my hand to her stomach and blasting her in the air, right before triple kicking her in the usual places. Temple, jaw, chest, unconscious.

I swung my sword back onto my back and walked back to Jess and Barukko.

'Hey guys.'

'Alfie, do you make your sword bigger when you lean on it?'

'The blade? Yeah.'

'Why?'

'Well cos it looks cooler, but it doesn't really fit on my back at that size.'

'Ohh.'

'Really, that's all you had to say about that fight?' Barukko asked.

She nodded, I laughed and put my arm around her, 'What wrong with that? Now come on, we've got to head back.' I said, exiting the arena.

We got back and sat down, 'Well, that wasn't that bad.' Barukko said.

'Well no! You two just stood there whilst I did everything!'

'Yeah, but you looked like you were having fun.' Jess said.

I shrugged, 'I did to be fair.'

She laughed, 'See!? So why should you care if you do everything?'

'I don't know! I just want you two to do something I guess.'

'That's very kind... But I'll pass.'

I laughed, 'Nope! For that you can fight the next lot.'

'Aww.' She pouted.

I glanced around and saw everyone glaring at us, 'What's your lot's problem then?' I called, 'Why do you all look so glum?' I joked.

Everyone turned away. I put my arms behind my head and smiled, 'You're one cocky kid you know that?' Barukko said in admiration.

'Yep!'

He shook his head and closed his eyes, presumably going to sleep.

'How does he do that?' I whispered.

'What... Just fall asleep instantly?' I nodded, 'Not a clue.'

I closed my eyes, 'Don't fall asleep Jess otherwise we'll miss our match.'

She nodded and I fell asleep.

After what felt like a second Jess woke us both up, telling us that our match was in 10 minutes.

'We're up against this team from Brazil, I think their main guy is called Gabriel, but that's all I remember.'

'How many guys?' I asked.

'Just the one.'

'Lucky guy.' Barukko and I mumbled. Jess glared at us, 'Sorry.'

'Anyway Jess you're fighting, I don't even know why you bothered to wake us.' Barukko yawned.

'Because I want you to at least watch me fight!'

I yawned (because Barukko yawned, I still don't know how that works), 'Do we have to?'

She started to glow, 'Yes!'

'Okay I'm sorry!' I said getting up.

'Whatever.' She grumbled.

'Oh stop being a baby.' I said, kissing her.

'You make me act like one.' She whispered.

I laughed, Barukko coughed, 'Ahem!'

'Yeah sorry, okay so erm, there's not much to say it's not like we've got a plan. Jess just shout... Or something... If you need any help.'

She smiled and nodded, 'Sure Alf, thanks for the support.'

I sat back down, 'You're welcome.'

Then they called us up to the arenas, which had increased by about a metre in every direction...

'Really? They get bigger?'

She shrugged, 'Hey I didn't say they got a lot bigger.'

I turned around and summoned a couple of chairs, I sat in one and Barukko sat in the other, 'Go on Jess!' I shouted.

The enemy three stared at us in disbelief, I could see them whispering to each other, I decided to throw up a shield just in case.

The horn sounded for the start of the match, Jess glanced back at us, we gave her a thumbs up then she lit up the stage,

literally. She blazed with light as she ran at the trio, punching one in the jaw and sending him sprawling onto the floor, the other two ran around her and towards us, Barukko tensed.
'There's no need, watch.' I said as they closed in on us. They both went for the punch at the same time, they both punched the shield at the same time. They were sent flying back into the wall, 'Idiots.' I grumbled.
Barukko laughed, 'You're mad!'
I turned my attention back to Jess, who had knocked out the first guy and was running at the girl to our left who was still climbing out of the wall.
'Aah!' She screamed, blasting a beam of light at the girl.
'Does she seem angry to you?' I asked Barukko.
He shrugged, 'Maybe she's just letting off steam.'
I turned back and found that she wasn't there anymore, she was on the other side of the arena beating the other girl up.
'Is it because of what we said earlier about the guy being lucky?'
'I have no idea.' He replied as Jess knocked the last girl out and walked over to us, 'I'm done.'
I pointed to Gabriel on the other side of the arena, who had woken up and was climbing to his feet, she glared at me, 'I'll do it.' I said, sticking my hand out and clapping him with a massive lightning bolt. The siren sounded for the end of the match and Jess gasped for breath. I put my arm around her to support her and we walked out of the arena together.
'I'm so tired!' She complained.
We laughed, 'You did well! Barukko's turn next.' I said.
She sighed, 'Can I sleep?'
I let out a pained smile and nodded, 'Sure.' I replied, picking her up.
'Thanks Alf.' She whispered, closing her eyes.
We walked back and sat down, Barukko went to sleep as well so I just sat there, in silence, waiting for the next match to be announced.

After what felt like forever, they announced the next matches, we were up first. We were up against fellow Brits, a couple of

Scottish guys who looked ripped as anything. Good job we had powers because we would not win in hand-to-hand combat (well, I would).

I woke Barukko up and we agreed to let Jess sleep, so I carried Jess as smoothly as possible over to where he was fighting.

I summoned a couple of chairs and put Jess in the other one, just in case Barukko needed help, then sat down, 'Go for it B!' I shouted.

He shot an angry look at me, 'Don't call me "B"' He called.

'Yeah whatever.' I replied, signalling him to pay attention to the 3 in front of him.

He spun around and the siren sounded, Barukko immediately summoned a wall of darkness, cutting us off from him and the enemy. I sighed and teleported past the wall, 'Really you won't let me watch?'

He laughed, 'Just looking out for my friends.' He shouted, slamming his fist into the lead guy. I levitated off the floor to watch the battle from above, out of the reach of the battle below. But the third chap decided overwise, he flew up and tried to hit me from behind. I flicked my fingers and a chunk of rock slammed into his back, sending him back down.

'You're battle is with him, not me.'

He staggered to his feet and spat the blood from his mouth, 'We've got to beat all of you to advance!' He yelled, flying at me again.

I sighed and kicked him to the floor. I descended, 'Hey you don't mind if I take this one do you?'

'Na, go for it!' He replied, knocking out the first guy with his darkness.

I smiled and turned back to the flying Scotsman, I cracked my knuckles and ran at him whilst he clambered to his feet again, I yelled and put all my strength into my fist, smashing it into his jaw. ***BANG***

He fell to the floor, his eyes had rolled to the back of his head and his face had a dent in it, 'Yep he's out.' I muttered, looking down at him.

I glanced over to Barukko, who had cornered the last guy.

I teleported over and swung my sword off my back and over my shoulder, 'How are we doing this then?'

I stared at him, I watched the fear grow in his eyes, it grew and grew, it was almost funny.

'Like this.' He replied, knocking him out with his darkness.

'Oh come on! That's no fun!' I complained.

'AJ calm down, we're here to fight, not mess around.'

'Yeah but we should have fun whilst it's easy, besides did you not see how scared he was?'

Barukko shook his head, 'You're a psycho man.'

'Na I'm just creative and bored.' I replied, putting my sword back on my back.

He stared at me, then chose to ignore my answer, 'Why do you even have the thing, you barely use it.'

I shrugged, 'I don't know, it just looks cool, and I imagine I'll have to use it at some point.'

I glanced back at Jess, who was looking around rather confused, 'Oh she's awake.'

We walked back over, 'Hey... What happened?' She asked.

'Well, we're through to the next round.'

'What? You left me sleeping whilst there was a fight? What if they attacked me?'

'Jess you had two separate shields around you, mine and Barukko's you were fine.'

She pouted, 'Yeah but still...'

'Anyway, now you're awake you can walk out of here on your own two feet, come on!'

She groaned but climbed to her feet, we walked out of the arena together, the teams were getting better, this tournament was looking like a fun one.

We sat down and took a deep breath, not really sure why but we all did, 'Hey should we all fight in the next one?' I asked.

'Na I'm alright, it's your turn next, you'll be fine.' Jess replied, bumping her head against me.

I sighed, 'Okay, but after that?'

'Yeah sure why not.'

I smiled, put my head back and stared at the ceiling, 'Hey guys? Do you ever wonder what would happen if you became too powerful?'

Barukko scoffed, 'I imagine that's only a problem you'll have.'

'Like, what if it becomes too easy, I just, do whatever I want... What do I do then?'

Jess smiled and stroked my hair, 'You'll find something.'

'I hope I don't need to.'

Barukko looked at me, 'In theory though, wouldn't it be better if you needed to, because then it means that the world would be safe because you'd be so strong that it wouldn't matter what happened.'

'Yeah, I guess you've got a point.' Jess replied, 'If he was that powerful, we'd never have to worry about supervillains ever again.'

'Exactly.' He replied, 'So there are two sides to that coin.'

I sighed, 'Yeah I guess.'

Jess wrapped her arms around me, 'Besides you've always got me, you'll be fine...'

We talked about that until it was time for our next match, our 4th out of a maximum of 7.

'Alrighty then! I'll do this shall I?'

Jess and Barukko nodded as I walked forwards. My opponents were three Spanish brothers, one in every year, they were known in Spain as the "Armada" (because they all had water powers) and apparently they were pretty famous over there. I cracked my knuckles and started summoning electricity, it crackled all around me, I kept generating more and more until storm clouds had formed overhead, and lightning bolts rained down.

'The perfect counter to water, electricity.' I said, gathering it in my hands, 'Good luck *amigos*.' I growled.

They all stared at me, blinked, then ran around me, I sighed then launched myself at the front guy, knocking him to the floor and blasting the chap behind him with a lightning bolt, before knocking out the guy I was stood on. I turned the final guy, who was staring at me from across the arena, I swung my sword off

my back and launched it at him, impaling him against the wall it
sunk to its hilt, he couldn't move.

'Hey, do one of you guys want to finish this?'

'Na we're alright!' Jess called.

I shrugged and walked towards him I held my hand out and
gathered so much lightning in my hand I could morph it into a
sphere of not-very-niceness. I held it out, 'Bye-bye.' I said,
before knocking him out with it.

Jess and Barukko burst into applause, 'Bravo!' She said, 'A truly
magnificent performance!'

I bowed to them and walked out.

Jess and Barukko glanced at each other then followed me out.

I put my sword on my back and went back to the waiting area, I
walked down the row of teams towards our bit, listening to the
whispers as I walked down.

"Scary", Meh, that didn't bother me.

"That kid there", Not a clue what they were on about, so don't
care.

But then there's my favourite, I heard this guy call me a
"thunder god" which I liked, so I shot him a look of approval
and carried on walking.

'Hey Alfie!' Jess said, catching back up to me, 'What's going on?'

I put my arms behind my head, 'What do you mean?'

'Well to say you just beat up three guys you don't seem very
happy.'

'Should I be?'

'Well, you normally are.'

I sighed, 'Yeah well... Its... Nothing...'

'That's a lie.'

I stayed silent.

'Hmph! Fine then!' She said, stomping her foot and sitting down
across from me. Right before closing her eyes.

'What'd you do?' Barukko said, sitting down next to me.

I shrugged and closed my eyes, 'Wake me when the next fight
comes around.'

He nodded. And before I knew it I was fast asleep.

Finally, dreams came to me, sadly it was nothing new, I awoke in the destroyed city I'd been in before, I was lying on the ground again and I only just got up to see Jess and Barukko get blasted to nothing, I screamed in rage again, I screamed and screamed till I could no more, then my vision went black again, I awoke in a house, on my knees, a picture of Jess smashed on the floor, I had a rope in my hand...

My vision went black again and I awoke in front of Jess and Barukko, I screamed in rage and blasted the guy to dust. A brilliant white beam of power blasted from my hands... So much power...

'Hey... Alf!'

I sat up. Eyes wide. Breathing heavily. I glanced around the room, my eyes were blurry but I could still tell what was happening. A lot of people were staring at me, *Great. This will spread like wildfire.*

I focused on Jess and Barukko in front of me. They were both studying me, worry in their eyes.

'Alf are you okay?'

I gripped the arms of the chair, trying to calm my breathing... I nodded slightly, but they weren't convinced, 'You can sit out this fight if you want. We've got this.' She continued.

I shook my head, *Why do my dreams bother me so much? They're just made-up things in my head, right?*

I took Barukko's outstretched hand and he pulled me up, 'Come on, we've got a fight to win.'

I nodded and put my cloak on. Swinging my sword over my shoulder I walked out onto the field and into the sunlight, 'Let's finish this.' I said, taking a deep breath.

They both nodded and we climbed into our arena, a now 50-metre square area surrounded by concrete with the boxing arena sides built on top of that. It was getting big enough to have some fun in.

These 3 girls entered the other side, they were dressed all posh and... Vibrant. One was wearing pink, another blue, and the third purple.

'What on Earth?' I muttered.

Jess gasped, 'Aww! I know these three! They're all sisters, third years! And they're famous for fashion design, I'm a huge fan! They travel all over the world for their shows!'

Barukko and I stared at her, *Really?*

'Okay… So what are their powers?' Barukko asked.

'One can control ribbons, the other has powers of the aurora, and the third and most powerful has the enchantment of love, so don't fall for it.'

'Powers of the aurora?' I asked.

'Yeah, I think it's just like healing abilities and some magical barriers.'

Barukko nodded, 'So more of a support than an attacker.'

Jess agreed, 'So shall we?'

We all nodded and activated our powers, Jess lit up and Barukko did the opposite. I grinned and began building up electricity, deciding to stick to the "thunder god" name for as long as possible.

I pointed my sword at the three of them and saw the fear in their eyes, we sure were a terrifying sight.

A lightning bolt erupted from the tip of my sword and forced the girls to scatter, we all attacked simultaneously, each going for our own opponent, Jess blasted the ribbons girl into the wall, then dived in, Barukko shrouded himself and his opponent in darkness, thinking that without light she'd be powerless.

I stared my opponent dead in the eye, electricity flickering around me, I launched my sword and forced her to duck, too slow to move she couldn't avoid the forthcoming bolt of lightning, which struck her body.

'Aaargh!' She screamed, collapsing to her knees. I walked up to her, yanking my sword out of the ground behind her I gripped it.

'You know, I don't normally like hitting girls, but right now I couldn't really care less.'

She spat at me and struggled to her feet, 'You're a monster.'

I grinned and had a flashback to when Jess called me a God.

'Na, I'm just a god.' I replied, right before she kissed me…

Ahhh, so that's how the love thing works, I was right then. I thought, right before I swept her off of her feet with my sword and punched her back down, embedding her in the ground.

She coughed up blood, 'How... Did my power... Not work?'

'Because I watch movies.' I said, pulling a bit of clear tape off of my lips, 'It's not quite what I saw, but it did the job.'

I raised my hand and summoned a lightning bolt, knocking her out.

I took a deep breath and looked around, Jess was beating the living daylights out of her opponent, Barukko wasn't having as much luck...

It turns out that her power is almost a perfect counter to Barukko's, the aura she summoned was fighting Barukko's darkness. I sighed and leapt into the fight, literally, I slammed into the ground next to Barukko and blasted her with a lightning bolt before she could put a barrier up.

'You struggling?'

He laughed, 'Yeah... I guess we aren't the best matchup for me.'

I twirled my sword, 'No kidding, but you don't look hurt.'

'Because her attacks do nothing, she just defends and heals herself!' He complained.

I nodded and glanced around, 'So... Any ideas?'

'Well I was hoping you could just beat her.'

'I mean, if I build up a lot of power I probably could do it in one, but it'll take a minute to build up.'

He nodded, 'I'll cover you then.' He said, before blasting one of her barriers.

I nodded and started to build up power in my right hand and formed a plan.

It went like this; I'd build up power in my hand, then once ready I'd attack, opening her up and then activating superstrength, hitting her ridiculously hard, then, in the moment of impact, I'd release all my power into her, basically hitting her twice, that was sure to knock her out... Right?

I planted my feet and hoped I didn't kill her, 'Barukko! I'm ready!'

He nodded and blasted down the barrier between myself and her. I charged forward, running through another barrier with my shoulder, then arriving within punching range I smiled, and slammed my fist into her jaw, more like an uppercut than I'd planned, but oh well.

The initial hit lifted her off of her feet, and the eruption of power... Well, that sent her flying.

Fwoosh!

Barukko and I watched her fly straight up, I had to block out the sun with my hand, 'I think you hit her too hard.' Barukko said.

I nodded, 'Wait! She's coming back down.'

'Well I'd be worried if you hit her into orbit.' He grumbled, 'Are you going to catch her or...?'

'Ermm...' I held out my hand and summoned a massive body of water.

'You know it's going to be like concrete if she hits that right?'

'I know but I think I can mess with the surface tension a little...' I replied, holding my hand just above the water.

'She's coming...! 3...2...1...Now.'

Thwoom!

I gave Barukko a thumbs up and dived into the water, gathering the girl up off the bottom and bringing her back up before dumping her off onto the side, I climbed out of the water and grabbed my sword, dripping wet I stood next to Barukko.

'You aren't going to dry yourself?'

'Huh? Oh yeah!' I said, increasing my body temperature and drying myself. We both stood there, watching Jess exchange blows with her opponent, 'Do you think we should help her?'

She glanced over and saw us watching her, 'You could help! Aah!'

That last part was because the ribbons wrapped around her and lifted her off her feet, 'I think we should assist, don't you?' I asked Barukko.

He chuckled, 'Yes, I guess we should.'

'HEY! We're a team aren't we?' Jess shouted.

I swung my sword over my shoulder and we started to walk towards her, well, it was more like a stroll. We took our sweet time, whilst Jess struggle and the girl watched us.

'How can you be so cocky? My teammates will…'

'I'm sorry? What was that?' I asked, 'You're teammates will what? I saved one from drowning and the other I fried, how can't I be cocky?'

Her face paled, then it turned to rage, she spun Jess upside down and tightened the ribbons, 'But I've got a hostage!'

We stopped 10 metres from her, 'And…?'

Her face paled again, 'Wha… I'll knock her out!'

'And then what? If anything you'd be better leaving her awake so she can actually be of use to you because once you knock her out we're free to do what we want.'

She frowned, 'Wait… Are you helping me?'

I shrugged, 'I mean, it's not like you can win, even if you're teammates wake up we'll just knock them out again.'

She grinned, 'That's what you think.' She growled, tightening the rope even more, making Jess go red.

I looked at Barukko, 'Shall we finish this?'

He shrugged, 'Sure.'

I held my hand out and set her ribbons on fire, causing her to drop Jess in panic, I caught her, 'Hey Jess.'

She frowned and crossed her arms, 'Jerk.'

I smiled and put her down before turning my attention back to ribbons on the overside of the arena, who was desperately trying to put out the fire in the water, I clenched my fist and the flames grew even more, her eyes widened and right before the flames hit her, she fainted.

Barukko winced, 'How are the fires burning on the water?'

I shrugged, 'I don't know but I'm not complaining.'

He high-fived me, 'Nice… But she only fainted do we need to knock her out or…?'

Almost in response to his question the siren sounded for the end of the game, Jess walked over to me and Barukko, still grumbling something under her breath, 'I can't believe you two!' She complained, 'You just left me hanging!'

'Could've been worse.' Barukko said.

'How?'

'Well, you could've been wearing a skirt.' He offered.

'Eww what?'

I looked at him, 'That is pretty weird.'

He shrugged and set off walking, 'Just being honest.'

Jess glanced at me, I shrugged and put my arm around her whilst putting my sword on my back, 'Come on... We've got to get out of here for now.'

She smiled, putting her head against my shoulder she said, 'How easy is it for you?'

'What?'

'To win this thing?'

'Oh, probably pretty easy.'

She laughed, 'You're amazing.'

'I know right?' I joked, entering the waiting area, where the numbers were dwindling. *Not many left... I wonder how strong these kids are...*

We decided not to sleep from now on, the matches were too close together for it to have any effect. I mean, half an hour, it's not that long, Jess still disagrees to this day.

Anyway, half an hour later we were staring at the screen, we were up against one of the teams that wanted me, Brandon, Harlequin and this other guy called Jeff, 'Their number two is called Jeff? Ha!' Jess shouted.

I smiled, 'Yeah whatever, let's just beat these guys alright?'

'We're second, also AJ the arena is full size, literally the whole arena so go mad okay?' Barukko asked.

I cracked my knuckles, 'Ooo yay. This will be fun.'

We walked up to the door and I leant against the wall, looking out into the arena I said, 'I can't believe so many people want to watch a bunch of teenagers fight.'

Barukko whistled, 'When you put it that way it sounds a bit like slavery.'

'I didn't know you could whistle.'

'Can't you?' I shook my head, 'Huh.'

We heard another roar from the crowd and we looked over, there were two nightmare-black dragons in the middle of the arena, the one furthest from us had a person on top, the one closer didn't.

307

'Hmm, I wonder if that's Cadmus.'

'Who?' They both asked.

'Our third year's number one, he can copy powers.'

'But how can you tell that it's him?'

'Well because there's no person on top, basically everyone with dragons needs to be in contact with them to control them, only the best can control them without touching them, because they're just so powerful.'

Jess stared at me, 'How... Do you know this?'

'Well because I want one.'

'You want a dragon?'

'Yeah why not.'

'Err, because it's a dragon.'

'I like it!' Barukko finally said, 'But this fight is pretty one-sided.'

I looked over, he was right, Cadmus' team were pounding the dragon, it was a 3v1, he stood no chance. Then finally, who I presumed was Cadmus opened his massive mouth and shot a bolt of jet-black lightning at the other dragon, knocking him and his owner out.

I stood upright and turned to the others, 'You two ready for this?'

They both nodded and we turned to look at the arena, we waited for Cadmus to come back, I nodded to him as he walked past, then we walked into the limelight once more.

We climbed into the arena and stood facing Brandon, Harlequin and Jeff (the name cracks me up every time).

'So... Who's fighting who?' Barukko asked.

'Well we need to be smart with Harlequin, we need to take her out in the smallest amount of punches possible, so we either all go for her or leave her till the end.'

He nodded, 'I think we should leave her.'

We nodded, 'I mean, she'll probably target me first, so we should be fine.'

The siren sounded and they started running at us, Jeff hung back, so I decided to focus on him, that was until the wings sprouted out of his back, pure white feathery wings that stopped me in my tracks. Both Jess and Barukko looked at me, 'What?'

I pointed to Jeff, 'That is not good.' I replied, ducking under Harlequin's punch.

I teleported behind Brandon and punched him in the face, only to find that he'd made himself super dense and that it nearly broke my hand, 'Ow!' I complained, leaping away and smashing him with a lightning bolt, before avoiding a ray of power from Jeff.

'This is a pain!' I complained.

Jess ran past me, blasting Jeff with her own beam of light, 'I know but get on with it!'

I sighed and swung my sword off my back, twirling it around I diverted one of Brandon's attacks and looked around, *What can I do?*

I decided to fight him head-on, I flew up to him and slashed, he dodged easily, 'God he's fast.' I muttered, deciding to just teleport everywhere. I kept chasing him, and chasing him, and chasing him, until I got one lucky punch, and then it was over for him, he hit the floor, I teleported again and hit him from the left, then the right, then from above, finally I uppercut him into the sky, 'Huh, nice.' I muttered, watching him come back down. I set off running and leapt into the sky, triple tornado kicking him, and sending him into the opposite wall, he was gone.

I turned around to see Barukko get smashed into the ground, I winced, he didn't get back up, 'Great.' I muttered, opening up the ground around Brandon and sinking him to his head. I walked over, 'Sorry Brandon.' I said, knocking him out, I turned around and saw Jess, breathing heavily, in front of me. I ran over, 'Hey you okay?'

She nodded, but didn't get up, 'Yeah... Just gimme a minute, or five.'

I nodded and teleported her into the corner, 'Stay down until you're good to go.'

She nodded and I turned around, Harlequin was glaring at me, 'I've never lost to a kid younger than me and I don't plan on that changing!' She shouted.

I shrugged, 'That's a shame isn't it.'

She bellowed, 'Aah!' And charged, I stood my ground, trying to build up as much power as possible before hitting her, I needed to take as few hits as possible, whilst not hitting her until I could finish her. It wasn't going to be easy.

I dodged every attack I could, teleporting around the arena and building up energy until I felt it was time. But then she ran up behind me, I had no idea where she came from, I spun around, too panicked to teleport, so I did what came naturally, I ran towards her and slid under her punch and past her, before leaping up and changing my direction, I twirled round and hit her in the jaw, reversing the momentum of her movement, it hurt, but it wouldn't knock her out, but then the power I'd built up erupted through my fist and she slammed into the floor, making a person-shaped dent in the ground.

Jess winced, 'She's got to be unconscious right?'

'I hope she is, I mean, I hit her hard.'

She climbed to her feet and walked over, 'Are you okay?'

I nodded, 'I'm fine, Barukko however...' I said, looking over, 'I think I should wake him.'

She nodded and continued to stare at Harlequin, I walked over to Barukko and knelt down beside him, holding out my hands over him and summoning the healing power, in a minute or so he was awake and able to stand up.

'Thanks man.' He said, standing up.

I nodded and stood up as well. It was over. 'We should move out, we've only got half an hour or so before our next fight.'

We all walked out of the arena and into the waiting area, where I healed the worst of our wounds, well, Barukko and Jess's.

'So then...' Barukko said once I'd finished healing him, 'What can you tell us about the third years.'

I sighed, 'Not much, I only know Cadmus, so the other two's abilities are a mystery to me. But Cadmus can literally copy any move and commit it to memory, he can also copy powers for up to about five minutes after they're used.'

They both nodded, 'Any counters?' Barukko asked.

'Other than just being stronger than him, I have no idea.'

Jess looked at me, 'You okay?'

I nodded and kissed her, 'We'll win this thing, I don't care how strong they are.'

She smiled, 'I know, because you're the strongest.'

'Ahem.' Barukko coughed, 'I'm here too.'

I laughed, 'Oh I know, now let's get out there and win this.'

We walked back out onto the field, where our enemy were already waiting.

'Shall we?' I asked.

They both nodded as the siren sounded, and with the roar of the crowd, we all ran into battle. The guy on the right disappeared immediately, *Invisibility?*

I switched to thermal vision and still couldn't find him, *No, complete camouflage, okay I'll have to listen out for him.*

I decided to focus on the other two, Cadmus had already copied Jess's power and was fighting Barukko, whilst Jess was fighting the other girl.

'Use your power!' I shouted to her.

'I...I can't!' She shouted, avoiding a punch.

I switched to power-view, *Power absorption, great.* I thought, diving in and punching her, she could hold her own against Jess, but with both of us attacking her at once, she had no chance. With my devastating martial arts and Jess's raw fighting style, she couldn't block both out blows at once, and eventually, she lost control of our powers. I felt all of my power surge back into me and I blasted her into the air with a blast of power, 'Jess!' I signalled.

She nodded and blasted her with a ray of light, sending her into the wall (we did that a lot).

'A little help over here!' Barukko shouted, he appeared to be being beaten by two people, even though I could only see one.

'Hang on!' I shouted, teleporting over and using superstrength to blast Cadmus across the arena, he staggered to his feet as I teleported next to him, right before launching him into the air with a massive geyser.

'Finish him so we can get camo!' Jess shouted.

I nodded and summoned a massive lightning bolt, right before it impacted another geyser of water erupted from under my feet and launched me into my geyser, right as the lightning bolt hit...

The electricity burned us both, we both screamed in pain, the geyser shut off immediately, we both fell to the ground.

Jess screamed, 'Alfie!' But we both climbed to our feet, my shirt was in tatters and I was burnt all over, but Cadmus was definitely worse for wear. His whole body was burnt and all his clothes were in tatters, I winced and went to grab some shurikens from my pocket before realising the cloak wasn't there.

'Great.' I muttered, teleporting over and pulling my sword out the ground, 'Alright then, if I can't beat you using powers, I won't use them.'

Immediately a geyser shot out from beneath my feet and I only just managed to dodge it, but I quickly turned it around, I redirected it onto Cadmus before diving at him, slashing my sword across his chest, ripping a line across it.

It didn't faze him, he dived back at me and tackled me to the ground, forcing me to drop my sword.

'Aargh!' I yelled and a shockwave blasted from me, sending Cadmus flying into the air. I shouted again and charged to where he was landing but Barukko and Jess beat me to it, they both blasted him with their power, knocking him out too.

I put my hands on my knees, gasping for breath, 'Are you okay?' Jess shouted.

I gave her a thumbs-up and stood up, but I still couldn't calm my breathing, I stood with my hands on my hips and watched Jess and Barukko try to fight camo-guy, I tried to figure out a way to fight him.

As I stood there, thinking about how I could see him, I realised something, I didn't have to *see* him, I just had to know where he was...

'Hey guys! I've got an idea!'

They both looked over, fatal mistake.

Bang Bang!

They both crumpled to the floor, 'Great.' I muttered, teleporting over and grabbing them both, putting them on the top of the wall, out of danger, then teleporting back down.

'Alright, then let's do this.' I muttered, setting my hands alight.
'Haha! What can you do? You can't even see me!' He bellowed.
I smiled and slammed my hands into the floor, fire slowly
spread across the floor, leaving just a thin strip for us to stand, I
began walking forwards, knowing that he was somewhere in
front of me, I glanced behind me, fire was spreading from my
footprints, he was definitely in front of me.
'Wha... What are you doing?' He shouted.
'I don't need to see you, I just need to know where you are.'
'O...Of course you do! You can't punch me if you can't see me.'
I shrugged and electricity crackled around my hands, there
must have been 20 metres between me and the wall, 'That's
fine.'
Lightning began raining down from above, the skies turned grey
and my eyes lit up blue, 'Who said I was going to punch you?'
He became visible, 'Okay okay! I concede!'
'You never read the rules did you, you can only lose in the final
by knockout.'
His face paled and I clasped my hands together, electricity
gathered from all around me, 'Bye!' I said in a cheery voice,
before blasting him through the wall and out of the stadium.
BANG... BANG... BANG… BOOM!
I peered through the hole at the park outside and winced, I'd
hit him harder than I meant to.
The clouds began to clear and I teleported up to Jess and
Barukko, healing them until they woke up then sitting on the
wall of the arena whilst they came to their senses.
Barukko came around first, 'What... Happened over there?'
'I'll tell you when Jess comes round.'
He nodded, 'So I'm guessing we won?' I nodded, 'So why are we
up here?'
'I had to get you out the way, and we're still up here because
they're getting out the trophy.'
'Hey guys.' Jess mumbled, sitting up and stretching next to me.
'We won.' I said.
'Yeah, I guessed that since you and Barukko are both awake.'
He scratched his nose, 'Yeah actually I got knocked out too, it
was just AJ.'

'And... What's that hole?'

'Yeah, that was my fault.' I said, rubbing the back of my head, 'There's a guy somewhere out there.'

She stared at me, 'Why?'

'Well because once you two got knocked out I put you on the wall, then set the whole arena on fire apart from one tiny strip of land, then blasted a lightning bolt down said strip of land, and did that.' I said, nodding to the hole.

'Did you need to hit him that hard?'

'Nope!'

She facepalmed, 'Hey look don't complain we won this didn't we?'

'Well... You kinda won everything.' She said.

'Na because you two won your own fights!'

'Yeah but that was like, you letting us have a turn on the console, you could easily do it yourself but you felt bad.' Barukko joined in.

I jumped off the wall, 'Fine, believe what you want to.' I said, walking over to the rest of the class.

'Alfie that was mad!' Jake said, everyone else agreed.

I rubbed the back of my head, 'Thanks, how'd it look from the stands.'

'Well, the media are calling you a "thunder god" because of you're performance in this tournament.' Zoe grumbled.

'Sorry I'm kind of stealing your thunder aren't I?'

'Ha nice!' Sam said, high-fiving me.

'Shut up shorty.'

'Hey you always take the mickey out of me why can't I do it to you?'

'You are one of the least Italian sounding people I've ever met.' I muttered.

'Hey! I'm basically only Italian by name at this point so shut it!' Sylvia smiled and rubbed her eyes, I glanced at Jake, who shrugged.

'You tired?' I asked.

'Huh? Oh me? Na.'

I stared at her, but she offered me no more information.

Jess joined me, 'You should probably put a shirt on since yours... Doesn't really exist.'

I glanced down at my pretty much non-existent t-shirt, I ripped the rest off and summoned my cloak and put my sword on my back, 'Will that do?'

'Yeah that'll more than do.' She said, staring at me.

'Yeah you look hot.' Maddison said.

'Hey he's mine!' Jess claimed, wrapping her arms around my arm.

'Yeah alright then let's go.' I said, walking over to the trophy area, where the Principal was waiting.

'Well... You've won another thing!' The Principal said, chuckling.

I put my hands in my pockets, 'Yep! What's the record?'

'By a single person? Four.'

'Ooo, so I can beat it.'

'And there's the invitational too.'

'Oh yeah, is there anyone even near my trophy count?'

'I think there's someone from India who's won two, but I think she's only competing in one more so all you've got to do is win one I guess.'

'Hang on though... What if I only win the doubles, but still have the most, because Jess will have the same number as me.'

'Well then you both go.'

'Nice!' Jess said.

'Okay well anyway, the press is down here and everything's ready, so go over there! Take what's yours!'

I smiled and nodded, we all walked over and I picked up the trophy, 'Well, it was fun.' I said, holding it above my head.

'Yeah for you.' Jess grumbled, taking the trophy off of me, 'We actually had to work for it.'

I laughed and knelt down, 'Get on my shoulders.'

'Why?'

'Why not?'

She shrugged and climbed on, I stood up and glanced at Barukko who was staring at the trophy, I clapped him on the back and glanced up at Jess, who had a huge smile on her face as she looked around at the crowd. I glanced at the Principal, who winked at me and pointed to the press.

I nodded but took my time with the other two before going to see them...

I said the usual hello and asking them for one at a time before accepting any questions, the first one was pretty routine:

'Hey Alfie, you've won another trophy today, you're third, how happy are you?'

'Yeah I'm delighted, I mean, it's always great to win something and to do it with my friends is even better.'

'Do you plan on going again?'

I laughed, 'What kind of question is that? Who wouldn't want to go again, I want to win everything I can.'

A girl popped up in the middle, 'Oh Jaeger,' (I liked that name), 'the media have been calling you a "thunder god" because of your recurring use of lightning in this competition, was that planned or...?'

'Well... Not originally no, but around the fifth or fourth match I heard someone call me it and I quite liked it, so I decided to stick with it as much as I could for the competition.'

Everyone nodded, 'Alfie, you seemed to hit your opponents a little too hard sometimes, is this a problem?'

I stared at him, 'What?'

'Well, you know, is it a problem?'

'I have no idea what you're on about, I admit that I did hit one or two people a bit hard, but is it a problem? No.'

'Okay and last bit from us I think Alfie, any word to the fans around the world?'

'I have fans?'

They laughed, 'Yeah you're pretty famous.'

'Huh cool, well erm, in that case, I guess I'd say... Never give up, I know I'm a one in a trillion case but look at me, I was hopeless at fourteen, and I'm not saying what happened to me will happen to you, but don't give up, the worst thing you can do is give up...'

'Sounds like you need a quote with that.' One joked.

I smiled, 'Well, I guess one quote comes to mind... Do you all remember the guy who gave up? Neither does anyone else.'

I nodded and walked away, leaving them in a sort of, dumb-founded silence, maybe because the quote sounded like it was a conversation starter and I had just walked off… Or maybe not…

I walked past Barukko and high-fived him as he went to talk to the press, 'Good luck.' I said, he nodded.

I walked over and stood next to the Principal, 'You're becoming a real pillar you know.'

I looked at him, 'What do you mean by that?'

'Well, you're sixteen and have already done what most dream of, people look up to you, even the older ones.'

I scoffed, 'Yeah right, it's not like I'm a realistic person to aim to be like, not because I'm so powerful but because I'm a one in a trillion case.'

He sighed, 'But you give people hope, hope that their life will get bigger. In the history classes they teach you that when the World Government was put in power that the whole world was happy and that's just…'

'Rubbish,' I finished, 'You can never have everyone in the world happy, it's just impossible.'

He nodded, 'But you can give everyone in the world hope, they may hate you, but you can give them hope.'

I looked around at the stadium, which was slowly starting to filter out, 'Yeah… I just don't see how people look up to me.'

The Principal started walking away, 'You beat the number one hero in a fight, remember that.'

I spun around as Jess walked past me and handed me the trophy, 'I can't be bothered to deal with these lot.' She said.

'They're not that bad.' I replied.

'Yeah but you actually did a lot, we just get grilled because we don't do a lot.'

'Look you asked me to do that.'

She sighed, 'I know but still.'

I kissed her forehead, 'Okay, I'll see you in a bit.'

She smiled, 'Okay.'

I watched her go and then teleported up to the roof with the trophy, I sat with my legs dangling over the edge and I watched the crowds slowly dissipate out of the stadium and back down the path behind me, I was up there for a good while before I noticed the cameras, some of the press had found me and I decided that it was time to move on...

Bzzz...

I pulled my phone out of my pocket, it was Alexia.

Alexia – Hey, we've got a prototype that we want to test in the battle royal of the doubles teams, can you do it?

Me – Yeah sure, do you have it with you now or?

Alexia – No but we will have it for the morning of the doubles so we'll give it to you then and explain it all.

Me – Okay

And with that I teleported back to dorm.

I teleported straight into the middle of the commune area, nearly smacking Nat in the face with the trophy.

'Ah! Alfie watch where you're teleporting!'

I apologised and put the trophy on the shelf, before sitting down on the sofa and taking a deep sigh of relief.

'What's up thunder god?' Sam said, Zoe slapped him.

I smiled, 'Not much, I need a sleep.'

'So do I.' Jess said, walking through the door, 'Where have you been?'

'Sorry I was on the stadium.'

There was a brief pause when everyone processed what I said, 'Wait… On the stadium?' Sam asked.

'Yeah.'

'Not in it, on it… Like… The roof?'

'Yeah… Why?'

'Estas loco bro.' Tiago said.

'Gracias mi amigo.' I replied, surprising him.

'De nada.' He replied cautiously, making me laugh.

'Ah yes!' Sam said, 'Words that make sense to me!' He shouted, we all laughed at him.

'But seriously where'd you learn that?' He asked.

'What you think I can't teach myself?'

'He's been using the internet.' Jess clarified.

'Ohh…' Everyone chorused, I stared at Jess, 'Why'd you have to spoil it?'

'Because… why not?' She said, sitting down next to me and putting her head against me.

I put my arm around her, and closed my eyes, falling asleep by accident.

I woke up sometime later completely alone, I sat up and looked around, it was dark outside and inside, with only the stair lights on. I sighed, *Great, I've been asleep for god knows how long and I won't be able to sleep now, might as well go play.*

I stood up and grabbed a basketball, heading outside and across the path to the basketball court, where I started putting up shots.

I was out there for a while before someone else came out, Jess wandered outside and began walking down the path, not even noticing me.

I swear there must be at least one person awake in our dorm at all times.

I tossed the ball by the door and jogged to catch up with her.

'Hey... What's up?'

'Huh...' She said, 'Oh... Not much, just can't sleep.'

'Why? What's up?'

'Nothing! Seriously, I just... I don't know I just can't.'

'Yeah I'm the same.'

'Yeah but we left you asleep.'

'I know! I was so confused when I woke up!'

Jess laughed but kept her eyes on the sky. I studied her, every little detail on her face, it all looked amazing in the moonlight.

'The stars are amazing.' She said in awe.

I sat down and rested on my hands, 'Yeah I guess, I've never really thought of it.'

'Why not?'

'Well... I guess it's because what you see up there, they don't even exist anymore.'

She looked at me out of the corner of her eye, 'What?'

'You don't know? Basically what you see is... Millions of years old, because the speed of light is so well... Slow, these stars are dead or dying really, I mean they last a while but they've never really interested me.'

'Why though, they still exist to us.'

'I guess... It's because they're not permanent.'

'Nothing is permanent.'

'I like to think some things are permanent, or at least, will always exist.'

'Like what?'

I sighed, 'I guess... Hope, determination.'

'What, so emotions?'

I nodded, 'What else is?'

'Death.'

I shrugged, 'Even that might not be.'

She scoffed, 'You can't be serious.' I looked up at her, 'You can't...'

She leant over and put her face in her hands, 'Jess...' I mumbled.

'You can't you'd be destroying the whole importance of life if you never died...'

'Life would have no meaning... I know.'

'But then again, if you live a life long enough...'

'Something good will come your way eventually...'

She looked at me and smiled, 'I think we've got something good.'

I kissed her, 'Couldn't agree more.'

She put her head against my chest and laid down next to me, 'Stories are permanent Alf.'

I smiled, 'The essence of stories are permanent, the joy of reading them, and experiencing them, that's the permanent part, the stories themselves, not so much.'

'Yeah but... We have stories from six thousand years ago.'

I shrugged, 'Yeah but, that's not forever.'

'It's a long time.'

'Everything's a long time depending on how you look at it.'

'You're weird.'

'You're the one who likes looking at dead things!'

She smiled, 'I might go to sleep.'

'If you go to sleep I'm teleporting us inside because I don't want us catching a cold.'

She rolled over onto me, 'Yeah whatever.'

I sighed and wrapped my arms around her, then waited for her to go to sleep then I teleported us up to my room, where I quickly went to sleep too...

The next morning I woke up to the patter of rain on the windows, my curtains were wide open but it was so dark I hardly noticed.

I rubbed my eyes and sighed, I could feel Jess laid next to me. I tilted my head to look out the window, it could've been midnight, midday, or armageddon, you could not tell.

My head fell against the pillow and I put my arms behind my head, Jess stirred next to me, her eyes opened and she looked up at me, 'Hey Alf...'

I smiled, brushed the hair off her face and whispered, 'Hey baby.'

She smiled and snuggled up against me, 'What time is it?'

'Not a clue. Could be morning or evening for all I know.'

'It is raining.'

'I know, the best kind of weather to do what we're going to do.'

'What are we going to do?'

'Absolutely nothing.' I smiled, putting my arm around her.

She shuffled on top of me and curled into a ball, 'Perfect.'

We spent half the day laid together, then I got bored and went on my pc, with Jess still asleep behind me I hopped on some competitive games and absolutely *slayed*. It's a shame I wasn't in a tournament because I was in top form.

Anyway, that day went by pretty quick, and we entered the day before the duos tournament (they allowed two days for injuries).

I was downstairs by 7 and having just eaten breakfast I headed out for training, without my Grandfather this time, I was sparring against Jess.

'You ready?' I asked, planting my sword in the ground and tossing my cloak on it, 'Okay let's put another added challenge in, if you grab the cloak you can...'

'I can ask you to do one thing and you have to do it?' She suggested.

I shrugged, 'Yeah sure.'

She smiled and hopped on her toes, from one foot to the other, 'So I can just grab it?'

I planted my feet, 'Well, in theory.'

She shot off, running straight for the cloak, I put a stop to that immediately, throwing a stone wall up that stopped right next to me.

She frowned, 'You want me to fight you, don't you?'

I grinned, 'Of course, it wouldn't be fighting practise if you didn't.'

I charged at her and slid under her light beam, knicking her leg with a knife as I passed her. She fell to her knee, grunting in pain. Then she spun around, eyes glowing a harsh red, she held out her hand and blasted another beam at me, I dodged it easily.

She smiled and spun around, running for the cloak on the other side of the wall, I sighed and teleported to the other side, right in front of her.

BANG!

I flew into the sword, taking it out and flying another 50 metres. I didn't think, I just teleported back and hit her through the wall, I winced. She staggered to her feet, her whole body glowing, 'Sorry Jess I didn't mean to...'

I stopped because she held her hand out, I stared at it, and in it, was my cloak.

I spun around to look behind me, 'Huh? Wait... Huh?'

I looked back at her, she smiled and fell onto her butt, 'I win...'

I looked back once more, still confused about what had happened, before sitting down next to her, 'Sorry if I hit you too hard.'

She spat out some blood, 'I'm alright.' She replied, putting her head on my shoulder. I put my hand to her stomach and healed whatever damage was there, she relaxed a little, 'So much for sparring practice then?'

I chuckled, 'I didn't expect you to win so quickly!'

She let out a pained smile, 'Yeah well... I get to choose now right?'

'Yeah, but you don't have to choose now!' I said, 'Don't rush it!'

She closed her eyes, 'Okay... I'll think about it.

I put my arm around her and stared at the sky, we sat there in peace, until Jess got bored... and hungry...

'Alf?'

'Yeah?'

'I'm bored.'

I sighed, 'Do you want to do something then?' Her stomach rumbled, '...Or do you want to go back?'

She smiled sheepishly. I groaned and stood up, offering out my hand to Jess, she took it and together we walked back to dorm.

'You're mad aren't you?'

I put my arms behind my head, 'What makes you say that?'

'A couple of things.' She replied.

I glanced across at her, 'Like what?'

'Just how you're acting, and that I won the challenge, and how I acted after, and...'

'And?'

'And the fact you aren't holding my hand.'

I looked at her, 'That bothers you?'

She nodded, 'You always do!'

I smiled, 'Yeah I guess...'

'Yeah what? You're mad?'

'I... Don't know...'

She grabbed my hand, 'Alfie... What's up?'

'Honestly... I'm not sure, I just feel like rubbish.'

She studied me, she gingerly wrapped her arms around me, 'You know you can talk to me right?'

I stood there, motionless, a knot in my chest, 'I know... I just... Can't...'

She pulled away, her eyes shimmering with tears, 'Come on... Let's go back.' She said, trying to keep it together, for my sake. We walked back in silence, my hand sitting limply in Jess's. We got back to dorm and I went straight up to my room, I felt Jess and Syl watch me go.

I walked upstairs and climbed into the shower, fully dressed again...

I lost it, I burst into tears, I'm not even sure why, but I did... I stood in the shower, tears streaming down my face, not making a sound. Eventually, I climbed out of the shower and into bed, trying to get the knot in my stomach to unwind, I curled into a ball and closed my eyes, hoping to go to sleep. And it did, but not without its consequences...

I awoke again in a dark room, sat at a table, there were 6 others at this table, it was too dark to make out any features. We were staring at this hologram of the world, red dots were sat in various places, Brazil, Japan, Italy, Egypt, Greece, China, and Isreal.

'We've got a problem.' An unmoving, male voice said to my right.

'No kidding,' Another voice that sounded surprisingly like Jess's replied, 'We aren't powerful enough to split up and deal with all these at once.'

'I mean… He is.' A younger girl replied.

'Well yeah, obviously.' The other girl replied.

'So what? We all travel together and AJ just teleports us everywhere?' The young one replied.

'I don't see why not.' The guy replied.

A younger boy's voice chimed in, 'But aren't we being a bit too reliant on Alfie?'

The whole room began to shake, everyone leapt up but me and ran for the door behind me. The room shook so violently my eyes went blurry, chunks of the ceiling fell onto the table, more chunks fell until rays of light burst through, I looked up to see a large part of the roof fall on my head, I panicked. My vision went dark, and I woke up.

My eyes flew open and I found myself breathing heavily, Jess snapped awake in the chair that she'd rolled beside my bed, she gripped my hand, 'You okay?'

I nodded, trying to steady my breathing, 'Yeah…'

'Another dream?'

I nodded again. She studied me, 'Are you feeling better today?'

I rubbed my face, 'I mean I've been awake a minute, but I feel better.'

She smiled, 'Good.'

I pulled her onto the bed and kissed her, 'You didn't have to sleep on the chair you know.'

'Yeah, but I didn't want to disturb you.'

'I don't care.' She smiled and I put my forehead against hers, 'I love you.'

She kissed me and smiled, 'I love you too.'

There was a knock at the door, 'Come in!' Jess called as I sat up properly, the door opened and Sylvia walked in, 'Good timing, he's just woken up.'

I frowned, 'Huh? What's going on?'

'Nothing.' Jess replied, 'Have you talked to the Principal?'

She nodded, 'Yeah, he's putting your match last but he can't delay it any more than that.'

'Okay, how long have we got?'

'Like an hour and a bit from now.'

'Wait... What time is it?' I interrupted.

'Half nine.' Jess replied, 'So get up, we've got to be at the arena soon.'

I sighed and climbed out of bed, showered, then changed, I met Jess downstairs, she was ready to go.

'Come on Alf, we don't have that long!'

I shrugged, popping a spoonful of cereal in my mouth, 'We've got at least half an hour, we'll be fine. We can always teleport.'

She looked annoyed but didn't reply, turning to watch the TV and leave me in peace.

A couple of minutes later the elevator doors slid open and San walked out, eyes bloodshot as if he'd been crying. We both watched him walk out the door, not even noticing us. We glanced at each other and shrugged, deciding it was better to leave him be.

After I finished we walked out the door and headed in the direction of the stadium, we were about halfway there when I remembered something.

'Oh sugar.' I muttered, pulling out my phone.

Jess glanced at me, 'What?'

I tapped through my apps until I found my messages, Alexia had sent me like 15 messages.

Me – Hey sorry it's been a long couple of days, can I meet you outside the stadium in 5?

She replied instantly.

Alexia – Yes!!!

I sighed and put my arms behind my head, 'You're going to meet Alexia and Phoebe by the looks of it!' I said as the stadium came into view.

'What?'

'We're… Or I'm… going to test their tech out, so I've got to meet outside the stadium.'

She nodded but didn't say anything, as we got to the stadium I found the girls and got the glasses. They told me just to leave it on "power reading mode" for today. I nodded and jogged back to Jess.

'They just look like sunglasses,' She noted, 'you actually suit them.'

I smiled, 'I know right? Now come on, we've got a tournament to win.'

We walked into the waiting area with all eyes on us, only 20 minutes before our first fight, a battle royal, again.

They called the last 50 teams forward (there'd already been three other battle royals) and I and Jess stood up.

'You know they'll probably target us right?' She said.

'Or run away from us.' I laughed.

She chuckled as we walked out into the sunlight, 'Either way-'

'I'm going to beat up some people.'

'What if you just put in minimal effort? Like just didn't move but zapped loads of people anyway?'

I thought about it… 'Hmm, I like it so why not?' I said, grinning as we took our place in the middle of the arena, yep, we made ourselves a target.

I left my cloak off and put my hands in my pockets, 'You ready?' I asked, looking over my shoulder at Jess.

She nodded and I put the glasses on, scanning the arena and comparing everyone's power to mine, not one came close…

The sire sounded and chaos ensued. Everyone either ran towards or away from us, just like I'd predicted. Jess ran off and I didn't move, an electrical storm gathered above my head, it kept building until lightning was raining down around me, it must have been a terrifying sight, everyone faltered at the edge of the clouds as they saw the first few get struck by the lightning and knocked out.

I sighed and put more energy into the storm, forcing it to expand and encompass the other contestants, forcing them to run at me. It was a barrage on the senses, thundering bangs, blinding flashes, and the blistering heat from the bolts.

Not one person made it within 10 metres of me, the game ended and Jess picked her way through the battlefield of unconscious bodies, I must have taken out 20-25 teams, and 34 went out altogether.

'Have you even moved?' Jess asked, standing next to me.

'Nope.' I replied, yawning.

She laughed and put her arms around me, 'That's ridiculous.'

I put my hand over hers, 'I know right?'

She pulled me back to the waiting area, where the screens were already showing the first-round matchups, who were we up against?

Only the tag-team that was set to win this thing, well, until we turned up.

We were up against two Italians, one was called Mario (of course, what else would he be called) and the other was called Monica, on paper they should hate each other, but this isn't on paper, so they worked perfectly together.

Mario was a fire-user, and Monica was a water-bender, apparently there's a difference, for Monica's to work there needs to be an existing body of water, whereas Mario can just make fire.

I had no idea how Monica was going to be able to use her power since there weren't any bodies of water in the arena, but who was I to complain.

We walked out onto the arena, another 25-by-25 metre arena, and stuffed my hands in my pockets.

'I hate the top-seeded teams, they've not really done anything to prove they have the best chance of winning this thing.'

'I mean, they have won this thing twice, out of a possible two times.'

I sighed, 'I know, but I mean, we're about to beat these kids without me even moving.'

'You do also know that we'll be the top seed for everything next year right?'

'I couldn't really care less.' I replied, beginning to gather a storm.

She smiled, 'Those sunglasses really suit you.'

I nodded and looked over to our opponents, their charts popped up with a comparison to mine, it was actually closer than I expected, well, until the storm exploded and then my attack and defence surged, *Huh, it fluctuates.* I thought, *Nice.* The siren had already sounded but the Italians had yet to move, so Jess forced them to, she held out her hands and beams of light blasted right at them, splitting them up and forcing them to run towards my storm, they tried to run at me but lightning stopped them in their tracks, and the few times they got past I just manipulated the bolt to follow them. All whilst keeping my hands in my pockets.

As Mario blasted Jessica and myself with fire, I began to notice small puddles of water forming after he'd fired. *Do they use science to make water appear?*

Now I'm not fully sure how they do it, but I think it's something to do with condensation.

After a minute of running them around they regrouped opposite us, they were both panting but Monica had a smile on her face finally.

I grinned, 'Oh are you happy now? Good.' I shouted, blasting every puddle of water with lightning, causing it to evaporate. Her smile faltered, making me laugh, 'Didn't like that, did you? I'm not dumb you know...' I turned to Jess, 'Hey can you grab my sword off my back and plant it in the ground please?'

She nodded and did as I asked, I concentrated all the lightning onto the sword until it was literally emitting electricity, I nodded, 'You can use that if you want.'

She stared at me, 'It won't hurt?'

'Na you'll be okay.'

She nodded and walked gingerly towards it, grabbing the grip and lifting it out the ground, 'It feels perfect.'

'Sick, I hoped it would, I messed with the weight a bit.'

'Yeah because you have yours ridiculously heavy.'

I nodded, signalling to the two behind her, 'You might want to watch them, not me.'

She spun around and immediately blocked a punch with the sword, which was a big mistake on Monica's part. Mainly because of the ridiculous amount of energy stored in the sword, which meant that when she punched it, she was immediately knocked out, cold.

Mario stared at us, Jess stood to the right of me with my sword over her shoulder, the sword back into its longsword shape, and me with my eyes glowing with electricity and the clouds above our head, he must've been wetting himself.

'Alfie you don't have your cloak on.' Jess stated.

'Huh? Oh yeah…' I shrugged, 'Oh well, I don't need it.'

She tossed the sword back into the ground by my feet and summoned a spear made of light.

I stared at her, 'Wh…?'

She smiled, 'You're not the only one with tricks.'

I laughed, 'You wanna see tricks?'

The sword lifted out the ground and hovered in front of me, Jess's jaw dropped, 'Perfect weapon control?!'

'Not quite, I can't get the sword to change shape or anything, it's more like telekinesis or something.'

She stared at the sword, 'Yeah… Still, it's cool.'

I smiled and the sword swung round so the point was facing Mario, 'Shall we finish this?'

Jess sprinted towards Mario with my sword tailing behind, she launched her spear at him, he blew it aside easily, but appeared to forget about my sword, he noticed it at the last moment and jumped to avoid the sword. It sliced through his leg.

'Aargh!' He screamed as the electricity discharged into his leg. He fell to the floor then struggled to his feet, his right leg was limp, the electricity had paralyzed it, the match was as good as won.

I finally moved, I walked slowly towards Mario, who was breathing heavily and had that look in his eyes. The look of a wild animal trapped in a corner, desperate to get out, there was only one look worse…

I stood next to my sword when the hilt touched me and it morphed into the massive broadsword/longsword combo I've grown to love. It spun onto its side and the side of my mouth tugged up, right before clattering the side of his head and knocking him out.

Jess winced, 'That sounded painful.'

'When does it not?' I replied, turning back to the waiting area. She shrugged and caught up to me, making her spear disappear as well. I caught my sword and swung it over my back. Jess put her head against me and we walked back into the waiting area in silence.

Another hour and a half later (I was, and still am, fed up of waiting for fights by this point) but it was going to be worth the wait, or we hoped.

It wasn't.

We were up against these two newbies who, as far as I knew, had never seen combat before until this tournament. Jess wiped the floor with them, I just watched I'm not going to lie.

The round of 16 match after that was definitely a good one, I can tell you that. Jess was asleep next to me when the matches were announced.

Barukko Knox & Gabriella Ramirez Vs Alfie Jaeger & Jessica Verose

'Oh sugar.' I woke Jess up and explained the situation, and we were the third fight, so we were up on the field in 5 minutes, looking across at a rather happy-looking pair of people.

'This will be fun.' I muttered, planting my sword in the ground and putting my hands in my pockets again.

She looked at me, 'You're still going with the "no movement" thing?'

I shrugged, 'Yeah why not?'

The siren sounded and they both stood there, watching us. I was quite okay with this because it allowed me to build my storm up (I know right, original, but it worked so shut up). Suddenly the whole arena was swallowed in darkness, I sighed and dispersed the storm, instead summoning a ring of fire around me to fight Barukko's darkness, I could see Jess on the opposite side of the arena too.

Bang!

Suddenly Jess's light disappeared.

'Jess?' I called out, no reply. *Oh great, a 2v1.*

I drew upon my massive reserve of power and expelled the darkness, revealing Barukko and Gabriella, 10 metres away from me on opposite sides, in front and behind. They both looked very confused.

I grinned, 'Surprise.'

Boom!

A massive shockwave blasted from within me and blew them both of their feet, I pulled out 6 shurikens and flicked them at Barukko and Gabriella, sticking them to the wall. They both struggled to release themselves, Barukko managed to wriggle out of his shirt but Gabriella was stuck whether by choice or not I don't know.

Barukko slammed his hands into the floor and a wave of darkness erupted. I flicked my hand and a wall of rock emerged, blocking his attack, I swung my arm upwards and the wall came apart, shaping the stones into spikes as it did so. Then I made a pushing motion and the spikes launched themselves at Barukko pinning him into the ground, with spikes impaling themselves in his hands and feet, I winced. I knocked him out quickly then strolled over to Gabby, who was still struggling on the wall.

(Now I'm going to hold my hands up now and say this before you carry on, I don't know what came over me, I was probably a bit harsh.)

I put my hand over her face and her eyes widened, 'Bye-bye.' I said, before sending a wave of power through my palm and into her head, knocking it against the wall with incredible power and knocking her out cold.

I teleported over to Jess and picked her up, carrying her out of the arena without looking back.

I woke her up when I got back inside and told her what had happened.

'So you had to move?'

'Just a little bit.'

She smiled and put her head on my shoulder. I put my arm around her and went to sleep.

An hour later it was the quarter-finals and the matchups were being announced, one by one the names appeared on the screen, then it was us, the last match, and we were up against two chicks (ugh, that's an ugly word), from a school all the way in Japan, one was Japanese and the other Korean, they were both ninjas (it was a ninja school). We walked up onto the field and knocked them both out in under a minute, they weren't any good, just quick.

Anyway, the semi-finals were basically the same, we were up against some British kids in the year above, we beat them too.

Before we knew it we were in the final... I walked out onto the field and blasted myself with lightning, finally putting on the cloak. Jess caught up and stood next to me, 'Glad you're finally deciding to try.'

I shrugged, 'Not really, I'm just putting on a show.'

Our opponents in the final were old ones, well for me anyway. We were up against Tan Orugun and the sleep girl from the tournament who knew Barukko.

'Jess? Don't let the girl touch you, at all.' I emphasised.

She glanced at me, but nodded, 'The Tan guy can increase his speed right?'

I nodded, 'But only for a short period of time.'

She nodded and summoned her spear of light again, I gave it the once-over then turned to face the pair.

The siren blared as I tossed my sword into the ground and did what the world was loving, I began to gather a storm. The sleep girl (whose name I just found out was Carena) ran straight for me, I sighed and levitated 15 feet in the air, out of reach from both, which was both a smart and dumb choice, depending on whether you're Jess or myself. They both ran at Jess, forcing her to burst into light and run towards me.

'Alfie!' She shouted.

I sighed and lightning began pounding the ground around me, I flicked my finger and a couple bolts darted past Jess and at Tan and Carena behind me, forcing them both to halt the chase and dodge the lightning before they got blown off their feet.

Jess ran underneath me, 'Thanks.'

I nodded and closed my eyes, 'Let's do this.' Instantly hundreds of bolts of lightning hurled themselves at me, charging me with millions of volts of electricity.

I dropped to the ground next to Jess, little arcs of electricity erupting from within me, and striking the ground around my feet. Jess took a step back and stared at me, 'After you then.'

I opened my eyes and grabbed my sword, swinging it over my shoulder I walked towards Tan and Carena, who were paralysed in fear.

I got within 15 metres and stopped, tossing my sword into the air, where it lodged into the ground, they both stared at me, the electric-blue glow had disappeared from my eyes.

'See ya.'

Boom!

All the electricity I'd stored in the sword exploded outwards at once, Tan had tried to run away but only got 2 metres before being knocked out, Carena was out cold too. I brushed myself off and spun around, Jess was staring at me.

'What?' I asked.

'You're scary.' She replied, unblinking.

'I know right?' I grinned.

'That's not...'

My face dropped and I walked over, 'What's up?'

She took a deep breath, 'Maybe just... Dial it back a bit.'

I stared at her, she took another, shaky, breath, I was watching her bravery dissipate before me, I wrapped my arms around her.

'I'm sorry.' I whispered.

She clung onto my shirt, 'It's okay.'

I kissed her forehead and pulled away, 'Well, we won.'

She smiled gingerly, 'Yeah we did.'

I grabbed her hand and lifted it into the air, the whole stadium roared.

'How many trophies now Alf?'

'Four... I think.'

She rubbed her face, 'You're unbelievable.' I stared at her, she stared back, 'What... Ohh, yeah okay I see why you're staring... Back... Yeah.' I laughed.

'Go talk to everyone if you want, I'm going to talk to the Principal.'

She nodded and went to talk to everyone, thankfully everyone else who'd competed in the tournament was fine and had been watching from the stand.

'So! That's four.' The Principal said as I stood next to him.

I nodded, 'Just have to win the solo tourney next to beat the record.'

'Well, you could just win the invitational.'

I smiled, 'I could win both.'

He shrugged, 'You could, but then it just gets harder for you to break the record next time around.'

I laughed, 'What if I just be a one-season wonder? After this festival I just retire?'

'Something tells me you're too competitive for that.'

I put my arms behind my head and glanced behind me, Jess was still talking to the others. I said goodbye to the Principal then teleported over.

'Yeah he's ridiculous, honestly I almost feel helpless because he just does everything...' Jess finally noticed I was here.

'What's up guys!' I said, choosing not to comment.

'Not much.' Barukko grumbled, his hands and feet still bandaged, making me wince, 'You did well out there, even though you hardly tried.'

'You weren't so bad yourself, I mean you knocked out...' I stopped when I caught Jess glaring at me.

He chuckled, 'Anyway I'll talk to you later, now go get your trophy.'

I smiled and nodded, pulling Jess out of her conversation with Zoe and Sylvia, past the Principal and over to the trophy stand.

'Ladies first.' I said, bowing, jokingly.

She stuck her tongue out but grabbed the trophy anyway, giving it the once over before holding it in the air, the whole stadium cheered, when she passed it to me I told her to stand still and put it on her head, much to her discomfort.

She glared at me, 'Really Alf?'

I winked, 'It looks good on you!'

She crossed her arms, 'But you need to hold onto it so it doesn't fall off my head! It's not practical.'

'Really, you're not bothered about the fact that you have a trophy on your head, just about how practical it is?'

She shrugged and turned around, walking away as I took it off her head.

I spun around and saw the Principal stood there, my face dropped, 'Press again?'

He shook his head, much to my relief, 'They're fed up with speaking to you!' He joked.

I smiled and gripped the trophy in one hand, 'I'll be off then!'

He nodded and I walked out the arena, going to catch up to Jess and the others, but I still had to hand the glasses back to Alexia. I found her and handed them back, she said the data and testing had proved "useful" but I'm not sure how, I mean I wore them nearly the whole time but still, I don't get it.

Anyway, I set off walking again, down the path and past the first and second set of dorms, past the groups of kids, wandering around the park, until I got to my dorm, I was about to turn towards the front door when I noticed Jess, alone, on the floor of the basketball court, facing the sky.

The thought of leaving her alone crossed my mind, but I decided against it, I put the trophy down at the entrance and put my hands in my pockets, she didn't notice me come in and sit next to her. I studied her face, there was a sadness in her eyes, after a while she blinked back to reality and noticed me sat there, watching her.

'Oh... Hey Alfie.'

'You okay?' I asked.

'Yeah it's just... I feel so helpless when I fight with you...'

'I know...'

'But you don't! You don't have that problem!'

'I spent the first fifteen years of my life hiding behind others.' I grumbled.

She looked at me.

'I know... Believe me, I know.'

'I've been at the top for so long, but now...'

I put my arm around her, 'But I'm a one in a trillion case, you know that.'

'I need to get stronger!' She complained.

'You will! I mean, you beat me didn't you?'

'But you weren't going all out.'

'Wasn't I?'

She sighed and closed her eyes.

'Look... Jess... You're extremely powerful, you can't be comparing yourself to me because no one is like me, it's like comparing a dwarf to a seven-foot-tall centre at shot-blocking.'
'I know but still, it hurts.'
I kissed her, 'I'm sorry.'
She smiled gingerly, 'It's not your fault.'
'But still, you shouldn't feel this way.'
'Oh please, even you can't be perfect.'
I sighed, Jess put her head on my shoulder, 'I'm going to get stronger, I know I will, I'll work harder than anyone else.'
I looked at her out of the corner of my eye, slightly worried, 'I know you will.' I replied.
We sat in silence for a while, my hand over hers, eventually my legs went numb and I went inside, leaving Jess to think, I presumed she was anyway.
We spent the rest of the evening messing around, Jess came in after a while and sat down next to me, and did what she did best, stuffed her face. Without saying much though...

Anyway, after like, 6 hours I went up to my room, leaving everyone else to do whatever they were doing. I showered and climbed into my chair, switching on my PC and entering the solo invitational tournament I'd been invited to last week, I put my headphones on and joined the lobby. Once the game started I popped off, well, kind of, I ended up placing 4th and won like, a grand, but I wasn't due any tournaments for a long time so I'd have to make it last a while.
Almost immediately after I'd finished Jess walked through the door and fell back onto the bed.
I spun round in my chair, 'Hey you okay?'
She put her hand to her forehead and sighed, 'Yeah I'm alright.'
'That's a lie.'
'Yeah it is...'
I got the feeling that she didn't want to talk about it, so I climbed onto the bed and Jess put her head on my lap, I stuck on some random movie that Jess liked, I didn't watch it, just her, watching her face go through all the emotions whilst watching it, it almost made me laugh.

Eventually, she went to sleep on me and I had to put her under the covers so she wouldn't catch a cold, I went too shortly after, and another night of dreamless sleep came and went...

30 - I lose a fight, well, you'll see...

I woke up the next morning expecting to do nothing but sleep all day with Jess.

That whole plan was ruined when I woke up and realised that Jess was not with me, and in fact had left me a note saying that she'd gone off to train. I sighed and sat up, rubbing the tiredness out of my eyes I looked outside, it was an alright day, a blue sky with splotches of unmoving clouds. I yawned and went to get changed, sticking on the usual joggers, jacket and high-tops before heading to the roof to find where Jess was at. I looked out across the park, scanning the numerous clearings for any signs of training, after 30 seconds of looking I noticed a fairly large group of people, 7 or 8 maybe, in a clearing directly out the back of the dorm, a couple of hundred metres into the forest. I jumped off the roof and walked into the forest, trusting that I'd find them in the endless swaths of trees.

Eventually, after 5 minutes of walking I came upon the group, they were in fact my fellow dorm mates, but I didn't walk into the opening immediately, I hung back, just behind the tree line and watched them all train. They were all working so hard, blocking, dodging, punching and blasting each other, they were surprising even, except Jess, who seemed a lot stronger than everyone else, and honestly, I thought she was holding back. Eventually, I stepped into the light of the sun and leant against the tree, letting them train in peace until one of them noticed me.

After a *long* time they decided to take a break and Jess glanced around and noticed me, arms folded with my back against the tree, her eyes widened and she walked over.

'How long have you been here?' She asked.

'Not too long.' I lied.

'You should've joined in.' She replied.

I shook my head, 'I'm good, it's my day off.'

'Work hard until it's your day off right?' Barukko called.

'Oh shut up you! It's not like I need it.'

He shrugged and turned back around, I smiled and put my hands behind my head.

'Be nice.' Jess chided, 'They're working hard.'

'I know.'

She raised her eyebrow, 'I thought you hadn't been here for long.'

'You know I've been here for a while, but I don't mind I only came to watch.'

'You could at least help, you know, offer tips and stuff.'

'Yeah I can do that, I mean, I don't know how much help I am with powers, especially with yours and Barukko's since I can't do them yet.'

She smiled, 'And I'm thankful for that, now come on, you can at least give them tips on hand-to-hand combat or something.'

I shifted my weight off my back and onto my feet before standing next to Barukko and offering some advice on Jess's technique with her spear. We spent the next 5 hours training, it started off as no-rules combat but it eventually became hand-to-hand because I was so "adept" at it.

'I'm telling you guys if I got my grandfather over here he'd be a better teacher than me, and he knows more.'

'Yeah but we like you.' Queenie replied, taking a sip of her water.

I shrugged, 'I know but still.'

Jess rolled her eyes, 'Stop saying that!'

'It is quite annoying.' Queenie agreed, 'You could just stop speaking.'

I chose to be silent that time, much to the annoyance of the girls, which confused me profusely.

As we walked back to dorm I had a chat with Queenie and Tiago.

'So, you guys ready for the solos competition?'

They both nodded gingerly, 'I guess so,' Tiago replied, 'but honestly it scares me when I fight, usually I've got a couple of very powerful teammates by my side, but with the solo tournament I won't.'

'You'll do fine.' Q replied, 'I mean, we can always help each other in the battle royal right?' I nodded, 'Are you teaming up with anyone Alfie?' She asked.

'Depends, if Jess or Barukko want to then I will, but I'm not particularly fussed.'

Queenie sighed, 'Must be nice to not be "fussed" about needing a teammate.'

I laughed, 'It's only our first year! You've got plenty of time, I wouldn't worry about it, and remember in the battle royal the aim isn't to win, it's to survive.'

They both nodded and walked away.

I put my arms behind my head and made my cloak and sword disappear before turning the corner to the dorm and stopping, everyone walked past me and into the dorm, even Jess. I sighed and followed them in...

The next morning came after another night's dreamless sleep. I woke up, changed and ate breakfast before heading to the arena, over half our dorm was in our waiting area.

There were four separate battle royals, each with over a hundred people in, that number would be cut down to 64 by the time we were done, then it was a bracket-style tournament, last man standing wins.

I was in the third battle royal, the majority of us had made it through already, with only Ulva and Darius not making it through (well, of those that had already fought), me and Jess were the only two from our dorm in the third battle royal.

We were all called up to the field and I walked out into the sunlight, much to the disappointment of everyone in front and behind me, who were hoping to face anyone but me (which made me smile a little bit). I glanced at Jess and we locked eyes, I gave her a nod of encouragement before walking into the middle of the field, everyone else moved to the edges.

The interesting thing about this battlefield is that it wasn't flat, there were jagged spikes of rock everywhere, caves too, *it'll be a pain to find people.*

The siren sounded and all hell broke loose, well, no one ran at me.

I sighed and gathered a storm before building a massive 30-foot-tall spire beneath me, lifting me above the battlefield and giving me a bird's eye view. I put my hands in my pockets and directed lightning all over the place, zapping kids and knocking them out, all whilst avoiding Jess.

When my back was turned to her I heard an ear-piercing scream and I instantly knew who it was. I spun around and teleported to her, who was out in the open, some random kid stood above her, Jess was bleeding through her stomach. As soon as I arrived (aka instantly) I blasted the kid into the sky and tossed him aside with a gust of wind before carrying Jess under some cover.

'You okay?' I asked.

She glared at me, 'Do I look okay? No! It really hurts!'

I sighed and sat her on me, holding my hand above the cut on both sides, whatever he used had pierced her through, thankfully missing all the major organs, but she was bleeding badly, all the colour had drained from her face. I threw up a shield and began healing her.

Her breathing was rapid and uneven, 'I don't... Feel... Good...'

I stared at her, 'Stay awake, you'll be fine I can stop the bleeding but you need to stay awake.'

She nodded but swayed from side to side, I really had to stop the bleeding, I could finish healing her once the match was done.

Eventually I managed to stop the bleeding, but the colour wasn't returning to her face, I kissed her forehead, 'I'll heal you fully once the battle is done, I've got you covered till then.'

She nodded weakly and leant against the wall, I stood up and dropped the shield, stepping out then putting it up again.

I summoned a huge amount of water and soaked everyone around me, right before blasting myself with a lightning bolt, knocking out at least 20 people. I went on a rampage, anyone I found I knocked out in whatever way I felt like, lightning, water, air, martial arts, whatever, if it worked, I used it.

After 2 more minutes of fighting the siren sounded and all the fighting stopped. I dropped the shield and ran over to Jess, picking her up carefully and carrying her inside, where everyone was waiting.

I laid her down on a sofa and knelt next to her, the colour still wasn't returning to her face and she needed to be at peak capacity for her next fight, I couldn't protect her from then on. 'What happened?' Sylvia asked, kneeling next to me. 'Some guy stabbed her right through, I got rid of him but well... This is my main problem right now.'
She nodded and cleared everyone out of the way. It took too long, but colour started to return, so I let her sleep, but I didn't stop healing her.
Sylvia looked at me, 'What happened? Weren't you teammates?'
I shook my head, 'She didn't want to be, so I planned on letting her be, of course I was always going to help if I needed to.'
Zoe nodded, 'Yeah you were basically all we saw on the screen, and the damage you were causing...'
'Yeah, well anyway when I had my back turned I heard her scream as she was fairly close to me so I immediately spun around and blasted this random blond guy into the air and out the way, then stopped the bleeding.'
'Then you went on a rampage.' Sam replied, 'I think you knocked out forty kids in two minutes.'
I chuckled, 'Really?'
Everyone else stared at me, I shrugged and put my head back, 'She'd better be okay for her next fight.'
Sylvia chuckled, 'Yeah... It'd be easier for the rest of us though!'
Everyone laughed, even I cracked a little smile.
Pain flared in my hand, causing me to wince and pull it away.
Sam frowned at me, 'You okay?'
'Yeah just... Felt a pain in my hand.'
Sylvia looked at me, 'You're probably over-extending your healing ability, Jess will be okay, worry about yourself now.'

I nodded and put my head against the back of the sofa, bored and waiting for my first match, which, as it turned out, was going to be one that I really wanted...

Half an hour later they announced the matches, but I was asleep for that so I didn't catch the name of the guy I was going to fight, but another 20 minutes later Barukko woke me up because my fight was in 5 minutes time, Jess was still asleep but her fight wasn't for a while, and she looked fine anyway.

I got to my feet and cracked my knuckles before walking to the massive door that faced out into the arena.
'Do you want me to wake Jess up?' Barukko asked behind me.
I shook my head, 'She needs to rest for now, it'll be fine.'
He nodded and walked back to the rest, I took a deep breath and stepped into the sunlight, greeted by a huge roar I walked out into the far corner, where my opponent was already waiting.

I got to the arena and stopped; it was him, I smiled.
It was the guy who stabbed Jess, *Guess it's time to get revenge then, for Jess of course.*
I stepped into the arena and decided to go all out on this kid.
The siren sounded and I blasted myself with lightning, summoning my cloak and sword, and generating a massive electrical storm.
I flicked my hand and lightning began raining down all around the arena, a constant thundering of sheer power, and it was only just the beginning.
And he knew it.
I watched the fear grow in his eyes as I slammed my hands into the floor, jagged spikes of rock erupted from the ground, creating a hazardous wasteland where it was impossible to run in a straight line.
Then I unsheathed my sword, glowing with electricity I held it out in front of me, 'Shall we?'
He panicked and spun around to run away, *Too slow.*
I teleported to him and slashed his leg, he fell to the floor.

345

'Not so fun now is it?' I asked.

The storm converged on us, forming an impenetrable barrier around us, he climbed to his feet, his hands bleeding from the stones that littered the ground. He pulled out his knife regardless.

I laughed and began to twirl my sword, 'Come on! Breakthrough this defence with that knife of yours!'

He disappeared.

I spun around and slashed, slicing through his wrist, cutting his hand clean off (not purposefully).

'AAH!' He screamed, falling to the floor and clutching his wrist, I winced, 'So you can teleport huh?'

He disappeared again, so I spun around again, this time grabbing him by the throat, he swung at me with both fists, yep, both fists.

'Ohh, that was a clone… But you can't make more than one, so this is the *real* you.'

He scrabbled at my face, trying to get me to drop him, so I did. He disappeared again, but this time I didn't spin round.

'AAH!' I heard again.

'Can't teleport through energy barriers apparently? Dodgy powers.' I replied, pulling an arrow with a boxing glove on the end of it out of my pocket, and summoning a bow in the other, 'Or shall I try and force you through it?'

I let the arrow fly and it impacted him right in the chest, I'd filled it with my explosive power, so as soon as it hit him it blew him back into the wall, sending another wave of pain through him.

He fell to the floor, I walked over to him and planted my sword in the ground, making him wince.

'You done?' I asked. He nodded his head feebly, 'Shame.' I replied, dropping the storm and launching him into the air, I followed him with my eyes, waiting for him to come back down. The dot in the sky rapidly grew bigger, until it was a human-sized human in front of me.

BANG

He flew into the wall on the opposite side of the arena, which then promptly collapsed on top of him, I sighed and put my hands behind my head, walking out of the arena and back to the waiting area.

I walked back into the dimly lit room with all eyes on me, I put my hands back in my pockets and walked past every one of them, looking straight on, before sitting down with the rest of my dorm. Then they continued their conversations.

'You are one scary dude.' Sam said.

'Yeah, you're actually terrifying at times.' Queenie agreed.

I said nothing and put my head against the back of the sofa, 'How's Jess doing?'

Sylvia glanced over at her, 'Fine but her fight is soon, so we'll have to wake her at some point.'

I nodded and closed my eyes, but not for long.

'Ahem.' A voice said above my head.

I opened my eyes and everyone turned around, it was the official in the suit with the really boring brushed-over hairstyle from earlier (not the blond dude, the first guy), 'Oh hey what's up?' I said.

'The higher-ups want a word with you.'

I sighed, 'Really? Why though...'

Everyone stared at me, 'Yeah alright fair enough, cut me some slack!'

I got to my feet and started walking away before turning back, 'Wish Jess luck for me.' I said, following the official out.

We walked through another maze of corridors before reaching the executive boxes on the other side of the arena to the competitor's entrance. The guy knocked on the door and a voice on the other side rang through, 'Come in!'

He opened the door and walked in, I followed immediately after and looked around the room.

It was a pretty lavish place, leather chairs facing the windows and their own personal bar sat alongside a table of food, there was like, 10 or 11 people in the room and they all looked pretty important.

I leant against the window and kept my hands in my pockets, 'So... What's the problem?'

'The problem is you beat the hell out of one of my students!'
This decrepit old guy with no hair and a nice looking, wooden, walking stick shouted.

I sighed, 'And?'

They all stared at me, my Principal (I assumed the rest were principals of other schools) stammered, 'Wha... What do you mean, "And"?'

'Well, what's the problem, it's a fighting tournament.'

'The problem is!' The old guy continued, 'That you haven't gone this hard on any other student!'

'Yeah, I didn't like that kid.'

'Why?' He demanded.

I sighed, 'He stabbed my girlfriend and nearly killed her, is that what you wanted to hear?' He opened his mouth, then closed it again. 'Exactly.'

'Why didn't you take her to the emergency room here?' Another guy asked, he was built like a tank, easy 7 foot, 300 pounds of pure muscle, probably a martial artist, *I kinda want to fight him.* I thought.

'Because I had to stop the bleeding on the battlefield, which is why I disappeared for like, three minutes because if I took her to the ER in the middle of the battle, we'd both be out, so I dealt with it.'

They all stared at me, 'Are you that powerful?' The big guy replied.

'I bet I could beat everyone in this room.' I replied, unmoving.

This woman scoffed, she was covered in scars and muscles, definitely ex-military, she had a scary stare too, 'Not true.'

'Why not then?'

'Cos there's special ops in here.'

I stared at her, 'Special ops?'

'You don't know everything about the world Alfie.' The Principal replied.

'Can I fight one of the special ops?' I asked.

They all gasped, the battle-hardened chick (ugh, hate that word) came to her senses first, 'No... For two reasons, 1. You aren't allowed to. And 2. We've got to keep their identity a secret.'

I scanned the room, 'Really? It's not that hard to figure out, I'm guessing you're ex-special ops, that dark-haired guy at the door is one, and that red-haired girl at the back who hasn't moved this whole time is the other one.'

Another stunned silence, 'H...How?'

'They're the only two that know their worth, they don't hold themselves up, all high and mighty, even though those two alone could probably beat up all of you. So they're special ops.'

'Bu... But still, we need to sanction you!' The old guy demanded.

'Will you shut up man? You're just salty cos you had your student beaten up by a kid who has no history.'

'I agree though, he needs to be punished.' The ex-special ops woman said.

'Well... We can disqualify him.' The Principal suggested.

I stared at him, 'And what? Replace me with the other guy? I put him in a coma. He couldn't beat Jess whilst she was asleep, it'd just cause an upset for the fans when they get a d-list replacement.'

He shrugged, everyone began murmuring amongst themselves, I got bored and decided to test my special ops theory. I kept my hands in my pockets but made my eyes glow an electrifying blue, immediately the two special ops guys flew at me, and before they knew it they were on the floor, and the guy who was camouflaged in the wall next to me? I had my hand round his throat.

'Oh, so I was right, there were three of you. Nice.'

Everyone stared at me, the ex-special ops lady spoke up (again), 'H...How?'

I tossed the guy on the ground, they all clambered to their feet, putting them in between me and the leaders.

I made the light disappear, 'Oh please calm down I was never going to attack them over something stupid like this, I was just testing my theory.'

The old guy cleared his throat, 'Ahem... Anyway, we're disqualifying him, right?'

I sighed and stared at the ceiling whilst they all discussed the various punishments...

'Okay then!' The Principal finally declared, 'I'm sorry to do this Alfie, I really am, but we are disqualifying you from the competition...'

I rolled my eyes and walked towards the door.

'Also...' He continued, I stopped, 'All further competitions this year, including the invitational, let this serve as a lesson, to not treat specific students unfairly.'

My eyes lit up for real this time, 'What?'

They all stood their ground, holding firm, but inside I knew they were wetting themselves.

Fine then, just wait till next year. I thought, walking out the door, much to the relief of just about everyone in the room, I turned the corner and strolled down the corridor, spinning around at the end of it, 'Oh quick FYI, I can see you all.' I said, to the members of special ops who were, trying, camouflaged against the walls, shoving open the door and walking out of the row of boxes. I made my own way through the maze of corridors before (somehow) emerging out back at the waiting area, I walked back to the dorm group.

'How'd it go?' Barukko asked.

'I'm disqualified, for the rest of this competition.' I replied.

Everyone stared at me, not saying anything, 'Anyway... I'm going to watch from our stand so, don't let me down.'

They all nodded and I teleported away.

I was the only one in the stand, which I found weird, but it was pretty peaceful, especially since the whole crowd thought I was still competing, so they didn't even bother me.

I sighed and put my feet up on the chair in front of me...

The rest of the day passed pretty quickly, they announced my disqualification and I think half the stadium had emptied out by the quarter-finals. Jess and Barukko both made it to the quarters before getting knocked out, no one else even made it that far so I was back at dorm by 4.

I threw myself on the sofa and waited for everyone else to come back in, after a couple of minutes they did, everyone walked in and went about doing their various things. Finally, Jess, Barukko and Syl joined me on the sofas.

'So… What are you going to do now? Syl asked.

I shrugged, 'Dunno, just watch the fights that you guys are in and train in between.'

'More martial arts?'

'Na I want to develop a new power.' I said, 'A real game-changer.'

Jess nodded, 'Like what?'

'Not sure, I'm thinking about either gravity manipulation or dimension alteration.'

They all stared at me…

'I know you said "game-changer" Alfie but really, there are like, 2 people who can do those in existence, they're amazing! And even they can do limited versions of it!' Sylvia said.

'I know and I think that's why I want to do dimension alteration first.'

'Because you can develop into domain alteration and extension, right?' Barukko asked.

'Yeah.'

The girls looked at him, 'What's domain alteration and extension?'

'Well… You know how with dimension alteration; he can change the environment of an area around him? Well, he can only change it to a pre-existing dimension, so his options are limited. BUT… With domain alteration and extension…'

'He can create his own.' Helena finished off, sitting down across from me, I nodded, 'But there's only one recorded case of domain manipulation ever, and some rumours say that isn't even true so it might not even be possible.'

'It is.' I said.

They all looked at me, 'How do you know?' Helena asked.

'Because I'll make it happen.' I said, 'Because I can.'

Barukko chuckled, 'Well if anyone can do it it's this guy.'

'I think I can learn to do dimension alteration in about a week, probably closer to two, but for domain manipulation it might take a year, but I'm thinking closer to around four months, because it's basically a completely new power.'

351

'Yeah but wouldn't you be better learning Domain manipulation last?' Helena asked, 'Because it only gets better as you learn more powers.'

'Well… Yes… But no… Because of how powerful it is, it'll be basically unstoppable at my current level anyway, and as I become more powerful, well… You get the picture.'

Barukko stared at me, 'So you actually think it's possible?'

I held out my hand and gathered a massive amount of power, which eventually became visible, a glowing blue ball that even made Jess skirt to the opposite side of the sofa. Then, **Fwoosh** it imploded on itself and became a bizarre, window-like space, where you could see into what looked like an alien world.

Everyone stared at me, 'Is that…?'

'Yeah… It's a complicated way of doing dimension alteration.'

'So you can do it already?' Helena asked.

'Yeah but it requires a huge amount of energy to do, even for me, and it's pretty unpredictable, I had no idea what it was going to look like on the other side.'

I clenched my fist and extinguished the power.

Everyone blinked back to reality, Jess glanced at me, 'So… What happens now?'

'Well… You go to the invitational alone, since I can't. I train whenever I can, especially over the summer, and I come back and show off to you all!' I said with a beaming smile on my face.

Barukko chuckled, 'You know we all won't just sit back and chill either right?'

'Errmm…' Sylvia said, Jess and quite a few others agreed.

'So just me and you Barukko!' I laughed, 'It'll be fun, maybe you'll even overtake Jess again.'

Jess's face immediately changed, her tone became very serious, 'Okay no I think I'll train too.'

The next day I got up early and went out to train, but made no real process since I was just trying to figure out how to do it without wasting a ridiculous amount of energy.

The day after it was the invitational, we all rocked up to the stadium at 9 in the morning and were done by 12, Jess got her butt handed to her by the previous winners, especially the older ones, they were good...

I went back out to train with some others in the afternoon, I sat in a tree whilst the others fought rigorous training exercises, I again, made basically no progress.

31 – Oh yay, it's the end of the school year... And you know what that means...

The next day, whilst we were having breakfast, there was a knock at the door, it was the Principal.

I opened the door and he walked in, 'Hello everyone!'

He was met by a half-hearted chorus of greetings.

'Ahem, anyway, I have something to tell you all... As of next week, classes will not be resuming, I know it's only two weeks early but because of all you're hard work this year we're giving you an early break!'

An excited chatter broke out amongst everyone.

'Alright, you can discuss it later! We've got something else to talk about.'

Helena held her hand up, 'Is it the tests at the end of the week Sir?'

We all stared at her, 'Tests?!' Jake shouted.

The Principal nodded, 'Indeed, tests, over the last three days of the week there will be tests that you undergo, on the Wednesday, mental tests, so your maths and English skills. Then on Thursday and Friday, your combat or practical skills.'

Zoe sighed, 'Well, we all know who's going to win that.'

I smiled and put my arms behind my head.

'It could be worse, he could have figured out dimension alteration by now.' Jess said.

'Hey look, I've got what? Five days to figure it out?'

'Even I doubt you'll do it in that time.' The Principal agreed.

'Oh great thanks.' I grumbled.

He smiled, bid his farewell, then walked out. And all hell broke loose, nearly everyone just lost their minds.

'Seriously? A test in 3 days?' Jake shouted.

Jess, Barukko and Helena all came and stood by the door with me, watching the carnage unfurl together.

Then, something I don't think has ever happened before well, happened, the entire dorm went up to their rooms or out in the park to practice, and we were all still stood there by the door. I turned around, 'I know we're top of the class and all, but we should probably still go and practise.'

Everyone nodded and walked outside and into the park, we practised literally all day, Jess managed to create a light shield as well as her spear, Barukko did something but refuses to tell me, he just says, "You'll see" and walks off.

I actually finally got somewhere with my new power, I managed to do it in a space about the size of my finger for about a second, it wasn't much but it was progress. I didn't tell anyone though, it was going to be my surprise (if it worked).

Everyone spent as much time as possible over the next couple of days studying or practising, I hardly saw anyone, even Jess. But by the time of the tests we were pretty much ready. The day of the mental tests came and went (I'm assuming you don't want to hear about how I found the circumference of a blast zone using only my eyes do you) and before we knew it the day of the combat test was upon us.

We headed to training area Beta, but instead of us being in one of the practice areas, we were in the combat arena, a concrete platform 50 metres across in both directions, and there wasn't just us.

I walked into the arena ahead of anyone and saw two other groups also making their way into the arena.

'Oh great.' Jess grumbled behind me, 'We're up against everyone else from our year too?'

I cracked my knuckles and blasted myself with lightning (and you know what that means), 'Oh come on! It'll be fun.' I said, glancing at everyone else, who looked like they just wet themselves.

'You won't beat the living daylights out of everyone here will you?' Barukko asked.

I shrugged, 'Depends on whether anyone annoys me or not, if one annoys me, I'll hit everyone.'

Natalia rolled her eyes, 'Great, it's all or nothing then?'

'Exactly! I mean, what do you expect?'

Everyone looked mildly ashamed of me, I smiled and turned my attention back to the middle, where the Principal, Rocky and One Hit were stood.

'Hello everyone!' The Principal called, 'And welcome to your combat test, if you can't tell already you will be fighting your fellow classmates in this tournament.'

A series of unhappy murmuring erupted from the other two classes but it died down quickly.

'Now for the tournament rules,' Rocky said, 'It will be a one on one, bracket-style tournament. Matches will be random and you can, and probably will, come up against students from the other two dorms!'

The number one from class 2 raised her hand, 'But what if we come up against like, Jaeger in the first round, surely we'll get a rubbish grade?'

'The difficulty of your opponent will also be taken into consideration when judging your grade.' Rocky confirmed, 'Now! May the tournament begin!'

We were all told to get off the arena and watch the matches, I breezed through all of mine, beating a couple of kids from each dorm and Tiago from ours to get to the final, without really trying to be honest...

So there I was, leaning against the wall at the back of the arena waiting for my opponent to enter, Barukko was stood next to me.

'I really don't want to fight her you know.' I said.

'You know that she'll be disappointed if you don't at least try a bit.' He said.

'I know, but I don't want to hurt her.'

'Meh she'll be alright, I mean you're literally fighting her if you do anything serious you can just stop and heal her.'

I shrugged, 'Okay fair enough, let's do this then.'

He nodded and climbed out the arena, 'Don't lose to your girlfriend or you'll never hear the end of it.'

I smiled and gave him a thumbs-up before shifting my weight to my own two feet.

The siren sounded and I clasped my hand together, forming a triangle.

'Dimension alteration!' I shouted.

Instantly the landscape around me changed, becoming a scorched, blackened land with lava flows and pools. Jess stared at me, trapped in all but one direction by lava, 'H...How?'

I smiled and lit my hands on fire, 'Why are you so surprised, I told you I'd be able to do it.'

She stepped forward, already sweating from the blazing heat, 'Come at me.' She growled.

'Oh I wouldn't be so confident.' I replied, slamming my hands together, 'Blazing Dragon.' I growled.

The lava pool behind me erupted and from it emerged a dragon-like shape made of pure fire. I followed it as it advanced upon Jess, who summoned her spear and drove it into the dragon, which simply disappeared as it flew into her. What didn't disappear was the bolt of lightning which blew her off her feet afterwards. She flew into the wall and out of my dimension alteration, but it didn't matter. In her daze she threw her spear, I caught it and snapped it.

'I don't want to hit you again.' I said.

She smiled weakly, then spat out the blood, 'You don't have to... I concede!' She shouted. I smiled and pulled her up, she put all her weight on me, 'I didn't know you could do that.'

I kissed her forehead, 'No one did so don't worry about it.'

'That was insanely powerful.' She replied.

'I know, it would've hurt more if the dragon actually attacked.'

'You... Cheeky...Zzz...'

And with that she was out cold, I smiled and picked her up, carrying her back to the others I passed the other two groups, who were staring at me in awe. I winked at the number one in class 2, who I'd knocked out earlier, *See? This is what I can do.* I thought.

Sylvia and Zoe jogged over to me, 'Is she okay?' Syl asked.

'Yeah she's fine, just needs to rest.' I said.

They both nodded, relieved, and we joined the rest of the group as we were walking out of the arena.

'She'd better be okay for tomorrow's practical test.' She grumbled.
I laughed, 'She'll be fine trust me!'

And of course, as usual, I was right. An hour later she was up and everyone was drilling me about dimension alteration, and how I'd managed to learn it in such a small amount of time. We chilled out for a couple of hours, Helena quizzed us about possible scenarios tomorrow, and then we all went to bed early, excited for the next day.

32 – Oh no! A prison escape?

We woke up, changed, and went down for breakfast, we'd been told to be ready for 8, and that we'd have to wait for further instructions (and God knows what that meant).
So there we were, everyone sat in the commune area just before eight, I glanced around the room, every single person was on edge, checking their phones for the time. All the clocks turned to 08:00 and instantly all the TVs turned on and began flashing ready. Immediately everyone leapt to their feet, but we all had no idea what to do, so glanced at the TV where a message was showing.

RED ALERT: HEAD TO TRAINING AREA DELTA WHERE A MASS PRISON BREAKOUT IS UNDERWAY

As I read the message I sighed and grabbed onto Barukko and Jess, who were stood next to me, and teleported to the tallest building in Training area Delta. Where there was indeed a mass breakout of second years, they ran rampant as they went to their individual areas. We all looked at each other, 'Shall we try and clean this up before everyone else arrives?' I asked.
'So we've got... Five-ish minutes?'
I cracked my knuckles, 'Sounds about right, let's get to it then.'
We all jumped off the roof and onto the ground below, completely catching off-guard the whole of class 2-A, who were running into the city, Brandon saw me first, his eyes widened and his arm shot out, 'Oh for God sakes.' He muttered, 'Everyone! Prepare to fight.'
I smiled, Jess caught my eye and I sent her a silent message, *Leave them to me, go and sort out the other areas.*
She nodded and ran off, dragging Barukko with her.
Brandon laughed, 'That's cocky of you!'
Harlequin smiled, 'Or smart, it's better to lose one than to lose three.'

I grinned, 'Nah, it's just cocky.'

I clasped my hands together in a triangle again, 'Dimension alteration!'

Instantly the area surrounding me was converted into the same, scorched battlefield as before (it was the easiest one to summon for me), but the area of effect was bigger this time, *Huh, nice.*

Everyone took a wary step back, Brandon and Harlequin stared at me, 'What is this? What's "dimension alteration"?'

I smiled, 'This.' My hands burst into flame and I slammed them together, this time interlocking my fingers, 'Five Blazing Dragons!'

Harlequin realised what was happening and glanced around, 'Get out of the affected area!' She shouted, but it was too late. The five dragons made of pure fire erupted from lava pools around them and began circling the group, faster and faster, each time they spun round they added a layer to the wall of fire that was beginning to encompass them. They all looked around, panicked, Brandon looked at me, eyes wide, 'What the…?'

'Oh don't worry, it won't kill you.' I said.

Once they were distracted by the wall of fire around them I leapt into action, knocking out every one of them before they even knew what was going on, but then Harlequin noticed, she looked around and saw everyone on the ground, then she saw me, charging at her.

She knew too late, right as I was about to punch her, I teleported to the other side, and hit her from there. She crumpled to the floor and I dropped the dimensional alteration. Just before leaving the scene I glanced around and saw Brandon struggling to his feet.

I sighed, 'I knew you'd be the one I didn't get straight away.'

He got to his feet and held up his hands, 'Yeah well the fight's only just beginning.'

BANG

A flash of lightning shot from my outstretched hand and impacted him in the chest, launching him off his feet and flying 20 metres further away.

'Yeah you're out now.' I said, teleporting over to where Jess and Barukko had run off to.

I found them about a kilometre away from the city, stood on the edge of a cliff, panting heavily and surrounded by 10 or so kids. I flew in and landed behind them, 'Hey guys.'

'Did you run away or knock them all out?' Barukko asked.

'You know the answer to that.' I replied, 'So... Do you need some help or...?'

'Well, we took out like, 25 guys by ourselves but now we're tired.' Jess complained.

I laughed, and put my hands in my pockets, 'Is that a yes or no?'

She rolled her eyes, 'Yes! It's a yes!'

'That's all I needed to hear.' I said, gathering a storm and electrocuting everyone in front of us.

'Couldn't you have used dimension alteration?' Jess asked.

'Well... Yes but doing it twice in one day really takes it out of me and there is no guarantee you two wouldn't get hurt.'

They both nodded and turned back to the sea of unconscious bodies, 'That looks grim.' Jess said.

'I know right? It's a good job no one is actually dead.' I admitted.

'Mhmm.' Barukko agreed.

'Seriously B, is that all you've got to say? "Mhmm"?'

He cracked a smile, 'Yeah whatever.'

We all turned around and I teleported us to the tallest tower again, where I knew someone would be waiting.

'Where have you three been?' Helena shouted as we all materialised onto the roof.

'Just... Light-ning the load.' I said.

'Nice.' Jess said, high-fiving me.

'AHEM!' Helena said, 'So, what have you actually done?'

'Well... I took out the entire of 2-A, these two took out 2-B?'

They nodded, Jess shook her hand like, *kinda*, 'And we left you 2-C!'

'What about the people in the city and mountains?'

'Oh they're fine, we got there before the enemy did.'

Helena sighed, 'As annoyed as I am at you for running off, at least you did it right.' She turned to the rest of the group, 'Well, it looks like we've got it easy! On to the lake!' She said, 'You three! Stay here!' She shouted at us.

'Sheesh.' Jess complained.

'Oh please, we're not staying here, we're going to watch!' I said, 'Come on!'

I jumped off the roof and teleported over to the highest spot by the lake (aka the "sea"), where the gang of "criminals" had taken over a boat. Soon enough the class came charging in and leapt into the water, after a couple of minutes the class was at the boat and beginning to get on board.

I turned to Jess and Barukko, 'Hey should I spice it up a bit.' Barukko glanced at me and yawned (I don't know whether I should take it personally or not) 'Yeah sure why not?'

I smiled and began to stir up a storm, not a big one, just big enough to rock the boat about a bit and to cause a small issue for those still in the water.

They handled it pretty well though, it slowed them down in gaining control of the boat, but it also didn't make it easier for the guys controlling the boat, as they were all too busy trying not to fall over, so we were done in about 15 minutes, all escapees either in custody or knocked out (you'd never guess whose guys had been knocked out and whose had been put in custody).

I teleported over to the group who had just clambered back onshore, 'You did good out there!' I said, right before realising that half the kids were throwing up.

'Ooo.' Jess said, scrunching her nose (did I say she looked cute when she did that), 'You guys don't look so good.'

'Yeah well we got hit by a freak storm! And half of us are seasick.' Jake complained.

I glanced at Barukko, we were both trying to contain our laughter but when Queenie bent over and threw up for the third time we lost it completely. We both burst out laughing (much to Jess's surprise, who was stone-cold calm) and just couldn't stop.

Now, I'm not saying what happened next was our own fault, but it was.

Zoe put 2 and 2 together and finally made 4, 'WAIT A MINUTE.' She shouted, causing another wave of laughter between me and Barukko, even Jess cracked a smile, but probably more at us than with us.

Soon enough everyone caught on and were NOT very happy about it. They were all glaring at us, Jess acted like she had nothing to do with it, but of course we tried to get her in trouble too but *no*, they were not having it.

Eventually, it got so bad that Barukko and I had to make a run for it (aka, we teleported away) and decided to let everyone cool down before even venturing out of our rooms.

We didn't come down from our rooms that day.

Jess came up later though to check on me and make sure I hadn't died...

33 – Home Time!!!

Knock Knock...
'Come in!' I said as I laid on my bed, scrolling through social media.
Jess walked in and sat on the edge of my bed, 'Hey.'
'What's up?'
'Nothing much, just making sure you haven't died.'
'Thanks, as you can see I'm not dead!'
She smiled and laid down on top of me, 'Thanks for the clarification... You ready to go home tomorrow?'
I nodded, 'Yep...! Oh actually... Whilst we're on that topic I've got something to ask you.'
She looked up at me, 'Oh yeah?'
I stared at her, 'You already know what I'm going to say don't you?'
'Yep! But I want to hear you say it.'
I chuckled and stroked her hair, 'Do you wanna come home with me?'
She wrapped her arms around me, 'Of course, why wouldn't I?'
'I don't know! Maybe you're getting fed up with me?'
She laughed, 'I would never! Now on *that* note, I've got to go pack, you should too.'
I nodded and swung my legs off the bed, sighed, and packed my stuff up, I somehow managed to fit all my clothes and stuff into two suitcases.
'Wow, I must have washed all my clothes weekly or something because Jess will have at least twice as many cases as me.'
I left my PC at the dorm along with all the bigger items I didn't need. And the next day we were all sat around the commune area at 9 in the morning, waiting for the moment when we could leave. We'd all said our goodbyes to each other, we were all pretty much going to our own places, but some would be staying at other people's places.
Jess came down lugging 4 suitcases behind her, I took one look at them and sighed, 'Give them here!' I said.

She gingerly passed them over and I picked the first one up and tossed it into my dimensional storage.

'Wai…! Oh… Ohhh… Smart, I like it.'

I kissed her, 'I know right, I'm a genius.'

'Well, I wouldn't go that far.' She said, wrapping her arms around me. I glanced around and suddenly everyone started heading for the door.

I looked at her, 'Well, I guess it's time to go.'

She smiled, 'It definitely is.'

I stepped outside and felt rain splash against my face. I looked up at the sky, it was a dark, gloomy, wet British day. I sighed and put my hood up. Jess pulled an umbrella out of nowhere, one of those little ones all women seem to always have, and pulled up next to me, 'Lovely day.'

I smiled, 'It is.'

I glanced around, everyone was walking in their own groups. Each with their own umbrellas, or some without. We all walked in the same direction, excited, but also sad. A lot of us wouldn't see each other for another couple months… We walked through the campus and into the entrance building, not stopping for anyone. I saw Brandon talking to someone out of the corner of my eye but didn't stop.

We walked to the gate with everyone else, said our goodbyes, then I teleported us to the train station to avoid the worsening rain…

Now, you may be wondering *"Alfie, why didn't you just teleport home and save the money?"*

Well because quite simply because I'm not actually that good at teleporting, the longer the distance I have to teleport (in this case, 150-ish miles) the less accurate it is, so I could get it spot on, or I could be in the next city over, and since it would also take a lot out of me, it just wasn't practical.

Anyway, we boarded the first train to Central Manchester and found seats, some people recognised us and snapped some pictures, but I didn't really care, I put my arm around Jess and closed my eyes, I knew how long it would take to get there.

I woke up an hour later as the train entered Manchester, Jess was asleep on my shoulder but I left her until we arrived in the station.

We got off the train and teleported out of the station to avoid the crowds and before we knew it we were out in the local neighbourhood that I grew up in. Jess found it weirdly fascinating, she'd grown up in one of the richer parts, always had done, so she'd never really seen this side, the weather had cleared up so I was giving her the tour.

I mean, it's not like we're **Broke** broke, we're just not rich, if you catch my drift.

We wandered the streets, our fingers laced together, and after another half an hour we ended up on the long street towards my place. Jess was literally bouncing with excitement. I was about to turn onto our block when I heard a scream that sounded awfully similar...

'Is that?' Jess asked, glancing at me, panicked.

I looked around then flew up to my door, over the railing and onto the second floor, blowing it down I entered the apartment, where I found my mum, facing me, on her knees, staring at the girl in front of me.

She kind of looks like me, blonde hair, yellow-y eyes, tall build but fairly muscular... WAIT...

I stared at my Mum, 'Erm, who is this?'

She glanced at me, then turned her attention back to the girl in front of me. I heard Jess arrive at the door behind me, just in time.

'This... is your... this is your twin sister...'

Coming Soon

Alfie Jaeger – Book two!

Name: Alfie Jaeger
Age: 16
Height: 6ft 1inches
Birthday: September 1st
Appearance: Blonde hair, yellow eyes, pale skin, lean
Power: God Complex

Name: Jessica Verose
Age: 16
Height: 5ft 10inches
Birthday: October 14th
Appearance: Long, blonde hair, green eyes, tanned (annoyingly), slim
Power: Light Manipulation

Name: Barukko Knox
Age: 16
Birthday: December 21st
Appearance: Dark hair, midnight black eyes, very pale, muscular
Power: Darkness Manipulation

Name: San Wukong
Age: 16
Height: 5ft 11inches
Birthday: March 11th
Appearance: Brownish-red hair, red eyes, fair skin, muscular
Power: Superhuman

Name: Zoe Zane
Age: 16
Height: 6ft 0inches
Birthday: January 20th
Appearance: Long, brown hair, blue eyes, pale skin, fairly muscular
Power: Lightning

Name: Jake Wilson
Age: 16
Height: 5ft 6inches
Birthday: January 28th
Appearance: Blonde hair, blue eyes, pale skin, short and skinny
Power: Fire Manipulation

Name: Tiago Sanchez

Age: 16
Heigh: 5ft 9inches
Birthday: July 25th
Appearance: Crazy brown hair, brown eyes, tanned, skinny
Power: Bone Manipulation

Name: Queenie (Q)
Age: 16
Height: 5ft 1inches
Birthday: September 19th
Appearance: Short red hair, bright orange eyes, tanned, lean
Power: Phoenix Transformation

Name: Paris Palmer
Age: 16
Height: 6ft 4inches
Birthday: July 14th
Appearance: Short, brown styled hair, grey eyes, pale skin, well built
Power: Gravity Manipulation

Name: Helena Leroux
Age: 16
Height: 5ft 6inches
Birthday: March 14th
Appearance: Long, frizzy brown hair, honey-coloured eyes, tanned, skinny figure
Power: Enhanced Intelligence

Name: Sylvia Chapman
Age: 15
Height: 5ft 9inches
Birthday: August 2nd
Appearance: Crazy pink hair, almost rainbow eyes, pale, almost pink skin, slim figure
Power: Aura Reading

Name: Maddison Pagina
Age: 16
Height: 5ft 4inches
Birthday: February 21st
Appearance: Long brown hair, blue eyes, pale skin, slim
Power: Holographic Projection

Name: Alexander Pendrakon
Age: 16
Height: 5ft 8inches
Birthday: April 4th
Appearance: Curly brown hair, brown eyes, fair skin, skinny build
Power: Mechanical Genius

Name: Alexandra Pendrakon
Age: 16
Height: 5ft 7inches
Birthday: April 4th
Appearance: Curly brown hair, brown eyes, fair skin, slim
Power: Psychic Shield

Name: Samuel Di Roma
Age: 16
Height: 5ft 6inches
Birthday: January 9th
Appearance: flat, brown hair, green-brown eyes, tanned, skinny
Power: Paralysis

Name: Ajax Reid
Age: 16
Height: 6ft 4inches
Birthday: November 25th
Appearance: Straight, black hair, green eyes, pale skin, big build
Power: Life Manipulation

Name;: Troy Petit
Age: 16
Height: 8ft 8inches
Birthday: April 1st
Appearance: Curly black hair, dark brown eyes, fair skin, muscular build
Power: Size Control

Name: Talia Bronze
Age: 16
Height: 6ft 3inches
Birthday: June 1st
Appearance: Long, curly brown hair, bronze eyes, bronze skin,
muscular

Power: Telekinesis

Name: Gabriella Ramirez
Age: 16
Height: 6ft 0inches
Birthday: October 12th
Appearance: Long, black hair, dark brown eyes, tanned, muscular build
Power: Enhanced Combat

Name: Bianca Ramirez
Age: 16
Height: 5ft 11inches
Birthday: October 12th
Appearance: Short, black hair, dark brown eyes, tanned, skinny build
Power: Sharpshooter

Name: Natalia Ramirez
Age: 16
Height: 5ft 10inches
Birthday: October 12th
Appearance: Shoulder length, black hair, dark brown eyes, tanned, slim build
Power: Skill Duplication

Name: Ulva Hoights
Age: 16
Height: 5ft 8inches
Birthday: May 8th
Appearance: Long, black hair, blue eyes, pale skin, muscular
Power: Energy Manipulation

Name: Kareem Mosas
Age: 16
Height: 6ft 2inches
Birthday: July 27th
Appearance: Short, black hair, fark brown eyes, olive skin, lean build
Power: Exorcist

Name: Darius Jackson
Age: 16
Height: 6ft 0inches
Birthday: February 2nd

Appearance: Long, black hair, honey-gold eyes, dark skin, lean build
Power: Sound Amplification

Name: Shanelle James
Age: 16
Height: 5ft 10inches
Birthday: January 12th
Appearance: Frizzy black hair, green eyes, olive skin, slim build
Power: Flight

Name: Alda Larson
Age: 16
Height: 6ft 1inch
Birthday: November 17th
Appearance: Long, blonde hair, blue eyes, pale skin, lean build
Power: Viking Mentality/Ability

Name: Jason Webber
Age: 16
Height: 5ft 0inches
Birthday: December 1st
Appearance: Short, blonde hair, electric blue eyes, pale skin, skinny
Power: X-Ray Vision

Name: Brandon
Age: 17
Height: 6ft 2inches
Birthday: June 12th
Appearance: Long, white hair, blue eyes, pale skin, lean build
Power: Density Manipulation

Name: Leo
Age: 17
Height: 6ft 3inches
Birthday: February 5th
Appearance: Short, brown hair, light brown eyes, fair skin, muscular
Power: Unknown

Name: Principal
Age: Unknown
Height: 5ft 7inches
Birthday: Unknown

Appearance: Grey hair, dark grey eyes, pale, wrinkly skin, skinny
Power: Power Amplification, Enhanced Intelligence, more?

Printed in Great Britain
by Amazon

72181273R00225